S.L. CHOI

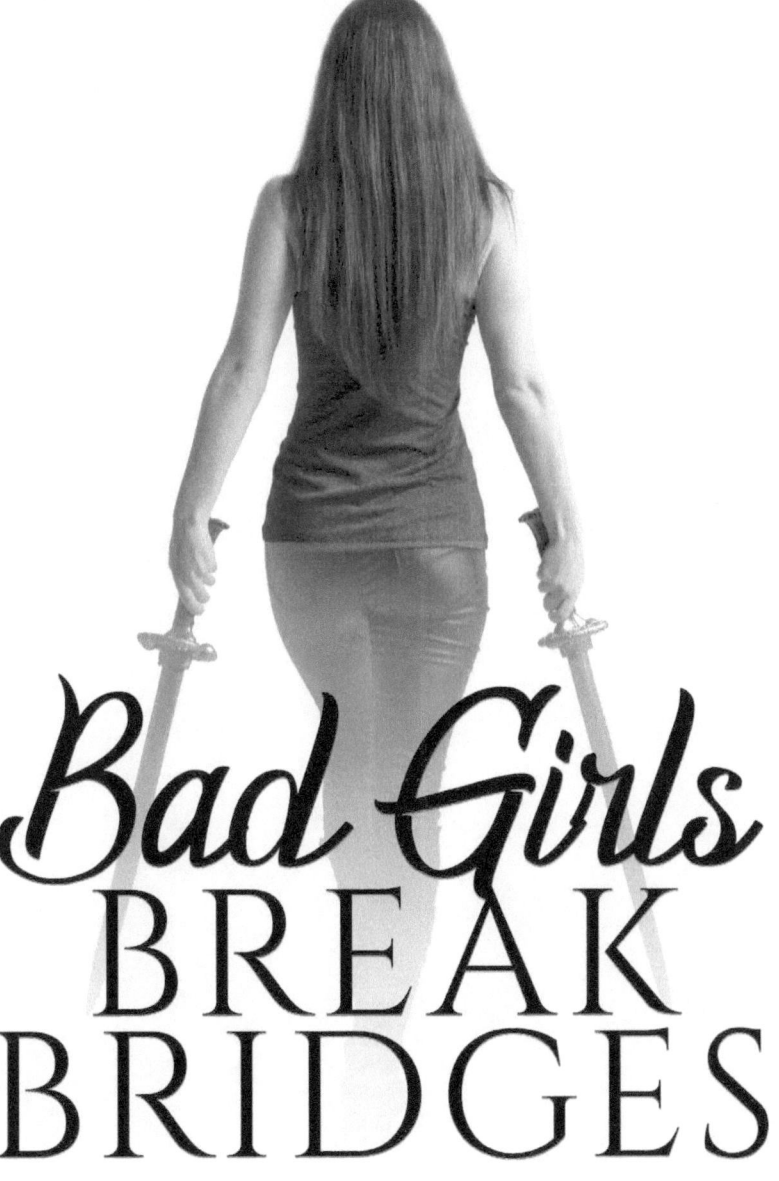

Bad Girls
BREAK
BRIDGES

BLOOD FAE DRUID | BOOK THREE

S.L. CHOI

Bad Girls BREAK BRIDGES

BLOOD FAE DRUID | BOOK THREE

BAD GIRLS BREAK BRIDGES
Blood Fae Druid, Book 3

CITY OWL PRESS
www.cityowlpress.com

Cover Design by MiblArt. All stock photos licensed appropriately.

Edited by Heather McCorkle.

For information on subsidiary rights, please contact the publisher at info@cityowlpress.com.

Print Edition ISBN: 978-1-64898-415-0

Digital Edition ISBN: 978-1-64898-416-7

Printed in the United States of America

PRAISE FOR S.L. CHOI

"FANTASTIC SERIES! EACH BOOK IS A MUST READ!" — *Faith Hunter, New York Times and USA Today bestselling author*

"With tantalizing hints of a wolfy blood tryst, a heavy dose of sisterly love, and plot twists to make the ride a surprise, S.L. Choi's, *Bad Girls Drink Blood* is too much fun. This brand-new world and mythos are a pleasure to explore. Solid world building, easy to grasp politics, hints of future romance and plenty of snark are the perfect scaffold to a story about finding that your scars are only the signposts of your hidden abilities, and that the part of you that brings you the most pain, can also be the wellspring of your deepest satisfaction. If you like the Hollows, you will love this." — *Kim Harrison, #1 New York Times bestselling author of the Hollows series*

"S.L. Choi, please hurry up and write the next book in the *Blood Fae Druid* series!" — *Lisa Edmonds, author of the Alice Worth series*

"Choi loads her debut and *Blood Fae Druid* urban fantasy series launch with snark, action, and characters who will steal readers' hearts. Lane Callaghan is a hybrid blood fae, which makes her an outcast in the fae world. She and her sisters, Mae and Y'sindra, operate a struggling private investigation firm on the edge of Las Vegas and the mystical Interlands... Choi delivers plenty of fast-paced action, but it's the individual characters who steal the show. This promising series premier will leave readers wanting more." —*Publishers Weekly*

"Welcome to a sexy, *new* spin on the fae. Deliciously gritty and full of snark, you'll find your new hero in Lane Callaghan." – *International and award-winning author of the Weird Girls UF romance series, Cecy Robson*

"*Bad Girls Drink Blood* is an action-packed good time that delivers wit, grit, and an unforgettable heroine." – *Kat Turner, author the Coven Daughters series*

If you are reading this, this one is for you.

AUTHOR'S NOTE

Dear reader, my sincere thanks for giving Blood Fae Druid series a shot! This is a slowburn to spicy truemate urban fantasy romance set amidst plenty of action and laughs. Expect the language to be salty, the violence stabby, and the romance to get hot!

1

I UNVOLUNTEER

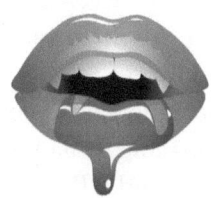

MUSIC PULSED FROM A MULTITUDE OF SPEAKERS HIDDEN AROUND THE amphitheater. It slipped through my body, pulling excitement to the surface and teasing all my tingly girly parts.

It had the same effect on my sisters. Eyes bright, Mae looked at me over her shoulder as she skipped down the front row. "This is such a great idea. I'm surprised you thought of it."

"Thanks," I said in a flat voice.

Her eyes rounded, and her glossed lips formed a horrified O. "I didn't mean it like that, Laney!"

Y'sindra snorted. "I mean it. This isn't exactly your style. The only half naked man you ogle is your boy toy."

I shot a glare at Y'sindra bouncing along behind me. Diminutive my sister might be, but her opinions were not. "First, you could show a little respect and stop referring to Teddy as a boy toy." Though he totally was. I climbed that prime piece of man meat like a jungle gym on the regular. "Second, I can appreciate a good-looking male—or female." I winked at Mae. "This is a mixed revue, ya know?"

Blue eyes shining like polished sapphires, she turned in a circle, taking in the large space. "Where are the girls? I thought you invited them?"

"I did. Zee messaged this morning to say she, Eli, and Pru are driving here together." I dropped onto my seat, sinking into the plump memory foam cushion. I didn't do well with crowds, and the closer we got to the big night out I'd purchased tickets for on a crazy whim, the more I had come to regret my decision. "Tickets are at will call. There's still plenty of time before the show."

"All together?" Mae stopped turning long enough to ask. "Dangerous. Who's driving?"

She wasn't wrong about the danger. Elisette was a sun fae who'd recently run away—I'd call it escaped—from Eodrom. The snooty seat of sun fae power in Ta'Vale. Pru still lived in Ta'Vale, and I doubted she'd ever even been in a car. Zee was just a terrible driver.

"Jason is dropping all three of them off here. They'll take resort cars back." Eli's fiancé was a gem. He'd get them here and home safely. In Pru's case, she'd use one of our father's portals to get home. I bounced in my seat. The thing was cushy and comfortable. It had to be expensive.

"Probably a good idea," Mae said. "I'm glad Eli stayed. She's been a big help to me in the garden, and Jason is a gem."

"I'm blown away you invited the blood fae." Y'sindra climbed onto the chair and stood on her cushion to watch the doors at the rear of the large, rapidly-filling space. "It was a good idea. She's cool."

I grunted. It hadn't been my idea. After my attempt to infuriate Prunettia with an obnoxious level of kindness went awry, Teddy low-key pressured me into getting to know the female I'd accidentally befriended. She might be a member of the Royal Fae Guard, he'd argued, but she was also the only blood fae aside from my mother I'd ever met.

I'd agreed, mostly because I hadn't expected her to accept. But she had.

"I'm glad Zee's coming. She seems stressed lately." Mae finally stopped staring and took her seat. "Do you think it's about *Blood and Wine?*"

When my ancient great many times over grandfather and the namesake of the resort and casino the Blackthorne, suggested Teddy open a high-end bar in the establishment we—my sisters, Teddy, and Lo—had taken up residence in, I'd wanted to refuse. Then I woke the fuck up and realized my man would be working a mere elevator ride away.

"No, at least I don't think so. I noticed she was a bit wound up too and thought maybe she was worried about the move. But Teddy said she was the first member of his staff who signed on."

I rubbed my bare, goosebump-covered arm as I glanced at the crowd flowing into the theater. It was cold as the undead in this place, which seemed at odds with the lack of clothes the performers would be wearing. Shrinkage and all.

"Are they really only serving blood and wine? They better carry berries." Y'sindra spun and dropped into her seat. Alcohol alone could not compete with a snow fairy's metabolism. Berries combined with alcohol delivered inebriation.

"Or you can just bring berries down from the penthouse," I said and touched my tingling lips. "Are my lips blue?"

I'd been a sucker and let Mae dress me. I had on so few clothes, there was a strong probability of frostbite in my near future if this place didn't warm up fast.

"Pretty powder blue. They match your fancy breastplate." Y'sindra chortled and tapped the wyvern scale embedded in my chest, on full display thanks to the scandalously low-cut tank top.

"Still, I'm confused as to why Dexter is taking over The bar in Interlands instead of Zee. She's the senior bartender." Mae didn't want to let the topic go. We'd been friends with Zee for years, and Mae was protective. It was cute.

"She'll be here soon. You can ask her." I shrugged. Teddy's choice had surprised me too. Dexter, the only moon fae without the corruption who lived outside of Ta'Vale was the next logical choice to run the bar in Teddy's absence.

"There's the blood fae." Y'sindra waved her hands wildly to catch Prunettia's attention.

Pru and I were similar, yet worlds apart. Teddy might believe it was a good idea for me to get to know another blood fae, but I wasn't so sure how much blood fae was left in me.

"Wow," Mae breathed the word. "I've never seen her out of uniform. She's stunning."

I looked again. Though only five-feet-tall like me, she seemed to tower above those she passed in the aisle. The female exuded confidence and power. She wore black, mesh leggings paired with a long-sleeved, silvery tunic. The slinky material was baggy on her lean torso but bundled tight across her hips. As opposed to my deeply auburn hair twisted into a tight braid and laying heavy along my spine, her silky, onyx tresses flowed and fluttered like a curtain down her back. Her only nod to makeup was her deep red painted lips. With high cheekbones set in an oval face, she didn't need anything else.

Resentment for her blood fae perfection bubbled up inside me but popped and faded just as quickly. Not so long ago it would have gnawed and festered my insides, but now I understood my hybrid nature didn't make me less than blood fae. It made me more.

"She is," I agreed at last, and meant it.

Pru reached the front row and gave us a shy wave. With her other arm, she held a flat, rectangular box against her side.

"What's she carrying?" Y'sindra asked.

I didn't answer because I didn't know.

"Oh good, there's Zee and Eli." Mae waved at the other two females coming toward us. A petite, but powerfully built woman with a broad smile and curly, blonde hair led the way. A tall, willowy, golden-haired sun fae with an equally bright smile followed behind her.

"Zee must have shifted recently," I said. "She had pink hair when I saw her the other day." Werewolves returned to their "natural state" with each shift.

The short, loose slip of shiny, multi-hued fabric came to a stop well above Eli's knees. It looked remarkably familiar. I poked Mae in the shoulder. "You loaning out your closet?"

Mae beamed. "Doesn't she look amazing?"

It was a rhetorical question. Anyone with eyeballs would see the stunning sun fae hurrying toward us, oblivious of the stares following her.

Y'sindra hopped off her seat and fluttered around me, toward the aisle Zee and Elisette made their way down. Though not yet strong enough for extended flight, her wing had grown to almost full extension in only the last few months. Mom's medicine and salves might be stinky, but with them she could turn impossibility into reality.

Pru shimmied past my sisters to the seat Y'sindra had vacated next to me. She looked at me as if asking permission.

"Go ahead," I told her and gestured to my other side. "We have those four seats."

"Thank you." She looked toward the stage and then around the large space.

This was the first show I'd attended inside the Blackthorne, and the theater was impressive. If this was Pru's introduction to the world outside of

Ta'Vale, I had to show her the elevators before she left. I knew a certain dungeon in Eodrom that could really use one. Electricity might not work there, but I was convinced someone could magic up a solution.

"Oh, I brought this for you." She held the box she carried.

My brows climbed in question, and I carefully accepted the box. As if it were a snake. Pru had given me no reason to mistrust her, but she had a multitude of reasons to hate me at best, stab me at worst.

I'd raided her closet. Took and then ruined some sweet, red leathers— which I deeply regretted. Borrowed several weapons still residing in my collection, where they would remain. I also broke into her home and stole her official Royal Fae Guard jacket.

Her shy smile slipped into a full-fledged grin which showed off her fangs. She chuckled, a unexpectedly sweet sound. "It's not a trick, I promise. I wanted to show my appreciation for the invite." She nodded toward the box. "Go ahead, open it."

I hesitated, pulling the corner of my lip beneath a fang and then ran a talon along the seam of the box, slicing through the tape. The lid opened to a neatly folded, red leather jacket. I gasped. "For me?"

She shrugged and ducked her head in an adorably bashful manner. "We're the same size, so I put in an order for a second set with my tailor. You can't get the same quality Earthside."

I traced my fingers over the butter-soft lapels. My chest grew tight. "Why would you do this?" Suspicion and hope wrestled inside of me. Hope for what, I wasn't sure. A friend? I had my sisters. I had Teddy. I hated people, I hated fae, especially sun fae...didn't I?

Or had I only believed they hated me? Elisette had only ever been kind, and I liked her.

"It's cold as the Driftas in here. The jacket might come in handy." Pru fanned her hands on her arms, the silver material of her sleeves catching and reflecting illumination from the bright lights from far above.

"It's freezing." I laughed and met her pitch-black eyes. Blood fae eyes. The obvious distinction to my one black, one violet iris didn't hit as hard as it used to. "Thank you."

I peeled the jacket from the box, revealing the folded pants beneath. "You didn't!"

She shrugged. "What's a jacket without matching pants? Don't worry, I used the Royal Fae Guard bank account. Call it payment for all the work you've done. Odo agrees Duskmere hasn't done enough to thank you."

"You got that right." I snorted and slipped into the jacket. It fit as if tailor-made for me, and well, it was. "Send Odo my thanks."

While Duskmere was the Royal Fae Guard captain, I'd recently learned gruff, scarred, Odollom was the RFG general. There was a time I'd have preferred to punch the guy than say hello, but now he was my best drinking buddy. Another fae I liked. What was wrong with me?

"Oh, snazzy." Y'sindra fluttered by my side, caressing the sleeve of my new jacket.

"Pru brought it for me. Isn't that nice?" I gave Y'sindra a crazy-eyed "help me" look, because all this *nice* felt really uncomfortable and confusing.

"Sure is. What were you thinking, girl?" she asked Pru, settling onto my seat cushion. "Have you seen what my sister does to her clothes? Holes. I'm not sure she owns anything without one."

I rolled my eyes, squeezed past Mae, beamed at Elisette, and gave Zee a quick hug. I wasn't a hugger, but Zee was, and I'd long ago learned you don't refuse a werewolf. At least not one you liked.

"Glad you made it." I waved the box at the group. "I'm going to have this delivered to the penthouse. I'll forget it if I don't."

I'd be damned if I lost another pair of those sweet red leathers. They made my ass look great.

Mae's gaze traveled from the box to my sleek new jacket to Pru. "Good idea," she agreed.

I made my way up the aisle, weaving through the crush of bodies still flowing into the theater. The lights flickered before I reached the doors, signaling the show was about to start.

By the time I located someone to run the box to the front desk and have it delivered to the penthouse, the lobby had cleared out. The doors were closed, and an amplified voice replaced the music.

Crap, the show started. I'd be the idiot running solo through the aisle. Holding my breath, I cracked the door and slipped inside. A gush of cold air and hormone-heated anticipation hit me in the face.

The lights were down. No one noticed my entrance. All eyes were focused on the bare-chested, dark-skinned man in a long black cape dancing around a woman seated on a throne center stage. She'd been fitted with what looked like the skimpiest wedding gown I'd ever seen. Poor girl had to be freezing.

The valet inside the door put a hand on my arm. "The Dark Prince is almost done. You can go during the transition," she whispered.

My brows shot up at the name, but I nodded and backed against the wall to wait.

"I will make you my dark queen." The man's voice boomed from the stage with a British accent even I could tell was fake. He slunk behind the woman, trailing his hands over her shoulders. His fingers grazed dangerously close to her breasts, and she thrust her barely constrained chest forward, as if straining for his touch.

"She knows there's people watching, right?" I mumbled and looked above the stage at the large screen showing up-close action. How mortifying!

He stopped in front of the lust-drunk woman and faced her. The cape draped from his broad shoulders facing the audience. His long braids were bound in a queue at his nape and trailed over the cape, down his back.

"It is time," he said, and then gave something hidden from the audience a violent tug.

The woman saw it. Her eyes bulged, and she licked her lips.

With a dramatic twirl, the man spun to the side. The cape flared across his torso and then revealed not just his broad, bare chest, but also thick, muscled legs.

Women screamed, as did several men. I sure hoped this place employed bouncers as well as valets, because this crowd was going to rush the stage any minute.

A true showman, the Dark Prince tossed his pants to the side. His black thong didn't hide a thing. My gaze shot to the big screen for an up-close and very personal view. I couldn't blink. My eyeballs burned. My hearts pounded. Heat raced beneath my skin. No wonder they kept it so cold in here.

Dear gods, what was happening to me? I needed to find Teddy, right now.

"I must prepare you." The Dark Prince's molten voice melted over the audience.

"Prepare me!" someone shouted. Someone from the front row, who sounded a lot like Mae.

The moment the man straddled the woman's lap, my laugh turned to sawdust in my throat. He flipped his cape to the side, revealing rock-hard butt cheeks to the crowd. The tight indents flexed and worked as he ground himself against her.

"Holy stars." I swallowed and pressed a hand to my thundering hearts.

Noting my flustered state, the valet whispered, "And I get to watch this for free every night."

"Are you ready?" The man on the stage asked.

"Yes!" The woman's shout melded with the audience's chorus of agreement.

I snorted, but who was I kidding? With his smooth, obsidian skin, all those muscles, and the not insignificant package inside his thong, I'd be tempted if I didn't already have perfection in Teddy.

All sinew and coiled power, the man spun once again with unnatural grace, stopping behind the woman.

Anticipation swelled. The enormous space, alive and buzzing with palpable energy, suddenly felt cramped.

"Wait for it," the valet whispered.

I looked from her to the stage.

"You are mine." The man's deep voice rumbled his claim. He threw his head back and when his pitch-dark gaze returned to the audience, fangs showed. Even from this distance, I didn't need the screen. I could see them.

Holy hot cakes, he was a vampire! I knew what made this revue special were the paranormal entertainers. But holy hot Cheetos!

Incoherent shouts and voices rose. The amphitheater pulsed with desire.

He was going to bite her. Right there.

"No..." I breathed.

"Oh, yes," the valet answered.

I shot her a stunned look.

She winked. "Wait until you see the next act."

On the stage, the Dark Prince sank low behind the woman. His hands came around to cover her ribs, fingers grazing beneath her breasts. He bent forward until his mouth hovered over her pulse.

This was an extremely intimate act I performed with Teddy. I didn't want to watch, but I couldn't look away. No wonder this show raked in so much cash. It also explained the revue's name: *Taboo*.

The spotlight trained on centerstage revealed every movement, every detail.

With his vamped out, ebony eyes on the audience, the vampire licked the woman's neck, numbing it. She writhed. Her legs fell open beneath the full skirt of the wedding dress. For her sake, I hoped her friends weren't recording this.

Slow and deliberate, like foreplay designed to tease, the Dark Prince slid his fangs into the woman's exposed throat. She jerked and then virtually melted beneath his hold. He drank, slow, shallow pulls. When he withdrew his fangs, he didn't immediately lick her throat. Instead letting a few beads of crimson escape the punctures to trace erotic evidence of the act on her creamy flesh.

At last, he ran his tongue over the punctures, using the natural numbing and healing components in his saliva to seal the wounds. "My queen," he declared, and drew the woman up from the seat.

"Isn't he a prince?" I muttered as the shaky-legged woman was led off the stage, followed by the nearly naked, but satiated and clearly aroused vampire. He certainly didn't suffer from the cold theater.

Bright lights burst to life and bathed the audience, replacing the moody reds and golds. Thunderous applause and screams bombarded the stage.

"I don't think anyone here cares about the storyline." The valet laughed and gestured down the aisle. "They're between sets. You can go now."

I hustled toward the front row, hoping to escape unwanted attention. If I wound up on the stage with a vampire at my throat, it would not end well. I'd bite back.

A woman in a slinky, diaphanous gold dress sauntered from behind the curtains. She praised the Dark Prince and his new queen while all around her things were wheeled off stage and replaced with new set pieces.

When I reached the first row, I made myself as small as I could manage and hurried to my seat.

"Took you long enough," Y'sindra hissed as I passed.

"You missed a good one," Mae said.

"I saw it." I made a vague gesture toward the back of the theater. "They made me wait until the performance was over."

"This was a great idea." Her eyes crinkled with her smile.

"Glad you're having fun."

Pru began to rise from her seat next to Mae, but I waved her back and began to shimmy past. "Stay, I'll take the other seat."

"It looks like we have our sacrifice for the Beast." The woman said from the stage.

Suddenly, a net of floodlights captured me. They came at me from every angle, blinding me.

Oh no. *No, no, no!*

Despite not being able to see a thing, I recognized Y'sindra's cackle. Mae squealed and grabbed my hand, tugging me away from my seat.

A hulking form eclipsed the floodlight coming from the stage. I blinked right, left, and then to the hooded man coming at me.

"I'll pass, thanks." I backed up until my legs bumped the seat.

"No, you don't." Mae grabbed my arms again and propelled me toward the man.

Dumbstruck, I went rigid when he swept me up and over his shoulder. Thank the gods I'd won the skirt versus leggings argument with Mae. I pushed up from his back and glared down at her as he mounted the stairs to the stage.

"You're dead," I mouthed.

Mae blew me a kiss while Y'sindra gave me two thumbs up.

Elisette and Pru appeared dumbstruck, while Zee put two fingers in her mouth and let loose an earsplitting catcall I had no problem hearing over the roar of the excited, hormonal crowd.

The man crossed the stage and climbed more steps. I twisted for a glimpse around his thick, muscled torso, but couldn't see a thing. Where was he going?

At last, he set me on what turned out to be a raised platform and spun me to face the audience.

"What? I don't get a throne?" I joked and looked toward the audience, hidden now by the lights of the stage. "Seriously, though. What do you expect me to do?"

Still saying nothing, the hooded man moved behind me. He took something from a pole mounted on the side of the small platform. It elicited a rattling sound and clanked. He reached for my arm.

Sluggishly, I caught on to what he was doing and backed away. "Nope. No thank you. I unvolunteer."

I didn't make it more than a step. His ironclad grip reminded me all the performers, not just the ones who shed their clothes, were some sort of paranormal. I could probably break his hold, but I wasn't certain. Despite regular nips of Teddy's blood, my blood fae abilities didn't hit the way they used to. Only my family knew, and I wasn't willing to out myself to escape five minutes of embarrassment.

"Come on, lady. You paid to be here." The anonymous man finally spoke, pulling harder.

Yep, he'd definitely win if I put up a fight.

"Fine." I closed my eyes, prepared for the mortification, and let my arm go loose. "Let's get this over with."

"Time to get some panties wet and get paid." His gruff voice was muffled by the hood.

"Helluva motto."

He grunted, slapped the shackle around my left wrist, and then moved around to my right. "Don't worry, you'll enjoy it. They all go wild for Beast."

For the audience's sake, he made a show of tugging on the chains. I rolled my eyes. Whistling beneath the hood, he hopped off the platform and positioned himself to the side of the stage, arms crossed over his barrel chest.

The lights in the theater cut out. Everything went dark. A collective gasp left the audience, followed by excited murmurs. Anticipation rose, palpable, like the zing of electricity.

With a pop, the floodlights came on again, all of them aimed at me. I blinked, my eyes watering against the wash of bright white light.

A deep primal drum beat swelled. My blood spurt through my veins in time with the rhythm. Whoever created this soundtrack knew what they were doing. Could I get a copy for my personal collection? The things I could do to Teddy with this music...

A tall, shadowy figure moved across the stage. It was barely a smudge in my blurry vision—a hulking smudge. Whatever, or whoever it was, had the audience shrieking.

I swear, if a vampire tries to bite me, I'm biting them first.

A howl rippled through the air. The fine hairs on my neck rose. My muscles clenched, and I froze.

Beast was not a vampire.

2

FUZZY BUTT

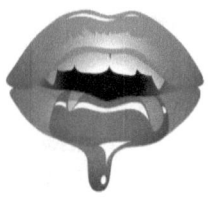

"THIS IS A GIRL'S NIGHT OUT. RELAX. HAVE FUN," I REPEATED THE mantra to myself over and over while I struggled to track the figure moving about the stage. I couldn't see much beyond a large, masculine silhouette, but whatever he was doing, the audience was going wild.

The vampire bit someone, so what could a werewolf do to elicit a similar response? I didn't think going furry would get anyone horny, but what did I know? With a name like Taboo, it could all be about repressed fetishes.

An image of a massive wolf humping my leg flashed into my brain. "No." I shook my head and gave my arm a jerk. "Nuh uh."

Being caught in the stage lighting's high beams was bad enough. I was on display for hundreds of people, fae, and who knew what else. I would not have a werewolf nose in my crotch.

Still facing the audience, Beast slid in front of me, blocking the spotlights. I finally got a good view of the guy. As far as human male specimens went, the tawny-skinned man was exceptional. Mile-wide shoulders resembled rolling hills, thighs strong and stout tree trunks. His biceps flexed and bulged with his dance moves, which frankly, weren't very good.

He could swivel those hips like *Magic Mike*, and I still wouldn't want any piece of him. The longer I remained chained here, the stronger the idea of anyone aside from Teddy touching me filled me with enough revulsion to send my sour stomach heaving.

A thought struck with brutal clarity. I stopped struggling and my mouth fell ajar. Could this be a mate thing? We only recently sealed the deal. Beyond a very serious interpretation of "until death do us apart," I didn't truly know what the bond entailed.

My mouth snapped shut, and I smiled. If I had this reaction, it gave me a measure of assurance Teddy wouldn't succumb to those wily nymphs who were always trying to seduce him. I didn't have a confidence problem, but nymphs were built for seduction. I'd been told more than once my come-hither face resembled constipation.

I yanked my right hand and then my left, rattling the chains. They didn't give. Not even a little. This was ridiculous. Wouldn't silk scarves have been sexier?

Thick billowing fog rolled across the stage illuminated by moody gray lighting. I twisted to look over my shoulder. Was that a castle? They'd rolled a whole-ass castle onto the stage. The dark and foreboding type.

The idea of this man touching me mixed acid into the pitcher of margaritas and plate of tamales sloshing around my gut. This was not going to happen—could not happen.

A woman, flanked by two large wolves, approached from side stage. Flinging her arm wide, she gestured in my direction as she bowed low. "The sacrifice has been prepared."

The what now?

I flexed my left arm, pulling my hand toward my shoulder until the leather of my new jacket pinched my biceps. The chain didn't break. Son of a swamp ogre, why did these stupid chains have to be so real?

So Beast here could look all beastly while he broke them, of course. I huffed, stomping my foot in frustration. This was stupid. I would have to reason with him. I'm sure the guy would want to wear my dinner as little as I wanted to end up as a meme.

"Hey, Beast!" I called, but it was no use. I could barely hear myself over the heavy, sensual pulse of music and chorus of shouts and screams. The beat was deep enough to turn my knees weak. It wasn't low enough to incapacitate me like the magic horn my dear old great grandpa used on me, but I could feel the effects. The bass combined with booze probably factored into my inability to break the chains.

Those weren't the main reasons. My blood fae strength, or lack thereof, was. Despite a steady diet of my sugar snack's red stuff, those abilities had yet to make a reappearance.

Beast body-rolled toward me. His groin thrust in my direction and retreated, eight-pack abs flexing with each hip pulse.

My stomach heaved. I folded my lips together and gave my arms another vicious yank. Thank the stars for the fuzzy velvet lining inside the cuffs, or I'd be bleeding. These dumb things had to be designed to snap dramatically under werewolf power. Of which, apparently, I lacked.

This was a swift kick to the ego.

The half-naked man mounted the small platform where I was chained. His eyes glowed as he approached. His white dress shirt had been torn open to reveal his zero-fat abdomen and broad, muscly chest. Nice view, but I preferred to take it in from the audience.

"Can we talk?" I asked and gave a closed-lip smile. Probably best to avoid flashing fang, looking like a threat. Werewolves were annoyingly dominant things.

Beast closed in. His head lowered in an animalistic manner. He smelled musky and wild. Not unpleasant, but there was something else distinctly wrong.

A thread of alarm drilled through my revulsion.

In a blur, he reached out and grabbed my chin. His fingers pressed into my flesh, pushing the hold into the wrong side of painful.

Threat be damned, I bared my fangs. A rumbling laugh answered my display. He pressed his nose against the base of my throat and inhaled deep enough I felt the pull of air and then the tickle of his quivering nostrils as he continued one long sniff up the column of my throat.

For a moment, my knees turned to jelly, and not from lust or the music. White hot rage ripped through me, terror on its tail. A memory pounded to the forefront of my brain. Teddy's brother Dacian smelling me, who had me believe he could make me his mate against my will. Who tried to kill me and almost killed Teddy.

A low growl vibrated from the man, loud enough to overpower the pounding music.

Snap out of it, Lane! I shook my head. This was a strip show, not a dungeon. Dacian was long gone, far away, in a different realm. He didn't have access to Earth. This was fine. Everything was fine. I just needed to get out of these chains and off this stage.

With a rough jerk, Beast pushed my head to the side and let go of my chin. He eased closer, towering over me. An unnatural heat rolled off him. Werewolves ran hotter than the average human, but they shouldn't feel like an active furnace. Sweat beaded between my breasts.

"You've got the wrong girl. I didn't volunteer for this." I glared up—way up. My five feet zero-inch height wasn't helping matters. "Unlock me."

"No." His voice scraped over his vocal cords, barely human.

As we stared at one another, yellow so pale it was almost white flared around his pupils, nearly enveloping the irises. I went still. I'd been around enough werewolves to know Beast was fighting his inner wolf. Or was he calling it forth? Either way, I wanted off this stage right now.

He grabbed for my hips, but I twisted, evading his hold.

"No," I snapped, as if speaking to a dog. To be fair, it was how he was behaving, and weren't wolves canines?

Beast gave no indication he either heard or cared I was not a willing participant in this. He wrapped an arm around my back and drew me against him, making it impossible for me to twist away. His unnatural heat enveloped me. Perspiration ran from my temple to the corner of my eye.

The smell of his musk sank into my nostrils, expected coming from a werewolf. Another scent pushed past the not-unpleasant aroma of wild animal. Beast smelled like a lightning storm.

Wrong, wrong, wrong! My brain screamed as he bent his head and buried his face in my hair, making weird snuffle-growls. Impossibly, his heat grew more intense.

Why wasn't he responding? What was wrong with this guy? It could be drugs, but I didn't think it was something so simple, so human. I tried to focus on the man pressing against me and jerked in surprise. The air around him vibrated. Through the neon haze of stage lights, it looked like puddles of watery paint bouncing and rippling atop a drum.

That was...new. I'd witnessed enough werewolves provoked into a shift during a barroom brawl to know this was not normal. In general, not normal was never far off from not good.

As if to confirm my thoughts, a crack, the snap of bone, sent my hearts into overdrive. I flinched. Beast's hands gripping my hips were frozen hooks, but a quick twist and I was free of his hold. He was too distracted by his change to notice.

With his back to the audience, no one seemed to notice what was happening. The snap of bone wasn't louder than the pounding soundtrack pumping from the many speakers or shouts of spectators.

From my vantage point, I had a clear view of the silver tipped obsidian pelt sprouting across his broad chest. The same chest which moments ago was shaved and smooth. His already impressive physique bulged.

In moments, I'd gone from looking at his furry pecs to his pelted navel.

"You really should see a doctor about whatever this is," I mumbled and tried to pull back even further. The fuzzy-lined cuffs pinched my wrists. He growled, a sound less sexy and more I'm-about-to-eat-your-face. "Or maybe a veterinarian."

Something warm and wet hit my cheek. I angled my head for a view of what appeared to be somewhat wolfy jaws jutting from a mostly human face hovering above me, agape, panting and drooling.

More bone crunched, and his shoulders widened. His arms convulsed with the transition, and he stepped back. A tug and pull at my side drew my attention to the claws snagging my new leather jacket.

"Son of a troll turd. I just got this."

Beast's head snapped up at my voice. An icy light blazed from his eyes—like werewolf white-gold cranked up to one thousand. His arms weren't the only things to transition. Despite being on two legs, I'd been right, and he sported a short, canine muzzle filled with very large teeth. His thighs had thickened to the size of small tree trunks, splitting the side-seam on pants meant to be ripped off mid-show.

Time to make my exit. I rolled my wrists, rising onto my toes as I gathered a length of chain into my hands. A second and third roll lifted me from the ground. My arms trembled and shoulders strained. I needed to work out more.

Beast threw his head back and a bone-shaking howl erupted from him. He'd grown taller, wider. His muscles had muscles. If he wasn't so close I could smell his breath, I might've been impressed.

I raised my knees to my chest, flexed my abs, and kicked forward. My feet hit Beast's furry chest, eliciting a grunt from both of us.

He stumbled backward. The collective voice of the audience rose once again. Beast had transformed into a strange cross between human and wolf, and his large ears swiveled toward the sound.

Spinning, he put his back to me and faced down the crowd who only raised their voices. His Velcro-pants flared, revealing not a tail, but a blood-red thong flossing pelted butt cheeks.

Lust from the overheated audience rubbed uncomfortably against my skin, thick and heavy, like humidity. The excitement from the amphitheater of viewers was a physical thing. I could almost feel them pushing closer to the stage for a better look.

This isn't part of the show, people! It couldn't be. Werewolves were supersized versions of their Canidae cousins. Not so with this guy. We would've heard about a bi-pedal werewolf.

A few legitimate screams rose from the white noise of shouts and whistles. Audience members not blinded by a rock-hard ass and abs on abs on abs had obviously reached the same conclusion I had.

Even as I watched, Beast swelled and grew in small steady increments. Too subtle for the audience to recognize his unusual change.

He threw back his head and released an inhuman howl.

My worry shifted from myself to my sisters and friends in the crowd.

He took a few lumbering steps toward the front of the stage.

My stomach twisted. If he made a move on the audience, things would go very bad, very quickly.

"Hey!" Fighting my instincts and bizarre revulsion, I shouted for Beast's attention. "Hey, Fuzzy Butt! Where ya going? We were talking."

His head whipped around, and those unnatural high beams glaring from his eye sockets landed squarely on me.

3

HAVING A CONSCIENCE SUCKED

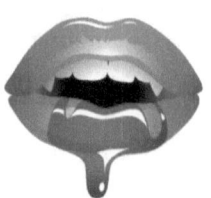

HEAD DOWN, WITH SLOW, METHODICAL STEPS, BEAST CAME TOWARD ME.

He's stalking me. My brain blared the warning, recognizing the pace of a predator.

This brilliant plan had only run as far as getting the raving werewolf's attention. It worked, I had it. Now what?

I narrowed my eyes, watching the heavily corded muscles covering his body bunch and roll with each step he took toward me.

Well, shit.

Keeping my movements slow as not to startle, I rolled my wrists once again to grab the chain.

One massive spotlight bathing the stage and others following the unhinged werewolf's movements made it impossible to see into the crowd. I licked my lips, gaze darting toward the area where my sisters and friends were in the big black void of the audience.

Beast reached the dais where I was chained and slowly mounted the platform. Instinctively, my hold on the chains slackened, and I tried to back away. I made it one small step before the links clinked and pulled taut.

A sickening symphony of popping bones and undefinable, slightly nauseating sounds accompanied his approach. While still remaining human, the bone structure of his face had taken on a distinct lupine appearance. Everything elongated outward, as if he'd begun to shift, and then stopped.

Rather than turning a beautiful man horrific, it only accentuated his best features. The hollow between his high, slicing cheek bones and strong, angled jaw stood out in stark relief. His round eyes cut higher at the outer edges.

His wolfy lips lifted in a smile and yikes, there was the scary. Bleeding gums revealed canine teeth too big for his face.

My gaze dropped and scoured the stage floor, landing on the bloody bits of bone he'd left behind. *Gross!*

I was no expert on Earth paranormals, but in my expert opinion, this was fucked up.

In an awkward, but unnaturally fast move, Beast's hand—nope, paw— shot out and grabbed for me. With a nanosecond to spare, I swiveled my hips to avoid being impaled on claws twice the size of mine. Talon-envy aside, I didn't want those things anywhere near me.

Despite recognizing the guy was beyond reason, I had to try to stop this. "Listen, you've made your point. Why don't you waggle that thong, collect your tips, and call it a show?"

In answer, he grabbed for me again. I twisted, but his claws caught the fluttering side of my jacket. I pulled. The fuzzy insides of the cuff ground against the delicate bones of my wrists.

Fabric tore, and my eyes popped wide. I shrieked in Beast's beastly face. "This is a new jacket!"

His mouth gaped, tongue lolling to the side in a super creepy, wolfy grin.

Nope. *Do not want any of this*. I pulled again. More shredding fabric sounded above Beast's snuffles and pants and the audience's continued roar for more.

Another pull, more tearing. Both furious and relieved, I gained another few inches. Stars take him—no, stars were too good for him—sun scorch him, my minutes-old new fucking jacket was ruined.

Irritation rose from my toes and erupted through my body. I screamed in his face. He screamed back, but with bigger teeth.

What big teeth you have. I snorted at the inappropriate thought, but then he snapped at me. Things got real serious, real quick.

I barely moved in time, and his fangs grazed my shoulder. They caught on the seam and he bit down. Pain tunneled through my synapses and shot fireworks across my vision. It felt like his teeth hit bone—my collarbone.

A fiery sensation seemed to flow with my blood, tumbling through my body in time with the pounding beat of my hearts. A halo of the purest white flared around my vision.

Instinct finally kicked in. The pain dropped to a distant buzz as I twisted in the chains and pulled my legs up to serve as a wedge between us. Digging my booted toes into the werewolf's rock-hard abdomen, I poured every bit of focus I had in me into my legs and pushed.

His body folded like a book. Air exploded on a grunt, and he flew backwards, landing with a thunderous crash. The audience's cheers finally turned to legitimate screams.

Beast rolled and then skidded to the edge of the stage. He surged upright and gave himself a full-body shake. Throwing back his head, the howl he released sent electricity over my bones.

I wasn't afraid. I was pissed. With another scream I yanked at the chains. At last, a *clink* heralded a small victory.

The bolt connecting the left chain hung precariously from its mount.

At the front of the stage, now pantless, Beast's massive quads bunched, and he sprang toward me.

I would not go down without taking a chunk of him with me. I bared my elongated fangs at him.

Five feet from the platform, Beast launched himself into the air, a furry torpedo headed right for me.

Tensing my arms, I gave the chains another colossal yank. The fluff-lined steel cuffs ground against my wrists. My left arm came free. A bolt hit the floor with a *plink*. I gathered the chain in my fist and swung my arm up, using the cuff like a flail.

The broken metal hoop hit Beast's jaw with a wicked uppercut and an audible *crack*. Warm blood sprayed my face. A feral shout tore from me.

Beast's head snapped up from the blow until his muzzle faced the ceiling. He staggered back, falling off the platform. Unable to get control of his legs, he stumbled toward the edge of the stage.

Frozen in place, I watched Beast gnash and snarl as he windmilled his arms, struggling for balance. As if gravity got sick of waiting, he suddenly fell backwards into a sea of darkness.

Into the audience.

"No!" The word scorched my lungs. *No, no, no!* Frenzied, I yanked my right arm. It was too weak to do what I wanted. Warm-wet soaked my shirt beneath the torn jacket. I couldn't believe he fucking bit me.

Another loud scream of pure rage scorched a path up my throat as I grabbed my right wrist with my left hand and pulled. My arms, my neck, my shoulders all felt close to popping something vital. Despite the typical cold casino air designed to keep patrons awake, alert, and spending cash, sweat beaded on my brow. The metal cuff on my wrist grew slick beneath my damp palm.

Terrified screams erupted from the audience. Pained shouts abruptly cut off—the sound of death. At last, someone turned on the amphitheater lights, bathing the chaos in stark white light.

I stopped struggling and scanned the front row—Mae, Y'sindra, Zee, Eli, Pru all on their feet. Relief swept through me strong enough to bring me to my knees. If I wasn't being held up by a gods' damned chain.

"Mae! Y'sindra!" I shouted for my sisters, but they couldn't hear me over the thunderous beat of hundreds of feet fleeing for the exit.

Pru's head swiveled, and our gazes locked. Like me, she had slightly better than average hearing. As a pure blood fae to my hybrid nature, hers would be better.

The stage was almost taller than she was, but she vaulted up with ease and raced for my platform. Ever the soldier, her dark gaze scoured me from head to toe, assessing my condition.

"You are hurt," Pru said. She leaned in to sniff the wound and her nose wrinkled. "It smells."

"I don't know. He bit me. Maybe he had a lot of garlic for dinner?" I rattled my right arm. "Get me out of here."

She nodded and moved to evaluate the strength of the chain. It rankled that she thought she could break the links whereas I could not, even if that was probably true.

"Zee says this werewolf is moonbit." Pru's black eyes met mine as she reached over my head and took hold of the chain. "Are you familiar?"

"Moonbit? Sounds itchy. Never heard of it."

With a grunt of acknowledgment, she focused on the link connected to the hoop affixed to the pillar and pulled. Her shoulders bunched and biceps flexed. Metal scraped against metal but didn't give.

Brows furrowing, she paused and relaxed her grip. "There must be a secret release around here. If I can't break it, a werewolf in human form would not succeed."

While the declaration sounded arrogant, she received no judgement from me. Pru was simply stating a fact. I hated it, but I knew it to be true. After all, I'd grown up with a blood fae mom. I was strong, at least I used to be, but true blood fae had very little competition in the pure strength department. At least when they were hopped up on blood, which Pru was, judging by her delicate blush.

She crouched, but rose slowly, giving the metal pillar my arm was still attached to a level of attention I was almost uncomfortable witnessing.

"It's impolite to feel up poles without first asking permission," I said dryly.

She shot me a scowl and stalked to the post I'd broken free of.

The other pole got the same treatment. Not finding what she searched for, Pru rose and shuffled methodically around the small, square platform. Laser focused on the glide of her feet across the wooden stage, she didn't look up as she passed me for a second time.

"What are you doing?" I asked, because surely time was better spent breaking the chain while a half-form werewolf rampaged through the crowd.

"I am searching for a button or catch." She glanced up, first at me and then at the retreating audience, finally to my sisters and Elisette chasing Beast through the aisles while he pursued fleeing patrons. Pru returned to her search. "Your friend Zee says this moonbit is a sickness, and this form is not natural. If he had been a wolf in his previous performances, the floor would be the most likely location for a latch."

"Maybe," I agreed, but my brain circled back to my sisters, Elisette, and Zee still in the audience. Where was Zee?

As if summoned by my thoughts, Zee's pony-sized wolf with a rare golden-blonde pelt launched over an aisle on a collision course with Beast.

Front paws connecting first, Zee hit the big man's chest. She torqued her tankish body in an astonishingly lithe, feline-like twist. Her hind paws followed as she turned, jackhammering into the off-balance man-wolf's chest. Powerful hind quarters gathering and flexing, she pushed off and sailed in the opposite direction from Beast.

He careened backwards. The stadium seats connected low on his legs, and he toppled. Seats folded and crumbled beneath his bulk, creating a dark gap in the connected row of seats.

Shock rooted me to stillness. I'd seen Zee in her wolf form, but never in action. She was powerful, graceful, and exuded the unmistakable alpha energy. A mantle she'd run from, far and fast. I made a mental note to dig deeper into her suddenly much more interesting history.

"There you are," Pru said, pulling my attention back to her.

She stood in front of me, looking not at me, but at the platform beyond my reach.

I narrowed my eyes. It took a moment, and then I saw it. A tiny, displaced shadow from a button embedded flush to the ground.

When Pru stepped on the button she had to tip her foot forward just so for her toe to connect with the release latch.

Clever. It would take good eyes and a deliberate touch from something stabby, like a wolf claw or the narrowed toe of a boot. She had to try several angles before a quiet *snick* came from my right. The chain relaxed but didn't release.

Pru reached up, once again wrapped her hands around the steel links above my raised arm and pulled. The links held for a breath and then snapped free at the hook.

I imagined a wolf rising onto its haunches, ripping loose the chain with its jaws. Yep, that would make a dramatic show for the audience. Dumb, in my opinion, but dramatic.

"Done." She gathered the dangling chain and handed it to me. Her gaze traveled first to the length I'd broken and held in my left hand, to my face. "I am unsure how you managed to break that."

Because she couldn't, remained unsaid.

I rolled my shoulders, stiff and achy from all the hanging and pulling. "I was trying a lot longer than you. Either it loosened it, or that side was faulty. I couldn't break the right one either." I tipped my head toward the implied chain.

Nodding, she visibly relaxed.

I took no offense. My lack of strength compared to a true blood fae was no secret. Only a handful knew my strength hadn't returned to my version of hybrid blood fae normal. Pru knew, not because we were bffs and I'd told her, but because her rising rank in the RFG—the Royal Fae Guard—made her privy to those sorts of private conversations.

Side by side, we leaped from the platform. A pile of clothing kicked to the side of the stage caught my attention. I switched direction, dropping to my knees by Beast's discarded pants to rifle through the pockets.

"What are you doing?" Pru paced toward the noise erupting from the amphitheater floor and back.

I raised my left arm, letting the heavy chain fall from my hand and clatter onto the stage. "This is going to get in the way." In the second pocket I searched my fingers brushed against a small metal object. "Got it!" I jabbed the key into the left cuff and let both it and the chain fall from my wrist.

Brow bent in a thunderous scowl, Pru's gaze traveled from the key to the pants. "I should have thought of that."

"Didn't occur to me either," I said. "Let's go." Together we jogged toward the edge of the stage and made the jump to the amphitheater floor.

Several rows up, Beast rose from the broken seats. Chest heaving, he threw his head back and released a bone-trembling cross between a roar and a howl.

My muscles pinched. Prepared for battle, all my connective tissue pulled taut while my joints felt oiled and loose. Movements controlled and smooth, I vaulted over row after row of seats, aiming for the man-wolf.

Ahead and to my side in the right aisle, the sole focus of Beast's attention, Y'sindra and Elisette were tucked in close to Mae inside her nearly translucent gold bubble of protection. As I watched, Y'sindra stumbled and dropped to her butt, looking magicked out.

Skirting Beast's peripherals several rows up, Zee stalked a wide arc to position herself for another attack.

Instinct told me he would be ready this time. Panic skulked along the edge of my brain, but I slammed the door on that reaction before it could fully form.

Faster, I have to move faster!

Pushing power into my legs, I leaped. My feet sank into another cushy seat, and I went up and over, landing in the next and then the next. At the edge of my vision on my left, I spied a swiftly moving shadow. Pru. She matched my pace but had pulled slightly ahead. We would get there at the same time, but from opposite directions.

Another row, and another, and I was there, flying over seat backs and slamming into the enraged, man-wolf's shoulder. I buried my talons into his flesh and hung on.

The punch of my body to his ribs shoved a huge rush of air from his compressed lungs. A breathy, whiny howl escaped his muzzle. He flailed, trying to catch his balance. Only a beat behind my collision, Pru rocketed into his other side.

Beast's breath left his body at the double impact. The slightly sour scent of old meat bloomed around us. Strangled growls vibrated his massive chest. His movements turned jerky and uncontrolled. Frantic, he twisted, stumbled, and swayed.

The crusty cold pelt beneath my palms told me Y'sindra had tried her winter magic thing. What would it take to bring were-zilla here down?

Like me, Pru's talons found flesh and she hung on. I gripped with my thighs to avoid a broken leg from flailing limbs as he twisted. Pru had the same idea. Our knees bumped, but just barely. This was like climbing a Sequoia sapling.

"Don't let him bite you!" A naked, now human Zee shouted.

Too late for that.

For a split second I marveled at Zee. Werewolves could shift outside the full moon, but it took power and control. Maybe it was all her alpha energy?

I blinked, bringing the situation back to focus, and answered her concern. "Fae can't be infected."

On the opposite side of Beast, Pru's fangs lengthened, and she drove them into his throat. In nearly the same instant, she reeled back and spat. "Smells sick."

Shit. We—and by we, I meant Pru—couldn't drain him of blood. Y'sindra had already tried her thing. Mae's magic was defensive, not offensive.

Recovering from being sandwiched between Pru and me, Beast gave a violent twist.

Where my talons dug in, flesh tore. I slipped an inch. Hot blood beneath my palms made my grip precarious.

"Don't make this worse. Just go down," I pleaded through gritted teeth. Worse for him, or for us?

Zee was suddenly there, lithe and fluid, dodging Beast's lethal-looking claws. She launched an uppercut I heard and felt. *Damn!*

His head whipped back, but it was only a moment of distraction. Zee now had his full attention. She moved like a seasoned boxer, dancing backward into the aisle. Mae grabbed Y'sindra and scrambled to get out of the way, Elisette on her heels.

The crazed man-wolf stalked after Zee, wearing Pru and I like accessories.

"This is ridiculous." My abused muscles strained and screamed. The bite at my neck radiated heat. Pain had begun to overtake adrenaline. A deep tremble vibrated my limbs. I wouldn't be able to keep this up much longer.

Pru and I locked gazes.

"Any ideas?" I yelled the question to be heard over Beast's growly breaths.

"We must put him down," she answered, not sounding one bit winded.

Put him down. Inwardly, I winced. I wasn't opposed to killing. Generally speaking, I was a big fan. But if this moonbit thing was real, it hardly seemed fair.

"Avid." Fatigue slurred whatever Y'sindra said.

"Huh?"

"Abid."

"What are you talking about?" I shot her a quick look over my shoulder. My focus slipped, and so did my hold. Scrambling, I tightened my knees and flexed my biceps. The motion sent a new ripple of pain into my nerves.

"Rabid. She's saying he's rabid," Mae yelled.

I blinked at the side of Beast's head. How would they know?

Bouncing on her toes, Zee moved in.

Of course. Zee witnessed the transformation and would have known.

Resignation and pity renewed the acidic churn of margaritas and tamales in my belly. The sour taste clung to the back of my throat. Having a conscience sucked. When had I acquired one of those, and could I return it?

The extra weight of Pru and me slowed the big guy down, turning his movements jerky and awkward. Reluctant to let go, I focused on Zee. "Right thigh holster."

Golden-brown gaze darting to the tri-blade dagger sheathed there, Zee nodded and darted in, ducking below Beast's awkward swipe. Touch so light, I didn't feel a thing, she snagged it and danced back into position. She gripped the slim, twisted blade at her naked side that sported bruises and abrasions from sliding on the floor.

I'd almost brought my smaller push daggers, but I'd capitulated to Mae who threatened to pour water over all my cheesy poofs if I covered my shirt with a weapon belt. I regretted that decision now. With their corkscrew blades that left behind gaping holes, it was tough to not land a death blow using the tri-blades.

"Go for the legs," I told Zee, still hoping we could bring down Beast without ending his life.

Obviously confused by the idea of stabbing someone in the leg, her brow creased. Being more of the stab-first-ask-questions-never kind of gal, I was confused too, but here we were. "If we can't bring him down, we'll do it your way."

Zee's mouth folded into a stubborn line.

A deep growl rumbled from Beast, vibrating his chest and belly against my limbs. The guy was coherent enough to understand, but not thinking clearly enough to free himself of my and Pru's barbed octopus grips.

In a zip of movement, Zee leapt forward, aiming not at all for the leg.

With more agility than he should possess, Beast twisted to the left while lashing out to the right.

The crack of flesh preceded Zee's body spinning away in an out-of-control spiral. She hit the row of chairs with a sickening crack.

Beast followed and bore down on my friend struggling to disengage herself from the stiff seats bent around her body.

Mae raced toward us—toward danger.

No!

I ripped my talons free of Beast's chest. Crimson sprayed through the air, onto my face.

Off balance by the sudden shift in weight, he stumbled to the left where Pru still held on.

I hit the ground. My knees went soft as I sank into the fall and then channeled the absorbed energy to dive for the blade Zee dropped.

Still focused on Zee, Beast didn't react, didn't get out of the way as I spun on my knees and lashed out with the dagger.

The twisted, glinting length of steel speared Beast's ankle. He canted to the side, roaring, and swiped at me.

I rolled out of the way, torquing the blade as I did. The crack of bone and tearing of vital tendons was loud. Hot blood coated my hands. The dagger handle turned slick in my palm.

Pru dropped from his other side and darted away with grace I would never possess.

Tightening my grip, I yanked the dagger free of Beast's ankle. It released with a ripping, slurping sound.

He dropped like a sack of wet cement.

I scrambled back, his flailing limbs barely missing my legs.

A guttural roar filled the theater to a painful decibel.

Oh, yeah, I'd fucked his ankle up good—but I hadn't killed him. Point for me, and my new, stupid, incredibly inconvenient conscience.

I scooted back against the closest seat rest and took a breath, keeping a close eye on Beast. It would take more than a shift to heal a wound like that in a healthy werewolf, but I didn't have a clue what the effect of this moonbit had. So far, he only rolled on the floor, howling and harmless when out of his reach.

Wrapping my arms around my knees, I relaxed against the broken chair.

Zee stepped forward and drove a length of wood that looked suspiciously like a seat armrest through Beast's skull. It sank in with a crunch. His big body spasmed and jerked as if he'd rolled onto a livewire.

Beast went still as death.

Because he was dead. *Gods damnit!*

My bewildered gaze met Zee's who crouched over the man-wolf's body.

Wiping her hands together, she fell back onto her butt and shrugged. "There's no coming back from being moonbit."

4

THE PROVERBIAL SACRIFICIAL LAMB

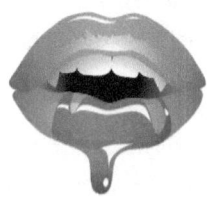

A GURNEY SAT IN THE AISLE, THE BRAKES ENGAGED TO PREVENT IT FROM rolling down the slope to the stage. Six EMTs weighed down with Beast's body staggered toward the black padded gurney way too small for its intended occupant. But he was dead, so it wouldn't matter to him if his legs hung off the end. It might make it difficult to navigate turns on tight corners.

The authorities questioned each of us. They had moved on from me and my sisters to a, thankfully, clothed Zee. Before the mob had descended en masse to investigate the scene, I'd cornered one of the hotel security guards and sent her to procure clothes for Zee.

Vaughn, the head of hotel security, and Mae's current boy-toy was all business. After a quick appraisal of Mae's condition and confirming she was fine, he got to work directing the bulk of his security team to move audience members to a convention room for questioning while he sent a smaller team to retrieve a copy of the video feed of tonight's events for the local authorities.

However, he told the police, before he could release the footage, he needed to place a call to the casino owner—Andrew Black, aka Angus Blackthorne, aka the really old evil-ish druid, aka my many times over great grandpa.

A scowl pulled hard on the corners of my mouth as I stalked toward

Vaughn intent on slapping the phone out of his hand. This was my hotel—sort of. I would say whether or not and to what extent we cooperated.

Still holding the phone tight to his ear, he looked toward the officer seemingly in charge. "We will turn over all video evidence, but we require the body."

I stopped. "We require what now?"

His dark gray gaze flicked toward me. "Mr. Black would like to investigate the body."

Stunned, at a loss for what to say, I gave Vaughn a blank stare. In typical haughty vampire fashion, he dismissed me and returned to his conversation filled with a lot of yes, sirs.

Finding my voice, I blurted, "Why?"

Vaughn's smokey gaze didn't flick, but rather slow-swiveled toward me. The guy was a master of projecting annoyance and disdain. Tough. I'd been the proverbial sacrificial lamb chained to a pole, and I'd also been the one to end Beast's rampage. The least he could do was give me an answer.

"Well?" I asked, meeting Vaughn's deadpan stare with one of my own.

Mae slipped a gentle hand under my elbow and steered me away. "Let the man do his job."

"Vampire," I corrected, because there was a difference.

Even in profile, her eye roll was obvious. "Let Vaughn do his job. He'll answer questions later."

With a meaningful look from my sister, Vaughn nodded.

Pleased, Mae turned up the wattage on her smile and threw him a saucy wink.

I made a gagging noise.

"Stop that," she chided.

"Stop flirting," I countered and asked, "Y'sindra?"

"She threw two powerful spells at Beast, both of which he shook off." Her nose crinkled delicately. "She knocked herself out, but she's okay. Eli is with her over there."

I followed the direction Mae nodded toward and found Y'sindra's puff of white curls in a seat on the opposite aisle, next to Elisette.

"Why do you think Blackthorne wants the body?" I asked.

Mae lifted one shoulder. "You could call him and ask."

"No."

A wet squelch accompanied my foot sinking into squishy, slippery carpet.

Blood had stained the red carpet nearly black. So much blood, it bubbled and stood on the surface around my foot. *Gross.*

Like Pru had said, it smelled wrong. Not unpleasant, but wrong. It reminded me of decaying leaves in a wet forest. I scented ozone and honeysuckle, rain and sunbaked grass, charred meat and toasted spices. Too many smells coming from a single source, almost none of which I'd ever scented on a werewolf. Unfailingly, I'd only ever associated woodsy, wild places in their scent. And dog—I couldn't forget the undertones of man's best and stinkiest friend.

What could I say? I preferred cats.

Without the crush of an audience, it occurred to me I might just be scenting other, varied sources of blood. I'd witnessed plenty being spilled in the first act, after all. Not to mention the damage Beast inflicted before we'd distracted him from a fleeing audience. I'd counted into the high teens of injured, and at least three sheet-draped bodies had been rolled out.

Zee joined us at the end of the row and fell into step as we moved into the aisle. "I know you were trying not to kill him, but it had to be done. I'm sorry."

Hearing Zee, Y'sindra, awake and coherent now, turned to face us. She knelt on the seat rather than stood, so not entirely back to herself. "Yeah, you're so stabby. What in Freya's loins were you thinking?"

"That whatever it is wasn't his fault," I snapped, but pinched my lips together and shook my head. She didn't deserve me biting her fluffy head off. "Zee said he was sick, and I didn't think he should die for that."

"Still." Eyes narrowed, Y'sindra dragged out the word, clearly conveying her doubt. "Not like you to show restraint."

It was my turn to lift a shoulder. I looked away, unsure why I'd felt bad for a guy who hadn't tried to do anything more than hump my leg before he'd...changed. "We live in the human world, not Interlands."

Lame excuse, but it was as good as any. The truth was, there were a lot of new people in my life. New people I cared about, and those tender feelings seemed to be rubbing off in different ways. I hated it.

Turning away from Y'sindra and her questions, I faced Zee and asked, "Is there really no cure? Some sort of wolfy antibiotics?"

"No. It's a rare condition. No one knows why it happens, but no one has ever come back. I've only seen it happen to werewolves, but there have been rumors swirling lately of it happening to other paranormals." She looked at me in question. "I don't think fae have experienced it?"

I shook my head. If it wasn't for a magic-born disease, Earth would be a magicless realm. Spending time around more human paranormals—as the altered humans referred to themselves, not as supernaturals—I'd learned most were now born this way. Children were born with the magic their parents' generations ago were infected with. Also, mages and witches were not synonymous, but that was a whole different thing I still couldn't wrap my brain around. Bottom line, it tracked this moonbit thing would be exclusive to humans.

"Right. Didn't think so." She crossed her arms, dropped them to her side, crossed them over her chest again. The fidgety reaction was so unlike Zee, it made me wonder if this moonbit business was the source of her recent stress.

Behind me, metal groaned and squealed. I turned my head to see some very exhausted paramedics covering Beast's lifeless body. One arm hung over the side, fingertips close to the ground. The bottom of the gurney hit him mid-thigh and his legs dangled at a weird angle.

Vaughn's security had replaced the EMTs and having recruited Pru's assistance, wheeled the stretcher and its somewhat furry, too-big-for-a-body bag passenger up the sloped aisle toward the exit. Beast's blood trailed along behind them, a wet line beneath the lights.

A weird pinch pulled deep in my chest. I needed to shake these tender feelings. Maybe go swing a sword at a tree or punch a bag. Teddy had turned a portion of the garden into a covered sparring ring, complete with protected, weather-resistant weapon racks and punching bags. He was delightfully thoughtful.

When I looked back to Zee, her mouth twitched to the side as her gaze shifted to follow the slow-moving progress of the gurney.

"If there was no helping him, you did the right thing," I said gently. From the brief glimpses of her past Zee had shared, I knew she didn't harbor any warm, fuzzy feelings for her kind. Still, Beast was already down when she'd scrambled his brains. Paranormal or not, she was still human, and this would be hard on her. Before moving to Vegas, I'd lived Earth-adjacent long enough to understand humans rarely had an easy time killing someone who did not pose an immediate threat to them or theirs.

She blew out a pent-up gush of air. Her shoulders slumped. "I know, but..." Pausing, her forehead pinched. "You made me think."

I snorted. "Not exactly what I'm known for."

A half-smile pulled up the corner of her mouth. She glanced at the retreating gurney once again.

I followed her gaze. They'd made it to the top of the aisle and were moving toward the exit.

Now that they were no longer struggling to push uphill, Pru broke away from the group and came toward us.

Zee crossed her arm over her body, gripping her biceps. "You asked if any have ever come back from moonbit?" She spun the statement into a question, stalling.

As a big staller myself, I supported this tactic. "I did," I agreed, because she seemed to be waiting for an answer.

Tongue darting out to trace her lips, she swallowed. "To my knowledge, no paranormal ever has."

"You told me. It's cool. I get it." I patted her arm awkwardly. I didn't do pep talks.

Her eyes, round and wide from some sort of unpleasant epiphany, met mine. "But what if no one has ever really tried," she whispered. "He was already down. Maybe someone could have tried."

Crap. I was not equipped to soothe someone else's conscience. I'd only just discovered I had one of my own.

"Don't second guess your choice," Mae said and guided our friend into a hug. "As I often tell Lane, follow your instinct, and your instinct told you it was the right thing to do."

Whew. Trust Mae to step in and save me from the mushy, emotional stuff.

I began to back away discreetly, only half listening to Mae and Zee along with Elisette and Y'sindra who had joined in. Dreams of a hot shower and maybe hot, soapy sex with Teddy in said shower filled my head.

"...more werewolves than usual. Most of them alphas. What if it happens to me?"

Zee's fear-filled voice drove into my eardrums like an icepick. I stopped and closed my eyes. That was not something I could unhear.

Moonbit anything didn't seem like something under YML Investigations purview, but this was Zee. If she feared for her life, there was absolutely nothing that would stop us from trying.

"All right," I called down the aisle. "Let's move this party upstairs."

When Zee stepped away from Mae and looked toward me, I made sure to paste on my most reassuring smile.

Sitting on a seat back just out of Zee's line of sight, Y'sindra pointed to her front teeth.

Oh, right, fangs. I pressed my lips together and stretched my smile.

Zee's pierced brow arched.

"Come upstairs and tell us everything," I said, giving up on the smile. "We're not letting anything happen to you."

Suddenly, my legs felt like sandbags as the weight of the entire incident and Zee's concerns finally hit home.

Dreams of getting dirty in the shower would have to wait.

5

PROMISES WERE LIKE TIME BOMBS

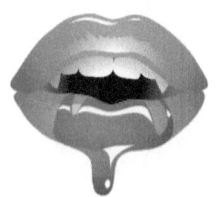

"Zee was right. You showed a lot of growth today." Mae set a large mug in front of me. Curls of steam rolled off the fragrant, dark liquid. When the light hit it just right, turning the surface a deep brown against the white walls of the mug, it reminded me of Teddy's beautiful eyes. How had I ever believed them to be black?

I sighed, missing him. He'd been in the bar with the work crew, putting the final touches on *Blood and Wine* when I'd called. He'd be up soon with takeout from Three Peppers Cantina, my favorite restaurant in the Blackthorne. We might have eaten platters of food from there only hours ago, but as I've always told Teddy, my appetite truly had no limits. Besides, adrenaline made me hungry, and I'd just had a mega dose of the stuff.

"You're all growned up," Y'sindra quipped from across the table.

Plucking a sugar packet from the little caddy, I tossed it at my sassy-mouthed sister. It hit her on the cheek.

"Ow," she cried dramatically.

I rolled my eyes.

"We should have insisted Pru and Eli stay after the shock of tonight," Mae called from the kitchen.

"Nah," I said. "Dad's portal made it easy for Pru, and Elisette wanted to be home with Jason."

We'd met Elisette, a runaway sun fae, purely by accident when her fiancé,

Jason, an earth mage with a dubious connection to my Great Gramps and an unfortunate case of idol worship, hired YML Investigations. He'd wanted us to track down a stolen ring he'd planned to use to propose.

The RFG had also hired YML to find sun fae who had been going missing. We'd found both in the most unlikely of places, but it all worked out. Though, the ring had been through an aloughta's digestive tract, thanks to Jason's vindictive ex. I still cringed a little every time I spotted it on Elisette's lovely, long-fingered hand.

Mae returned to the table with an espresso-size cup for Y'sindra and set another mug—not quite as large as mine, but not as small as Y'sindra's—in front of herself as she slid into a seat. After a sip, she finally broached the subject we'd been avoiding while we let Zee clean up and calm down. "Did you hear what Zee said earlier? About this disease, moonbit, and how it's happening more frequently?"

I nodded.

"What are your thoughts?"

Hands curled around the warm ceramic, I stared into the second-best elixir of life—first being Teddy's blood—and thought about my answer. "I don't think I know enough about the disease to say one way or the other."

Mae tilted her head slightly. A swath of golden hair fell across one eye, and she tucked it behind the elegant point of her ear, so unlike my short, almost rounded tips. "What is your gut telling you on how we should approach this?"

My gut had very little to say, other than it might need an antacid. Taking my time, appearing more thoughtful than I actually was, I pulled a sweating glass of ice water to me and took a sip.

The fancy round ice cubes bobbed and clinked. I gave the glass a swirl and watched the frozen orbs dance. "We need to determine how often, and how much more than normal, this is happening. Is it natural, or is something causing it to happen?"

Still Mae waited.

Finally, I shook my head. "That's all I've got. We need to wait for Zee to fill us in. Maybe you can find some information in our father's library. The great Finnlay Callaghan," I said with a mocking wave of my hands, "has all sorts of clandestine info on creatures all over the worlds."

Her blueberry-blue eyes widened. "I didn't think of that, but you're right."

The elevator slid open and moments later the rich, spicy aroma of Three Pepper's signature molé preceded my sugar buns. My salivary glands went into overdrive, from both the scent and the view. Teddy—aka sugar buns—set the two bulging brown paper take out bags on the counter, winked at me through the pass-thru and got to work setting out plates, utensils, and anything else we might need.

Something about watching a six-feet-four male who radiated fuck-with-me-and-find-out energy but knew his way around the kitchen made my hearts go pitter patter. Not so long ago I was horrified by these types of reactions. Now I leaned into them, and onto Teddy, if I got lucky.

I went to the kitchen pass through, pressed my palms to the cold marble and hoisted myself forward until I stretched across the counter, toward Teddy. A smile tilting his lips, he slipped his hands under my arms and pulled me across the counter. The moment my feet slid free of the marble and he lifted me into the air, I wrapped my legs around his waist. "Hi," I said, and wove my arms behind his neck.

"I thought you were hungry." He gave me a squeeze and then backed me toward the counter until I was seated between two incredibly aromatic, overstuffed takeout bags.

Hooking my ankles at his lower back, I pulled him closer and teased, "I'm hungry for all sorts of things."

"Really, Laney?" Mae strolled into the kitchen. She shot me an arched look over Teddy's shoulder. "On the counter?"

"Wouldn't be the first time," Teddy said.

Heat tore up my body, so swift, I thought the tips of my ears might ignite. Mortified, I buried my face in his shirt. "Oh, gods."

"Huh," Mae said. "Didn't think Lane had it in her. Just clean up after yourselves."

"I've seen Y'sindra and Lo walking all over every surface in this penthouse. Whatever Lane and I might do is hardly the dirtiest thing that happens on these counters."

"You make a good point," Mae said.

I pushed Teddy back and hopped down, grabbing one of the bags. "Okay then, I'm officially done with this conversation."

Laughing, Teddy swung me around to face him. "Not so fast." The paper bag crinkled between us as he took hold of my hip and pulled me to him. He leaned in for a kiss. His satiny lips met mine. A knot buried somewhere deep behind my breastbone tightened and then unraveled.

This was home. This was where I belonged, forever.

His tongue traced the seam of my lips, asking for entrance.

I opened for him.

Our tongues brushed against one another and retreated.

My breath left me in a stuttered rush, and I melted into him. Everything but Teddy fell away. An overwhelming need swelled inside of me, too enormous to be contained. I always wanted Teddy, but not like this. This rivaled oxygen.

Sensing, or maybe scenting my wild need, a low growl rumbled from him, and he pushed closer.

Paper crinkled and something popped. A spicy, salty, pungent aroma of melted cheese exploded from the bag I still held between us. Something hot and wet gathered against my chest. "Shit! The queso."

"No harm done. I got it." Teddy took the bag, set it on the counter, and dug out the queso. Cheese oozed from beneath the lid, coating the sides. He retrieved a bowl and dumped what was left of the ooey gooey cheese into the bowl.

My gaze slid to Mae, standing next to the coffee machine, smirking.

"What?" I snapped.

A grin bloomed from her smirk, she shrugged, and hit the grind button on the fancy coffee maker, getting a second pot brewing. Next, she filled a pitcher with water from the refrigerator.

Not a drop of booze in sight. Wise choice, as we needed clear heads.

Teddy placed a large aluminum tray filled with Mae's favorite duck and plantain enchiladas on the pass through, between the kitchen and the dining room. Biting my lip, I watched him. With everything that happened— berserk werewolf on a rampage—I'd forgotten my initial repulsed reaction when I'd thought Beast might touch me. In a sexual way, not a tear-a-chunk-of-flesh-from-my-face sort of way. Maybe that was what was responsible for my swift, intense reaction to Teddy's kiss?

Thinking about the bite, I rolled my shoulder and returned to the dining room to begin transferring the food to the table. A bottle of Mom's special medicine had taken the edge off the residual ache. Mae had bandaged the wound. These days I sipped directly from Teddy more than the bottled stuff, and my healing had returned to normal even if my strength had not. But

Beast had gone for my shoulder like I went for the last strip of meat on BBQ ribs. I'd felt teeth hit bone. It was pure luck he'd missed the vital bits, and I'd retained use of my arm.

On bare feet, Teddy came around from the kitchen and joined Mae and I as we filled our plates. No one said a word as we got to work appreciating the food. Eventually Zee, Y'sindra, and Lo joined the feast.

After scarfing down a large portion of carnitas drowned in a tangy salsa verde and a generous helping of rice and beans, Y'sindra let out a burp which had no right coming from such a small body.

"Rude," I said.

She scrunched her nose at me and to no one's surprise, dug into the takeout containers, serving herself seconds. Moments later, Lo did the same.

"Where do you two put all that food?"

"Fast metabolisms." Teddy grinned at me from his seat at my side.

"Faster than an angry grounder," I said, but when I looked into his eyes, my smile slid off my face. I set my fork on the plate and sat back in the chair. "I guess I need to tell you what happened."

Teddy shrugged. "I saw the tape, but you can tell me what happened in your words." His gaze slid down the table to Zee, a wiggly line of concern creasing his brow, and his tone turned gentle. As if the strong werewolf might suddenly shatter. "And I suspect we need to hear from you?"

Licking greasy, delicious hot sauce from her fingers, Zee nodded. She waved a taco in my direction. "I want to hear what happened from Lane's point of view first. Beast's—"

Teddy choked.

I arched a brow and asked, "Water?"

He shook his head and made a motion for me to continue.

"I know, dumb name." Zee said and chuckled. It was a husky laugh. I'd tried to emulate it once, but Teddy only asked if I had gas.

"Mo worf van va bark prinf," Y'sindra mumbled incoherently around a mouthful of shredded pork and beans.

"Don't talk with your mouth full," Mae chided, sounding a lot like Mom. It was cute.

"The vampire's name was bad too," Zee agreed, somehow deciphering what Y'sindra had said. Her nose wrinkled. "I can't believe people find blood drinking sexy."

Teddy's expression could only be described as a leer. "You should try it sometime." He winked at me.

Heat stampeded across my cheeks. I scowled.

Gaze locked on Teddy, ready for a reaction, I steered the conversation back on track and asked Zee, "So, you couldn't see what the exotic male werewolf dancer was up to? You couldn't see the change?"

Teddy only smirked. My sugar snack knew he had no competition.

"No," Zee said, but then wagged her taco again. "Well, not exactly. We saw a little, but it was distorted by the lights and all the screaming. There are rumors *Taboo* uses some great special effects, so I didn't think anything of it."

"Humans be crazy." Y'sindra accompanied her declaration with a fork drop on her plate. She sat back, hands on her very full belly.

"I could see you were angry," Mae said.

"The people in the nosebleeds could see that." Zee laughed, shoved the rest of her taco into her mouth and like Y'sindra, sat back.

"If you're all done," I grumbled.

"Lighten up," Y'sindra said and threw a tortilla chip at my head. She loved throwing food. "A werewolf tried to hump your leg. We've all been there."

Jaw dropping, I gaped. "When…never mind. I don't want to know."

Try as I might not to think about it, the image in my mind of a tiny werewolf going to town on Y'sindra's leg still formed.

"Anyhow," I drawled. "The short of it is I tried to reason with the guy, but he kept coming."

"That's what she said!" Y'sindra shouted and banged on the table, snort-laughing. Next to her, Lo giggled.

"Anyway," I drawled again, then proceeded to summarize the entire event, from pelvic thrust, to bite, to Beast ending up in the audience.

Zee nodded. "Pretty much what we saw, but we couldn't tell what was real."

"And like Zee mentioned, the lighting camouflaged much of his change. Until the very end," Mae added.

"I heard screams. I assume that's when some of the audience clued in?" I asked.

"Probably. I know I did." Zee's mouth twisted to the side. "It was pretty obvious. I can't believe I didn't see it sooner."

Looking at my still half-full plate mournfully, I pushed it away and sat back. My appetite hadn't fully returned after the upheaval the contents of my stomach went through earlier, and I knew when to admit defeat—with food, at least.

"Don't be so hard on yourself. You said it's rare. You've probably never seen it happen." I pulled my napkin off my lap and tossed it onto my plate.

The silence stretched into the realm of uncomfortable. I glanced around the table and found everyone watching Zee.

She cleared her throat. "My mom went moonbit." Her statement was little more than a breath.

Her words shot through my hearts. If I wasn't already convinced we'd look into this for Zee, that would do it.

Mae, bless her soothing soul, rounded the table, took the seat next to Zee, and wrapped her in a comforting embrace. My sister was awesome.

"I'm sorry," Teddy said, and everyone voiced their agreement with the sentiment.

Snuffling, Zee sat up. She used her napkin to wipe her nose and then smiled at Mae. "Thank you." Facing the rest of us, she repeated her thanks. "It was a long time ago. We weren't close, but I guess the shock of seeing it tonight kicked in. You know I'm not a crier."

"Girl, everyone deserves a good cry," Y'sindra said and then pointed at me. "Especially that one. Weepy all the time."

I shook my head at the blatant lie. It was cool she was trying to lighten the mood, but I wouldn't hate it if she aimed her bone-cutting quips at someone else once in a while.

Zee chuckled. "I'm pretty sure Lane is incapable of being *weepy*."

Sitting a little straighter, I beamed at my friend.

"You've never seen her when someone takes her last Ho Ho," Mae said.

"It was one time," I snapped. "And I didn't cry."

"You totally cried," Y'sindra said.

"I was hungry."

"Hangry," Zee said and popped a tortilla chip into her mouth. "I get it."

Grinning, I shrugged, but then I followed this thread back to the conversation it had unraveled from. "Moonbit," I said gently. "Explain to us what it is, and what you think is different this time."

Zee's forehead wrinkled. The gold hoop in her brow caught the light and winked. "I'm told moonbit can happen to any paranormal, but like I said, I've only seen it in the were-community. It's more like an infection, not a disease, and not too different from an animal who contracts rabies, or a human on PCP. Or a combination of both, I guess."

"How so?" Mae leaned her elbows onto the table. Sitting forward, she folded her hands together and rested her lips against her fingers.

Mouth twitching to the side, Zee said, "Oh, yeah, you probably don't have either in Ta'Vale, huh?"

"Unlike these yahoos, I watch TV," Y'sindra said. "I know what you mean."

Looking down my nose in my best impersonation of the one the sun fae called queen, Iola, I said, "Half-naked horned up singles on a beach don't count."

She slouched into her seat and shot me a black look. "Hey! You're right there watching with me."

"Which is how I know there are no rabid beasts, or whatever PCP is, on those shows."

"I watch other things," she grumbled.

"Let's allow Zee to finish," Mae said, using a far gentler tone than I did or would.

In a snit, Y'sindra slung her arms across her chest and slouched even lower. If she kept that up, it was only a matter of time before she disappeared beneath the table.

"Rabies and PCP," I said, hoping this time we stayed on track. "What is PCP?"

"It's a drug. It gives humans excessive power and an immunity to pain," Teddy said.

I started to ask how he knew that, but he'd been around humans a lot longer than me. It wasn't that strange he would know what Zee meant.

"They aren't stronger," Zee said. "PCP inhibits pain receptors, which gives mundane humans a sense of invulnerability. To an observer, it might look like more power. It also makes them highly aggressive."

"Like rabies," I said, finally getting the connection. I glanced back and forth between them. "This feels like weird knowledge for both of you to have."

Zee let out another throaty laugh and smiled. "I'm a lot older than you, babes. I've been around the block. I was also a counselor for the at-risk and vulnerable at one point in my life. I saw a lot of shit."

"From counselor to bartender," I said, a little in awe of Zee's versatility.

"Girl's gotta do what she's gotta do. And you'd be surprised. The two professions aren't so different."

Teddy grunted his agreement.

"The truth is," Zee continued. "After I walked away from my pack, I was empty inside. Part of an alpha's responsibility is to care for and nurture those who belong to them. It's something I was missing, so I applied the sociology degree I thought would help me as an alpha into helping others."

The naked truth and raw vulnerability in Zee's admission lanced me, all the way to my bones. She might be a badass beast, but she had a mushy heart. She was far better than me.

"You are a good person." Mae echoed my thoughts and squeezed Zee's hand.

"Okay, I think I understand what we're dealing with, or rather what happened." I paused and traced my fingertips over my lips in thought. "I'm not sure what we can do though."

"You're staying with us, of course," Mae said. "You'll be safe here."

"Not to be that asshole, but if what Zee says is true, we can't make that promise."

"You are exactly that asshole." Y'sindra glared daggers at me, squishing her nose in an angry sneer and spun toward Zee. "Ain't nothin gonna happen to you on our watch."

Promises were like time bombs, ready to explode when the promise, while well-intentioned when made, was broken. I rolled my eyes to the high ceiling overhead. There was no point in arguing.

"Lane is right," Zee said.

My gaze snapped to her and then to Y'sindra. I wasn't above giving her a smug smirk. I could be petty. I also didn't care.

"Exactly that asshole," Y'sindra muttered again.

I chuckled. She wasn't wrong.

"We aren't putting you down if something happens to you," Teddy said. "I refuse to lose my best bartender."

"You got it, boss." Zee winked. She reclined against her chair back and laid her forearms on the arm rests. The beat Zee tapped with her fingernails was steady and even, obviously lost in thought. At last, she said, "I got a good whiff of Beast tonight, and while there is no other explanation for what we saw, he didn't smell right. The infection might be evolving. It would explain the more frequent cases."

The horrific realization she knew what moonbit should smell like because she'd been there when it happened to her mother unsettled me.

Spinning the tiny loop in her brow, Zee's gaze went unfocused. "Your grandfather requested the body." Her eyes, the unusual shade of liquid butterscotch, deep and yet translucent, slid in my direction.

"There are about a gazillion greats in front of grandfather. But yeah, he did." I shrugged because I didn't know why he made the strange request. Vaughn had followed us up here and gone to the roof garden, apparently intending to send the body through the druid circle. He'd returned and left without the corpse, so either we had a new garden ornament, or it was gone.

It had been weird, but so was this entire night.

Zee released the loop. Her gaze sharpened and met mine. "Can you ask him to find out if there is anything unusual? If that isn't what he's already doing?"

Leaning to the side in my seat, I folded my legs beneath me. My seat didn't have arm rests, only those at the head of the table had those uncomfortable things. "Sure. I can't imagine what else he's doing with it." I didn't want to imagine what else he was doing with it. Maybe he had a necromancer in his employ?

I'd found out the hard way Gramps had necromancers on the Blackthorne payroll when I got nosy and wandered to the hotel's industrial laundry. There had been a guy in a bedazzled, eggplant-shaded robe sitting in a comfortable chair, reading while dozens of zombies ran the machines, transferred loads, folded, and sorted. If you could ignore the stitches and, in some cases, very obvious reasons for death, the zombies had been pleasant to chat with. The necromancer not so much. Pompous jerk.

"Why don't you get some rest?" Mae's voice was soft and gentle. "Take the guest room you used the shower in. We'll collect anything you need tomorrow." She rose and began to clear the table, purposefully bumping Y'sindra's seat as she passed in a not-so-subtle hint to help.

Muttering incoherent but clearly profane comments under her breath, Y'sindra popped out of her chair and climbed onto the table, collecting the small plates as she went. Lo followed, picking up empty to-go containers, of which there were many.

We might have no rent and no mortgage, but with our expanding household, the food cost was astronomical. I wrinkled my nose and glanced at Teddy. "Shouldn't we get a discount on food?" I waved a hand indicating the room. "Penthouse. Technical owners and all that."

Teddy chuckled. "We do." With a quick kiss, too fast to savor, he rose to help with the table clearing.

Holy Ho Hos! I'd seen the food bills we'd racked up since we moved in. That had been with a discount?

"I can help." Zee stood with her plate just as Mae reached her and took it from her.

"You had a shock. Get some rest," Mae urged.

Zee wasn't the only one who'd had a shock.

How easily they forgot I'd been the one chained up. Suddenly reminded of my revulsion at the idea of being touched by Beast, my gaze slid to follow Teddy's phenomenal ass as he made his way around the table. I made a mental note to ask him later. Pillow talk seemed like the right time. After the dirty, steamy shower sex.

A smile creased my mouth, and I pulled my lip beneath a fang, hiding the heated reaction to my thoughts.

When I looked at Zee, she was watching me with raised brows and a knowing smirk. Ugh, how had I forgot? Werewolf. Even if she wasn't privy to my thoughts, she could guess by my scent change.

Feeling the burn on my cheeks, I frowned and pressed my fingers to my face. "Mae's right, you should rest," I told Zee. "I'll call Blackthorne. If he has any important news, I promise I'll wake you."

Very little extra convincing was necessary before Zee capitulated and headed for her room.

I rose and stretched across the pass through for a towel to wipe down the table. Lo and Y'sindra stood side-by-side on stools washing dishes while Mae loaded the dishwasher. Teddy was busy taking care of the garbage.

It was all so...domestic. Almost surreal considering the past year, or even this past evening.

I padded to the sliding glass doors. The wood floors were cool against the soles of my feet, even through my thick socks. I enjoyed feeling the floors. Though sanded smooth and polished, the natural texture, the ridges and whorls of the wood were evident. Not long after we'd moved in, I'd realized this entire penthouse had been like one massive focus for Blackthorne. The wood acted as a buffer between his brain and the magic, so he could avoid frying his gray matter.

A harsh trill rang through the comfortable sounds coming from the kitchen. In the reflection of the glass door, I caught sight of Mae reaching for the phone.

My brow creased with annoyance. That line had a direct connection to the front desk. Goosebumps pulled at my flesh, and I hugged my arms tighter across my middle. Mae's eyes widened slightly, and her gaze landed on me. She spoke quietly into the receiver and hung up. The bulky plastic earpiece clacked loudly in the cradle.

"Who was that?" I asked, still watching her in the reflection.

Mae glanced furtively over her shoulder, toward the entry. "No one."

Suspicious, I said, "It was obviously someone."

"Just the front desk," she said and walked from the kitchen, out of my line of sight.

Eyes tight with suspicion I turned to follow. Halfway across the living room, I heard the quiet thump of the elevator reaching our floor followed by the whisper-soft hiss of doors opening.

A sudsy plate in her grip, Y'sindra craned her neck to see the entry. She burst out laughing. "Freya's frozen fruitcakes, what are *you* doing here?" Her gaze shot to me, and she smirked. This did not bode well. "Lane is going to lose her shit."

The too-tight, prickly feeling pulled another round of goosebumps onto my skin. I increased my pace, walking faster toward the archway leading to the entry. Suddenly, those whorls and ridges in the wood weren't so comfortable. They ground uncomfortably under my feet.

I rounded the corner into the hallway leading past the kitchen to the elevator and froze. My muscles clenched and joints locked. Irrational fury rocketed through me. My fangs tingled. Well, from my perspective, it was very fucking rational.

The delicate woman with a river of blue curls falling over her shoulders sent me a shy smile and waved. "Hi."

"Fate," I snarled. Sure, a lot of people said Fate was a bitch, but they didn't know her. I did, and they were right. I hadn't seen her in almost ten years. It wasn't long enough. "What the fuck are you doing here?"

6

WANT A COOKIE

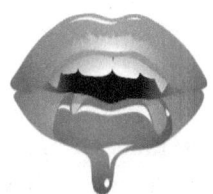

FOR SUCH A REVERED, POWERFUL SEER, FATE STOOD THERE LOOKING LIKE an unsure, afraid, overgrown child. I was fifteen when I saw her last. She towered over me as a teen and was even taller now—taller than Mae. Whip thin with delicate bones, she hadn't grown into her height.

Like me, her hair reached her waist. Unlike me, her tresses were the natural blue of a cloudless sky, full and bouncy. Her dark complexion was the perfect canvas to set off such an amazing shade. Mae would call her ethereal, and she was.

Fate had an unreal quality, like a cross between a goddess and a human hippie. Her thin-strapped tank top, multitude of bangles, and skirt with its hem dusting the floor really sold the hippie vibe.

"What do you want?" I repeated. Anger strangled my vocal cords, my voice tight and vibrating in the uncomfortable silence filling the penthouse with tangible pressure as everyone waited for me to react.

They probably thought I might explode into a thousand raging pieces and were prepared to dive for cover. It was still a possibility.

When I managed to unclench my jaw, I repeated my still unanswered question for a third time.

Fate blinked. If her hair resembled a cloudless blue sky, then her eyes were the sun, bright yellow and weirdly complimentary to the rest of her features. Right now, those expressive eyes were huge and round in her heart-shaped face, lending her a wounded appearance. I felt as much as saw my sister's surprised expressions slip into scowls aimed in my direction.

Taking up the length of my unbound hair, I twisted it around my hand and tugged. Of all the beings—fae, human, or otherwise—I thought might show up on my doorstep, she was the last I would have laid money on.

Stars give me strength.

I blew out a breath and asked something different. "How did you even find me?" Why would she even want to?

A tight smile pinched the corners of her mouth and she pointed to herself. "Iomas, or did you already forget?"

I snorted. "Your track record with me would say otherwise."

Animosity hadn't always lived between Fate and me. We'd been friends, almost like sisters. After everything Y'sindra and Mae had been through together before I came into the picture, they were naturally closer to one another than to me, but I'd had Fate. Until she'd tried to kill me—or at least she hadn't stopped someone else from trying.

Fate stomped her foot, a gesture that reminded me of how similar we had always been. "I told you it would change your life. I didn't say to go."

"You also didn't say not to," I snapped. "And then someone tried to kill me. They almost succeeded too."

"Oooh!" Y'sindra's astonishment pierced the palpable tension.

I had never told my sisters this part of the sun bridge story. I had never told anyone. From the corner of my eye, Mae's golden head swiveled from Fate to me and back.

At the sink, Teddy had straightened, unsure if a threat had just walked into our home. The only threat he should worry about was me pouncing on Fate and ripping all those perfectly coiled curls from her head.

As if hearing my thoughts she shook her head, sending those curls into a new cascading wave over one shoulder and then the other. "I was too young, too inexperienced, and my gift too weak to shape the *see* I received when you showed me the note. You knew that."

"Note?" Mae asked.

Grimacing at the conversation to come, I shot a quick glance in her direction. "Later."

She narrowed her eyes but nodded.

I'd spent all these years keeping details of that day to myself. My family said they believed I hadn't remembered what drew me to the central apex of the sun bridge, a loop in the sky overlooking the sun garden far, far below, but deep down I knew they were only respecting my wish to stay silent on the subject.

No longer. Everyone would insist on the full story.

Angry at having my past forced into my present, I lasered Fate with my best glare.

Reflexively, she drew herself up. She was tall enough to look Teddy in the eye. Even as a child, she'd used her height as a defense mechanism. "I told you whatever awaited you on the sun bridge would change your life, and it did."

Eyes narrowed, I ran my tongue over my teeth, pressing against one fang and then the other until I felt the subtle, sweet sting of pain. "Do you want a cookie?"

"What kind?" she asked.

Y'sindra chortled.

The remark caught me by off guard. I almost laughed, but instead pressed my lips together and looked away.

"Lane." Fate took a few tentative steps into the foyer, reaching toward me before she thought better and flattened her hands against her side once again. "You came to me and asked for my help. I only ever wanted to impress you, to be your friend, so I told you what I felt from the note. I have regretted it every day since."

Discomfort settled over my shoulders. I shifted awkwardly from one foot to the other. A bubble of what might have been sympathy, but I sincerely hoped was gas swelled within the heat of my long-held rage. Mentally, I reached for the fraying ends of my anger.

"What do you mean, *you only wanted to impress me?*" I latched onto that lie and threw it back into her face. "I was the outcast and you, the future Iomas Príomh, had legions of admirers. If anyone wanted to do the impressing in our relationship, it was me."

Fate shook her head. Her long, loopy curls caressed her bare shoulders.

Suddenly, feeling exactly like the self-conscious child I described, I ran a hand over my head until I'd gathered my hair at my nape and began the centering practice of braiding.

"They watched. They judged." Fate dropped her gaze to the floor. Her slim feet, encased in handwoven sandals peeped from beneath her hippie hem. She dragged one foot in a small arc, back and forth. "Any attempt at friendship was made only for who I was and what stature they might gain from the future leader of the Iomas."

Gah! I would not fall for this wounded puppy, vulnerable act. She had to want something from me. What, I had no idea.

"Poor you," I said, earning a disapproving *tsk* from Mae. I huffed and dropped my half-braided hair to plant my hands on my hips. "So why are you here, Fate? To clear your blemished record?"

"Of course not." Her gaze snapped up, fierce and fiery, burning into mine. "I was not wrong. Your life changed, but you suffered for the inaccurate, immature *see*."

Shrugging I said, "It happened. It's done. I'm doing great." I swept my hands wide in a broad gesture to encompass our lux surroundings.

"I see that." Fate smiled softly.

"Ha!" Y'sindra laughed. "You see that. I get it. Good one."

I rolled my eyes to the high ceiling and sighed. "Well, you've unburdened your guilt. Feel free to send a letter if you get the urge to do any other unburdening"—I made air quotes—"in the future."

"This is not easy," Fate snapped, her whip-fast temper rising again.

Inexplicably, my hearts squeezed at the memories. She'd been my fiercest defender, ready to throw down in my defense at the smallest slight. And vice versa. *Like sisters*, I thought again. The weight of sadness substantial. "Then why do it? For the last time, why are you here?"

"I am here to rectify my mistake." Confidence fusing her spine into a steel rod, Fate strode through the short hallway until she stood a breath away. My sisters' heads popped out from the kitchen entry behind Fate, watching.

"It's done. I survived." I tried to meet her gaze, but it had become an iridescent kaleidoscope of color, like a fractured whirlpool of stained glass. Shit. She was *seeing*. My muscles pulled and pinched with tension. Anticipation sizzled over my nerves. "Don't," I whispered.

"I have *seen*." Fate's voice took on a hollow, booming quality.

"Don't," I repeated, but I knew it was too late. She'd *seen*. She was here. Her words were an unstoppable force.

Behind Fate, Mae and Y'sindra's eyes were wide.

Uncertainty rippled across Lo's cherubic face, but he took his cue from my sisters' anxious reactions and pressed close to Y'sindra's side.

I licked my lips and looked at Teddy behind them, watching me with concern.

Sighing, I accepted the inevitable. "Well, get on with it."

Chin raised, eyes unfocused, Fate spoke. "What once awaited you on the Sun Bridge has been set free with malevolent intent upon the sun fae."

Cold settled in my middle.

"Puppet strings they held have been severed. They are desperate. They chip away at Eodrom's stability. The kingdom rests on broken crutches, ready to collapse."

A chorus of gasps came from the kitchen.

Hoarfrost crept through me, reaching into my extremities, numbing me. Pieces of information began to fuse into a horrible realization. This was something I'd have to turn over in my brain later.

I licked my lips, struggling to keep the dread from my face. "Well, message delivered. Bye now." I gestured toward the elevator.

Fate's gaze, while still intense, had focused—on me—and returned to normal. "I can sense whoever this is blames you for their failing plan."

"Nothing new. My job tends to put me on people's bad side, and I've been hard at work."

"Impressions tell me all those years ago, they knew you would have a hand in whatever is happening now. It cannot be an Iomas, I would know. Whoever they are, they are very powerful."

The cold hunkered in my middle turned sharp and biting. I thought I'd burned all those bridges to the past when I left Ta'Vale, yet here we were again. "It seems like you should be telling a whole lot of fae who aren't me this news."

"I have. However, I am aware of how the RFG works. They will look inward to fix any problem before reaching out. That is, if they even bother to contact you. I came here so you could hear the *see* for yourself."

Unlike every other fae—mainly Duskmere—in Ta'Vale, who failed to tell me anything of importance, Fate, who knew the reception she would receive when she darkened my doorstep, was here. She had made what was probably her first trip cross-worlds to deliver news she could have called with.

I ordered myself not to soften toward her, but I could feel it happening.

"Listen," I said and curled my chilled fingers against my sides. "I did my job. I don't want anything else to do with the sun fae or their problems."

"Good." Fate rolled her lips together and studied me. "Because if you return to Eodrom, they will be waiting. Do not come back."

7

YOU'RE STILL A SELFISH ASSHOLE

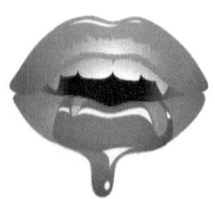

Alone for the moment, I sank into my favorite chair, the deep cushions welcoming me. I stared blankly at the huge television mounted on the far wall. It was turned off.

I curled in on myself, planting my feet on the seat and pulling my knees to my chin. I was itchy and uncomfortable. Beneath my skin, nerves continued to jump and twitch from a deluge of adrenaline and anxiety. A combination triggered from buried memories seeing Fate forced to the surface, and the latter by her dire warning.

My sisters had insisted Fate and her sun fae escort who had been left to wait in the casino lobby, not return by whatever means they arrived by. Instead they used the platform set up on the balcony to return to Ta'Vale. The flat rock, a small piece of the larger stone pad in our parents' garden, only helped focus the coordinates our father's portal discs were tuned to. A device was still required, but maybe not for much longer.

After being claimed by the sun stones, and since I had one stone planted here, in the rooftop garden, Mae's power had grown exponentially. She and our father had been working on linking the two devices, which blew my mind.

And terrified me for the uncertainty of what my sister was becoming.

Until we come to it, I thought, repeating my newly forged mantra to myself.

A blanket fisted in my hands, I wrapped my arms around my legs, drawing the soft material over my body. A fuzzy shield of false security against the conversations I knew were coming.

My sisters were taking their time with Fate. I glanced down the hallway toward the elevator. I could still escape.

No. Time to tell the unfiltered truth. I puffed a breath and dropped my chin onto my knee, watching the neon-lit night outside the sliding glass door, waiting for my sisters' return.

Part of me longed to be surrounded by Teddy's strong arms rather than the blanket. I always craved his calming presence, but I also appreciated how he knew when to excuse himself and give me time with my family. Lo had taken his cue from his best bud. They'd both turned in for the night, but I doubted either were asleep.

I rubbed my chin back and forth across my knee, the velvety fuzz of the blanket soothing. Teddy would need answers too, but it wouldn't be the same. I hadn't lied to him for nearly ten years, as I had my family.

Had I lied, though? I told them I couldn't remember what happened, which was a half-truth. I didn't remember what happened after I fell.

Fingers feeling stiff, I picked at the blanket's hem curled around my feet, talons catching and pulling.

Fine, I lied, but my family hadn't needed to know the sucker I had been. That the pivotal moment in my life which sent me running from Eodrom had been as much my fault as it was the fae who pushed me from the sun bridge.

A wash of buried shame burned across my chest.

Now they knew. Thanks to Fate.

I wanted to weave the unraveling ends of my anger back together. Yet, inexplicably, I'd grown a bit of wisdom over the last few years. The sharp edges of my grudge had dulled.

Despite my initial violent reaction to seeing Fate, a deep ache had settled against my hearts. I sat back and pushed a talon between my teeth. Stars take me, I had missed that girl. Worse, I had no defense for the truth in her words.

Gnawing on my talon, I annihilated this morning's expensive manicure. Deep down, I realized I'd always known I couldn't blame Fate. All those years ago, I'd put her on the spot asking for a *see*, fully aware she was too immature in her powers to be accurate.

Only she had been accurate, so maybe precise was a better word choice.

I recalled the note, its expensive natural leaf parchment soft against my fingertips. When I'd unfolded the small square left on my windowsill, it had fallen open like a cotton handkerchief. No sharp creases, but smooth and rounded folds. I could still smell the sweet scent of honeydew wafting from the page. The sharp, confident writing. The confession of someone who claimed to have admired me from afar but was ready to reveal themselves.

I'd been so desperate for acceptance. I hadn't listened to the warning in Fate's voice when she'd told me what she felt. *Whatever awaits you will change your life.* No poetic flourish, only uncertainty.

Scowling, I moved onto my thumb claw. Fate had even said she didn't know if it was a good idea, but I'd waved off her concern. My brow pinched. Funny she hadn't brought that up. Was she trying to make me think she was the better one of us?

Knowing I wouldn't treat her kindly, she'd still made what had to be her only trip out of Ta'Vale, maybe away from Eodrom, to issue a warning. And she apologized. Maybe she was better. Probably. I closed my eyes and let my head thump onto the seat back. Definitely—she was definitely a better fae than me.

My sisters' voices drew closer, rising above the white noise, an ever-present pollution in Las Vegas, despite us being over seven hundred feet above the Strip. The scrapes and hollow clomp of their footsteps hitting cement transitioned to a soft whoosh from the hand-woven throw rug laid inside the sliding glass door, and finally the solid thump of hard wood.

Softer steps led to my chair. I knew it was Mae, because despite her size, Y'sindra stomps were like an Aloughta charging into battle.

Not bothering to lift my head, I cracked an eye and squinted up at Mae.

"You treated Fate unfairly." Her lips pressed into a tight, bloodless line.

"You're going to get wrinkles." With a lazy swirl of my index finger, I indicated the general direction of her mouth.

Eyes narrowing into slits, she puffed an breath from her nose, but her mouth relaxed. "Lane, you were mean."

"I know." It sucked just as bad saying the admission aloud as it did thinking it. "I miss the days when I was blissfully unaware of other people's feelings and could go through my day being a selfish asshole."

Y'sindra snorted. "You're still a selfish asshole."

"Thanks," I said with genuine appreciation.

She held up a small hand, and I leaned forward to fist bump my sis.

"If you two are done," Mae said flatly and did her huffy walk to the sofa where she settled into the cushions and gave me her best deadpan-stare.

As far as looks went, it wasn't bad.

I matched her stare with my own while Y'sindra crossed between us and flounced to the opposite end of the sofa from Mae. She hopped up and looked between Mae and me. Neither of us spoke.

Silence would not break me. This was something I'd been practicing. I hinged forward at the waist, getting closer to prove it.

Mae's judgy eyebrow arched. The right one. It had a slightly sharper peak, and she knew it.

I smiled, letting my fangs lengthen slowly.

"Oh, you're getting good at that," Y'sindra said.

"Thank you."

"Gotcha!" Y'sindra knelt on the seat cushion, pointing at me.

I yanked a small pillow from behind my back and threw it at her.

Mae's hair ruffled as it zipped past her face and smacked Y'sindra with a satisfying whumph. Her white curls puffed up, back, and then settled.

"Troublemaker," I said and caught the pillow she threw back at half the velocity. "May all your Sno Balls be missing their cream filling."

She gasped. "Take it back."

"No," I said stubbornly and crossed my arms.

"Enough, both of you." Mae narrowed her gaze first on Y'sindra and then pegged me with a withering look. "It's time for the truth, Lane."

My spine softened, and I hunched over the pillow. "Yeah, I know." I worked my talons over the pillow's seam. *Thwipt, thwipt, thwipt.* A thread popped.

My sisters sat quietly, waiting for me to speak.

I looked away. Against the backdrop of night in the glass doors I could see the reflection of the room. Mae and Y'sindra watched me.

I licked my dry lips and spoke. Despite this happening almost ten years ago, it was the catalyst for me leaving Ta'Vale. Every detail had been etched into my brain. "I found the note on my windowsill."

My words were a wrecking ball crashing through the dam I'd built against the memory. The story poured out of me. I told them everything, from the scent and texture of the note to the feel of the hands hitting my back.

"Oh, Laney." Mae came to my side and squeezed next to me into the overstuffed chair. Her weight rolled me toward her, and she wrapped her arms around me. I tilted my head onto her shoulder, and she stroked my hair over and over. "You shouldn't have carried that alone."

"Now I understand why you're always so quick to stab everything." Y'sindra perched on the seat's armrest, creating a Callaghan sister-sandwich. Despite her snarky comment, which, frankly, I took as a compliment, her smile radiated so much love it almost hurt.

Not for the first time, I thanked the stars and whatever forsaken gods set these girls in my father's path. Though I used the term *adopt*, that was a human practice, not fae. The fae *claimed*. Mae and Y'sindra had been claimed by the Callaghans. They were my sisters of the heart, which, for me, meant a helluva lot more than blood.

At last, I sat up and said, "Stabbing relieves a lot of stress."

"I hear sex does as well," Mae said. She twisted this way and that, trying to get comfortable in a chair built for one. Giving up, she returned to the sofa. "Which begs the question, how are you not living in bliss?"

"Ha!" Y'sindra stood on the armrest and gyrated like a dashboard hula figurine. "Lots of stabbing and sex. I get it."

I swatted Y'sindra with the pillow. She tumbled off the chair. A moment later she rose into the air, hovering. My loose hair swished over my shoulders from the breeze generated by her wings.

"We all heard you and Teddy going at this morning, so when was the last time you stabbed someone? Two weeks ago? Maybe it's time." Y'sindra fluttered back to her end of the sofa. My gaze followed her progress. Her dips in the air were already less and less. Whatever she was doing in her free time, her almost repaired wing was rapidly gaining strength.

"Last week," Mae answered. "In the rear end."

Technically, it was a couple hours ago, but I didn't think any of us wanted to talk about that yet. I shrugged. "The guy shouldn't have run."

"Mmmhmm," Mae said, sounding unconvinced.

"It's true. He didn't want to return the money he owed Rip and tried to make a break for it. I threw a torpedo." My favorite throwing daggers. No barb, so they got the job done without causing too much damage. "Why else would I stab someone there?"

"It's fun," Y'sindra said.

"Yeah it...er...." I caught Mae's glare, and my agreement withered on my tongue. Best change the subject before she decided to find out how much fun it really was and put the act into practice on my lovely derriere. I cleared the amusement from my throat. "Right, well, you both know everything. What's next?"

Mae gave me her hard stare, long enough I once again began fidgeting with the pillow seam. "First." She paused for emphasis, making the one-word declaration a sentence. "You heard Fate. We are going to heed her warning."

"Agreed."

A quick smile of approval fluttered over her lips. "Y'sindra will take Zee to Mom and see if there is anything she can test for. You aren't going anywhere near Ta'Vale."

Hallelujah. I'd been trying to escape that place for years, and now Mae insisted I stay away. "Agreed," I said again. "Are you going with Y'sindra?"

"To Eodrom, yes, but I plan to pay Dad's library a visit. That was a good suggestion. There must be something in there about moonbit." She stood and took my chin in her hand, tilting my head to the side. Cool air rubbed over the exposed edges of what remained from Beast's bite. "I will look for something on fae bitten by human were-creatures."

The mostly healed flesh along my neck and shoulder seemed to crawl. I pulled my chin from Mae's hand. "I'm not going to go furry and howl at the moon. If fae could be changed, we would have heard about it by now. Fae and human paranormals have been mingling for years."

"I agree, but it doesn't hurt to check." Mae pressed the back of her hand to her mouth and yawned. "Your job is to visit Blackthorne. The druid, not the lobby, just in case you decide to play dumb."

"Sounds good... wait, what? Why?"

Her expression turned to granite.

Ducking my head, I scratched my neck. Unease settled on my skin, itchy and uncomfortable.

"You made a promise to our friend. Did you not mean it, or have you already forgotten?"

"Of course not." I totally had.

"Cut her some slack." Y'sindra bounced into the air and hovered at my side. "Girl had a rough night. First, a mutant werewolf used her as a chew toy and then her childhood bestie slash nemesis stopped by to say don't come home."

A delicate snort escaped Mae.

I shrugged and almost asked Mae why she expected me to visit

Blackthorne, but then I remembered. "Can't I just call and ask why he wanted the body?"

"You could." Mae picked my cell phone up from the coffee table and dropped it into my lap. "But I would prefer not to replace another phone."

My brow pinched. "It was one phone."

"Three," Y'sindra not-so-helpfully supplied. "Plus, the house phone you ripped off the wall last week."

"Room service lost my order," I mumbled.

"Phone breakage aside, you are very good at reading more from what a person doesn't say than what they do." Mae stood and looked pointedly at the digital clock below the television. "It's late. Let's try to get some rest before the sun comes up."

Wings flapping, snow spraying from them, Y'sindra shot up the stairs. She stopped at the top and called back, "Don't worry, Lane. If you do go furry, I got you covered. The shop in the lobby sells gourmet milk bones."

I sent my throw pillow spiraling for my smartass sister, but she was already gone.

Mae chuckled and hugged me. Her warm hands brushed over my back. "You take care of yourself. I don't believe Blackthorne will hurt you. He seems to take pride in your relation to him, but don't let your guard down, okay?"

"Don't go day drinking, you mean?" Smirking, I stepped back.

"Oh, no, do that." Mae laughed and led the way toward the stairs. "You deserve it after the night you had, just..." She shook her head, her golden hair swishing across her back in front of me. "I'm not sure what I mean. Maybe just don't believe everything he says."

I hummed my agreement.

We reached the second-floor landing. She faced me and shrugged. "Or do. He is the only one who has been completely honest with you."

Surprised, I inhaled sharply. "You aren't wrong, and isn't that sad?"

"It's something to consider." Mae yawned again, pressing the back of her hand to her mouth.

"Sleep." I shooed her toward her room. "No vampire booty calls."

Eyes hooded, head tilted, her full lips melted in a smile that practically screamed sex. "I told him to come up when he finishes his shift. Don't worry, I'll get a few hours before he finishes handling the Beast situation."

My eyes made a tour of their sockets. "You two are worse than bunnies.

Or grounders—there are a lot of grounders. They must be as bad as bunnies, right?"

Laughter like pure magic filled the air. "Maybe. I never thought about it."

"I don't blame you. I sort of hate myself for putting that image in my brain."

More laughter bubbled out of my sister. It was good seeing her happy. The uncertainty of her situation with the sun stones had stripped her bare of her usual joy. Ever since the mysteriously sentient power source of the sun fae had anointed my sister a keeper, she'd been struggling to find her way.

Silver glinted beneath the fingers Mae curled around the doorknob to her bedroom. "Besides, you're one to talk. You and Teddy are very enthusiastic. We all hear you."

A blush ignited my flesh. I couldn't hide my embarrassment. My pale complexion always ratted me out. "Maybe it's a really competitive game of Twister?"

Still laughing, Mae closed her door with a soft snick.

I continued to the end of the hall and passed through the double doors into my suite. All the second-floor bedrooms were suites, but mine was the largest. When it was evident Teddy would be joining us, my sisters insisted. Who was I to go against their wishes?

Dim light shone from the table lamps next to the bed. The sheets and blankets were thrown back, but the oversized king bed Teddy had insisted on was empty. The glass wall beyond the far side of the bed revealed nothing but night. Neon lights glowed far below. The foot of the bed also faced a wall of glass that opened onto a smaller, private patio.

Soft light spilled from the crack in another set of double doors to my right. Steam swirled inside the room. Tendrils reached toward the open door but dissipated before they escaped.

Belatedly, I heard the water running. My stomach dipped toward my toes, and not in a bad way. It was a weird weightless flutter of anticipation. Smiling, I began to strip, leaving a trail of clothes on the floor as I padded toward the bathroom and the hot steamy shower sex I'd been craving.

I shoved open the doors and waded into the thick humid air. "Who's up for Twister?"

8

I WASN'T TOO PROUD TO BEG

THROUGH THE FOGGED GLASS WALL OF THE LARGE, WALK-IN SHOWER, I had a great view of my sugar bun's perfect sugar buns. After basically assaulting those muscular, dimpled butt cheeks with my eyeballs, I moved on to his V shaped torso, to the hills and valleys of his upper back. The ripple and roll of muscles flexed across his shoulders as he lathered up the suds.

My stomach disengaged from my body. It floated away, a weightless fluttering thing.

Teddy swiveled his torso, turning his face toward me, and he let loose a weapon-grade smile. A slow delicious expression promising wicked delight.

I was so in.

Stepping out of one fuzzy slipper and then the second, I peeled what remained of my clothing off as I crossed to the shower. Despite the humidity, cold air blasted my bared flesh. The sudden tightening of my nipples skated the line between pleasure and pain.

Ravenous need pulsed through me, all the way to my tingling fingertips. My breath hitched with quivering pants. Despite my sisters' jokes, my and Teddy's sex life had cooled from Olympic level to a healthy normal. Yet right now, if he tried to say no, there was a very real chance I would lose my sun scorched mind.

My need was powerful, unnaturally so. All I could think of was sinking onto Teddy's soapy length. He'd angled himself toward me in profile, putting the appendage in question in direct line of sight. Even as I watched, or maybe because I watched, his dick twitched and thickened. My core clenched, and I'd be damned if I didn't whimper.

Want was too weak a word for what I felt. This was a necessity, like hunger, like thirst. Like air. I'd never felt anything like it. Not even when we'd forged the mate bond. At this moment, if anyone stepped between us, I would tear my way through them.

I stepped out of the last piece of clothing on my body—my panties. Leaving the small pool of silky red fabric on the floor, I angled toward the open walk-in to steamy paradise on the right. A large rectangle, the decadent shower, took up the entire far wall with an open entry on both sides and a sheet of glass in between.

Soap suds slid down Teddy's glistening flesh, the hot water coming at him from six strategically placed shower heads lent his tanned flesh a deep flush. He turned to face me fully and slid his hands down his powerful chest. My breath hitched as he paused their descent to draw sudsy circles on the muscled ridges and dips of his abdomen.

Eyes half-hooded, he watched me as I stepped inside the shower. His hands finished their journey, and he gripped himself. Slowly, he stroked his soapy, silky length.

Unsure what to do, I just stopped walking, my own hands clenched at my sides. I'd never seen a male touch himself before. If I had, I suspected I wouldn't feel this sharp jolt of lust. It was an ache. A need. A demand.

Teddy continued to slowly glide his hand up and down his length. Meeting my transfixed gaze, he swiped his thumb across the broad head.

My breath struggled to escape. At last, my knees unlocked, and I crossed the tiled floor. Licking my lips, I reached for him.

He shook his head and looked pointedly to the apex of my thighs. "Back up. Let me watch you."

Oh, gods. Anticipation rocketed through my body. If his fingers followed the direction of his gaze, I would instantly come undone.

I stood there, beneath hot water licking over me from several directions, shaking and unsure. Throw mortified and nuclear level turned on into a blender, and you'd end up with me right now. No one had ever watched me touch myself. I'd never watched my partner pleasure themself, but holy hotcakes, now the idea was in my brain, and I couldn't shake it loose.

With a small, jerky nod, I backed against the shower wall opposite him.

The cold tile shocked my overheated flesh. Closing my eyes, I drew my hands down my body, across my breasts. My palms skimmed over my nipples. Awareness arrowed straight to the bundle of tingling nerves between my folds. Surprised, I gasped.

Self-conscious, my gaze snapped to Teddy's face. Focused solely on my hands, he hadn't noticed—or hadn't cared. Or was completely aroused by it. His arms moved, hand stroked. I couldn't help but follow those bulging biceps, down his arms, to the hand working his length. Intense desire shook my legs.

Though his face was angled down, his eyes rose to meet mine through the fall of his hair across his brow. Once our gazes locked, I felt the tingle from my fangs to my center as he purposefully looked lower, telling me without words where he wanted my hands to go.

We weren't unadventurous. I fancied us pretty wild in the sheets, on the sheets, and with no sheets at all, but this felt more intimate. More exposed. More...just more. I'd never thought of myself as shy, but right now I was grateful for the hot water turning my pale flesh pink, hiding my blush.

The desire to squeeze my legs together was almost as overwhelming as the one to tackle him to the shower floor. Instead, I let my hand drift from my breasts to my belly.

Teddy's hungry gaze followed, and his motions slowed as he watched. As if he forgot what he was doing.

Finding myself emboldened by my captive audience, I widened my stance and let my fingers drift closer. So close. "Like this?" I asked, shocking myself.

Though he didn't look up, that crooked smile curled one side of his mouth. "Not quite."

"Maybe you should come here and show me?" Okay, who possessed me? Because this was so not me.

He shook his head. "You first."

I dipped my hand lower. My entire body clenched in anticipation. I swallowed and glided my finger to that throbbing, desperate place. The moment I touched myself, my fangs nearly vibrated from my skull. All thoughts of play and teasing scattered like the stars. "Oh, gods."

His hands flexed around his manhood. Bracing himself, he rocked his legs wider. The muscles of his thighs were rigid. Loosely held in his palm, his length thickened and grew even more.

"I need you," I whispered. And I did. So badly. It had been a thing lurking in the shadows since Beast had been so close. It had been dormant, crouched, waiting, but now refused to be ignored.

Him. I wanted Teddy. Needed Teddy inside of me. The image filled every crevice of my brain. Insistent. Demanding.

"Not yet," Teddy said, his voice gravel and grit. "Again," he commanded, and with another gods damned whimper that refused to be contained, I did. He groaned and moved his hand faster.

I did this to him. It was a heady thing.

The sight was powerful and seductive. Up and down, up and down. When his hand reached the tip of his cock, he rubbed his thumb over the broad head once again. Down, up, rub. Down, up, rub.

Deep inside of me, sensations crashed together in a hazy tangle of want. The swirl of my finger on that painfully sensitive spot increased to match his pace. Need pulled, swelled, and skittered just out of reach, over and over. So close, so elusive. My legs threatened to give out. Sensation beat against me, so intense it demanded I squeeze my thighs together. To stop. To keep going.

Feeling brave and oh-so-naughty, I brought my hand to my mouth. Teddy's eyes, nearly black and blazing with intensity, tracked the movement as I slid my finger into my mouth and withdrew it slowly.

"I need you," I said again and dipped the wet finger inside myself, this time showing him what I wanted.

Something between a groan and a growl left him. His motions quickened.

He was trying to kill me. Unbidden, I pumped my finger faster, matching his pace. My legs were so weak, it was only a matter of time before I hit the shower floor.

I wasn't too proud to beg—not for this. "*Please*." My voice broke and so did his rhythm.

Striding with purpose across the wide shower, Teddy didn't pause when he reached me, but lowered himself enough to grip me beneath my hips and then he stood, sliding me up the shower wall. Without soap, it wasn't an easy ride up the tile. It was sort of squeaky.

Without conscious thought, my legs found their way around his waist. His cock pressed against my center and rose to lay against my belly. The weight felt right, but it wasn't enough. He shifted just enough to reach between us.

I licked my lips. watching as he once again took hold of himself. Angling his hips away from mine, he guided his thick erection to my entrance. Both of us watched as he slid into me, each of us so slick, he went slow and smooth until I finally felt complete. Until I couldn't tell where I ended, and he began.

Water beat against his shoulders from the side, from behind him, from behind me. It ran down his chest, across his abs, diving into those ridges, until it created a pool where we were joined.

"Lane. Fuck." Teddy said on a rough groan. "You feel so good."

My gaze rose to his, and our eyes met briefly. Gods I loved this male. I'd never imagined him in my life, but I knew, with absolute certainty, I could not live without him. I tried to project all of that through my gaze, but as he started to move, sliding out, teasing me with only his tip inside my entrance, I looked down.

I watched.

Ecstasy was right there. I was ready to break apart around him. I was so full, but I needed...something. "Teddy, please," I said again, and looked up to find him watching his length slide inside of me—stretch me.

Push, pull, push, pull. Faster, harder, until the slap of our flesh and panting breaths rose above the water hitting the shower floor.

"Oh, gods. Teddy." I was desperate for something. Something so close.

"Give it to me," Teddy demanded, voice tight. "Come for me."

This wasn't the lovemaking of pretty poetry and delicate flowers. This was raw and carnal. I bounced against his thighs as he pounded into me again and again. I was on the crest of something. My thoughts were a jumble, focused on one thing. One sensation. Building and building. Painful and exquisite.

He curved his spine to allow room between us. Pulling one hand from beneath me, he pressed his thumb against my clit. Rubbed once, twice, and suddenly everything inside of me went taut. His thumb made another circle.

With an incoherent scream, I came undone. My thighs locked against Teddy's sides. My feet flexed. I dug my fingers into his shoulders, distantly realizing my talons broke flesh.

My inner walls spasmed around Teddy, milking him to completion. His pace grew furious. I was limp, along for the ride.

"Lane," he roared and followed me over the precipice.

White noise filled my ears. I was fairly certain I blacked out, only dimly aware he continued to move with jerky thrusts until he was completely spent.

Still buried inside me, his broad chest heaving, Teddy crushed me against him and carried me to the bench running the length of the back of the shower. He crouched, his semi-rigid length finally slipping from me as he gently placed me onto the water-warmed seat.

Deeply satisfied, I hummed sleepily and settled back against the wall. I felt claimed. I felt like I'd claimed my mate. Ecstasy soaked into my bones, made them heavy. "That was nice."

"Only nice?" Teddy asked, still kneeling in front of me. He worked his hands between my knees and pushed them further apart. "We can do better than *nice*."

Eyes closed, I felt a smile I knew was disgustingly sappy and sweet curve my lips. My body hummed with satisfaction from a completion I somehow knew I needed with Teddy—only Teddy—from the moment Beast's intention to touch me had become clear.

Like a candle flickering in the distance, the thought that I should ask him about my reaction, about this insane sexual need danced at the edges of my foggy brain.

Teddy's hands stroking my legs lulled me to the brink of sleep. His long fingers brushed over my skin. Heated breath washed against my thighs. I smiled, feeling like the proverbial cat who got the—

Soft hair brushing against my belly was the only warning I had before Teddy's hot tongue stroked over my still humming center.

"Holy shit! What are you..." I gasped and tangled my fingers into his wet hair. His talented tongue did a little circle. It hurt so good. "You can't."

Face buried between my thighs, he laughed, low and oh-so-sexy. The brush of his breath over my sex sent my eyes rolling back into my head.

"I can." He licked again, his tongue flicking over me.

"You wouldn't."

He murmured, an erotic hum as he rubbed his cheek against me and looked up. His lips spread in a deliciously evil smile. Stubble pricked my inner thigh. "I will."

My legs tried to close but his broad shoulders filled the space.

Working an arm up, he pushed a finger inside of me, and then two. He turned his hand over and curled his fingers up while he continued to play me like a guitar with his tongue.

Pieces of me came back together, only to prepare to come apart. I squirmed, away or closer, I wasn't certain.

Just beyond the lip of the seat I saw Teddy's cock, once again thick and hard. It rocked and bounced from the motion of his fingers plunging in and out of me.

Our gazes locked. He changed hands, putting his free hand to work on me while moving his sex-slicked hand to his lap. Beneath my fingers, his shoulders flexed as he took hold of himself and began to stroke in time with his fingers moving inside of me. His tongue worshiping me.

It was too much, in the best possible way. My world had fallen away, leaving that single sensation. Bright lights flared behind my tightly squeezed lids. Even with the water falling against the tile, against us, my ragged, desperate breaths were the loudest thing in my head.

Suddenly, he drew the intensely sensitive, swollen part of me he'd been playing to perfection into his mouth and sucked.

"Oh, gods. Teddy!" My back bowed. He continued to suck, and I shattered against his mouth, on his finger. Sparks burst across my vision. I curled my fingers against the bench. Tile cracked beneath my talons.

Teddy's climax followed mine. He shouted, his hot seed landing on my thigh and then sliding off in the running water.

Eyes closed, bones liquid, I slumped against the shower wall, drifting on the edge of sleep. At some point Teddy washed me with our lavender and honey-scented soap. He ran his large hands, so strong but so gentle, over every inch of my flesh. Drawing me to my feet, he washed between my legs. The sensation hit like an electric jolt, almost sending me out of my skin.

He turned off the water and led me from the shower.

Cold air. A towel. Cradled against Teddy's chest, and then he was laying me in our bed. He scooted in behind me, unceremoniously rolling me to the middle. Once settled, he pulled me to him, sprawling me half across his body. I worked my thigh over his.

I tried to rally for questions I couldn't quite remember but knew I needed to ask. My tongue felt too thick, my eyelids too heavy.

"Mate," he said, and I felt like maybe a question had been answered.

Beneath the sheets, Teddy stroked a hand down my naked back. His calloused fingers traced over my spine. They passed between my shoulder blades, tickled over my ribs, dipped into the depression of my lower back before reversing the path back to my nape, only to do it all once again.

Contented, bones melting in pure bliss, I slipped into satiated sleep.

9

MY BLOOD, MY LOVE, MY LIFE

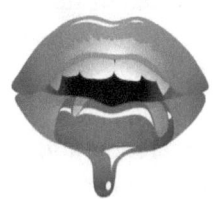

TEDDY SHOOK A SMALL FRYING PAN, GETTING THE TWO OVER-EASY EGGS sliding, and then he executed a flip with a quick wrist flick. He returned the pan and moved to the griddle side of the fancy stove we inherited with the penthouse. Once turned, the first slab of buttered bread revealed its perfect golden-brown side. A multi-tasking professional, Teddy finished turning the remaining bread slices and then slid the cooked eggs onto a plate. He cracked two more into the pan, and then moved a baking sheet from the oven to the island counter.

"Can you put these on the plates?" He pointed the spatula from the rows of bacon laid out like delicious little soldiers on the parchment paper lining the baking sheet to two paper towel covered plates.

A rare moment of perfect contentment filled me soul-deep. My lips curled into a smile, and I grabbed the tongs to do as Teddy asked. It was the least I could do for all this perfect male did for me.

I got to work transferring the bacon, muscle memory moving my arms as I thought back to this morning. Watery pink-and-gold light had leaked into the room, announcing dawn, I'd woken up, my sexual need more than satisfied. Satisfied so well, I felt another blush heat my cheeks. I'd curled into Teddy's side and snuggled. We spoke briefly about what led to our shower escapades. My instincts had been spot on. Our mate status meant no part of me wanted anything to do with anyone other than Teddy.

It was what Teddy once told me—*from now until the end, I am yours.*

After slipping from the sheets, he threw on flannel PJ bottoms—and whoa boy, that ass—and headed downstairs to get breakfast started. He was so deliciously domesticated, and I was utterly spoiled.

Finished with my one breakfast task, I slid the baking sheet with its still-hot grease back into the oven to cool and turned to watch Teddy work the frying pan. I was greeted with the glorious vision of his bare back. He hadn't tied the apron, only looped it over his neck and let it drape over his front. Watching the natural bunch and flex of his shoulders as he shook the frying pan surpassed even the trashiest of trashy reality television.

When did I get so girly? I shrugged to myself. It happened, and where Teddy was concerned, I found I didn't care.

"Food's ready." At the stove, Teddy added four slices of griddle-toasted bread to the plate with eggs and held it out to me. "Dig in."

I took it and headed for the bacon while he cracked two more into the frying pan and added another four slices of bread to the griddle.

"Can't imagine why you're so hungry this morning." I bit off the melty end of a piece of bacon and grinned.

A quick shimmy of the pan, and Teddy flipped his eggs. "Try not to get pawed at by werewolves too often. I don't have the same stamina I had fifty years ago."

Pointing my bacon at him, I flashed a fangy grin. "Old man." There was no way I could repeat last night on a regular either, but I wasn't about to admit that.

The second set of eggs joined Teddy's plate. He piled on the remaining toast, grabbed his bacon, and headed out of the kitchen. Taking up my plate, I followed to the dining table, and took a seat across from him. Sitting next to each other was sweet and all, but I liked to look at someone when I spoke to them, and no one else was home.

"Where is everyone?" I snapped a piece of bacon in half. I'd grabbed six slices. Too many?

"Mae asked me to let you know they changed plans. She's going alone with Zee while Y'sindra and Lo visit Beast's old pack. Beast—what a name." Teddy shook his head, chuckling. He tore off a bit of crust and dragged it through the thick, gold yolk. After chewing the mouthful, because my man had manners, he said, "They already called and said no one saw anything worth mentioning and they're off to Outerlands."

"What's up with those two spending so much time there? Y'sindra wanted to be done working there so badly, I'm pretty sure at some point my ears actually bled from her constant whining. Now, those two can't stay away."

"It's a mystery." Teddy laid his fork on his plate, wiped his fingers, and drank down his orange juice. I'd been aghast to learn that was his preferred breakfast drink. At least he squeezed the stuff himself. It wasn't coffee, but it was pretty good. "Mae tells me you'll be paying Blackthorne a visit."

My mouth screwed up of its own accord. An involuntary reaction, which was better than the hot flash of rage that used to sweep over me at the mention of Great Grandpa's name.

Chuckling, Teddy dragged his last piece of toast through the golden goodness decorating his plate. "Your expression says it all. Considering your opinion of him, why the visit?"

"You disagree with my opinion?" Always one to save the best bite for last, I pushed the final piece of bacon to the side and got back to the bread in egg ritual.

"I don't really have an opinion." Plate squeegeed clean with his final piece of toast, Teddy leaned back in his seat and tossed his napkin on the empty plate. "I'm not one to judge someone based on their past."

"What about the fact that he caught us in some bullshit net and you almost died?"

"It only knocked me out."

"Are you actually saying you don't care about what happened?"

Teddy threaded his fingers behind his head, and I was momentarily distracted by all that flexing and bulging. "Fair's fair. We were there with worse plans for him. He ended up in a dungeon."

In my opinion, fair was never fair where Blackthorne was concerned. "It was more like a mildly unpleasant vacation in a one-star motel. We checked him in, and he checked himself right out."

"Aside from the first meeting you told me about," Teddy said. "When you first broke into his place and he didn't know who you were, he seems all right. Pretty supportive of you. Proud, in fact."

I tore off a bite of bread with more gusto than necessary. It stuck to the back of a fang. "I'm his creation, of course he's proud."

"You are a result of his creation, and sweet fangs, I like who you are."

Warmth seeped all the way to my toes. I shoved a forkful of fluffy egg whites into my mouth, suppressing a smile fighting to be free. I would not express pleasure about anything related to the old druid. "His potion killed countless fae who couldn't survive the change."

"Ugly things happen during war." Teddy's statement was shockingly matter of fact. "I haven't been through one, but living on the edge of Earth, I've witnessed plenty."

"You aren't wrong, except he told me he created the potion, a potion—I might remind you—that forced the moon fae into an evolution, not for a cause, but because the fae he loved asked."

One side of Teddy's mouth rose. "Isn't that a cause? Whatever you want from me, all you have to do is ask, and I promise it's yours."

"Don't." My fork slipped from my fingers and clinked onto my plate. "Don't make promises like that."

He shrugged. "It's the truth. Anything in my power to give is yours. My blood, my love, my life."

My breath hitched, and I shook my head, refusing his words. "Your blood, your love, I'll take those, but under no condition do you ever offer your life." I wasn't certain I could exist without this male.

Standing, Teddy slid his plate from the table. "How about an extra bag of cheesy poofs instead?"

"Deal." I laughed, relieved at the lighter shift of conversation. Shoving the piece of bacon I'd saved into my mouth—because I did not have manners —I took up my plate and followed Teddy to the kitchen. "You know me so well."

"Well enough to know when you are avoiding a subject." Instead of using the fancy dishwasher, Teddy washed his plate by hand and reached for mine.

"I'm not avoiding, I was distracted."

"Okay then, I'm listening." Teddy wiped his hands dry on a dish towel and faced me. He leaned back against the counter, looking both ridiculous and delicious, still wearing only the flannel pajama bottoms and apron.

I crossed my arms over my chest. "I'm going because Blackthorne requested Beast's body. I want to know why, and Zee suggested a few things to test for."

Nodding, Teddy rubbed a hand across his mouth, looking thoughtful. "Smart. If this is an epidemic, we want to do what we can to protect Zee."

"Exactly. Now about that apron." I pushed off the island and employed the new sexy walk I'd been practicing.

Suddenly, something large and fuzzy bowled into my calf before winding through my legs.

I wobbled and leapt back, half-climbing onto the island. A fuzzy, orange, black, and white *thing* yowled up at me. I jabbed an accusing finger at the orange-eyed beast. "What the holy Ho Hos is that?"

Teddy's rich laughter cracked through my shock. I glared.

"That, my brave little monster, is a cat."

"I know what a cat is," I snapped. "What is it doing in my house?"

The enormous feline sat back on its haunches and launched itself onto the hip-high island. It padded to me and bumped its head against my shoulder. Much larger than a typical house cat, it stared at me eye-to-eye.

Awkwardly, I patted its head. Wasn't it last night I'd thought I preferred cats to dogs? What sounded like a diesel motor erupted from the cat.

"She likes you."

"Who is she, and how do you know her?" I looked for a collar but saw none.

"Mae said Vaughn brought her up with him last night." He pointed to the raised lip of the island which served as a kitchen eating area. A piece of paper sat in the middle.

This had to be the vampire's idea of a joke. I hopped off the counter and moved to grab the note.

TALULLA WAS THE FAMILIAR TO A WITCH WHO WAS ONE OF BEAST'S VICTIMS. *Vaughn asked if she could remain with us while he locates an appropriate home. I told him we'd be happy to keep her as long as he needed.*

XOXO Mae

I PEEKED OVER THE SHEET OF PAPER AT TALULLA, WHO HAD REMAINED ON the countertop watching me with solemn, intelligent eyes. "We don't have a litter box."

With a graceful, noiseless leap from the counter, the cat landed on the floor and padded past me into the hall, tail erect and waving. A moment later the toilet flushed. My jaw dropped open, and my astonished gaze shot to Teddy.

"Familiars are smart." He came toward me. Wrapping his arms around me, he folded me against his chest. All that naked flesh beneath the apron warmed my cheek.

I knew a little about familiars. Something about a witch passing on a piece of their essence to a familiar when they left the mortal realm. Often, many witches infused one familiar, which was super creepy.

"I'd ask about food, but I assume if Vaughn delivered the cat, he also provided cat food?"

Talulla pranced back into the kitchen, bumping and twining through our legs.

"Mmhmm." Teddy's hummed response rumbled in his chest. It tickled my ear, and I couldn't help but smile.

"Hopefully Talulla can entertain herself without destroying the furniture."

"Or you can take her with you," Teddy suggested.

I pictured Blackthorne's face when I showed up with a gigantic cat smart enough to poop in his potted palms, if I asked. "You have the best ideas."

10

WEREWOLF. MOONBIT. BODY.

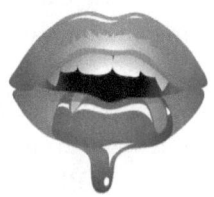

Talulla dove from one dune to the next. Plumes of pale sand shot into the sticky, humid air. I watched her antics from my peripherals as I made my way up the wooden slat walkway to the deck affixed to the back of Blackthorne's beach hotel. He still hadn't changed the name from Shadwe.

Though it felt like he'd escaped—aka walked right out of—Eodrom's prison years ago, and that I'd known him even longer, it had only been a year.

Furry patchwork face covered in grains, whiskers twitching, Talulla raced away from her most recent dune conquest, back to me. So far, aside from the toilet trick, I wasn't convinced this familiar bonded with the brightest witch.

"Remember, the big palm in the pot that looks like a giant coconut? It's in the sitting area. To the right when we go inside. Got it?" I felt dumb, but she blinked her big, round eyes, and I got the weirdest feeling she understood. Time to find out if she could do more than flush.

We reached the steps to the deck. Talulla pranced up the stairs ahead of me, straight to the doors. She stopped and waited. The cat was the size of a medium-sized dog. I couldn't wait to see Blackthorne's reaction. Hopefully he didn't use that nasty druid magic I knew firsthand he had at his disposal to zap the feline familiar. Mae would never let me hear the end of it.

I pushed the first door open and crossed the few steps it took to reach the second set of doors. As soon as they slid wide, Talulla bolted into the air-conditioned lobby. Her claws clacked across new flooring. Where the last time I'd visited the place had plain white porcelain squares and beachy throw rugs, this new stuff looked like wood, but was tile. Things had gone fancy in this joint. Okay, this might not have been the best idea. I chased after the cat.

"Wait," I yelled, but too late. Talulla stared with her big orange eyes from where she squatted in Blackthorne's prize potted palm, tending to her business. She locked eyes with me as she created a mound of rich potting soil. Whiskers twitching, chest puffed, and tail waving behind her like a flag, she pranced to me and took her place at my side.

It was juvenile, but looking from the cat to the palm, I giggled. Maybe it wouldn't be the worst thing having a feline familiar around, after all.

The smell of fresh paint tangled with a multitude of mouth-watering food aromas. The disorienting celebration of scents worked their way over my senses. Yeasty bread, sweet and spicy cinnamon, grilled meats.

"I see Vaughn delivered Talulla?" Blackthorne emerged from a large archway that led into the dining area, wiping his hands on a napkin. His appearance snapped me out of my food trance.

"Yeah, last..." Hands planted on my hips, I narrowed my eyes on Blackthorne, who was completely unsurprised and unperturbed by Talulla's presence and actions. "How did you know? And how do you know her name?"

Dabbing his mouth with the napkin, he crumpled and tossed it into a trash can. "Vaughn apprised me of the situation. I suggested he leave Talulla with you until he can locate a witch candidate to bond with the poor girl. You know shelters cannot take a familiar? Afterall, they are—"

"I know what they are," I bit off my retort. "Of course, it would be your idea."

Next to me, Talulla looked from me to my great grandpa. As if understanding my emotions or just as likely my words, she hissed at him. "Good girl," I murmured.

Blackthorne's brows rose, and his lips melted into an all too self-satisfied smile. "Well, this is unexpected. Vaughn might not need to look for a home after all."

"What's that mean?" I scowled.

"Why are you here, Granddaughter?" he asked instead of answering.

Typical. Gods knew this man infuriated me. Stars take me, but I'd also come to understand he was much smarter than I was comfortable with. In terms of chess, he didn't think a few moves ahead. He didn't have to. He already knew the outcome and was thinking about the next match.

Lips pressed into a tight line, I pulled a deep breath in through my nose, held it, and then exhaled long and slow, letting calm energy replace my irritation. At least I tried to. Mae and her daily sun stone meditation tricks didn't work on me.

Talulla rammed her head into my calf and then trotted to one of the sofas arranged in the upscale, beach-themed sitting area. Gone were the rattan furnishings. In their place sat elegant carved pieces of driftwood furniture with removable cushions displaying soft, beach images which could easily double as artwork.

An extra-long bench with a somewhat ergonomically curved back, the centerpiece of the collection, took up the bulk of the space and must have cost a fortune. The image on the cushion was a landscape of a beach, soft waves rolling in, sun on the horizon, seagulls in the sky. Talulla chose that seat. She leapt onto the bench, executed a circle, kneaded the cushion, pricking and pulling with her long claws, and finally curled up. Her focus shifted to grooming, but I didn't miss the way her tufted ears swiveled in our direction.

"Granddaughter?" Blackthorne repeated, drawing my attention away from the strange cat.

I cleared my throat, following the threads as to why I'd come. Oh yeah —*Werewolf. Moonbit. Body.* "You asked for the werewolf's body. I came to ask why."

He chuckled and shook his head, brown-and-silver braid swishing against his back and brushing the rim of his belt. The silver in his hair was the only indication of his ancient age. "We do live in the era of the mobile telephone. Brilliant device, you could have called."

As always, Mae had been right. I would have busted another phone if I'd called this guy. He had a talent for pricking my temper. "But I didn't, so how about you answer the question?"

"You caught me in the middle of interviewing a new chef." He stepped to the side and swept his arm toward the dining area. "We'll need to move the conversation in here. Chef Leblanc is testing a breakfast menu. I hope you brought your appetite."

The delicious scents drew me, not the promise of conversation. I might have finished breakfast only a few hours ago, but there was always room for good food. "I could eat."

"I'm sure you can. You cleaned out my fully stocked kitchen—an industrial-sized kitchen—in the week I lent you the hotel."

For reasons I still did not understand, Blackthorne had offered this hotel as a place for Teddy and me to escape to after we returned from Shadwe with a corrupted moon fae imprisoned in the Eodrom dungeons and a rescued sun stone planted in the penthouse garden. Teddy and I had the run of the place —and the kitchen.

Try as I might to hate Blackthorne, his persistent affable attitude and weird desire to cling to the DNA that bound us made it really hard. It also wasn't lost on me that approach was how I had unintentionally won Pru over.

I passed through the large opening into the dining room and stopped short. Without the filter of space from one room to the next, the full spectrum of delicious breakfast food aromas mingled with fresh paint and drywall hit me hard. Paused on the threshold, I glanced around, taking in the changes. The room had been expanded to accommodate many more diners than the previous eating nook, where I'd had a showdown with Nyle—the corrupted moon fae who'd eventually taken Y'sindra's wing before I took his head.

During the fight, Nyle's deadly dark magic had dissolved not only pieces of furniture, but a large section of flooring. A dark hardwood floor replaced the bland tiles that had been destroyed. Of course, Blackthorne couldn't just patch things up, he had to turn the place into a fine dining joint.

Placing his hand on my back, Blackthorne propelled me into motion. He followed me into the room and made his way to a large, rectangular table set for six. A smattering of plates already sat on the table. He rounded the table to a seat pushed away on the far side and gestured toward the chair opposite his. It put my back to the open doorway, which I hated.

"Try that benedict," he said as I slid into the chair. There were three versions of eggs benedict, but he pointed to a plate near my right elbow. "The one with the pepper gravy, not the classic. Brown sugar pork belly—you won't regret it."

"Sure, why not. Second breakfast is a thing, right?" I pulled the plate he'd indicated from the gourmet smorgasbord laid out in front of me, and then used the knife and fork he provided to cut off the perfect bite.

An explosion hit my tongue. Caramelized sugar, smoky meat, creamy gravy with a spike of black pepper, melded with slightly sweet, buttery goodness of a runny yolk and pillow-soft biscuit with a hint of salt. "Divine," I said around a second bite, though Teddy's eggs were better.

With a wide sweep of his hand, Blackthorne gestured to the eight or so other plates of food on the table. "Save some room. This is meant to be a tasting to set the menu. There's still all of these and more to come."

Reluctantly, I pushed the benedict aside and pulled a thick French toast adorned with fruit and whipped cream into its place.

"So, about that werewolf body." I made a little circle in the air with my fork and then used its edge to cut through the tender bread. A thought hit me, and my hand froze, stopping the fork just in front of my mouth. Syrup dripped onto the plate. "Tell me he's not stored in the freezer?"

Chuckling, Blackthorne pulled the French toast plate toward himself. He cut off a piece and dragged it through the syrup and cream before taking a bite. "Nope."

"Whew." I ate the forkful. "So why did you request the body?"

"What do you think of the French toast?" he asked. "Help me with the menu, and I'll answer your questions."

"Delicious, but not as good as the benedict. Why the body?"

"Try this next." Blackthorne pushed a new plate toward me. The dish was arranged as some sort of stack with shredded potatoes on the bottom. "To answer your question, I plan to run tests."

I rolled my eyes. "That much is obvious. Tests for what?"

He gestured to the plate.

Annoyed, I took a bite. Spicy peppers hit my tongue, immediately mellowed by another runny yolk. "Unexpected. Good." I nodded.

"Menu?" Blackthorne asked.

"I'd order it again."

"Excellent."

"Tests," I reminded him as he pushed yet another plate in front of me.

Blackthorne sat back, folding his hands on his flat belly. The guy was in great shape for someone his age—however ancient that might be. "I am checking for particular additives in the blood."

"What additives?" I ate the next bite, finding it bland compared to the first three.

"Menu?" Blackthorne asked.

Catching onto his one answer for every two of my questions, I smiled. "Additives?"

He chuckled and shook his head. "Would a list really mean anything to you?"

"It might." It totally would not, but Mae or Zee might know. I should probably write this down. Knowing how hot it was here, I'd left my jacket at home, so I didn't have my ever-present notepad. I did, however, have my cell phone. I pulled up the note feature and waited.

Blackthorne raised a brow and smiled. "Look at you embracing technology. Living at the penthouse is doing wonders for you."

Thumbs poised over the screen, I gave him a blank stare and waited.

Accepting I had not taken the bait, he began to rattle off a list that sounded both medical and medicinal. Mixed in with the boring litany of words I mostly didn't recognize, the names of familiar herbs jumped out at me.

I frowned, put an asterisk next to the familiar names, reminding myself to ask about them when he was done.

"Traces of moon fae."

A fissure of shock rocketed down my arms. My hands seized and head snapped up. "What did you just say?"

"Menu?" Blackthorne asked, and I barely resisted launching myself across the table and choking answers out of him. Mostly because I was certain he could kick my ass.

"No," I answered simply. "What did you just say?"

"Why not?"

My fangs tingled in irritation. I rubbed my tongue along the back of my clenched teeth. "It's bland."

"Really? I didn't think it was that poor. Thank you for your opinion." He slid the plate away and replaced it with another.

My nostrils flaring on a deep breath, I asked again. "What did you say?"

"I am testing the werewolf for moon fae genetic material."

Words failed me, which didn't happen often. My mouth opened and closed.

"Try the omelet. It's a vegetarian option."

"Seriously?"

"Very serious. Every restaurant needs a vegetarian option." He pointed at the omelet. It had two bites missing. "I need the menu set for the grand opening."

"Ugh!" I grabbed the fork and shoveled a bite into my mouth. I raised my brows, silently demanding he explain.

"What is your question?" Blackthorne asked.

"I think it's obvious."

"It is not." He tapped a finger on the plate in front of me. "And it's my turn. What did you think."

With a harsh shove, I pushed the omelet away. "No."

"If you want an answer—"

"No," I cut in. "I don't like it. Now can we stop playing games?"

Green eyes solemn and steady, he stared for a long moment. "Excuse me. Let me tell Chef to hold the next tasting. I'll meet you on the deck."

He stood and disappeared through the far door I'd guessed led to a kitchen.

For a long moment I didn't move. I felt drained. Pushing back the chair, it stuttered across the new floor, leaving faint scuff marks.

None of this should have come as a surprise. Nothing about Blackthorne was ever easy. Worse, he seemed to enjoy my company. The skin across my neck tightened. I rolled my shoulders. Hopefully, the games were over, and he'd give me straight answers.

"You coming?" I asked Talulla as I strode across the lobby.

She rose and followed me, slinking through the automatic doors off the sitting area before they slid shut. The short hallway between doors was designed to keep the humid air out and the perfectly chilled air in.

Then the vacuum sealing the door to the deck popped, and Talulla trotted past me, the long hair of her multi-colored tail flaring in the beachy breeze. I looked around and settled on a seat at the large square bar that took up more than a quarter of the deck.

I slid onto a stool. The cat leapt onto the seat next to me and then onto the bar. She stood perfectly still, peering at me with those big orange eyes.

"What?"

She slow-blinked and then looked from me to the back entrance.

"I know, I didn't need to bring you. It was a silly, petty plan."

Head tilting, her tail rose and fell once in an undulating wave.

Scowling, I turned toward the beach and the circle of stones. "Do you know how disconcerting it is to apologize to a cat?"

Talulla didn't answer, but somewhere I'd swear I heard laughter. Or maybe that was just in my head.

I glanced from the feline to the lobby. The tinted windows reflected the mid-afternoon sun, disguising anything but vague movements inside. Waiting, I drummed my fingernails against the bar top. The dull thump reverberated like footsteps rushing, fast, fast, fast, and pause.

At last, the inner door slid open, and Blackthorne stepped into the short walk to the deck door. He pushed, and it opened with a sucking pop.

"I don't suppose you chose this seat for drinks?" he asked.

"Nope."

He took the stool next to me and remained silent long enough I thought maybe he forgot why we were here. His unfocused eyes seemed to watch the horizon. "I've tested two other subjects recently who were suspected of contracting the moonbit infection."

Unease squirmed down my spine. I shifted in my seat. "Suspected?"

Blackthorne nodded, his lids fluttered, and he inhaled deeply before his green gaze landed on me. "Another werewolf and a vampire."

"A vampire? Is that...normal?" Zee had said she'd never seen it in other paranormals, but she'd heard rumors.

"No," he said. "I have been a part of Earth's paranormal community for a very long time, which is the reason I began studying this infection. Until recently, I have only witnessed were-creatures succumb."

Hope was a painful knot in my chest. Did Blackthorne know what this was? "I have a friend. She's scared. Do you know what the infection is? Do you know how to stop it?"

Absently, he rubbed his forehead. "What is happening is not the moonbit infection."

The knot of hope shriveled, but it didn't quite die. "How do you know?"

"What paranormals refer to as moonbit happens when their human bodies reject the infection."

"You know a lot about humans," I drawled, though I wasn't surprised. A learner, a practitioner, I saw a reflection of my father in Blackthorne. He'd lived on Earth long enough to have seen this happen before. Probably many times before.

Blackthorne rose, circled the bar, and went behind the counter. He punched the code into a panel on a long, stainless-steel refrigerator and pulled out a beer. "Want one?"

"It's still morning."

"You need a mimosa or something?" he asked as he came back around the bar.

I snorted.

Sliding onto his stool, he popped the top of a dark green bottle and drank deep. "Perhaps I am being unfair. I have lived among the human paranormals for some time. You have not."

"You're older than dirt, I know." I couldn't resist.

"And one day, you will be too." Blackthorne saluted me with his beer and took another drink. "That's not the point. What I am getting at is I understand there is much you might not know about the human species."

Wood squeaked beneath the finger I dragged in a circle on the bar. "I'm learning."

A feeling of inferiority swept through me. *Ugh, gross!* What in the nine stale twinkies of Hell did I care about Blackthorne knowing more than me? It made sense he would. Maybe I was coming down with the flu.

"The thing you need to know right now is only were-creatures are *made*," Blackthorne said with zero judgement. "They pass the paranormal gene—they no longer refer to it as an infection or disease—through their saliva into the clean blood stream of another mortal."

Only were-creatures. His words penetrated whatever tantrum my brain was throwing. "Vampires can't..." I left the implication hanging.

He held out his hand and rocked it side-to-side. "They can, but despite the romanticized lore, they do not turn humans—not without consequences —and they don't need to. Their blood can do many things, including extending, or even saving the life of their bonded mortals. So even if a rare *made* vampire was infected with moonbit, I expect the blood would cleanse it."

I was both keenly interested in knowing what Vaughn's blood did for, or to Mae, and appalled by what he might be doing with my sister.

"It can be done, but the vampire council is very strict and must be petitioned for the change. Permission is rarely granted, but when it is, the change is performed in secret." Absently, Blackthorne swiped his hand through the bottle's sweat ring glistening on the bar top. "Were-creatures, however, are ruled by packs. There is one wolf, or cat, or bear, or whatever were-creature you are thinking, who oversees the large regions. For smaller issues, such as how the change is handled, it is determined pack to pack."

"What about lone wolves?"

"There aren't many. If they can survive on their own, they answer only to the territory alpha."

That confirmed what Zee told my sisters and me on our first girls' night out. Lone wolves were rare. "I assume you did more than just test for random genetic material. You studied the bodies, which is why you wanted Beast's."

"Yes. Until the recent vampire, it was always a were-creature, mostly commonly a wolf, and always one *made* not *born*."

I jerked, realizing the implications. It made so much sense. Were Zee's parents *made*? No, Zee was *born*, which meant one of her parents was also a *born* werewolf. The blood disease that turned humans into paranormals had been around for so long, it was now a genetic trait passed from *born* parent to child.

Setting the bottle on the bar, Blackthorne slid it from palm to palm. He remained silent for a long while, watching the slip and slide of the green glass and the slosh of liquid.

Throat suddenly dry as the Mojave, the final piece of this twisted puzzle clicked into place. "You found something, didn't you?"

Blackthorne dipped his forehead toward the bottle. "Someone has replicated my potion, the one I used to create blood fae, to create you."

To create you. His words landed like a punch to the gut.

"Some fool is out there trying to change human paranormals into something new, and there is only one reason to do that."

Words threw themselves at the barrier of my brain, but they didn't escape my lips. There were too many questions, but no answers I actually wanted. So I didn't ask.

He told me anyhow. "They want to create their own army."

11

MISS ME ALREADY

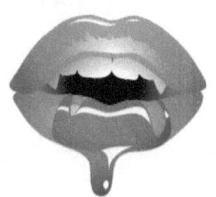

AT SOME POINT I'D MADE IT FROM THE DECK TO THE CIRCLE OF STONES. My entire being had absorbed the weight of what I'd learned, and I moved slowly, my steps dragging. I leaned heavily against one of the pillars.

They want to create their own army.

Blackthorne's words swam in circles around my brain, taking little nips of my sanity. How could someone be using his potion? It was *his* magic.

"I can't be certain, but I plan to find out," Blackthorne said from behind me.

My head whipped up. I blinked at my many generations removed grandfather, realizing I'd asked the question aloud.

Eyes narrowing, looking me directly in the eyes, he shifted close enough our noses nearly touched.

"Boundaries, man," I griped and tried to move.

"Shh. Be still." His focus shifted from my purple eye, to my black, and back to purple.

"What?" I leaned back and this time he didn't protest.

He shook his head. "Your left eye looks irritated. It's a little red."

I pressed my fingertips to my eyelid, as if I could feel what he saw. Dropping my hand, I shrugged. "Probably allergies."

The slow nod he gave me said agreed, but his tone did not. "Probably. Were-creatures cannot pass the were-pathogen to fae."

"I know."

"But this event did not involve a simple a werewolf, nor a moonbit werewolf," he said. "Did he bite you?"

Like the reflex to rub my eye, my hand went to my mostly healed neck. "I'm fine."

"Most likely, but you will let me know if anything changes."

What would change? I shook my head and pushed away from the pillar. "Whatever. I need to think. Alone. I'm going home."

"Home." Great Gramps' smile was full of amusement. "You have settled in rather quickly."

"It serves a purpose."

"A comfortable purpose," he teased.

"That too." I didn't bother hiding my smile. "You'll tell me if you find anything else?"

"I will tell you if I find anything you need to know."

Which wasn't much different from what Duskmere did with his half-truths and omissions, but this felt different. For some bizarre reason I trusted Blackthorne would tell me anything I needed to know.

"Thanks." I reached down to scratch Talulla between the ears. "I need to get back and figure out what to do with this thing."

"You could keep her." His suggestion stopped me on the threshold of the druid circle. No accidental porting for me.

"Why would I do that?"

Blackthorne crouched to eye level with the cat. They stared at one another. "You know druids were the first to adopt a familiar?"

Shock zinged along my nerves. "No."

He tilted his face to me, squinting in the glare of the sun. Absently, he ran a hand along Talulla's back. She arched into the touch while her purr motor rumbled to life. "I had arranged for Jason to offer her a home, but I think she should stay with you. At least for a short while."

"Why?" I asked again, watching Blackthorne as he rose. If druids had a connection to familiars, Jason and his obscure implication that Earth mages descended from druids made sense.

Talulla trotted away from Gramps, past me, and into the circle.

"Have you never..." Blackthorne pressed his lips together. His jaw worked as if chewing on his words. "Have you never felt you communicated with an animal?"

"No," I answered automatically. But it was a lie. The picture of Ayo, the dragon whose cave my father had mistakenly ported me into, rose in my mind. Those midnight scales rimmed with shades of a million nebulas that made up my most precious possession.

A knowing smile tilted Blackthorne's smug mouth. "Let her stay with you a week. See if you learn anything."

"From a cat?" I scoffed.

"From a familiar."

I pointed at the feline in the center of the circle, one hind leg in the air, grooming her nether regions. My brows rose to emphasize my meaning. "From that?"

Blackthorne just smiled. *Argh!* He was so annoying. I pinched the bridge of my nose.

Exhausted, head swimming with everything I learned, so much more than I'd shown up intending to discover, I acquiesced. "A week, fine. Then Jason comes to get her, right?"

"If you still wish."

"I will."

"Fine, fine." Blackthorne shooed me into the circle. "Will you contact me if you learn anything new about the infection?"

Somewhere deep inside me, pleasure bubbled like fizzy champagne. He hadn't ordered me to do anything. He'd asked, as if I might learn something he did not know. As if I were his equal.

"If you're honest with me, I'll be honest with you," I said.

"Fair enough."

Grinning, I held up two fingers, making a V. "Peace out."

In a controlled teleport, the beach spun away. A blanket of darkness enveloping colorful shooting stars surrounded me, and then I was back on the penthouse rooftop garden. I was getting good at this druid business. While I hadn't visited the hotel, I had been visiting Blackthorne's beach, practicing going and returning.

Talulla, with her half black, half orange face, shook her head and then pranced toward the stairs at the other end of the garden.

"Well, that's bullshit." I was seriously annoyed at how little the feline had been impacted by what I could only describe as interstellar travel. On my first trip through the circle, I'd lain on the beach puking my guts out, which had happened to contain Mom's secret recipe cookies.

Back inside, I found a bowl of food and water in the hallway leading to the kitchen. Someone had been home and put things out for Talulla, but the space felt empty now. It wasn't any special gift telling me no one was here. Homes just had a sort of cold, vacant feel when there was no one else inside.

I checked my phone—no calls. This silence made me uncomfortable. It itched beneath my skin. The time display on my phone confirmed I had only been gone a couple hours. It felt like a full day, but here on the West Coast it wasn't even noon.

Fingers frozen over the phone, I watched as Talulla found her bowls, daintily ate a couple pieces of kibble, lapped at the water, and then went back to the patio. She hopped onto one of the loungers, completed a few turns, and settled back to take in the sun.

Shaking my head, I set the phone on the counter and rather than shooting off texts, I decided to start a pot of coffee. There was a lot of information I needed to sort through. I wanted to feel everything out before I brought the others into the equation.

Mae always said I had good instincts. The sad truth was, I had to learn to trust them. I didn't know how long I would have my sisters to lean on. Something was happening with both of them. One was growing into something new, the other was simply growing.

Y'sindra was closed lipped about whatever she and Lo got up to when they flew away. I never pressed her, but anyone could see it was more than just Outerlands patrol, especially since we no longer had any sun fae obligations.

It might have something to do with Lo. He had lived in Outerlands alone, waiting for Teddy's return who had been shut out of the realm when the sun fae closed the door from Outerlands to Ta'Vale. The same door I recently cracked open. I could understand if Lo was more comfortable there, or more protective since the moon fae had been pushed back into Shadwe. Perhaps he wanted to be certain they stayed there.

I dropped onto the sofa, propping my head on a pillow and hugging another pillow to my belly. Pulling my lip beneath a fang, I stared at the high ceiling.

"It's more than that," I said aloud. There was no proof, and I had no plans to ask, but in my gut I knew they were away so often because of Y'sindra. She was up to something. I also knew she'd tell us eventually.

Mae was a different story. The floors below us were filling up fast with new residents, mostly sun fae. I shuddered and scratched my chest. *Hives.* The thought of that many sun fae so close gave me hives. It happened all the time.

They came through the house early in the morning. Gauzy robes flowing, sun fae passed from elevator to garden to worship and meditate at the sun stone with Mae. The swish of their billowing hems as they swept across the hardwood had become fingernails needling my brain.

From the corner of my eye, movement grabbed my attention. I rolled my head to the side. On the deck, Talulla stood, turned, and laid back down. Her massive, shaggy front legs extended onto an all-weather throw pillow, and she began to knead.

Yeah, like that. That was how everything related to the sun fae traipsing through my home, my safe space, felt on my brain. *Push, prick, tug.*

It wasn't fair. *I* wasn't fair. These sun fae had been nothing but courteous, deferential even, which was a whole new level of uncomfortable. But they were important to Mae, and apparently, Mae was important to them, so I'd been trying. Despite breaking out in a red, itchy rash every time, I forced myself to join their morning meditation at least once a week.

I saw who she was becoming in the light shining behind her bright blue eyes. The telltale sparks of gold power were hairline fractures splintering her blueberry irises. It would be a long time before they held the same power as Iola's eyes which always blazed like a sunset over a deep-water lake.

Still, day by day, week by week, Mae grew into a keeper—a protector of the sun stones. They had chosen her, and whether I liked it or not, she was edging closer to being something like Iola who, along with Torneh, were the current keepers in Eodrom. They were bound to the stones, tied to Ta'Vale, unable to leave the fae lands without suffering, and potentially without the stones suffering.

A sharp pain wrung my hearts like a washcloth. Mae had been saved that fate when we'd moved one stone to our garden. The stone and Mae were what drew the sun fae, curious about life outside of Ta'Vale. A life they could not lead without sacrificing whatever power they possessed had the stone not been right here on our roof.

Would my sister be able to remain here forever? Or would the stones demand she return to the land where they sprouted?

I sighed and draped an arm over my eyes. Whatever happened, it wouldn't happen anytime soon. Of all the things I should be thinking about, Mae and Y'sindra were not among them.

The conversation with Blackthorne teased...something. I had learned so much, yet I felt like I'd missed something too. I turned each word over in my brain. Nothing stood out as a Duskmere sort of half-truth.

Tucked into a cubby on the far side of the room, the tick of a clock seemed abnormally loud. I wasn't used to this level of quiet, and more noises that typically went unnoticed filtered in.

Distant shouts and laughter rising from the pool deck several levels beneath the penthouse. Even the faint sounds of Las Vegas Boulevard, so far below with its toy-sized cars and ant-sized humans. An occasional horn, a siren, the white noise of never-ending traffic.

I thought about the last thing Blackthorne had said. Someone was using his potion. They were attempting to create an army. It had to be related to the corrupt moon fae and their continued play for power. Who else would know and attempt to use such foul magic?

I'd hoped they'd crawled into some deep dark hole in Shadwe and were busy licking their wounds. We'd captured their last living prince. His accomplice, Hielmal, a sun fae war criminal and Mae's mother, might also be dead. Was this a last-ditch attempt, just as the creation of the blood fae had been?

The blood fae had turned on the corrupt moon fae. Apparently, some lessons weren't so easily learned.

Hugging the throw pillow to my chest, I picked at shaggy fibers along its side. My talons caught, pulled, and brushed through the soft threads. A thought surfaced. I swung my legs off the sofa and grabbed my phone from the coffee table.

I tapped on the name of the last person I expected to call today.

"Miss me already?" Blackthorne said by way of greeting.

"Not one bit, but I have a question."

On the other end of the line, he waited.

"How do you know someone is using your potion? What are you testing for?"

"I wondered if you'd get around to that." He sounded entirely too pleased, and I wasn't sure why. It was almost like he was...proud.

Nah.

I stood and paced across the room. "Well? What were you testing for?"

"Remind me never to invite you to a party." Blackthorne sighed into the phone. "Fine, among other things that might shed light on the infection, and what eventually led me to the discovery of what moonbit actually is, I've been running tests for traces of any fae DNA."

"Traces of..." my words trailed off and my feet stopped moving. "The fae whose blood you used. That's what you were looking for?"

"Markers, yes."

Goosebumps rose across my flesh. "You suspected before you knew." Statement, not a question.

"Yes. Both the symptoms and the end results seemed familiar," he said.

"And that's what you found? In the vampire? In Beast?"

Blackthorne's breathing filled my ear.

My stomach cramped. "What did you find?"

"It is my formula, but the slurry of genes are different. Many human paranormals. An assortment of were-creatures, vampire, witch, mage."

I dropped onto the edge of the sofa. "Aren't those the same thing?"

Somewhere across the country, Gramps snorted at my ignorance. "Absolutely not. You see—"

"Lesson for another day," I said, curtly.

"Don't think I'll forget, but yes, another day."

It was my turn to snort. "You forget? Of course not. I wouldn't dream of being so lucky."

"Quite the tone for someone looking for information," he teased.

I stuck my tongue out at the phone.

"Mature of you."

Gasping, I leapt to my feet and spun side to side. "Do you have cameras in here?"

Blackthorne laughed loud enough to hurt my eardrum. "No, but I imagined, and I was right."

I scowled. "By the gods, can you just tell me what you found?"

"Traces of shifter blood, and traces of blood fae."

Ice lanced my hearts. Cold raced across my skin. A noise, like a rushing river filled my ears.

"Granddaughter?"

Blood fae. Shifter.

The wafer-thin thread of hope I'd had that this was a human problem snapped.

"Granddaughter, are you still there?"

I ran my tongue over my suddenly dry lips. It didn't help. There was no moisture in my mouth.

"I'm here." I needed water. I needed a nap. I needed Teddy. "I appreciate your honesty. I'll let you know if I hear anything else."

We disconnected, and I texted Teddy.

Home. Where are you?

Nibbling on a talon, I stared at the screen and waited for his response. There were a million things I could be doing, probably should be doing, but with the seismic-level news I'd been hit with, I only wanted comfort. Specifically, from Teddy.

Downstairs at the bar. Join me?

Relieved, I let out a shaky laugh.

On my way.

12

LAUGHTER IS THE GLUE

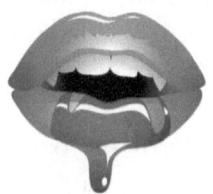

FRESH PAINT AND SAWDUST GREETED ME AS SOON AS I WALKED THROUGH *Blood and Wine*'s front doors. It wasn't terribly dissimilar to the scents at Blackthorne's beach hotel, minus the delicious food.

I'd looked up the chef, and damn if they didn't have two Michelin stars. I hadn't been living on Earth-proper for long, but I did live in Las Vegas. I knew what those stars meant. It meant I should have eaten more free food.

Teddy met me halfway across the room. He wrapped his large hands around my waist and deposited me atop the bar. Wedging himself between my legs, he delivered a deep, languid kiss. I inhaled shakily, and his essence flowed into me on a shared breath.

Excruciatingly, deliciously slow, he pulled away, leaving me all fluttery and breathless. My toes flexed inside my fuzzy slippers.

I rested my hand against his cheek. "I hate to say I appreciate anything Blackthorne does, but I do appreciate this bar. Anytime I need my sugar buns fix, you're only an elevator ride away."

Grinning, he tilted his head to the side and exposed the long slope of his throat. "Anytime, sweet fangs. Anytime."

A tangle of embarrassment and arousal heated the back of my neck, flamed over the short points of my ears. My fangs tingled with want. I pushed him—just a light shove.

He stumbled away.

"Don't be a drama queen." I reached for the hem of his plain gray tee shirt, stretching the material as I pulled him back to me. "Y'sindra is a bad influence."

"I was channeling Rip."

"A lofty goal." I laughed. "He is the biggest drama queen."

"Quite literally," he said referring to the ogre's seven-feet-plus height. Teddy rested a hand atop the bar on either side of my hips. "He's considering moving his business to *Blood and Wine*."

My brows ratcheted up my forehead, and I twisted to look around. Major construction was complete, but it was still undergoing final touches. Teddy oversaw most of the work. Who knew my sugar buns could cook and work construction. I was a lucky girl.

Despite the unfinished state of the bar, this was firmly in the upscale category. "No disrespect to Rip," I said. "But this doesn't seem like his scene."

The dark wood floors were covered with a fine layer of construction dust. According to Teddy, carpets would be the final touch on the space. I had my doubts about carpet in a bar, but he and the grapefruit-scented mystery concoction he'd used for years at his Interlands bar performed feats of cleaning magic.

When this bar opened, the floor to ceiling glass would offer a view of the interior from three walls. Currently, they were all blacked out with paper. Along the front door, dark red drapes fell in heavy folds from the high, dimly lit ceilings to the floor. Booths with extra springy seats and leather tufted backs lined the outer walls. Tables of all shapes and sizes were arranged a comfortable distance from one another around the large, octagon-shaped room.

In the center of the circular bar, a huge glass case designed to hold what had to be at least a hundred bottles of wine reached toward the shadowy ceiling. Some sort of rolling ladder and pulley system had been installed to retrieve those bottles. The walk-in interior of the wine wall was the refrigerated section for their chilled bottles.

On top of all that, large glass orbs were mounted at eight points around the wine wall. The barrel-sized, frosted glass containers would contain the "Blood" in *Blood and Wine*. I still had my doubts about the entire concept, but I couldn't argue with the reservations already on the books. Last I'd checked, the bar was booked out for a solid two months, and it had yet to open the doors.

"This place is *fancy*." I emphasized the word with a silly accent. "I'm getting *Dracula* meets *Great Gatsby* vibes."

"I was going for *Phantom of the Opera*, but I'll take *Dracula*," Teddy said.

"You plan to let Rip rent one of the booths like he does in Interlands? Those are some awfully nice seats for the big guy."

Teddy pointed to one of the four doors off the main room. One led to a kitchen, three led to private VIP areas. "I told him he can lease that room for a hefty fee. Privacy appeals to him. I think he's going to do it."

"How much?" I asked and nearly toppled off the bar at the obscene amount Teddy quoted. "Nice. If he can afford that, he should be paying me more."

"He already pays an obscene amount."

"He does, doesn't he?" I grinned. "It'll be easier on me having him so close, but what about kiwu? He won't move without his kiwu, and you said you'll only serve blood and wine."

With the exception of coffee, which Rip drank by the literal pot, I'd never seen him with anything other than the unpleasantly aromatic drink of fermented mushrooms, black garlic, and molasses.

Teddy huffed a laugh. "If he pays what I quoted, I'll give him whatever he wants."

"A dangerous thing to say."

"Lane, you didn't come all the way down here to discuss my future patrons."

"The elevator ride was rough." I pouted. Anxiety might have driven me down here, but now I didn't really want to talk about it.

He stared at me and then shook his head with that adorably crooked smile. "You're too much."

"Laughter is the glue that holds a relationship together."

"I thought it was really good sex?" He bounced his eyebrows suggestively.

"You look ridiculous." He looked divine, but I had to keep his ego in check. "Sex is important, but it's what's in here that matters most." I pressed his hand to my hearts.

"Could have fooled me last night."

"So much for romance," I grumbled and tossed his hand aside.

"I agree with the sentiment, but I also know you, and you're stalling."

Teddy traced his thumb along my cheek. He captured my chin and tipped my face toward his. "Something is bothering you. Tell me about your visit with Blackthorne."

Damn him and his perceptive nature. I did want to tell Teddy, but I also didn't want to voice the words. Speaking them to the Universe made them reality, according to Mae. She was into manifesting things. I didn't really buy it, but I also saw no reason to take the chance.

"Do I need to feed you first?" Teddy asked.

"No." I sulked. "Maybe. Wait, no. Blackthorne was testing a menu—you should see the changes he's made—anyway, he forced me to try the food."

"Forced you?" Teddy pulled me from the counter, took a seat, and tucked me onto his lap. "I doubt it."

"He did!"

"Okay, okay. I believe you."

"The rumbling against my ear says otherwise." Still, I left my cheek where it rested against his chest.

His rumbling chuckle turned to laughter. "Sorry," he said at last. "What did you say? Laughter is the glue?"

"Those were my words." I leaned away so I could see his handsome face "I'm not lying. For every question I asked, Blackthorne made me taste something and give my opinion."

"Sounds awful."

I almost said it was, but that would be a lie.

"You had fun, didn't you?" Teddy asked.

"Ugh!" I dropped my forehead to his shoulder and spoke into his shirt. "Yes."

Teddy stroked a hand down my spine and rested it on my lower back. Warmth radiated from his palm.

"I don't know him well, but from our brief interactions and from the stories you've told me, you are very similar, you know?"

I jerked with shock. Appalled, I leaned away. "You shut your mouth!"

He held his hands up in surrender. "It's just an observation."

"Well, it's a bad one. A very, very bad one." I wriggled on his lap, attempting to get up but he tightened his hold.

"This isn't a very private space, but if you don't cut that out..." Teddy's voice dipped. It took on texture, deep and gravely.

I stilled, feeling the weapon he threatened me with beneath me.

"Really? Your stamina is commendable, but I don't have it in me," I said. He opened his mouth, but I held up my hand to stave off the smart-ass remark. "Don't. I heard it as soon as it was out of my mouth."

"You're making this too easy." Teddy pushed me from his lap and patted my butt.

Muttering, I took another seat and slung my legs across his lap. "The conversation with Blackthorne scrambled my brain."

"So, you ready to tell me about it?"

"Yeah, but first, do you remember the palm tree in the coconut looking planter? The one Blackthorne specifically asked us to water and be extra careful with?"

"I do." Concern pinched his forehead.

I told him the story about our furry houseguest.

Teddy laughed, but quickly sobered as I relayed what I'd learned over second breakfast.

He rubbed a hand over his mouth in thought.

Weirdly, I found the scratchy sound of stubble sexy. Or maybe comforting was a better word. It made me want to slide my face against his, like a cat. Talulla was already rubbing off on me.

"First things first, how do you feel?" he finally asked.

In reflex, my hand half rose toward my right eye before I caught myself and crossed my arms over my chest. Sighing, I loosened my arms and laid my hands flat on my legs. "Fine, why? Is something wrong? I checked in the mirror, and I just looked tired. I think it's more obvious in that eye since it's lighter."

Teddy grunted. "Maybe, but don't make excuses if something feels off."

"Geez, I won't. I'm fine. Everything happening with the moonbit is a human thing. I'm fae, remember?" I gripped the barely-there points of my ears and gave them a wiggle.

Sitting back, he crossed his arms over his chest. "Don't take this lightly. If Blackthorne is concerned, there must be some merit."

"You give the old windbag way too much credit." I waved a hand, brushing away the topic. "What about everything else?"

"Your safety will always be my priority."

"Cute, but what about someone out there using a twisted version of the same potion Blackthorne used to create the blood fae?"

"It's a concern."

I scoffed. "A concern. Running out of coffee grounds is a concern."

"An apocalyptic-level emergency in our house."

"True. Bad example." I didn't miss his phrasing. *Our house.* My squishy insides went all melty and girly, which I hated, but it couldn't be helped. He did that to me. "Okay, it's like running out of peanut butter. Better?"

"Much."

"The potion and the potential army thing *is concerning*, as you put it." I flashed a fangy grin. "But what bothers me is where did whoever's behind this get blood fae and shifter blood? I'm the only sort of blood fae outside of Ta'Vale. As far as I know, you and Lo are the only shifters outside of Shadwe."

"We are. I'm sure you'll figure it out." Teddy patted my legs, and I lifted them from his thighs. He stood and arched his back. The thin shirt pulled tight across his broad chest and abs that rippled and flexed with his stretch.

"You have way too much faith in me."

"You don't have enough in yourself."

I had nothing to say to that, so I did what I did best and changed the subject. "If nothing else, learning what triggers moonbit made the trip worthwhile."

"You're right. I'm relieved we don't have to worry about Zee." Teddy blew out a breath and nodded. "Though you might want to ask him if there is still any danger if a *born* wolf is the product of a *born* and *made* pairing."

Heat burned down my chest, chased by a wave of cold from my head to my toes. If Zee's mom went moonbit, she was a *made* werewolf. Eyes round, I stared up at Teddy. "I didn't even think of that."

"It's okay. I don't think it's a problem." Teddy grabbed his flannel from the back of a stool tucked against the bar. He shrugged it on but left it unbuttoned. "Maybe ask to be sure next time you speak."

Yawning, I pressed my hand to my mouth as I nodded. It wasn't like me to be tired in the middle of the afternoon, but it had been a crazy two days.

Teddy held his hand out, and I took it. He pulled me up. "You look dead on your feet. Let's go upstairs and wait for Mae and Zee to get back."

"Good idea." I threaded my fingers through his and followed him out the door where he paused to lock up. "In fact, I'll use the crystal to contact Mae. If she's still with Mom, I'll ask her if she thinks a *born* werewolf with a *made* parent is at risk."

And avoid being forced to ask Blackthorne for more help.

"It's a plan." He wrapped an arm around my shoulders and steered me in the direction of the elevators. "Do you want to pick anything up before we go?"

"For once, I'm going to say no to food."

Teddy slapped his free hand to his heart. "Who are you, and what have you done with my Lane?"

"Ha. Ha. Just for that I'll grab a bag of cheesy poofs from the grocery."

Blowing Teddy a kiss, I executed an about face and marched toward the lobby.

13

THAT VILE DRUID

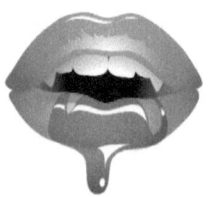

STRETCHED OUT ON A LOUNGER, COMMUNICATION CRYSTAL ON MY BELLY, I waited for Mae to return to her crystal. I was relieved to find she and Zee were still in Eodrom when I called. She'd placed me on the equivalent of hold and gone to get Mom.

I stared at the dining room table of my childhood. The long, well-worn but polished wood gleamed. A bouquet of fresh-picked flowers and herbs from Mom's garden overflowed in a wide-mouth, stoneware vase. Sun shards created an elaborate mosaic around the glass. The amber colored crystals, chips shed from sun stones, shone from most surfaces in my parent's home.

As chief royal wizard and the most powerful sun fae aside from the keepers, my father surrounded himself with the objects to feed his magic. Or rather, to feed his power through. Sun stones served as a source of power. Sun shards served as a focus which prevented magic-heavy sun fae from frying their brains.

Having never really looked at my family home with this in mind, I gnawed on a talon. My gaze jumped anxiously from one embedded sun shard to another. They had always been there, but for me they were decorations. They were so much more to my father. To my sister.

Would Mae need this? Thank the stars I'd managed to negotiate the relocation of one sun stone to the penthouse garden. With the stone, we'd bought my sister's freedom from Ta'Vale, but we still had so much to learn about her growing power and status as keeper.

Voices echoed from the depths of the house back to Mae's crystal. The domed ceilings made for great acoustics. Crouched in cubby holes, corners, and behind chunky furniture, Mae, Y'sindra, and I had eavesdropped on our parents. It never occurred to us how easy it was for them to do the same.

I shifted, pushing higher on the teak lounge chair's slatted back, and gently cupped the crystal to prevent it from toppling over, but not so tight as to break the connection.

"...couldn't your sister bring herself through the portal?"

Mom's annoyed voice drew closer. It was never easy. I closed my eyes and squeezed the bridge of my nose, the gesture pushing up my sunglasses. The retina-scorching Las Vegas afternoon sun beat against my eyelids.

"Lane had a rough night, and she's been very busy today," Mae answered.

Fizzy warmth, like a bubble bath, settled inside of me. A smile tugged at lips. My sisters' defense of me never failed to both humble and amaze me. I don't know what I did to deserve those two, but I thanked the stars, the gods, the universe, and everything in between that they had come into my life.

Inside my old home, shadows moved against the wall, just outside of the crystal's field of view. Footsteps knocked on the wooden floorboards, frequently muffled by the colorful throw rugs Mom used to decorate, most woven by her own hands.

This would have been faster if Mae had brought the crystal with her, but she'd said Zee was resting. Though I had good news for her, Zee did need to recuperate. She'd feel better when she learned the truth—probably. I supposed a lot would depend on Mom's answer, if she even had an answer.

Gods, I hoped so. I wasn't up for another round with Blackthorne. Teddy was right, it could be entertaining, but it was also infuriating and exhausting.

My view performed a disorientating tilt-o-whirl before it leveled and a close up of my mom's face came into view.

"I am trying to help your lovely friend. What is it you need, Lane?"

All the warm feelings Mae's defense of me stirred up evaporated. My brows pinched. "Same, Mom. Same."

She harrumphed, but her face softened. "I know you are. I am not sure how, but you have always had a knack for digging up the biggest bukbah nests."

Bukbahs—hornets on steroids who lifted weights in their spare time and ate werewolves for the protein. Ta'Vale was a world with beauty beyond compare where everything, including the insects, wanted to, and could, kill you.

"You enjoyed fixing the trouble I brought home," I teased.

"Well." Mom harrumphed again and absently brushed her sleeve. When she looked back at my image projection, her eyes narrowed to slits causing the barest traces of crow's feet. She leaned closer, as if she might see me better. "Are you wearing the sunscreen I sent?"

"Yes, Mom. I am wearing the sunscreen." I grabbed for the opaque, green glass jar off the small table next to my lounger and held it up.

"Good, good. You're too pale for desert sun."

I pushed down my sunglasses so she could experience the full effect of my eye roll. "You say that like you have a tan."

She tsked and thankfully, eased away from the crystal at last. "This isn't about me."

Sliding my glasses into place I said, "You're right, it's about Zee."

Somewhere out of view of the crystal, her sharp inhale was echoed by Mae. If Mom would just put the crystal back on the table, I could see them both. You'd think the communication technology hadn't been around for...I didn't know how long. Much longer than I'd been alive.

"Your sister told me where you went." Mom picked at a piece of lint on her sleeve only she could see. "I do not approve of you spending time with that vile druid."

"That *vile druid* is more closely related to you, than me, generationally speaking." I deposited the crystal in my palm and swung my legs off the side of the lounge chair. "Did Mae also tell you he requested the body of the werewolf who we suspected of succumbing to moonbit, which is the reason why I went?"

Lips pursed, she nodded. Strands of her onyx hair slipped from the loose bun piled on her head, and she tucked it behind a petite, pointed ear.

Despite being the only sun fae turned blood fae, she still had every physical characteristic of a blood fae, unlike my hybrid ass. Captured and experimented on during the Great Fae Divide, she was the only one who survived the forced evolution brought on by Blackthorne's spelled potion.

Chills crawled over my sun-heated flesh. And now someone was using a version of that potion on the human paranormal population.

"Of course, I told her," Mae said, edging behind Mom. "What did you find out?"

"He's been studying this for a long time."

"Why?" Mom asked.

My eyes widened. "I didn't think about it. I didn't ask."

Over Mom's shoulder, Mae leaned closer. "You didn't wonder why he was collecting bodies to experiment on?"

"He's hardly collecting bodies," I scoffed, appalled to hear the note of defense in my voice. "In a lot of ways, he's like Dad. A practitioner—always learning."

Mom huffed and stuttered. "How dare you compare your father with that...that..."

"He's a practitioner, and a very good one. Just like Dad."

"It makes sense," Mae said, staving off the oncoming argument. Girl always had my back.

"The Blackthorne, the place where we live, not the man," I clarified, "is a haven for paranormals. It would be in his best interest to understand the infection."

"You're right. It makes sense he would want to understand it." Mae straightened and glanced over her shoulder, in the direction Zee would be resting. "Well, this obviously couldn't wait. What did you learn?"

Quickly, I ran through the summary of what Blackthorne had shared on his knowledge of moonbit and what he'd recently observed. I left out the information about someone using his potion. It wasn't that I would never tell them, but it wasn't the priority of this call. Zee was the purpose.

"The good news is, we probably don't have to worry about Zee," I finished. "But when I discussed it with Teddy, he brought up a good point. Will the progeny of a *born* werewolf and a *made* werewolf also be at risk?"

At last, Mom slipped into a seat at the table and set the communication crystal on its surface.

Mae sat next to her, scooting close enough to be in the projection.

"I do not know about human physiology." Mom spoke slowly, as if sorting through her thoughts as she voiced them. "However, I drew some of your friend's blood. If you could retrieve a few other samples for me, I can run some comparisons."

"Anything for Zee," Mae said immediately. "What do you need?"

First, Mom listed the samples she would need. Then she surprised me by telling me to contact Blackthorne and ask for his research material. My reaction wasn't from her interest in his findings, but that she asked me to reach out to *that vile druid*.

The samples from a *born* and *made* werewolf would be relatively easy to get, but her final request would be a problem. Time to fess up about the rest of what I'd learned. "I can probably convince Blackthorne to hand over copies of his research, but there might be a kink in the moonbit samples—if I can even get my hand on any."

Elegant black brow arching, Mom said, "Shouldn't that druid have samples?"

"Unfortunately, no. At least, not from the recent cases." I steeled myself for the explosion I knew was coming. "Someone is using a version of Blackthorne's potion. It's what happened to the werewolf we encountered last night."

Eyes bulging, words flew from her mouth that turned my ears red. A sinking feeling dropped into my belly. She'd survived the potion, but it had been pure agony, comparing it to being flayed alive from the inside out, every hour of every day.

"How?" Mom screeched.

Murmuring words of comfort, Mae drew our mother's hand into hers. Rage slowly relaxed its grip on Mom's shoulders. The lines of her face softened.

Memories haunted her dark eyes. She closed them for a few seconds. When she opened them, her gaze was clear. She calmly repeated her question. "How?"

I shook my head. "I don't know. Blackthorne said it's not the same, but a variation. Rather than fae, it contains strands of human paranormal DNA."

"Will they never see?" she said.

My gaze met Mae's. We knew who she meant—the corrupt moon fae. It made sense, and also was who I suspected.

"I don't suppose your great grandfather volunteered any suspects?"

Convenient she forgot how as my mother, he was also her great—we left off a lot of greats—grandfather.

"He did not."

"Not surprising," she said.

Mae nodded. "That level of magic would have required several hands in the creation. Dad has a guild of wizards to produce large quantities of potions. Blackthorne probably didn't even know everyone involved."

"Precisely." Mom rubbed her arms as if chilled.

"Even if he thought he knew," I said. "It wouldn't do anyone any good. We can't exactly storm Shadwe. The best we can do is ask questions when we collect samples of a suspected moonbit case. If we discover a pattern, we might eventually catch them in the act."

"All right, I suppose any samples you can get will help." She sucked her lower lip between her fangs. The sharp points pressed into the soft flesh until it turned white. "We only have blood fae genetics to trace Blackthorne's spell. It would be informative to see this variation."

Meghan Callaghan might have lost her healing magic when she became blood fae, but she remained a healer. Like my father, she had an inquisitive mind.

"It's only been a day. I'll visit Blackthorne when we're done talking and see if I can get some samples."

"You know I do not approve of you being in contact with *him*," Mom repeated.

Mojave sun growing too hot for me to handle, I balanced the crystal on my palm and retreated to the air-conditioned penthouse. Talulla slit a single sleepy eye at me as I passed.

"Yes, Mom. I am aware."

"Hmph, good. You are going now?" she asked, and I was torn between laughter and pulling out my hair.

"I am."

"Let me know what you discover. Better yet, bring your crystal in case I have questions for him."

Who was this woman and what had she done with my mom? My eye twitched with the struggle to keep a straight face. "Um, okay."

Saying her goodbyes, she excused herself to check on Zee. Mae watched her go. As soon as Mom was gone, my sister whipped around to face me.

"In case she has questions for Blackthorne?" Shock strangled Mae's vocal cords, turning the question into anything but the whisper she was going for.

"I know!" Executing a full-body shrug with my shoulders and my brows, I threw the hand not occupied with the crystal in the air.

"This morning, after I left Zee with Mom, I met with Brenyn in the garden for meditation." Mae slid the crystal directly in front of her. "She didn't seem bothered you were with Blackthorne."

Leaving the door cracked for Talulla, I headed for the stairs to change. "Why would you tell her?"

Brenyn, Iola's sister, was no more than a phantom to me. The mysterious sun fae wasn't a keeper. She didn't live in Eodrom, but she tended the stones, gathering the shards they shed for the sun fae. She and Mae had grown close.

"We talk about everything." Mae rested an elbow on the table and her chin on her hand. She drummed her long fingers with their tangerine-shaded manicure against her cheek. "Brenyn said my energy felt unsettled. I told her what happened last night, which led to a discussion on what you were doing today."

The fact that Blackthorne was alive and not in the Eodrom dungeons was no longer a secret, neither was my convoluted relationship to him. Yet, Mae discussing any of this with someone other than our shared inner circle made me uncomfortable.

"I understand, but it feels weird I don't know her. I'd like to meet her sometime."

A sunshine-bright smile lit her features. "I would love to introduce you. Oh, and I didn't make it to the library, but I believe my conversation with Brenyn saved me the trip. She agrees with your thinking. You wouldn't be infected."

Oh no, I didn't really want to meet the fae, but I had to go and open my big mouth. I'd only been trying to make Mae happy. Maybe she'd forget I mentioned it.

I rushed up the stairs. "Okay, no problem. Gotta go. If you plan to skip the library, you'll probably beat me home. I'll fill you in when I get back."

My inner circle was expanding like a helium balloon, and I hated it. Not that long ago, secrets withheld from my sisters and me had tested my trust.

Deciding to dress for the beach and a little relaxation, I slipped shorts and a tank top on over a bathing suit. Before leaving the bedroom. I scribbled a quick note for Teddy, letting him know where I'd gone.

Since I knew he had to cover Dexter's shift at the Interlands bar—some sort of flu—I expected to beat him home. Still, I was learning how to do this relationship thing. I wasn't great at it, and if he did get home first, me disappearing without a word seemed like a bad idea.

The first time I'd accidentally crossed through Blackthorne's portal and vanished for days longer than I'd promised, Teddy had lost his mind. So had I, but for entirely different reasons.

Forgoing shoes, because who needed those at the beach, I put my phone and the crystal into a small bag and headed back outside.

"Ow! Ow, ow, ow." My soles felt like they caught fire only a few steps onto the deck. A quick U-turn, and I high stepped my way inside for flip flops. I wasn't a fan of flimsy shoes, but they were right by the door and were better than toasting my tender feet like marshmallows.

Outside again, I slid the door closed on its tracks, but turned to find Talulla watching me.

"Right, forgot about you." I left the door open just enough for her to slip in and out. This was going to take getting used to. "Please don't make me regret this."

In the garden, the midafternoon sun rested in the sky directly behind fruit trees at the far end of the roof. My steps slowed as I walked toward the illusion of a spikey golden crown resting atop the stone circle.

I wasn't looking forward to a second visit with Blackthorne, but I couldn't wait for that swim.

14

THE WEIGHT OF WORRY

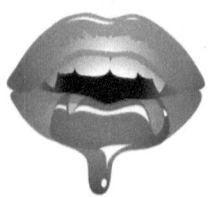

THE THINNEST LINE OF ORANGE BURNED ACROSS THE DARK HORIZON. So much for sunshine and swimming. One of these days I'd remember the existence of a time difference from coast to coast.

Flip-flops filling with sand, I shuffled toward the wooden planks leading to the hotel. Cheers rose in the distance. I squinted at the deck, barely making out three figures gathered around the bar. Something resembling a movie screen stood opposite the group.

The figures on the screen kept lining up and then piling on top of one another. Football. I didn't know much about the sport, but there were always bets greasing Rips palms at the Interlands bar. A trend I expected would see an uptick if he moved to Las Vegas. More collection jobs for me.

"That ref is blind!" A man bellowed and leaped from his stool. The silvery-gray complexion gave the moon fae's identity away before I could make out his features.

I stopped, tugged my phone from the tiny bag dangling from my wrist and shot a text off to Teddy.

Found your bartender. Is flu code for football?

Snickering, I returned the phone to the bag and headed to the party I wasn't invited to.

As I drew closer, I recognized Jason, Eli's fiancé, in the company of Blackthorne and Dexter.

My phone buzzed. I checked the message, laughing as I mounted the stairs. The three men turned toward me.

"Granddaughter! Two visits and a phone call in as many days. I am pleased."

I snorted. "Don't be. It's not a social visit."

"Alas, it never is." Reaching behind the bar, ice sloshed and clinked. He pulled out a bottle and held it toward me.

"Sure." I relieved him of the bottle, popped the top with a talon, and took a long swig. Smiling, I turned toward Dexter. "Teddy asked me to say hello."

"Shit," he muttered. "Am I in trouble?"

I shrugged. "Do you think you're in trouble?"

He pushed a hand up his face and then through his hair. "Probably. Shit," he said again. "I'm going to be scrubbing toilets for at least a month. You know last time he made me use a toothbrush?"

"Coulda been worse, considering what you'd been up to."

Unwitting as he may have been in his role, he'd helped the corrupt moon fae smuggle sun fae from Ta'Vale and into their ranks. Of course, if he hadn't, Jason wouldn't be engaged to Elisette, and I wouldn't have discovered some sun fae were all right.

"Truth." He pinched the neck of his near-empty bottle and gave it a spin. "Any news about the prince?"

Prince Miro, the most ruthless and feared, corrupt moon fae alive. Also, the last of their royal line. Y'sindra impaled him on a spear of ice, and I helped toss him into the Eodrom dungeon. Good riddance.

Brow pinched, I studied Dexter. I wasn't sure why he wanted to know, beyond fear of the prince. "If you're asking if he's still in sun fae custody, he is. Beyond that, no news. YML Investigations fulfilled their contract to the sun fae. We don't work for them anymore, not officially. Even if I did, by-the-books Duskmere isn't keen on sharing."

I often didn't find out someone escaped the dungeon until they were kidnapping my sister or trying to kill me.

Ever since I'd learned Duskmere's superior was Odo who had no problem sharing information, I'd decided the Royal Fae Guard Captain was just an asshole.

"Good, good." Dexter's nod was jerky. He tipped back his bottle and drained the beer. "We don't need that guy running around, am I right?"

"Uh, sure." I gave Dexter a sideways look. He was a weird guy, but the bar clientele loved him. I hooked a talon on a bowl of something in front of Blackthorne and pulled it toward me. "If the dungeon can hold him. Or maybe I should say, if no one lets him out."

I didn't think it was possible for a moon fae to visibly pale, but Dexter did.

"Why do you care?" I asked.

He waved a flippant hand. "I don't. He's just a dangerous dude, ya know?"

"Yes, I do," I said dryly. "I am the one who put him there."

"Right on." Dexter stood on his stool and reached over the bar for another beer.

Giving the snack bowl a shake, I looked down. "Chex Mix! I love this stuff. You know how to party, Gramps."

"Hey, Lane," Jason said.

"Hey, Jason." I twisted toward the mage. He wore faded denim and a beige T-shirt with his business logo. A black cowboy hat rested on the bar at his elbow. Despite his friendship with Blackthorne and supposed relation to drunken quasi-deity, Nuada, I liked him. He ran an animal sanctuary outside of Las Vegas and made an out-of-this-world green chili.

"I've been meaning to thank you for taking Eli out."

"You sure? You know what happened, right?" I asked and popped a savory puffed square into my mouth.

A wide smile creased his face, rough and tanned from the outdoors. "Absolutely. She had a great time. Couldn't stop talking about it. About how you and your sisters handled the situation. Shame about the young man, though."

I sipped my beer and slid my gaze back to Blackthorne. "It was. Terrible when you have no control over what happens to you."

Reading the implications in my words, I meant his potion, not moonbit, Blackthorne tilted the mouth of his beer toward me.

"That's what I came here to talk to you about," I told him. "Want to step inside?"

He relaxed, twisted on his stool to put the bar at his back, and hooked his elbows on the counter. "No need. These gentlemen know who I am."

"And what you've done?" I asked.

"Don't worry about us. We're just here for the game." Jason pointed at the large screen.

"And the drinks." Dexter gave me a boyish grin. He looked so young, but I had to wonder. Suddenly, he leapt off his stool.

On the big screen, a man launched into the air and pulled a ball into his arms from an impossible height. Before his toes met turf, he was torpedoed by another man and disappeared beneath a pile of bodies. The ball spun away from the group and another man dove on top.

"No! Come on, man. Hold onto the ball." Dexter dropped onto his stool hard enough to bruise his tailbone. "Damn. Another week's worth of tips to Rip."

"If you stopped skipping shifts, you'd make more." I said, dryly. "And Teddy wouldn't need to find someone else to run the bar."

Dexter's eyes rounded. "He'd do that?"

I snorted. "Probably not, but he should."

"This is the last time, I promise."

"Sure, whatever." I waved my hand. I'd believe that the day Y'sindra gave up berries in her booze. Facing Blackthorne, I said, "All right, you asked for it. I'm here to collect a sample of the werewolf's body you swiped from the casino."

"I stole nothing," Blackthorne smiled. "It's my casino."

"I live there," I shot back.

Raising his hand, as if asking permission to speak, Jason added, "It is his name on the building."

"Shoosh." Eyes narrowed, I shot Jason a *speak again and die look*. Very intimidating.

Dexter shrugged. "My man's right. Big green and gold lights. I remember noticing a bulb was out the other night and told Vaughn."

I swung around on my stool to glare at the peanut gallery. "By the gods, if you two can't keep your mouths shut, you can go inside."

"But the game..." Dexter whined.

"Quiet!" I snapped, irritated by their continued conversation and my failed attempt at intimidation.

When I turned back to Blackthorne, the grin on his face and mirth in his eyes didn't endear me to him, either.

Draining my beer in three long swallows, I thunked it onto the countertop. "Do you still have the body or not?"

"The important pieces."

Pieces? That was just nasty. "Okay, gross, but about those samples..." I drew my finger through the sweat ring on the bar top from my bottle.

"I will provide them if you tell me why you want them."

"What does it matter?"

"It doesn't." Blackthorne pulled the snack bowl to himself and dug out a handful of salty, crunchy goodness. "But I'm curious."

"Mom needs them." I hooked a talon into the bowl and pulled it back.

"Interesting." He popped his handful of crackers into his mouth and chewed. "She wants to see the potion's elements."

It wasn't a question.

"You have your answer." I pointed at him. A checkerboard-patterned cracker dangled from my talon tip. "How's about you get me those samples."

Nodding, Blackthorne swung off the stool. "Deal's a deal. Follow me."

"See you boys in a few." I slid the bowl to Jason and followed Blackthorne into the hotel.

My plaited hair quickly released from the sweat-slick skin along my neck when we entered the exceptionally cool hotel lobby. The prickly sensation of goosebumps replaced the sticky feeling.

Blackthorne turned left, heading toward the reception desk. I glanced out the back wall made mostly of glass as we strode past Jason and Dexter in a highly animated, one-sided shouting match with the big screen.

"How did those two get here? They didn't come through the druid circle."

"Not through your circle." Gramps hung a right toward the hotel's front entry and a door set in the wall opposite the check-in desk. "Through Jason's circle. With me in Las Vegas, he'd never had a need for one, but since I have been exiled here..."

He let the statement linger.

"Yeah, you've got it rough," I said, tone drier than the Mojave, and paused for emphasis. "On the beach. Anyhow, I didn't think he was... I don't know? Druid enough to build a circle."

"He couldn't build a circle on his own, but connecting it to mine on this end makes it possible. You should have noticed the extra stones when you arrived."

"It was dark," I grumbled.

"They have been here for weeks."

Implying I should have noticed them when I came through the circle this morning.

Blackthorne unlocked a door I'd assumed was a cleaning closet and walked inside, flipping on a light as he went.

"Whatever," I muttered, like any mature adult would, and trailed him into an elegantly furnished office full of rich wood and leather furniture, similar to the office he had at the penthouse. I gave the desk a doubletake. Son of an ogre turd, exactly like that office.

"How'd you move the desk here?" And how had none of us noticed it was missing? If this guy was going to waltz in and out on a whim, I needed to do inventory of the penthouse.

"Vaughn and a few other members of the security team moved it here." Blackthorne went to the wall and slid open a very clever false wall to reveal yet another door. Punching a key code into a discreet panel, he then inserted a physical key in another location and gave it a turn before the door slid open.

Curiosity drove me to follow. How often would I get to see a real-life super villain's lair?

"Fancy," I said, doing a slow spin.

The space was much larger than I'd expected. Even more unexpected, every solid surface—walls, floor, ceiling—was lined with wood that appeared to be the same petrified wood I now associated with the man digging through a commercial-grade, stainless-steel refrigerator at the back of the room. A door to my right broke up the solid wood surface. It opened on a small room with white tile and a drain in the floor. An empty, stainless-steel table the right size for a body lay in the center.

Two hip-high tables were between Blackthorne and I, with equipment like what I had often seen in my father's labs. On my left, glass-covered cabinetry ran from one end of the wall to the other. Containers of all makes and sizes, books, notebooks, and other items I didn't recognize cluttered every shelf.

I zeroed in on the notebooks. "Can I get a copy of the research material you have on moonbit?"

Placing a large, opaque container on the table behind him, Blackthorne closed the refrigerator and gave me a long, appraising look. "Your mother's request, I presume."

"You presume, correctly. Don't worry, she isn't asking to double-check your findings." I pushed a rolling stool to the opposite side of the table he'd placed the container on and took a seat. Hooking a thumb toward the side room, I said, "I can't help but notice the distinct lack of body in here."

Blackthorne patted the top of the large bin he'd transferred from the refrigerator. "Your werewolf is right here," he said and popped the top.

One by one, he methodically unloaded smaller, clear plastic containers with what appeared to hold various organic compounds. A lump of something I thought was a heart. Maybe a liver, or a lung, I didn't know. I stabbed innards, I didn't study them. A few more pinkish, globby things followed, and then a large piece of flesh. The bristly werewolf fur suggested I was looking at a chunk of Beast's thigh.

Sour bile coated the back of my throat. I covered my mouth—just in case. I wasn't squeamish, but that was just gross. Apparently, my gag reflex could tolerate dismembering, disemboweling, beheading, and a hundred other wounds, but it drew the line at sterile body parts. Specifically, hairy ones.

When he was finished, eleven containers in total formed a grisly line on the gleaming white surface.

Moving with efficiency, he retrieved a glass measuring cup from a shelf and two small tubes from a drawer. Blackthorne stood by the sink as he dumped the tube's powdery contents into the cup and then added water. He pulled a metal spoon from a canister, gave the concoction a stir, and then popped it into the microwave.

I rolled my seat to the right for a better view. As much as I hated to admit it, this was pretty interesting stuff. Faded memories, like old, blurry photographs, surfaced.

When I was very young, too young to be hurt by or understand other fae's disdain, my father would bring me to Eodrom, to his lab. A small smile tugged at my lips as I watched Blackthorne pull the glass from the microwave, stir, and heat again. With quiet focus, he repeated this process several times.

"There can be no lumps, Malaney," my father would tell me. I always left lumps, but still, he let me stir.

At last, Blackthorne deemed the mixture free of floaty bits. Next to each bin, he placed a petri dish. Opening the first, he poured the clear, slightly yellowish liquid inside, and then replaced the lid. He worked quickly, making his way down the line of samples and dishes, repeating the same process.

Finished, Blackthorne relaxed against the counter behind him, arms over his chest, legs crossed at his ankles. "If not to double check my research, research I have been doing for far longer than you have been alive I might add, why the request?"

I wheeled my seat closer to the table and reached for one of the little plastic discs.

"Don't," Blackthorne said. "If you want me to create these samples your mother requested, the solution must set. They need twenty minutes."

Oh my gods, how will I survive twenty whole ass minutes?

Pulling my hands back, I pressed them palms down on my legs and drummed my talons on my thighs. "You asked about Mom's request."

Blackthorne crossed his arms. "I did."

"I have a friend."

"How wonderful for you."

Eyes narrowed, I bared my fangs.

"Yes, that right there." He straightened and pointed at me. "That face is the reason I worry for your social skills."

"Who are you? My therapist?"

"Do you need one?" Blackthorne asked. "I have the number to a very good counselor in Las Vegas. She helps when there are trauma issues which impact the staff. I can phone Vaughn—"

"Argh!" I thunked my forehead on the table. "Can you not?"

"Only trying to be helpful. Please be careful not to jostle the petri dishes, or we will have start over." Fabric swished, rollers rattled on the floor, and I heard the telltale creak indicating Blackthorne took a seat. "You were saying you have a friend. This has something to do with the research material request?"

"It does," I answered, still face down on table. Sitting up, I crossed my arms and gave Blackthorne my no-nonsense look. "She is a *born* werewolf, so I was relieved when you told me the infection only impacts the *made*."

He made a humming sound of understanding. "To be expected."

"However, she must be the offspring of a *made* and *born* pairing, because she lost her mother to moonbit." I dragged a talon along the edge of the table, inexplicably nervous to meet his eyes as I got to the point. "The question I posed to Mom was whether a *born* werewolf with a *made* parent might be susceptible to the infection."

"The answer is no," Blackthorne said immediately.

Relief swept through me with a flushing sensation and a whooshing in my ears. My shoulders sagged, only now realizing the weight of worry I'd carried for my friend. *My friend!* Who would have ever thought I'd say that? Not me.

There was no way Blackthorne missed my reaction, but he said nothing for which I was grateful.

"As you can imagine, there is too much information to simply copy." He waved his hand at the multiple shelves filled with all shapes and sizes of notebooks and binders. "If Meghan is still interested in the research, bring me a communication crystal, and I will speak with her."

A sharp bark of laughter jumped out of me. The idea of Blackthorne and my mom chatting short circuited my brain. "Sorry." I cleared my throat. "Good idea. My sister is with her now. I'll ask her to bring a crystal home."

Better idea than handing him my personal crystal. It also wasn't lost on me he'd used my mom's name, meaning he knew who she was. It made me wonder how much more he knew about his family tree, but I wasn't curious enough to ask.

"You have time. The solution still needs to set, and I will need to prepare the samples." He made a rolling "go ahead" motion with his hand. "Feel free to step outside and place your call if you are more comfortable."

"Probably for the best." I headed for the lobby. True, Mom said to bring my crystal and contact her, but I had no desire to be present when she finally met her war criminal relative for the first time.

I dug the crystal from the small bag where I'd stashed my cell phone and made my way toward the sofa Talulla had napped on earlier. Making a last-minute decision, I went out the back doors, and into the sticky Florida night. While I didn't think there was any chance Blackthorne could overhear something he shouldn't, I didn't want to afford him the opportunity to listen on principle.

Engrossed in their game, neither Dexter nor Jason paid any attention as I crossed to the far side of the deck and scooted into a cabana. I placed the crystal on the mattress, brushed my finger over its surface, and spoke Mae's name. Her image rose only a moment later.

She gave my surroundings a quick once over. "You're still at Blackthorne's. Are you in one of the cabanas? Is everything okay?"

"Yes, yes, and I'm fine. Blackthorne's inside making the samples Mom asked for." I gestured to the hotel behind me, barely visible through the gauzy curtains. "I'll fill you in on the conversation later, but for now you should know he says Zee is not at risk."

A smile lit her expression. "If he's right, that's fantastic."

"I wouldn't say this in front of him, but he's probably right."

Mae chuckled. "I expect you wouldn't."

"Blackthorne says he'll talk to Mom about his research, but it's too much to copy."

The expression on my sister's face matched my initial thoughts. "I'm not sure if I want to be in the room when those two speak for the first time or not."

"I don't," I said quickly. "Which is why I need you to get a new crystal linked to Mom. I'll drop it off with Blackthorne later and whatever happens from there is not our problem."

"Good idea." Mae glanced over her shoulder, her features soft when she turned back to the crystal. "Zee woke up only a few minutes before you called. Mom is checking in on her now. I'll go give them the news and get that crystal."

"As soon as I have these samples, I'll meet you back at the penthouse." Closing my fist over the crystal, I stuffed it back into the bag and returned to the lab.

As I entered, Blackthorne was already at work. With nimble fingers he sliced a wafer-thin sample from one of the pinkish-red lumps with the precision of a master sushi chef.

"So, you and your sister don't think your mother and I can have a civil conversation?" Without looking up as he spoke, Blackthorne carefully transferred a slice of some sort of internal organ to the prepared petri dish.

I gawked. "How did you know?"

He placed the lid over the sample and pressed until there was a small click. With his scalpel, he gestured to something below the table on his side. "Do you really believe I would not have cameras outside the hotel?"

"Of course, you would."

With an unabashed grin, he moved to the final piece of Beast laid out on the table—the hunk of werewolf thigh. "As you like to remind me, I'm an old man, living all alone out here. I need the protection."

"Sure you do." Morbid curiosity drew me to my feet, and I circled behind him as he went to work on the mound of flesh. I blinked at the view. Below the table, six decent-sized screens each depicted as many different views. "Are you watching the entire beach?"

Blackthorne pressed the lid on the final dish. "Only what's mine."

Once all the dishes were sealed, he retrieved an insulated box from a shelf and a frozen white rectangle from the refrigerator which he placed inside the box. Next, he laid a layer of foam with two depressions the petri dishes fit into perfectly. He repeated the foam and dishes until he'd placed everything inside. After he closed the box, he ran a band of yellow tape around its edges.

He patted the lid. "One last thing before I turn these over."

"Of course, there is." I propped a hand on my hip. "What?"

"I would like a sample of your blood."

"What, why?" Reflexively, I slapped a hand over the inside of my elbow.

A smile creased the corners of Blackthorne's eyes. "You are the only hybrid in existence. Getting a look at those genes will help with comparisons on the suspected moonbit cases which are actually from my recreated potion."

Agreeing for no other reason than I didn't care, and it would get me home faster, I gave the blood.

While I held a cotton ball to the inside of my wrist, Blackthorne placed the five vials of my blood into something that resembled a pencil holder and set it aside.

When he'd finished, he handed me the box. "Please be careful. You'll need to send this to Meghan immediately. She'll know what to do."

Ready to get home and relax, I trailed behind him to the exit and waited as he closed and locked the room that disappointingly, gave off zero super villain vibes.

Back outside, Blackthorne returned to his seat at the bar and handed me a beer for the road—or the portal. Jason extracted a promise to come for Sunday barbeque, which took no convincing at all. I was always willing to show up for good food.

"Lane?" Dexter called as I jogged down the deck steps to the beach.

Carefully balancing the box of samples, I paused to look back. "Yeah?"

"Will ya tell the boss I'll be in tomorrow, and I'll bring a new toothbrush?"

I laughed all the way back to Vegas.

15

WHAT SOLITUDE

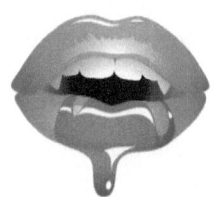

THE EXCHANGE WAS SIMPLE. A DOORWAY TO MY PARENT'S BACKYARD opened where Mae and Zee waited. Zee crossed quickly and went into the penthouse. I handed Mae the box of samples, and she gave me the crystal before the portal had time to close.

I looked up as Teddy came outside to greet me. "That was easy. Come with me to the beach? Just there and back." I wrapped my arms around his waist and rested my chin on his chest, face angled up. "We won't even leave the circle. Promise."

Running his hand over my braided hair, he took up the end and tickled my nose. "I can, but what are you up to?"

"Can't I just want your company?"

"No."

I made a face. "I want your company all the time. Meet me in the garden? I need something to hold this crystal."

Zee had a cupboard open when I entered the kitchen. She glanced at me. "Bowls?"

I pointed to a shelf to the right of the stove. "Bowls there, cereal is in the pantry. Y'sindra stashes her marshmallow stuff in the cabinet by the fridge. Help yourself to anything,"

Grabbing a plastic baggie, I thought better and grabbed a small brown bag instead. I texted Blackthorne on my way to the druid circle on the roof.

Have the crystal. Leaving in the circle. Paper bag.

He responded with the okay emoji. Less words—fine by me.

Make sure Dexter watches. Coming now.

Phone secured in my back pocket, I took the stairs to the roof and jogged across the garden to Teddy waiting in the portal circle. "I texted Blackthorne. He knows I'm dropping off the crystal. Wave at the deck when we get there."

"Why?"

"Just being friendly." I gave him a wide smile.

He shook his head. "I knew you were up to something."

"I make life fun." I winked. "Let's go."

The world spun away. A split second of darkness and shooting lights and we were across the country, on the opposite coast. I tossed the bag with the crystal against one of the pillars.

I heard Teddy laugh and turned to find him waving at Dexter standing on the deck.

What I wouldn't give to hear the conversation going on up there.

"You're such a troublemaker," Teddy said, still waving.

"Don't you mean I'm a good time? Back to Vegas."

Once again the world spun away with my intent, not the magical password I once believed was required.

"There and back, just like promised." I grabbed Teddy's butt and laughing, made a run for the penthouse.

When I slipped inside from the balcony, Zee was climbing the stairs to the second floor.

"I haven't seen a toothbrush or soap in at least twenty-four hours. Gonna change, shower, and wash this stank from my mouth. Not necessarily in that order." She disappeared down the hall.

"Dexter better not quit on me." Teddy came in from the balcony, leaving the door open behind him. I almost complained about him letting all the cold air out, but Blackthorne paid the bills. "Don't tell Zee, but he's the best bartender I've got."

"I heard that!" Zee shouted from upstairs.

"He's the best bartender I have in Interlands," Teddy amended. Leather creaked as he sank onto the sofa and hit recline on his seat.

Only Y'sindra used that feature, which was funny since her legs didn't reach beyond the seat. Mae and I were taking a little longer getting used to all the Earthside gadgets. In Interlands, we'd been exposed to what I'd thought was a lot. I'd had no idea how much bigger this world would be beyond cheesy poofs, cellophane wrapped snack cacks, and reality TV.

"You hurt our houseguest's feelings," I teased.

Teddy glanced up at me and patted the cushion next to him. "Zee knows she's my favorite."

I cast a longing look at my favorite chair and then curled up against his side. "I thought you said best?"

Leaning close, he lowered his voice. "Dexter works magic on the crowds. Zee is a great bartender. Dexter is a great showman."

"Still heard that!" Zee yelled. Girl was going to strain her vocal cords. "Werewolf hearing."

I smirked at Teddy.

"But it's true. Everyone loves Dexy-boy," she called. "And he ain't bad to look at. I'm gonna miss that view."

"Weren't you going to shower?" Teddy bellowed, blowing out my eardrums.

Wincing, I resisted plugging a finger in my ears. I'd learned the hard way what a bad idea that was. While my talons were semi-retractable, the point was always present, and they hurt.

"Volume, man," I grumbled.

"Sorry." Teddy kissed my temple, and it did not make it feel any better.

Wrapped in a towel, Zee popped her head out of the second-floor hallway. "You just want to talk about me where I can't hear."

"Never." Teddy had the grace to look sincere.

Zee winked and disappeared back into the hall. A moment later the shower turned on.

"Maybe you need to bring Dexter here too. At least he'd be less likely to skip out on his shift with you so close." I leaned forward to grab the TV remote from the coffee table, grunting with the effort. The weight of Teddy caused me to tilt toward him on the seat, and I couldn't quite reach. Tongue caught between my teeth, I strained, wiggled my fingers, missed.

"I've thought about it." Teddy took pity on my plight. Putting a leg on either side of the extended footrest, he leaned forward, snatched the remote, and dropped it in my lap. "There's something special about that kid."

TV suddenly forgotten, I angled toward Teddy, my knees poking his thigh. "How old is he?"

Teddy shrugged and took the forgotten remote from my hand. "I don't know. I call him kid, but he could be older than me. He acts young but that doesn't mean a thing. Take your grandpa, for example."

"You've got a point."

"He doesn't take life seriously, but when he's on, he's on. I can trust him with the bar." Turning on the TV, Teddy navigated to the vast library of shows Y'sindra and I record on the regular as he spoke. "He has a way of keeping the patrons in check. Dexter is the only bartender who hasn't called me for help when a brawl breaks out."

Struck silent, I blinked at Teddy while he scrolled through the programs on the DVR.

"Nothing but your reality romance," he complained. "Can't you and your sister watch a crime drama or something?"

Knees bent, feet tucked under my butt, I stared at Teddy. Dropping such a bold statement like it was no big deal, he had my full attention. Who needed TV drama when I had it right here? "That scrawny guy can handle the Interlands crowd? I saw him do some sort of magic once."

The magic had been small, but unconsciously done and controlled. Like sun fae, strong magic in the moon fae was rare. My father lamented all the powerful practitioners had turned corrupted and either been killed or banished. I'd meant to tell him about Dexter, but I kept forgetting. He'd be so happy when I finally told him, he might even smile.

Teddy reached an arm around my shoulders, turning me and pulling me against his side. "I've never seen it when we've been on shift together, but Zee has. She doesn't know why, but she says no one challenges him."

"Weird."

Ever so lightly, he traced his fingertips up and down my arm. Goosebumps pebbled my skin. My lids grew heavy. The hypnotizing friction of his hand was better than one of Mom's sleeping draughts.

"Hmm." Teddy made a rumbling sound of agreement. "Some of my people feared the corrupted. Until Duskmere, they were the only moon fae I had ever met. It must be an innate reaction to their kind."

His people. He meant Shadwenians, shifters. My brow creased. Until recently, I too hadn't met any moon fae other than Duskmere, but I knew those who remained in Ta'Vale lived in harmony with every other fae.

"I suppose," I said, snuggling against my sugar buns. Just because I'd never heard of or seen any fae have a reaction to moon fae didn't mean it couldn't be true. Ultimately it didn't matter. "Why would you bring him to *Blood and Wine* if he does so well in Interlands?"

Upstairs, the shower turned off. I lifted my head and looked outside. Mae was taking forever. Mom must have enlisted her help with the samples, or some other chore. Y'sindra and Lo had come and gone. I knew she was off working hard on strengthening her wing, but I missed that girl.

"Like Zee said, the people love him. He'll charm the credit cards from all the high roller's wallets." Teddy's gruff laugh vibrated his chest against my cheek.

It tickled and my lips slowly spread into a smile. "I don't think that's the kind of magic he performs."

"You never know." Teddy wiggled his shoulder for me to sit up. "I hear your stomach. Come on, let's go order food."

He had already laid out several menus when I reached the kitchen.

Sorting through the enormous stack, I tapped my finger on a glossy, trifold menu with an ooey-gooey, melty, cheesy pizza on the front. "This place."

A click and clatter on the coffee table drew my attention. My communication crystal was vibrating.

"Must be Y'sindra," I said and returned to the living room.

"What do you want?" Teddy asked through the kitchen pass through.

Dropping cross-legged onto the sofa, I called back to Teddy. "Surprise me."

The crystal continued to vibrate. I leaned forward and swiped my finger over the surface. It read my energy and Mae's image popped up. She should have been home an hour ago. Why was she calling? What was wrong? For a split second my hearts tripped and panic began to churn, but then she smiled.

"Laney, Dad asked me to help with an errand at the castle. Since I was here, I stopped by the Sun Garden."

Trees with multi-colored spade-shaped leaves framed my sister. A branch drooped with the weight of a pale-yellow orb hanging from it. That fruit, with its delicious deep purple segments, only grew in the sun garden. Meaning she was still there.

What was this about? "Okay..." I drawled, suspicion making me wary.

"I was surprised to find Brenyn here." Mae began walking. "Happily so, but I thought I could introduce you since you said you'd like to meet her."

Acutely self-conscious, my hand flew to the halo of flyaways that had escaped from my braid. I tugged the scrunchie free and shook out the length. I was still wearing my *Fang You* tank top. "I need to change."

"You're fine." Mae laughed.

I pointed at my shirt and tilted my head in an *are you sure* gesture.

"Hold the crystal up, no one will see."

Of course, what was wrong with me? I smoothed my hair again and then picked up the crystal, holding it so only my head would be projected on Mae's end. I spun to look behind me making a *psst psst* sound for Teddy's attention and waved him out of the frame.

"I didn't expect to see her again so soon," Mae was saying. "She's normally only here once every few months to collect the shards."

"Maybe she's there for the same reason you are."

"No." Mae looked past her crystal to the empty path in front of her and lowered her voice. "Brenyn cares less for the court than you do, and Dad's errand was certainly not something she would be concerned with."

"Oh?" I asked to be polite.

"It was nothing." She waved her free hand dismissively. "A shipment from the farms came in. Somehow the ingredients Dad uses in his potions were mixed in with items meant for a RFG ceremony dinner tomorrow. He asked for my help sorting."

"As if they need a ceremony," I said and then pointed at a tree Mae passed. "Can you grab some fruit?"

Changing course, she backtracked and plucked one ripe yellow globe from the tree. "While I was there, Duskmere explained they do this every year. Welcome new members, say goodbye to old. Strengthens loyalty."

A second smaller piece of fruit joined the first in her knit cross-body bag, and she continued down the path.

I'd only visited the sun garden twice. Once when I was pushed from the sun bridge and almost died, the second time to investigate the theft of the sun stones. The first trip to the garden left me unconscious. The second had been stressful. Not the best conditions to memorize the landscape, but I was fairly certain Mae was headed toward the first stone.

"May they forge many bonds that do not include us," I said.

Mouth curling up, Mae shook her head. "You know they'll only call if it's an emergency."

"Everything is an emergency to Duskmere."

Mae lifted a hand and waved at someone—Brenyn, I presumed—in front of her.

Stomach clenching, I pulled a pillow into my lap and waited. This was a fae who was rarely present at the Eodrom court. According to Mae, few even knew of her. I rubbed shoulders with the keepers, so I shouldn't be nervous about meeting Iola's lesser-known sister.

Yet, I knew why I was anxious. Mae liked her. It was that simple. Until recently, my sisters and I shared the same acquaintances, the same friends. These days Y'sindra was almost always gone. When Mae wasn't in the sun garden with Iola or training with our father, she spent most of her time with the new sun fae residents of Las Vegas.

Meeting Brenyn would be more evidence of my sisters' growth and my lack thereof.

Insecurity and jealousy crawled over my skin like a kicked ant's nest. I rolled my shoulders. The feelings were irrational and unfair. Nothing and no one remained the same forever.

Plastering a smile on my face, I waited for the introduction.

When Mae's gaze briefly dropped to me and then away, her head jerked right back. "Are you okay?"

"What? Yes, fine." I paused. "Why?"

Mae pointed at her mouth.

My brow creased. Did she mean my smile? "Too much?"

She nodded and giggled. "It looks like your face might crack into a million pieces any second."

Just like my hearts.

"Sorry." I rubbed my lips together, letting my mouth relax. My cheeks hurt. I'd definitely had that expression turned up to terrifying. "You know how I am meeting new people."

Light footsteps and the whispery swish of grass announced someone's arrival. Mae looked up, through my projection and smiled. "Hi, Brenyn. This is my sister I told you about, Malaney—Lane."

A tall blonde sun fae with a willowy figure stepped into the frame. Colorful beads that offset her golden hair, cobalt blue, burnt orange, silver, and black, as well as what appeared to be chips of stones, like sun shards, had been woven onto tiny braids in her hair. "Hello, Lane. Mae speaks so highly of you." The female smiled, but it lacked the warmth I'd expected.

Her expression was almost brittle. Although that wasn't fair. If she was the recluse Mae described, she'd be as uncomfortable as me, if not more so. She still lived in Eodrom. Most of the fae might not be as bad as I'd always thought, but the court, those who considered themselves part of a royal bloodline with a right to minor authority, were still a nest of spitting vipers.

Careful not to let any fang slip, I returned her smile. "As she does you."

There, I'd done it. Cordial, casual. Go me!

Time flew by, speaking of nothing and everything. A few anecdotes about my, Y'sindra, and Mae's childhood and trouble we'd gotten into. We spoke about Mae's training, about her time in the garden.

"I find peace here, but your sister has been a balm to my solitude," Brenyn said.

What solitude? Her sister Iola was a keeper and in the sun garden daily. Torneh too. The sun garden was enormous, but still. They had to bump into each other at some point.

I had no idea what happened between her and Iola, but it made me grateful for the amazing sisters I had.

The elevator doors opened on a quiet hiss. Thank the gods! This conversation had ventured into uncomfortable territory.

"It was a pleasure meeting you," I said, trying my rusty manners on for size. Not too shabby. "We'll have to meet in person the next time I visit for a family dinner."

Good segue, Lane. I gave myself a mental pat on the back.

"We shall," she replied.

I looked at Mae. "Speaking of dinner, will you be back soon? Food just arrived."

On cue, the heavenly scent of bread, tomato, and hot cheese filled the penthouse, and I was suddenly starving.

Mae looked past me. "Pizza? Nice."

I glanced back. Teddy had set a stack of five pizza boxes on the counter and was separating them one by one.

"I'm done here." Mae smiled at me and then Brenyn. "I just wanted to introduce you. I'll see you in about thirty."

We ended the connection. I made it two steps toward the kitchen before a whirlwind of white curls and snow blew past me.

"Just in time." Y'sindra landed on the kitchen pass-through counter and started flipping open box lids.

"Do I smell pizza?" Zee called as she jogged down the stairs.

For the first time since the whole crazed werewolf incident, things felt right.

16

NEED A TOP OFF

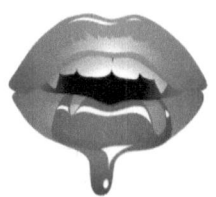

THE HAZY GRAY LIGHT OF PREDAWN WAS JUST CRESTING THE HORIZON, and I was awake. Something was very wrong with this scenario. Mouth minty fresh, fangs sparkling, I padded to the bed and crawled to the center.

When my lips met Teddy's temple, he came awake. He rolled over and tunneled an arm beneath my middle. He pulled me to the mattress and curled me against his chest. The sheets were warm from his body heat.

"Hey, you," he said thickly as he stroked his hand up my back and tickled his way beneath the hair covering my neck. Goosebumps rose in response. "You and Zee headed out?"

"Yeah. Which forsaken god did I piss off to be forced out of bed this early?" I whined, rubbing my cheek on his shoulder.

The sleep-roughened chuckle vibrating his chest sent a fresh wave of shivers through me.

"I'm no expert on werewolves," he drawled. "But if Zee, a werewolf, says this is the best time, you should listen to her."

"I listened. I'm up."

Teddy angled his head, presenting the long line of his bare neck. "Need a top off?"

I snorted a laugh and sat up on my elbow, looking down at him. "A top off? Funny guy."

Sheets ruffled and the mattress dipped as Teddy scooted to prop himself against the headboard. He reached for the bedside table and grabbed a bottle of water. The bedding fell to his waist, revealing a mouthwatering amount of naked flesh. My sugar buns slept nude, and I could just make out the outline of his semi-hard morning arousal. A phenomenon I'd discovered—and taken advantage of—sharing a bed from dusk to dawn with a male.

Stop it, Lane! Zee's waiting. Then again, it wouldn't kill me to be a little late. We could be quick.

Placing a hand on his thigh, I tried my new seductive look on for size. Emulating the way I'd seen Mae pull admirers to her in bars, I let my lids droop and poked the tip of my tongue from the corner of the coy smile curling my lips.

Teddy sputtered his water. He laughed. He coughed. His eyes watered.

"Ugh." I yanked my hand from his thigh and smacked him on the back before he choked. "No, I do not need a *top off*. I drank last night, remember? Because Zee said there might be trouble. Figured I needed to be ready."

"Don't be like that." Teddy gripped my waist gently and maneuvered me until I straddled his hips. I didn't exactly put up a fight. "We've talked about this. You don't have to seduce me."

"I didn't get the sultry gene." I sighed dramatically.

He bounced his hips and my nether regions stirred.

"You're sexy as you are. Stop trying so hard." He pressed his fingers into my hips and moved me over his manhood still infuriatingly hidden beneath the sheets. "See?"

My knees squeezed his sides. He pushed and pulled me against him again. Sensations spiraled from my center. My core clenched.

"You're naughty." My expression might have failed at sexy, but my voice finally achieved that husky note. "We shouldn't. I'll be late."

Releasing my hips, he bunched the hem of my shirt. His thumbs grazed the exposed skin at my waist. "We won't be long. You drank a little last night, but we fell asleep before anything else happened."

"Whose fault is that?" I teased. As he did most nights, Teddy had left to work with the late-night construction crew in *Blood and Wine*. When he'd returned, we'd snuggled, I'd sipped, and then the poor guy was snoring.

"Mine." His knuckles grazed my ribs as he dragged my shirt up and over my head. Cold air splashed against my bared chest. My breasts gave a sharp pinch as my nipples hardened. The soft cotton bra I'd purchased for on-the-job comfort was suddenly scratchy.

I held Teddy tightly, cheek to cheek, chest to chest, as if trying to absorb his essence. Or maybe just scratch my boobs.

"This new bar can't get done fast enough. Construction is kicking my ass." He gently detached me from where I'd glued myself to him and met my gaze. "I've missed you."

His words melted me, my insides warming as much as the molten heat trapped beneath me. "I've missed you too," I whispered.

"Let me make it up to you." The crooked tilt of his mouth should have warned me, but I was wholly unprepared for his wet mouth closing over the tight bud of my nipple, sucking through the cotton.

"Mother of hairy ogres!" I half stood up from his lap.

Laughing, he clamped his arms behind me and drew me back down.

"Okay, yeah. Zee won't mind waiting a few minutes." Because turnabout was fair play, I smiled into his beautiful dark gaze and shifted on his lap, just a little.

His smile was gone in an instant. His chest rising and falling, evidence of his arousal moved beneath me.

Feeling his reaction turned the air inside me light and fizzy like champagne. A damp heat built between my legs, right where he pressed against me. I drew my bottom lip between my teeth and moved again, rubbing up and down on his thickening length still trapped beneath the sheet.

Teeth gritted, the cords on Teddy's neck stood out. He licked his lips and smiled. "You are the most adorable mix of shy, curious, and shamelessly aggressive."

"Shy," I scoffed, unable to decide if the aggressive comment made up for the shy part. I gave a small swivel of my hips.

A rough half-chuckle-half-groan vibrated from him. At least he wasn't completely unaffected.

"I love you how you are." He took hold of my hips, and one side of his mouth curled up. His heated gaze went hooded. "But let me show you what I mean."

Uh, oh.

He grasped my hips and then he moved me against him with much more force than I'd moved myself.

"Oh, my." My head fell back. Was he doing that for me or for him? Because holy Ho Hos that indescribably delicious pulling sensation shot straight to my core. A little giddy and a lot lightheaded, I mimicked the movement, rubbing up and down hard enough to feel him through all the material between us.

"Yes," he said, his voice deep and strained. Those incredibly sexy veins stood out along his neck. "Like that."

A wicked sensation stole over me. He wasn't wrong about the curious part, and I was a fast learner.

He hissed a breath. Releasing my hips, his fingers deftly worked the button on my pants open and half undid my zipper. "This works better without clothes."

"Right." I leaped from the bed. The comforter had sneakily twisted around my foot and catapulted me toward the ground. Throwing my hands out, I caught myself before I performed a face plant.

"You okay?" Teddy sat up. The sheets slid low enough for the rest of him to stand and twitch hello.

"Yep!" I sprang to my feet, shoved off my pants and panties, and climbed back on top of Teddy, gasping at the feel of him wedged between my exposed folds.

Electric tingles coursed over my flesh as he slid his hands from my ankles to my knees and then up my thighs, thumbs brushing dangerously close to that spot I desperately hoped he touched. His length trapped beneath me pulsed, and my legs squeezed against him in response.

Before his thumb could start something I wouldn't have the will to stop, I swept his roving hand aside and rose onto my knees. "Not necessary," I said, and wrapped my fingers around his semi-rigid cock.

He hissed a breath and bucked slightly. The friction of his silky, steely length growing in my palm left me feeling powerful and dizzy.

"You undo me," he said.

"I'm already undone," I teased breathlessly. But it was the truth. This male had become my everything, in every way possible.

Eyes locked on his, a knee on either side of his hip, his tip at my entrance, I held myself above him and stroked his rapidly thickening length.

He jerked, the movement barely pushing his broad head into me. I was full and empty all at once. His fingers spasmed and dug into my hips. "I love your hands on my cock."

His words pulled at my control, and I almost sank onto him right then. I was wet enough, but he was so good at driving me wild. Could I do the same?

"I love the way you feel in my hands." Emboldened by our time in the shower, I dragged my palm through my wetness and reached for him again. Beneath the slickness gathered in my hand, I worked him. Slow at first, and then faster.

This might have backfired. The feel of him in my hand. The sight of his flesh against mine, quickened something inside of me. I felt so desperately empty, but I wanted to do this.

Thinking about how he'd worked himself, I squeezed the fully erect, thick base of his cock.

He let out a little breathy gasp.

I rotated my hand just a bit as I glided up, to envelope his head in my palm and then repeat.

His hips moved, demanding more. "Lane." My name was a warning through gritted teeth.

"A man of many words." I chuckled, but I couldn't wait any longer either. I knelt above him and guided him to my entrance. The laughter evaporated in my throat as he bucked into me, and I sank onto him completely in one swift glide.

Our shouts blended. Probably woke the house.

I rocked against him, started to rise, but he gripped my hips hard and held me still.

"Drink," he said and dragged me toward his throat.

I'd had enough last night, but I knew what it did to Teddy. Having experienced it during our mate bond, I knew what it did to me to be drank from.

"Drink," he said—no commanded—again, voice gruff and sexy as fuck.

He was buried deep, hot and thick. I was so deliciously full, but I wanted to move so badly. My legs trembled against his sides with my need. I traced my tongue along the backs of my aching fangs. I wanted this too much to be gentle. "It'll hurt," I said.

"Make it hurt." His grin was every shade of wicked. His hands were big enough to hold me torturously still while his thumb found that livewire bundle of nerves.

When I cried out, he loosened his hold but kept his thumb moving in tight circles as I rose halfway up his length, until I could reach his throat. My hips made little jerky movements as he rubbed me toward climax.

I leaned in, inhaling the intoxicating sweet vanilla and crisp woodsy scent cascading through the veins pumping nectar just below his skin.

Teddy bent his knees drawing his legs up. His hand fell away, but he pushed even deeper.

Beneath my fangs, his taut flesh resisted and then gave with a soft pop of pressure. The sharp points retracted to normal length, and I sealed my mouth to the wounds. His pulse beat against my mouth, and liquid sugar spurt onto my tongue. Smoky, salty, sweet, and divine, his blood came in a steady trickle. A tingle of power flew through my veins. Every nerve ending came alive.

"Fuck." Teddy rocked his hips. "Harder, Lane. Drink harder. I want to feel the pull in my balls."

Oh, gods. I moaned against his wet throat. I'd swear he reached the very center of me. He pulled out and thrust quickly. I bounced, the friction hitting just right. Again, and again, harder and faster, until all I could do was drink deep and hang on.

"Yes, like that." Teddy's voice was gravel and growl. His strokes matched my pulls on his vein.

Everything inside of me coiled. A knot about to snap. All sensation focused on one spot. Heat scorched my ears, my throat, and arrowed to my core. Closer, closer. In and out.

All at once, I shattered, shouting against his neck. Fireflies flew behind my lids. My inner muscles clenched and unclenched.

With a firm grip on my hips, Teddy drove deep once, twice. His back arched off the bed, muscles strained, veins standing out stark on his sweaty flesh. "Lane!"

At last, he collapsed on the mattress and pulled me down on top of him. I thought he'd fallen asleep, but then his fingertips trailed down my back to cup my backside. Deep inside of me he pulsed.

I pushed up onto my elbows to look at him. His eyes were closed, and as if he could feel my gaze, his lips spread into a satisfied smile. My hearts turned over, and I tucked my head into the crook of his neck. The scent of his blood hit me stronger than it should. I angled my face toward the crimson trail racing toward the sheets.

"Oops." I leaned forward, reaching for the napkin on my bedside table.

Teddy groaned at his slick withdrawal. "Are you trying to kill me?"

"Trying to save the sheets from being ruined." I dabbed at his throat, realizing I'd been wrong. It had already healed.

"I think we already did." He rolled me onto the wet spot.

"Gross!" I squirmed to escape his hold.

Laughing, Teddy climbed over me and out of bed. He scooped me up, tossed me over his shoulder, and carried me to the bathroom. "Let's get you cleaned up, you dirty girl."

17

DNA SOUP

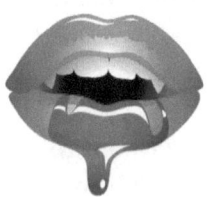

SQUEAKY CLEAN, I STEPPED INTO THE HALLWAY AND CLOSED THE DOOR behind me with a quiet snick. The smell of fresh coffee drew me toward the stairs. As I reached the first-floor landing, I spotted Talulla sitting by the sliding glass doors.

"You're lucky. You have no idea how much I need coffee." I slid the door wide enough for the large feline to squeeze through. A light nip rode in on the early morning air. I shivered and watched the cat—no, familiar—mount the stairs to the roof garden.

A yawn hit me. Hand pressed to the back of my mouth, my jaw cracked. I arched my back and stretched my arms wide as I turned toward the kitchen. And stopped.

Zee sat at the table, sipping from her thermos, watching me.

"Hi," I said.

"Hi." She gave the wall clock a pointed look.

"I...uh..."

A smile curled her lips and she laughed. "No need to explain, babes. I know. The entire house knows."

Heat raced over my cheeks, reminding me of Teddy's shy comment. Maybe he wasn't too far off the mark. "We need better soundproofing in this place." I stalked to the kitchen.

"Between your sister and her vampire, and you and the boss, it's a wonder anyone gets any sleep around here." She twisted in her seat to watch me through the kitchen pass. "I'm almost afraid to ask, but things are awfully quiet in Y'sindra's bedroom."

Steam rose in long, aromatic curls as I filled my thermos to the brim. "I've never asked. I think she insulates her door with ice."

Zee blinked. I could see the wheels grinding as she tried to picture it. "She can do that?"

"Maybe. I got a cold burn on my palm from the knob once."

Rivetted, Zee leaned forward. "What did she say?"

Judging by her reaction, I really needed to invite her over for TV night with Y'sindra and me. She'd love that stuff. Who knew, she might still be staying in the guest room.

"Don't know. Honestly, I never want to know. I wish I didn't know about Mae and Vaughn." I screwed the lid on the thermos and collected my bag with my phone and crystal from the counter. "Ready?"

"I never would have imagined of all the fae, a blood fae would be such a prude." Zee cackled at my affronted expression, swiped her thermos from the table, and swaggered toward the hall.

"I'm not a prude!" I yelled after her, and then muttered, "I'm just shy."

Waiting inside the elevator, eyes dancing with suppressed laughter, she watched me stomp toward her. Despite the joke being at my expense, I was smiling by the time we hit the lobby.

The air of the casino floor slid between the elevator doors when they opened. The fragrant blend of signature scents designed to seduce the senses and remind patrons of a wild forest greeted us. What I did not smell was the multitude of bodies and all the odors they possessed.

Zee handed me her thermos and a duffel bag. "Hold these? All that coffee, I should have used the bathroom before we left."

I slid the bag onto my shoulder and watched as she jogged toward the restroom. Saying Zee had dressed down was an understatement. She wore a baseball cap with a frayed bill over her braided blond hair. A fist-sized hole flapped on the right calf of her gray sweats. The white T-shirt had an assortment of faded, multi-hued stains on the shoulders, making me think she wore it while she colored her hair. There was no saving the once white sneakers.

Always one to dress for the job, whether I expected trouble or not, I'd strapped several blades to my body over fighting leathers. She'd said things might get dicey, but she looked like she was ready for a sleepover, not a fight.

Bells jangled and clanged from the endless banks of slot machines. Servers in tasteful but tight black uniforms patrolled with full cocktail trays. The limited number of open gaming tables was the only indication of the hour, the rest were dark and unmanned.

The first week living above a casino came as a shock. With the cold air designed to keep gamblers wide awake, the free drinks, lack of windows, and exactly zero clocks, dusk to dawn passed in a blink down here.

Zee returned and claimed her thermos and bag. She took a sip and winked. "Refilling the bladder. It's cool, the drive isn't too long."

Focused on navigating our way through the casino toward the exit, I steered us through the wide aisles, dodging early morning gamblers and cocktail servers in a rush. A few pit bosses recognized me and waved.

"Would you look at that." Zee pointed toward the farthest card table. From this distance, I couldn't quite make out the sign—Let It Ride or maybe Caribbean Stud Poker. What was she pointing...

The dealer moved, and I spied a halo of fluffy white curls. "Seriously? I swear she better not be charging those chips to the Penthouse."

We hung a left, away from Y'sindra and the gaming tables.

With a soft chuff of laughter, Zee asked, "She's down here a lot?"

I shook my head. "You have no idea."

"Mystery of why her room is so quiet solved," Zee said. "She's never there."

Colorful carpet designed to disguise fallen casino chips gave way to elegant marble floors as we crossed into the lobby. Explaining I kept my Bronco at the Interlands house, I headed for the concierge. Before I'd been sidetracked with Teddy, I'd called down and reserved a car while still in the bathroom—because I actually had a house phone in the bathroom. Wild.

Several people were in line, but one of the attendants spotted me. "Ms. Black," she called and waved me over.

I didn't correct her. Employees knew about my relation to Blackthorne— Mr. Black—so they assumed, and I let them. The benefits were endless. Who was I to squabble over a name?

No one in line objected as I sauntered past them to the front. That might have been due to the large sword sheathed on my back, or maybe the daggers in their various holsters. I could have gone around the queue rather than through it, but these power-plays brought me joy.

"I'm glad I caught you. I was just about to call up," the brunette desk manager said with way too much exuberance in her voice. Didn't she know it was dawn-o-clock?

I fought the scowl trying to form on my face. "Is the car still available?"

"Absolutely." The smile never left her face, even as she spoke, which was a tad bit creepy. What did they put in their coffee around here, and could I get some? Still smiling, she lifted the receiver. "I will call now and ask your driver to pull into the valet. He will have the privacy window raised, as you requested."

"Thanks." I headed to the valet drop off area outside. A dark green Hummer pulled up to the curb as Zee and I stepped outside. A beefy guy with close-cropped black hair and reflective sunglasses came around to open our door.

"Ms. Black." He nodded and I climbed inside.

The interior of the Casino Hummers were designed like limousines, not SUVs. Two bench seats faced each other with built in drink coolers on either wall. Zee followed me inside and took the opposite seat. Grinning she angled her back against the blacked-out car window and threw her legs up across the seat.

The driver leaned down, pointedly ignoring my friend's dirty shoes on the leather. "I have the address you requested, but I want to confirm you know it is the location of the Split Sands Pack? They don't welcome visitors."

He had it wrong. There were two large werewolf packs located on the United States west coast: Split Sands North and Split Sands South. However, I gave the concierge desk the address myself, so I knew he was taking us to the correct location.

"We know." I pointed to Zee seated opposite me. "Werewolf."

She turned to grin at him over her shoulder and waved. "Hi."

"Appreciate you checking, but we're good," I told him.

"Understood." He stepped back and shut the door. The interior lights slowly faded to a soft yellow glow.

Zee's head whipped towards me. She swung her feet to the floor and sat up. "Ms. Black?"

I shrugged. "They assume. And he is my grandfather. Why confuse them?"

She stretched out her legs and ran her hand over the supple leather seats. "Doncha mean why risk losing out on all these sweet, sweet perks?"

"That too." I took a healthy swig of coffee and then dropped the thermos into the drink holder. "Anything I should know before we get there? Protocol, behavior?"

My limited experience with werewolves taught me to ask questions. Being friends with Zee, a lone wolf, and rubbing shoulders with wolves out for a good time at a bar would be different than driving onto pack grounds where the wolves would be territorial and on high alert with strangers.

Zee turned her head toward the tinted windows. Understanding this was a difficult subject for her, I pulled out my phone and Googled information on the pack. The more I read, the wider my eyes grew. The driver had not misspoke. Formerly Split Sands North Pack, the South pack had been absorbed into the North pack after the South pack's alpha issued a challenge and lost. Split Sands Pack was now the largest werewolf pack in North America.

Fantastic. We were driving into a literal wolf den run by an extremely powerful alpha. Then again, I was hopped up on Teddy-juice. Could be fun.

"I will probably be challenged," Zee said.

"Oh, hell yes! I need a good fight." I held my hand up for a high five.

Zee shook her head. "I have to do this alone, or they won't talk to us."

Hand falling to my lap, I winced. "Sorry. Got excited, didn't read the room."

A smile flickered over her lips. "Don't worry, babes. I feel you. You know I'm always down for a good brawl."

"So this challenge will be a wolf thing?"

She nodded and made a sweeping gesture from my head to my toes. "Unless you've got a wolf hidden in that DNA soup of yours, this one's on me."

"DNA soup?" Panic pressed down on me. A spurt of adrenaline hit my system. My ears warmed and tingled. I crossed my arm protectively over my torso, hugging the opposite elbow to my side. My hybrid nature was no longer a secret, but old habits were hard to shake. "How'd you know?"

"I've got a great sniffer." Zee tapped her nose. "Your scent's wild. It's layered like an onion. Each layer masks another smell and is always changing."

"Ugh, why do people keep saying I smell? I do shower, ya know? Like, once a day. Sometimes twice!" I flopped against the seat.

Teddy's asshole brother, Dacian, really got in my head when he'd implied he could smell sex on me. It'd been months since the confrontation, but the remark stuck.

Laughter exploded from Zee, and she shook her head, the fuzzy tail of her braid thumping over the back seat.

"It's not funny." I scowled.

"Sorry, tension release." She patted the moisture away from beneath her eyes. "Girl, you don't stink, and that's sort of the problem."

My brows arched. "You compared me to an onion. Wanna explain?"

"So feisty. I said layers like an onion." Zee flashed a grin. "Okay, so everyone smells different. Werecats don't smell like werewolves."

"I bet," I muttered.

"Harsh, girlie. Not once have I ever smelled like dog." At my blank stare she wrinkled her nose at me. "It doesn't count if the wolf is in control, and I get wet."

I shrugged and her eyes rolled so hard, her eyelids flickered for a full three seconds.

"Do you want to know this stuff or not?"

Pressing my lips together to keep from smiling, I nodded.

The narrow-eyed look she gave me lasted way too long. "Not all were-creatures smell the same. But all weres of the same type—cat, dog, avian, fox, whatever—have the same core, identifying scent."

"In other words," I said, rubbing a hand over my chin. "All werewolves have the same base scent beyond their personal aroma. Sun fae smell the same, but different from moon fae. Like that?"

"Exactly like that." Zee put her elbows on her legs and leaned forward, hands dangling between her thighs. "You smell like everything."

Informational whiplash sent me reeling back in my seat. "How is that possible?"

She shrugged. "Don't know. Until the other night when I met Pru, I chalked it up to blood fae scent."

"And you saw the difference between us and knew," I finished.

"Not as much as you think." She relaxed into the seat, arms spread across the back rest on either side, an ankle on her knee. "The differences are subtle enough I probably wouldn't have ever noticed. But the smell." She tapped her nose again. "She smelled like danger."

I grunted. "Don't try to make me feel better or anything."

"You have that smell too, but not all the time. There are days you remind me of sunshine, like Mae. I've caught the scent of moon fae, like Dexter—a cold dewy night. Others a mossy oak, which I'd never smelled until Jason picked up Eli." She paused and tilted her head in question.

"Mage," I said. "Which according to him and Blackthorne, are traced back to druids."

A smile bloomed across Zee's lips. "And you're related to that rich druid. Makes sense. Listen, I don't know what you are. I just know you aren't *just* a blood fae."

My head fell back on the seat. "What the hell, it doesn't matter who knows." I lifted my head and steeled myself for her reaction. "I'm a hybrid. Pretty much what you just said—a little of this, a little of that. Until recently, my blood fae genes were dominant."

"So cool! I've never met a hybrid."

Shame crested inside me. I took a breath and beat it back. I was no longer embarrassed or angry about what I was, but years of conditioning could make it difficult to embrace. "You wouldn't. I'm the only one."

"Uh, one of a kind? Again, super cool."

Uncomfortable with the spotlight on me, I cleared my throat. "Sure. So back to this challenge. Is that the reason you're dressed like you shopped in a dumpster for those clothes?" If one could call it an outfit.

Zee looked down at herself. "Yep. Things can happen fast. Loose clothes are something my wolf can easily step out of—if they don't tear off."

"And the hair?"

"In case it comes down to fists." Zee grabbed the end of her braid and waved it at me. "The farther we are from a full moon, the harder it is for most wolves to change."

"And the earlier it is in the day, the harder?" I guessed.

The finger gun and wink she gave reminded me so much of Y'sindra. "Bang on, babes. I can change, but I don't know about this alpha."

I gave a rueful shake of my head and glanced out the window. We were deep in the desert with no buildings in sight. "This has been...interesting, but we should probably talk about what might happen."

Her golden-brown eyes grew serious. "Let me do the talking. If there's a challenge—when there's a challenge—you'll need to stay out of it."

"Okay but if things look bad—"

"They won't. Not for me."

Mimicking her earlier pose, I spread my arms across the seat behind me and smiled. "Awfully sure of yourself."

"If you don't believe in yourself, who will?"

"You read that on a bumper sticker?"

Stretching her legs, she kicked my feet. Not much taller than me, she barely grazed my toes.

The car turned and all amusement evaporated.

Zee sat forward, resting her elbows on her knees. Her gaze on me was intense. "Let me do the talking. Don't get involved in the fight," she repeated. "When the dust settles you can ask questions."

Everything in me wanted to object, but this was foreign territory. I trusted Zee. I would trust her in this. "I don't like it, but all right."

"Good," Zee said with palpable relief.

I was mildly offended. My strength had waned, but she didn't know. Even with decreased power, I was surely stronger than a werewolf.

The car rolled to a stop. A crowd was slowly gathering. They'd probably heard the car approaching for the last mile and come to investigate. Discomfort settled in my belly, and I went through my pre-battle ritual of weapons check, even if this wasn't meant to be my fight.

Daggers sheathed on my thighs. Sword in the new vertical sheath along my spine. I patted my chest and winced. Damn, I should have worn the bandolier of push daggers. Finally, I smoothed my hand over my braid, from the crown of my head to the nape of my neck, ensuring its length was tucked securely beneath my jacket and out of any would-be combatant's reach.

A buzzing sound startled me. My hands flew to the hilts of my daggers but relaxed onto the seat when I spotted the absence of the tinted window between us and the driver.

The driver swiveled to face me. "You need me to come with you?"

"No," Zee and I said at the same time.

"Hopefully this won't take long," I told him.

Zee cracked her neck and then angled toward the driver. "No matter what you see, stay in the car."

Brows arching, he looked at me in question.

"What she said." I pointed at Zee.

He shrugged and turned to face front.

Zee crossed to the door in a crouch. Hand on the door handle she gave me her serious look. "Remember, stay out of it."

The dry desert heat roared inside the SUV as soon as she opened the door and climbed out. It was still early, and not even close to the temperature the day would reach.

As Zee step away from the door, I shook my hands, flinging away the discomfort, and followed. My feet hit the ground in a puff of pale-yellow sand. The road was hard-packed dirt leading to this housing development in the middle of acres and acres of open desert. I rolled my shoulders and surveyed the dozen or so men and women gathered. More were heading this way from the weirdly suburban streets. Thankfully, there were no children present. Based on the time of day, probably in school.

"What brings you two bitches all the way out here?" A man asked and spat.

Someone needed to be taught manners. My palms itched for the feel of steel. I curled my fingers.

"Look, the cast-off brought one of them pointy-eared people." A woman taunted. People snickered and laughed.

"Who's in charge?" The power Zee put into her voice caught me off guard. Instantly, the laughter cut off. Eyes cast down.

A man shoved his way to the front and stomped up to Zee, putting them toe to toe.

"How dare you come onto my territory and *project*."

Based on the emphasis he put onto the word project, Zee had done something alpha-y with her voice.

Zee smirked. "I dare."

Eyes glowing eerie werewolf gold-white, the man ripped off his shirt. Muscles bulged in places I didn't know they could grow. Sweet Twinkies, he looked like he could bench the Hummer without breaking a sweat.

My brows dove into my hairline. I scooted closer to Zee and hissed, "You sure about this?"

Zee pulled off her own shirt followed by her pants and shoes.

Bones cracked, skin stretched, and I got the fuck out of the way.

18

LICK YOUR WOUNDS

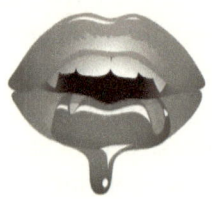

AN ENORMOUS GRAY WOLF NEARLY AS MUSCLE BOUND AS THE MAN BRACED his legs and shook himself. His head alone was so large, I doubted I could get my arms around it.

Only a few feet away, Zee threw back her head and howled.

Every hair on my body stood at attention.

The humans who had gathered around the pair took several collective steps back.

Comparing the two, worry wrapped around my ribs and squeezed. Zee's blond wolf was slimmer and smaller in stature. I didn't know a thing about werewolves, but bigger seemed better. At least, it was scarier.

Ears flat against his skull, the gray wolf dropped his head and snarled. He began to stalk a semi-circle around Zee.

I tensed and thumbed open the catch on my thigh holsters. Wrapping my hands around the hilts, I slowly inched them free. Despite the promise Zee pulled out of me, there was no way I'd stand back and watch—

She was across the distance and colliding with the much larger wolf in a heartbeat. Dust and fur flew. Jaws snapped. The crack of teeth echoed. Meaty thuds sounded as they slammed into one another over and over.

Daggers out, I circled the wolves. By the gods, I would put a blade through that guy's furry skull. If I could see him. The fight had churned up a billowing cloud of yellow dust.

A sharp yip ended the commotion. Blood sprayed across the dirt and a wolf whimpered.

Which wolf? My hearts thudded against my breastbone. Hurrying around the wolves, I inched as close as I dared, trying to make sense of the tangle of furry bodies. Slowly, the clouds of floating dirt and fur either fell or was carried away in a breeze.

I sucked in a sharp breath and stumbled, coming to a sudden stop. "I'll be damned," I grinned.

The surrounding group had the same shocked expression I felt on my own face. More people had arrived. They pointed to the two wolves.

Zee's jaws were clamped onto the gray wolf's throat. He'd been pushed onto his side. Blood seeped into his thick fur, turning all the silver and cream tones red.

I secured my daggers back into their sheaths before anyone noticed I'd had them out.

A growl rolled from Zee.

Neck still trapped in her jaws, the gray wolf kept his head still as he rolled onto his back, presenting his belly in submission.

My girl held on for a full minute longer. Her white-gold eyes rose and moved over the crowd, issuing a clear challenge. One by one gazes dropped. Zee was a bad ass. As a certified badass in a small package, with an even badder and smaller sister, I should know better than to judge someone by their size.

Zee released the downed wolf. She stood over him and licked his blood from her muzzle.

I became aware of the white noise of whispers around me. Snippets of conversation overlapped into a nearly indecipherable tidal wave of babble.

"...the lone Gunnulf."

"...she's real."

"...scary."

On and on it went. My brow furrowed. I knew lone wolves were rare, but this reaction seemed extra. Didn't werewolves around here know about her? She worked close by. Was Gunnulf another name for a wolf? I had so many questions!

Tail high, Zee padded toward me. Bones popped and shifted beneath her pelt. I'd seen my share of were-creature shifts at the Interlands bar, but I'd never seen one happen on the move. She approached with casual swagger and a bloody, wolfy grin.

I gawked at the shortening muzzle and reshaping skull. The transformation was slow and controlled, no sudden snaps. She was putting on a show. It was horrific and fascinating.

Across the open space between us and this pack, their alpha whined. Bones crunched. Unlike Zee, his shift came in jerky spurts. His weak howl died on a moan as his vocal cords manipulated into their human shape inside something between a wolf and human throat.

Rather than continuing to watch the gruesome display, I retreated a few steps and retrieved Zee's clothes.

Looking like a warrior-woman, she was fully human when I returned. Sticky, red blood coated the lower half of her face, down her throat. It splattered over her shoulders and bare breasts.

"Thanks, babes." Zee took the clothes, sounding exactly like she always did.

I was a little taken aback at the level of normal in her voice. It wasn't like I hadn't seen her as her wolf before. I'd seen her furry ferociousness many times. What I hadn't witnessed was her as an alpha. The ease with which she'd taken down the much larger wolf had been something else.

"Any yours?" I asked, making a *wax-on* circular motion in front of her with my hand.

"Nope," she said, and together we turned to the owner of the blood in question.

Still caught in his change, the man crouched on all fours. His head was mostly human-shaped. Spine elongating, muscles plumped his limbs as fur pulled into flesh. Naked, he sat back on his heels. Chest still pumping, he put his fisted hands on his hips and tipped his face toward the sky. There was no wound, but blood caked his throat, painted his chest red, and dappled his abdomen which rippled and contracted with his harsh breaths.

A woman pushed her way through the crowd and tossed clothes at the man. She made a tsking sound and brushed her hands together. Her head came up and she regarded us, gaze zeroing in on Zee.

"Becky," the man said, a note of warning in his ragged voice.

"You just sit there and lick your wounds." She shook her finger in his face and then strode for us.

"Shit," I muttered.

Zee sighed and started to shimmy her pants back down her legs. "Alpha's mate," she said to me under her breath.

Not like everyone couldn't hear.

"Don't. I'm not about that." The woman waved a hand at Zee's pants. "The moment I saw you, I knew who you were, so did my mate. Sometimes that man has rocks for brains."

She spun and shouted across the clearing, "Rocks for brains!"

Eyes widening, I bit my lip and turned to Zee. She shrugged.

"Sorry about the reception." The woman turned back to us, never quite meeting Zee's gaze. She had no problem giving me a thorough once over. Her gaze paused on my ears. "Huh."

Frowning, I touched my ear tips.

"Roger doesn't get a lot of challenges. He's gotten a little too big for his tail. Thought he'd try himself against a Gunnulf." She torqued to look behind and said again, "Rocks for brains."

Unable to hide her smile, Zee held out her hand. "Zee."

"Zeelaway Gunnulf, I know. The legend herself." The woman took my friend's offered hand and gave it an enthusiastic shake. "I'm Becky. Mate to the Split Sands Pack alpha, who got what he was askin' for messin' with you."

Zeelaway? Gunnulf? *Legend?* So many questions begged to be asked. I opened my mouth, but Zee squeezed my hand. I glanced at her and caught her side-eye expression. Right, let her do the talking. Fine, I could do that, but boy was she going to hate the ride home.

The big man lumbered up behind his mate, his gaze, too, never quite meeting Zee's. No mistaking the lack of challenge now. "Fair fight, good fight." His voice was overly gruff, I suspected to hide the embarrassment of the equivalent of a first-round knockout.

"That was no fight," Zee said.

His shoulders pinched and he winced, but he didn't look offended. Truth was truth. Big wolf of the west coast, he'd given it his best against an unknown and lost horribly.

It wasn't only lone wolves who were rare. Female alphas—pack or no— were unheard of. According to Zee, she was it, which was why she'd never fit into her clan. She couldn't be beta, and they couldn't stomach a female alpha. Which now that I thought about it, made her and I more alike than I'd ever acknowledged. The list of commonalities I was discovering between me and my friends was astonishing, and probably what made them my friends.

I studied her profile. Easy-going, fun-loving Zee had an apex predator lurking just beneath her skin. Grinning to myself, I looked back to find the man watching me. Using his shirt, he scrubbed absently at his bloody chest.

Like Becky, he eyed my ears and then jutted his chin in my direction. "We don't see many of your kind."

Nodding, I kept my mouth shut. That silent trick had been used on me so many times, I'd learned to use it myself.

"We heard about the new fae owner of the Blackthorne."

Damn if the silent treatment didn't work. I waited for him to continue.

"One of our boys..." He stopped, seeming to chew on his words. "You who run the hotel?"

I nodded. It wasn't precisely true. I didn't run anything except room service up and down the elevator all hours of the day and night.

"We heard about what happened with the werewolf there." Roger looked from me to Zee. "That what brings you here? He wasn't one of ours."

"No," Zee said. "But you had a case of moonbit last year."

It didn't take much to put together what Roger had been about to say. One of their boys had gone moonbit, like the one at the casino he believed I owned.

Showing the first sign of affection, Becky eased into Roger's side. He slid an arm over her shoulders. She looked up into Roger's face, pain contorting her soft features.

"We have a few questions about that," Zee said gently.

Roger's face flushed with anger. His lip curled.

Becky tightened her hold around his waist, and her mate dropped his chin to his chest.

With a deep breath he looked up and nodded. "I don't know how we can help. You know well as we do there's no explanation for moonbit, but ask your questions."

"I understand your reluctance to talk about this. It's a hard subject, but we could use your help." Zee crossed her arms over her chest and tilted her head in my direction. "This is Lane. I'll let her ask the questions."

I'd been looking over the group, studying their reactions. Hearing my name, my gaze snapped back to the pack leaders in front of us. They both stared at me.

"I'm sorry for your loss," I began.

They nodded and mumbled thank yous. Becky's shoulders relaxed a fraction.

In my line work for YML Investigations, I'd done my fair share of interrogations. I pulled my trusty notepad from my jacket pocket and clicked open the mini pen.

Putting her hand on my arm, Zee said, "I'm going to talk to the others while you speak with Becky and Roger."

The alpha pair stiffened.

Noting their reaction, I laid my hand over Zee's, stopping her before she left. "Why don't you stay here while I talk to the others?"

This arrangement was better. There was a good chance the alphas wouldn't be as open without Zee around, while pack members would be anywhere on the spectrum of starstruck to terrified talking to Zee. Too distracted to be reliable.

Leaving Zee with the alphas, I made my way from one person to another. Everyone was curious and, for the most part, friendly. There was a lot of interest in the casino, what kind of fae I was, and the fae in general. I fielded a few questions from each person before steering the conversation to my own agenda.

No one knew a thing. Not that anyone came across as deceitful, they just all had the same answer. Lincoln, the wolf believed lost to moonbit, had been young and single. Every person I spoke with had the same story. Nothing strange happened in the days leading up to the event. My pad was full of notes. Lincoln's favorite food, shampoo, even the fact that he wore boxers, not briefs. He preferred evening runs to mornings. He wasn't a big drinker, and he favored craps to poker. A lot words, no substance.

At some point, someone handed me a photo of a guy with a dark, flawless complexion that reminded me of smoky quartz, with eyes to match. His hair, worn in neat rows of braids, hung to the middle of his back.

Pocketing the photo, I returned to the Hummer. Disappointment added weight to my steps. I tapped a finger on the last word I'd written in my pad, *MADE*. Lincoln being *made* and not *born* meant there was a chance this was a true case of moonbit. I hadn't expected finding information about this person reproducing Blackthorne's potion to be easy, but it would have been nice.

"Ma'am." Footsteps scuffed the ground behind me, and the voice came again, louder. "Excuse me, ma'am?"

Turning, I found a good-looking guy jogging to catch up. He sported a healthy layer of stubble on his chin. A quick head to toe appraisal confirmed he hadn't been with the crowd I'd interviewed.

"Sorry, ma'am. I was late to the party." His boyish grin oozed charm, reminding me of Dexter. "I heard you were asking about Lincoln."

My gaze climbed toward the sun as I nodded. Squinting, I guessed we'd been here a couple hours now. Even with my super protective lenses, the sun seemed extra bright in the clear blue sky. Eyes watering, I blinked a few times to clear my vision. My stomach rumbled, and I grimaced. Please let this be about something other than his shoe size or favorite brand of beer.

I rolled my shoulders and lifted the pad, ready to add more innocuous notes. Tone droll, I asked, "Did you see anything out of character in the week leading up to Lincoln falling ill?"

"Not exactly."

It took the willpower of a saint not to whip the sword off my back and cleave the guy in two. I flipped my wrist, closing my notepad. "Okay, then. Thanks."

"I mean, I might have."

Something in his tone gave me pause. I waited.

He swallowed a few times, as if working moisture into his mouth. "Three days before…it happened, a bunch of us went to a nightclub for a bachelor party."

"Bachelor party," I mumbled and made a note. "Something weird happened?"

Clearly uncomfortable, he shifted on his feet. Glancing over his shoulder, he lowered his voice. "Lincoln got pretty wasted and brought a girl home."

Seriously? A young werewolf got drunk and got laid was the weird news delaying my trip to the In-N-Out we'd passed a few miles back?

"According to my notes here, he was a werewolf in his early twenties. Not exactly unusual behavior." Hunger and irritation made my fangs tingle. I ran my tongue along my teeth, tempering my tone. "I appreciate you letting me know." I even said thank you. Giving myself a mental pat on the back, I tucked the pad away and turned on my heel.

"Not Linc," the guy said. "He was a two-beer max kind of guy, and he never had one-night stands."

Now, that was weird. I turned slowly. "Go on."

Shoulders hunched, he tucked his hands into his front pockets. "Ma'am, he has—had—a girlfriend." The guy cast a sidelong look over his shoulder and inched closer. "Linc was crazy about her. He planned to propose this summer on her birthday. That guy was loyal as the day is long. We all gave him shit for it, but all of us were secretly jealous. Ya know what I mean?"

"Do you remember what the woman he left with looked like?" A tiny spark of anticipation ignited at last.

A sharp, short bark of laughter puffed out of him, and he shook his head. "Aside from being a leggy blonde? No ma'am. Linc might have been wasted, but he was the soberest of us all."

There went the spark. Unable to hide my disappointment, I blew out a breath and nodded.

"My brother runs security at the nightclub, though. He made a copy of the video surveillance from that night." The boyish grin was back, stamping a dimple in his cheek. "He did it so we'd have something to remember Linc by, but maybe it can help you?"

"It might." I searched what remained of the crowd. Excitement over, most of the pack had returned to their homes. "Where's your brother?"

"Lives in your neck of the woods. I'll give him a call when ya'll leave." His mouth screwed sideways. "You're at the Blackthorne, right? He can drop it off."

"I am." I scribbled my info in my pad, tore out the page, and handed it over. "And there's my cell phone at the bottom, in case you think of anything else."

Holy Ho Hos, the trip wasn't wasted. We could get out of here and grab some burgers. It had to be lunchtime. I would call Teddy and see if I should pick up food for everyone.

I was almost to the Hummer when my right butt cheek vibrated. Locking eyes with Zee, I nodded toward the car as I fished my cell phone from my back pocket. I saw Mae's name and tapped accept.

"Hey, we were just about to head home. Got some information, not sure if it'll help with anything, but it's something." I climbed into the SUV, Zee right behind me. "I was thinking about picking up some food. You guys hungry?"

"I'm starving," Zee said. "Shifting really takes it out of you."

Hearing the remark, Mae asked, "Zee shifted? What happened?"

"Tell you all about it when we get back. Oh, and someone should be dropping off a...I'm not sure what. Pictures? A video? Maybe one of those little sticks with information you put in the computer."

"Thumb drive." Zee dug a bottle of water out of the compartment. She found a little box filled with individual-size bags of crackers and cookies. "Score."

"A thumb drive," I told Mae. "Someone has video surveillance of a suspicious night out our most recent moonbit case, aside from Beast, of course. Can you call down to Vaughn and let him know to keep an eye out?"

"Sure thing. We'll have to watch it when we get back."

"Get back?"

On the other end of the line Mae was quiet.

I sat forward. "Mae..."

"Well, you know that RFG ceremony I told you about?"

This wasn't going anywhere I liked. "Mmhmm."

"Turns out some of the food must have been cross contaminated by Dad's supplies. Almost everyone is sick."

I absently flicked the hilt of my dagger. "Everyone? You've got to be kidding me."

"Duskmere is pulling the *in case of emergency* you promised." Mae paused. "He wants us on Outerlands patrol."

Sun scorch it. I knew better than to make promises.

19

I DIDN'T WANT TO TALK ABOUT IT

"This breeze is nice." Eyes closed, the picture of serenity, Mae tipped her face toward the Outerlands sky. Toes flexing and pointing, she rocked slowly in the oversized rocking chair on the front deck of Teddy's old bar. "I can still taste the salt in the air. Are you certain Blackthorne sealed the beach portal?"

"I'm certain he did not." My seat arced forward, and my toes tapped down. I shoved off hard, sending my chair rocketing back. Mae's feet barely touched the ground, so with my much shorter legs, it was the only way to keep the chair moving. "He might have put some sort of magic lock on it to prevent anyone from using it except him. But did he close a door he ripped open between two worlds? Nah. He's cagey."

Mae was quiet a moment. "You sound like you admire him."

"I might." I grimaced and rolled a fist against the center of my breastbone, over the scale lodged there. That admission caused me physical pain. Heartburn, at least. "I swear I'll spike all your food with sugar if you tell him I said that."

Rather than be outraged, Mae laughed. She rolled her head on the chair back to look at me. "Even the greens?"

"A thick layer of sugar between each leaf."

She shuddered.

"Might get me to eat lettuce if you do." Y'sindra swooped in from wherever she'd flown off to as soon as we'd arrived.

When my ogre-sized rocking chair rolled forward, I dismounted with very little grace. Momentum kept me stumbling to the edge of the porch. My shoulder cracked against a column bracketing the front steps. I stayed there, leaning against it. It was where I was headed anyhow.

"Smooth," Y'sindra said, face blank, tone droll. "How are you such a bad ass on the battlefield and a newborn aloughta...everywhere else?"

I popped a hip out and wagged my brows. "Not everywhere else, if you know what I mean?"

"I do not. Because if you mean the bedroom, explain how Teddy got that black eye last month?" Y'sindra asked.

A loud choking earned Mae a lethal glare from me. Eyes watering, Mae covered her mouth.

"It was his fault," I snapped and stomped down the steps to kick grass in the road.

The grass had grown ankle-deep in the absence of regular foot traffic from the corrupt moon fae and their shifter sympathizers. Royal Fae Guard patrols came in pairs, sometimes foursomes, but unlike my lazy ass, they marched up and down the border like good little soldiers.

"If by 'his fault' you mean you were doing the dirty in doggy-style and he got too close to your elbow, then sure." From the porch rail where she'd parked her fairy butt, she gave me a slow wink.

"That's not what happened," I grumbled, the heat in my cheeks spreading to the tips of my ears. It was reverse cowgirl, not doggy, and I didn't want to talk about it.

I sank onto the grass, laid back, and closed my eyes, letting the early day sun warm my face. Despite it being late afternoon in Vegas when we left, the time in Outerlands more closely aligned with the portal located on North America's east coast in Blackthorne's beachfront lobby.

"When did Duskmere say our relief is coming?" I asked.

The creak of Mae's rocking chair was the only response.

I rolled my head on the grass in her direction and cracked an eye. "Mae?"

Face scrunched, she rocked faster.

"Mae..."

She actively avoided meeting my eyes. "He didn't."

Annoyance welled inside me. "Why are all three of us here?"

She bit her lip. "I thought it would be fun."

"How exactly is this fun?" I surged to my feet and turned in a circle, waving my hands wildly at the ghost town.

"We used to be together every day. Now we have our own things outside of YML. I thought we could use the time together." One angular shoulder lifted and fell in a limp shrug. "With the accident at the Interlands bar and all hands-on deck there, I figured it was the perfect time."

While Zee and I were visiting the Split Sands pack, a call had come in from Dexter who had indeed shown up for his shift. He'd claimed a fireball had been dropped on the bar. Assuming he'd been drinking on the job, it could have been anything from a fight breaking out and someone throwing a candle, a drunken fire mage whose magic went haywire, or an inebriated patron crashing their car through the bar. It wouldn't be the first time any of those things had happened. Teddy, Zee, and Lo had gone to assess the damage.

"That's...thoughtful." Arranging for us to spend time together, even if it was patrol duty, wasn't what I expected. It should have been. Mae always put others first. Shame crashed into me.

Hopping off the porch railing, Y'sindra fluttered to our sister and hugged her neck. "You're a good egg."

The wooden stairs echoed with a hollow thump beneath my heavy steps. I crouched in front of Mae. Fabric wrapped around her hands as she twisted the loose folds of her pants in her fists. I placed my hands over hers. They were warm beneath mine. I ducked my head to meet her downcast gaze. "I'm sorry. You are right. We haven't seen enough of each other lately. This was a great idea."

"You're just saying that. I know you hate it here." A tentative smile tugged at her lips.

My knees were beginning to ache, and my legs were stiff from the prolonged crouching. I rose and backed up to lean against the porch railing. "I do, but I love you two more."

When Mae met my gaze, I pointed at Y'sindra and tilted my hand side to side.

Laughter, open and loud, burst from Mae.

"I saw that." Y'sindra made a face, but it quickly morphed into a grin.

Mae's rocking chair creaked into motion. She crossed her legs, pushing with one foot.

Concern drew my brows together. She seemed fine, but we were literal worlds apart from any sun stones. "Hey, are you okay?"

The quiet stretched, but then she dipped her head. "You know what? I am. Don't get me wrong, I can feel the pull, the stone's insistence I return to them, but for now, I'm fine."

I narrowed my eyes. Mae had been known to put on a brave face if she thought it meant Y'sindra and I would be happy. Like when she ate potato chips, or worse, my beloved cheesy poofs on movie nights. "Iola once said being parted from the sun stones is akin to severing a piece of her she can't survive without."

"Iola has been a keeper of the stones longer than most sun fae have been alive," Mae said, tone like over-toasted, unbuttered bread.

"Fair enough." With the railing against my lower back, or rather, against my fancy vertical spine sheath, I spread my arms to either side and drummed my talons. "What about the reaction you had in Shadwe?"

A few months ago, we'd ventured into that mysterious world to retrieve the remainder of the stolen sun stones. The trip had mostly been a success. However, it almost began with tragedy when Mae grew so ill, I'd worried I might lose her.

"It wasn't easy being away from the stones then, but you know my reaction was due to the unrooted stones. All the sun fae caught in the same realm as the unrooted stones fell ill." Mae bit her lip. "It hit me a little harder because the stones had claimed me. That was the reason I had to leave Shadwe."

"Unconscious. You had to leave Shadwe unconscious." I hooked a thumb at Y'sindra, still hovering next to Mae's chair. "Along with our champion ice spear thrower. You two do like forcing my poor hearts to live on the edge."

"Promise I'm okay. I couldn't stay here for days, but..." Mae bit her lip. "I can still feel the stones feeding me energy, diluted, but the trace is there. Maybe because we are between two realms where stones are rooted?"

Relieved, I nodded. "Okay, just tell us if you need to go back. Y'sindra and I can cover until those sun fae stop puking long enough to do their own patrols."

"Righto. Laney and I got this when you need to go." Y'sindra flew to the oversized rocker I'd vacated and dropped into the chair. While my feet had only whispered against the ground, hers barely extended past the seat.

I whipped my phone from an inner jacket pocket and snapped a picture.

The moment my thumb tapped the power button, something snagged my attention. I brought the home screen up again.

Two bars showed in the upper right of the phone. I didn't understand how any of these signals worked, but I did know to have reception, there had to be an active cellular tower around here. I said as much to my sisters.

"Weird," was all Y'sindra said.

My gaze met Mae's. I tilted my head, she shrugged, and we both turned to Y'sindra. I'd suspected the power supply was due to Blackthorne, but our devious sister knew something.

"Y'sindra..." I drawled.

She picked at her tunic. "Hmm?"

"What do you—"

A buzzing drone hit my eardrums. A shadow flew by in my peripheral. Something bone-cutting cold and wet hit my cheek.

Launching toward the blur, my arm arced through the air, talons coming down on... *holy stars!* I had a fraction of a second to adjust my aim and catch air.

It was a snow fairy. A male snow fairy. Pale blue wings the shade of polar ice flapped, spraying snow.

My shocked gaze bounced from the impossible newcomer to Y'sindra who...wasn't at all surprised. She glowered, visibly vibrating with annoyance. A thin coating of ice raced around her, covering the rocking chair where she now stood.

Was this a threat? He was too adorable to be a threat, but he was a snow fairy. They weren't supposed to survive outside of the Drifta Mountains. Y'sindra had been on the verge of death when my father found her and helped coax her winter magic to life.

A pale gold glow bubbled from Mae's pores. She'd stood, but like me, wavered.

Y'sindra obviously wasn't happy, but she hadn't skewered the guy on an ice pike, either.

"I understand you told us to keep to the forest," the male snow fairy said. His eyes, the same polar blue as his wings, darted quickly from me to Mae.

"Yes, ahwal'Tam." Y'sindra's tone was filled with as much ice as her magic. "I did."

Where "Y" was Y'sindra's surname, and both the length and placement before sindra indicated her family had ranked at the highest level of her clan before she'd been banished, the stressing of "Tam" implied the opposite of the new snow fairy.

Head bobbing, hair dancing in pale blue waves over his shoulders, ahwal'Tam, fidgeted. "There...there are big ones coming from the dark tree line. The one you told us to watch."

Told *us* to watch? What the hell was going on?

Snow sprayed from Y'sindra's wings as she rose into the air and shot out from beneath the porch. Hovering in the middle of the street she looked in the direction of the Shadwe border and then faced the male snow fairy who'd followed her. "Where? How many?"

Taking my cue from Y'sindra's reaction, I jogged into the street, pulling the sword from its sheath as I went. Still coated in a light gold sheen, Mae joined us. Any questions we had for Y'sindra had to be put aside. Whatever was happening was serious.

"We counted at least fifteen," the male snow fairy said. "Many of the corrupt moon fae you have pointed out, but there is also a female like her." ahwal'Tam pointed at Mae. "Big and gold, but with the same markings as the moon fae."

Hielmal—the most wanted sun fae, Mae's birth mother, and an evil ruthless bitch I'd tried to kill but had apparently failed—was on her way for round two.

Pulse hammering against my eardrums, my fingers curled on reflex. The sharp points of my talons extended beyond the sword grip to prick my palms, piercing through the anxiety playing havoc with my nerves. My gaze flew to Mae. "You should go."

"Absolutely not." Determination blazed in Mae's eyes—literally. A nearly imperceptible line of gold ran circles around her pupils. One paper-thin streak of amber shot out from the circle, across her blue orbs. The power living inside Iola had begun to grow inside my sister. Barely a trace, but it was present.

That settled, I tilted my head side to side, giving it a good crack and looked at Y'sindra. "You'll explain later." It wasn't a question.

She gave a sharp, quick nod. "This wasn't how I wanted you both to find out, but shit happens." To the new snow fairy, she asked, "Are the others close?"

Others?

"Yes, Ellri." He pointed farther down the street, in the direction of the

Shadwe border. "They are following the group, using the methods of evasion Lonwie has taught us."

Ellri. I recognized the word from tales of Y'sindra's youth. It was the honorific title for an elder of a snow fairy clan. Apparently, my sister was now the elder of a rag-tag group of snow fairy castaways, and Lo was holding "How To Be a Spy" classes. Oh, the questions I had!

Eyes in perpetual motion, Y'sindra watched every possible entry spot up and down the street. "We should go inside. Not the bar. That's what they'll expect."

I gestured to the building across the street. "Not that one, either."

"Really." Mae drew her bottom lip between her teeth and looked at the building in question. "I would think they'd assume we'd avoid that building due to the history we have with it."

The history being Mae had been kidnapped and held there in a cage by the same female on her way right now.

"Exactly why I think they'd check there—probably before they check the bar." I seated the sword in its sheath and removed the tri-blade daggers from their holsters. The sword was big, but the daggers were much more deadly. We needed deadly. "These fae are smart. The corrupt have been cooking up their comeback since the war ended a hundred years ago. They made big moves, somehow acquired connections right inside the heart of Eodrom, without anyone being the wiser until we accidently stumbled across one of their contacts."

"All true. These guys are S Tier assholes, but they aren't stupid." Only Y'sindra would use a video game reference in the throes of a life and death situation. "I'm with Mae, though. I don't see why they'd search that building."

"Precisely." Thinking better of running with blades out, I holstered the daggers but left the snaps open. "Because you think it's safe, my gut tells me they would assume we felt like they would avoid it. They have been making plans for too long not to think at least two steps ahead. We need to think three."

"Look at you, being all think-y," Y'sindra said, but her tone lacked its typical bite. Her nose scrunched. "Where to?"

"Let's move in the direction they are coming from. We have a better chance if we can get behind them so they don't see us coming." I pointed to a building on the far side of the street, two doors down.

Lifting into the air, Y'sindra and the other snow fairy flew toward the building. Mae and I followed the pair at an all-out sprint. We made it into the building before any movement appeared on the road.

Inside was a perfectly preserved slice of someone's cozy life. A small dining table sat on a burgundy rug. Assorted knickknacks cluttered shelves. A living area with a small sofa complete with a blanket and throw pillows in disarray were to my right, near the large front window. Thin white curtains were drawn back on either side, their length draped to the floor. A dainty teacup rested on the simple coffee table in front of the sofa, as if whoever lived here had only moments ago walked away.

Nothing about this place screamed moon fae, who were the last residents of Shadwe, but then what had I expected? Black furniture, spikes on the walls, a pit of acid in the floor for their enemies?

Careful to stay out of sight, I crouched at the edge of the window and watched the sunlit street.

"Are they coming because they know we're here?" I wondered aloud. "Or did we just draw the short straw and show up when they decided to finally return?"

Mae edged up next to me at the window. "I don't think they'd risk coming back without reason. It has to be because we're here."

"They must have spies," I said. "Like Lo's brother."

"It has to be that shifter dung sniffer." Y'sindra kicked a chair. It tipped over in a clatter. I winced and craned my neck, pressing my cheek against the windowpane. Thankfully the street was empty. No one had heard.

"Sorry." Y'sindra struggled to right the chair. Seemed like a weird time to worry about furniture that belonged to absolutely no one, but whatever. "I told them it was a bad idea."

The muscles of my neck tightened. I was ninety-nine percent certain that comment wasn't about the chair. "Told who, what?"

"The R-*we-know-best*-FG."

Mae spun toward Y'sindra, eyes tight with suspicion. "How did you speak with anyone from the Royal Fae Guard without us knowing?"

"Is this really the time?" Y'sindra's wings buzzed in agitation, dusting snow. Behind her, ahwal'Tam's hands knotted together.

"No. It is not," Mae snapped, as angry as I'd ever heard her be with our sister.

Jaw working, I peeled my glare from Y'sindra to check the street. "So, what you're saying is we should expect to deal with Enode?"

Y'sindra puffed a breath. "Yes. Long story short, Enode was the perfect prisoner. Played contrite. Knowing full well no sun fae would venture into Shadwe to act on anything they learned from him, he provided all the information they asked for. Those dumb dumbs at the RFG decided it would be a goodwill gesture to release Enode to the Shadwe ruling family."

"Teddy's parents," I said.

"Precisely. They think if the ruling family looks sympathetically on the sun fae, they'll keep their wayward wyvern son in check."

"Ha!" I barked a laugh because that right there was funny.

"Just wait, I haven't gotten to the best part yet. Those Royal Fae Halfwits thought they could track Enode, a shadow shifter, to any contacts he might have on this side of Shadwe." As she spoke, Y'sindra smoothed her frizzy curls back and secured them into a tight tail at her neck. "Lo warned them not only would it not work, it would backfire. They refused to believe Enode, a master spy, might be learning anything of value from them."

"Fantastic." A surprisingly flat response from Mae, the epitome of sunshine and rainbows.

"Shadow shifters are rare, and you and I took out two a few months ago. If they have a spy, it's Enode. We know how to track him, Lo showed us." Y'sindra gestured between herself and ahwal'Tam. "You two focus on the rest."

"The rest, right." I hunkered at the edge of the window, wondering how many and who "the rest" would be.

Mae twisted toward the snow fairy male and asked, "How far away were they?"

Wings humming, ahwal'Tam buzzed into the air, seeming startled to be addressed directly. "They, um...they crossed the border on the path next to the large boulder north of downtown and headed this way."

The path next to the large boulder. Not exactly helpful. I looked at Y'sindra.

"A little over a mile north." She smirked. "As the fairy flies. For you ground dwellers, maybe two. There's a large lake and heavy vegetation between here and there."

If they were two miles out, we had time. My legs were once again beginning to cramp from crouching for so long. I stood, shook off the pins and needles sensation, and hopped on my toes to get the blood flowing. Blood still pushing power to every nerve ending, thanks to my liberal use of Teddy's veins the last few days.

I looked at Y'sindra's new friend, acolyte, whatever he was. "You're certain Enode didn't see you? He's a sneaky little shit."

"Ellri Lonwie has been teaching us techniques for evasion." His enthusiastic nod sent his powder blue curls bobbing. "I am certain."

What the hell was going on here that this snow fairy labeled Lo, who was not a fairy, as a clan elder? I stared at Y'sindra who pointedly ignored me. When we got out of here, I would tie her to a chair and get some answers.

"Nothing else in the sky?" Y'sindra asked.

"No. We sent four teams out like we have practiced. I left immediately to find you after they all reported back."

Mouth twitching to the side, she looked at Mae and me. "No Dacian."

"Ellri, I will alert the others to your location."

Y'sindra nodded to the other fairy. He paused to dip his head to Mae and me and zoomed to the back of the building. Moments later a door opened and closed.

A bowl on the dining room table caught my attention. "Are those berries?"

"Must be plastic," Y'sindra said as she ran her hands down her tunic.

That little liar.

With an annoyed huff, her brows snapped together, and she glared. "Shouldn't you be watching the street?"

"You're sure your new friend won't fly right into a bunch of shadow shifters and their poison darts?" I asked.

Y'sindra wrinkled her nose up at me. "I just told you they are rare, and yes, I'm sure."

"Fairies." Mae pointed.

Taking to the air, Y'sindra flew to the window.

Across the street, three snow fairies stood atop the building. As soon as they saw Y'sindra, they leapt off the far side and disappeared.

"That's the sign. Hiemal and her followers are almost here. Once the fairies and I take care of Enode, we'll join you." Y'sindra jogged in the same direction ahwal'Tam had gone, but she stopped and ran back to hug each of us fiercely. "Don't get dead."

20

SUPERNOVA

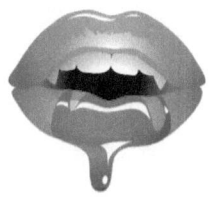

"She can't be allowed to live." Mae held my gaze, and my stomach dropped.

Who *she* was went unsaid, but I knew, and I agreed. Still, my sister had a soft heart. Did the amber-spiked determination in her eyes disguise pain?

"I've been preparing for the day we would meet again," Mae said. "Iola has been training me to harness my inner sun."

Unable to hide the whiplash surprise, my eyes widened. "Whoa, whoa, whoa. Training with Iola? Your inner sun?" I looked her over, searching for any trace of the bright gold light leaking from her pores. "And I thought Y'sindra had secrets."

A laugh bubbled from her. Smiling, she peeked out the window, as did I. The streets were still clear.

"I wasn't keeping it from you. I promise." She sucked on her bottom lip and then straightened, growing serious. "After I barely held onto my protection during the fight with Miro, Iola has been helping me focus my power. I should be able to maintain a shield through at least one hit from that awful magic now, maybe two."

"Should be able to?" My hearts were slowly gathering speed in anticipation of a fight. I began my pre-battle ritual—sword, tri-blades, push daggers, torpedoes, braid beneath the jacket. "There's no margin for error here. If that stuff hits us, we're toast."

For a moment we stared at one another, remembering the magic speeding over Y'sindra's wing. Eating her piece by piece. My sword cleaving her wing.

"I know." Mae's chin rose. "Yes. I can do it. You better take that bitch out before she gets a second chance."

I barked a laugh. Mae rarely cursed, but when she did, it was effective.

A smudge of movement appeared at the end of the street. "They're here." My gaze flew to the roof across from us. There were no fairies.

Backing away from the window, I turned the knob on the front door to disengage the latch so we could silently slip out behind the group when they passed. I flattened against the wall to wait. My fingers curled and flexed at my thighs. The desire to dig my talons into Hielmal's throat hummed through my veins. Teddy's blood infused a clarity I hadn't possessed since I'd ripped open the veil between Ta'Vale and Outerlands.

At the time, I'd had the fleeting thought that power did not come without sacrifice. Only recently could I admit to myself I'd given up almost every piece of who I was that day. But now I was something else. Something stronger, and I planned to ruin Hielmal's day.

I looked at Mae and gave her a savage grin, exposing fangs tingling with anticipation. "What Y'sindra said."

"You too." A smirk flirted with her lips.

Outside, two figures crept by the window. Both had dark hair. They had the height and build of males. Even though I didn't have a clear view of the corruption—a roadmap of black veins crawling across their faces—their pointed ears and slate complexions meant they were corrupt moon fae.

I hadn't expected them to be so close to the front of the house. Had I made a mistake cracking the door?

Doesn't matter, I told myself. What's done was done. There was no room for second guessing or panic. I breathed through my mouth, slow and steady. Tense, I focused on the tableau outside the window. With my hands hanging loose next to the tri-blades holstered on my thighs, I wiggled my fingers, ready for whatever might come.

A soft gold glow edged into my vision. I whipped my head toward Mae. Training or no, she still had trouble controlling her power...and that glow would draw attention from outside. I grabbed her and wedged her into the corner between the door and the wall.

Flung against the wall, she grunted. Her brows smashed together. She looked down at her hands—her softly glowing hands—and then up to me and nodded. Closing her eyes, she slowed her breaths. Unless she went supernova, no one would see her tucked there.

Though it still leaked from every pore, the intensity receded until only a dim glow shone through her clothing made from spider silk—an insanely expensive material which allowed her magic to pass through the weave. It provided more protection than cotton, but it wouldn't stop a well-placed blade.

A second pair of soldiers were passing out of view of the window frame when I turned back. Across the street, six soldiers crept two by two toward the bar. Unless I'd missed any during my brief distraction shuffling Mae, that made ten soldiers and no Hielmal.

As soon as they had passed, I darted to the sofa and grabbed the blanket. Tossing the covering to Mae, I resumed my place against the wall.

"Thanks," she murmured, and wrapped herself with the blanket.

Minutes dragged by without any more movement from outside. How long did we have to wait? Our enemy would eventually check those locations and discover them empty. Would they do a sweep of the other buildings on the street?

Patience and I, we weren't friends. I bounced on my toes and tilted my head side to side. *Crack.* In the quiet of the room, the sound hit like a firecracker. I grimaced an apology to a Mae.

"Nothing?" she whispered.

"I've counted ten. No Hielmal." My gaze darted to the still empty street beyond the window and back. "I might have missed something when I moved you to the corner, but it's unlikely. We were fast."

Nodding, she absently rubbed her fingers along the hem of the blanket she held together over her chest. Gold sparked and dripped from her fingertips...like the black death magic Hielmal possessed. My eyes widened. *That's new.*

"Do you think the others went down a sideroad?" Mae asked as she followed the direction of my gaze to her hands and the drips of magic. She curled her fingers into the blanket and gave me a sheepish smile.

"Probably." I eased toward the door and angled my ear toward the slight crack. Hearing nothing, I moved to the window. Still hidden by the bunched folds of the drapes, I looked toward the bar. The six other soldiers I'd seen remained outside, bracketing the door. None looked behind in our direction, only to the door they hid next to and occasionally across the street to where I assumed the four who had passed along the front of this house also waited.

What in the fried dill pickle were they waiting for?

Hearts thumping in my throat, I edged past the curtains and angled my head to look in the opposite direction, down the street. If anyone approached the window now, or if even one of the soldiers across the street glanced this way, I would be exposed.

Nothing stirred outside. I pulled back from the window and looked at Mae. "Most of their firepower is outside the bar. I'm betting the others we haven't seen are circling behind."

"I agree." She glanced at the window and then toward the back of the house. "How long should we wait?"

If we went on the attack, I would be forced to leave Mae's side. She'd have her shield to protect herself, but would that be enough?

"Weapons?" I asked. This was a terrible idea. We should have retreated and gone for backup as soon as—

The blanket slid from Mae's shoulders in a hushed whoosh. She crouched and pulled two long daggers sheathed in cleverly hidden holsters on the outside of her knee-high boots.

"Sneaky." I had to get me a pair of those.

She gave a cheeky wag of her brows. "I learned from the best."

"Hopefully, it won't come to you needing those, but I'm relieved."

Mae straightened. "Don't worry about me. My shield will compensate for my lack of weapon mastery. Though I'd prefer not to expend my power before we run into Hielmal."

"You and me both." I rolled my bottom lip beneath a fang, and looked toward the rear of the house. "It sounded like ahwal'Tam went out a back door."

"I heard the same thing." She glanced in the direction he'd gone. "What are you thinking?"

A shrill scream came from outside. I dove for the window. The group of corrupt from the bar were surging into the street, eyes trained upwards.

"What was that?" Mae asked from behind me.

"My money's on Y'sindra." I turned my face toward the sky. Nothing, but then I saw the small form with a puff of white hair sprawled on a rooftop on the opposite side of the street. They weren't moving. Terror grabbed hold of my hearts and twisted. My muscles clenched.

No. Wrong shade of white. The hair was closer to gray.

It wasn't Y'sindra. Not ahwal'Tam, either. How many snow fairies were out there?

I rubbed a trembling hand over the sharp ache in the center of my chest, feeling the solid resistance of the wyvern scale beneath the bandolier and jacket.

Not far from the fallen snow fairy, a blurry shadow moved along the rooftop. Squinting, I tried to focus. "Did you see that?"

"Where?" Mae leaned over me and peeked out.

"Across the street. Three buildings down." I rushed to add, "That's not Y'sindra or ahwal'Tam on the roof."

A breath rushed out of Mae, and she grabbed my arm.

"I know." I squeezed her hand. "We'll have time for sympathy later."

Against the rooftop across the street, a shadow coalesced into Enode. We locked gazes and he pointed. "In there!" His voice carried through the crack I'd left in the door.

Fight or flight dumped a bucketload of adrenaline into my system.

Almost in unison, the group from the bar angled toward our window.

Anticipation rolled an electric current down my neck. My shoulders pinched, and I forced them to relax. "Here we go," I murmured.

I backed away from the window, watching Enode, still hovering in plain sight across the street. My gaze jumped to the group from the bar moving toward us.

"Back door?" Mae asked, a little breathless.

"Probably—" I sucked in air, swallowing the rest of my response in a gasp.

A long, thin spear of ice erupted from Enode's abdomen. He was shoved forward through the air, rocked off kilter, but remained above the street.

"Mother Sun," Mae whispered.

The ice in Enode's belly immediately started to melt. Blood began to flow from the momentarily frozen hole. A slow trickle of pink water dripped into the street below the shadow shifter. He struggled to maintain altitude, turning the slow trickle into a spray. The group from the bar backed away from the gory rain falling from Enode.

We were momentarily forgotten by those outside, or they'd discarded the notion we were there at all. Enode was the only one who saw us, and whoever hit him was clearly outside.

A sadistic thrill shot through me. Y'sindra got her revenge.

Y'sindra!

Where was she? I searched the rooftops, the tree line, everywhere she could hide behind Enode.

There! Impossibly far away, I spotted something moving in the trees. The figure was all grays and browns. Was she wearing a hood? It might not look like her, but there was no mistaking the magic. I was even more curious to know what she'd been doing here.

Mae gripped my arm. "Is he...?"

The figure I watched in the trees stopped moving. For two long heartbeats nothing happened.

Something shot toward Enode. It glittered in the sun. A second spear of ice appeared in the shadow shifter's chest. He plummeted to the street. His small body bounced and jerked. All traces of inherent camouflage gone, he didn't move.

"He is now." Outside, the soldiers from our side of the street edged into view. "That's all of them. They're distracted, but we're still outnumbered. Going out the back door and coming around is still the best option."

"Agreed." Mae edged toward the hallway. Pores already leaking light, she faced me. The hairline fracture of gold twitched across her blue irises. "Remember, I can't throw a shield on a moving target, you'll need to be close."

"Understood." With a final look outside, I followed Mae.

Halfway across the room, shouts went up in the street. On instinct, I ducked. Had they seen us? Were they coming? I plastered my back to the wall. Mae did the same. My gaze shot to the window.

A tight cluster of ice shards pelted three guards clustered together. They screamed. Bleeding from numerous wounds, the group broke formation and scattered. Ice in all shapes and sizes continued to rain from above, seeming to come from everywhere. There had to be at least a dozen snow fairies.

"Change of plans." I pivoted toward the front door. "Let's finish what our snowy friends started."

Palming two torpedoes, I yanked open the door and spilled onto the porch. I moved aside to allow Mae room and took aim at a corrupt moon fae crouched next to a porch column across the street.

I pinched the weapon between my fingertips, bent my arm until the tubular dagger swiveled in my grip and rested against my shoulder. Aim steady, I channeled all my strength into the forward thrust of my arm.

End over end, the dagger spun toward my target. A breath later, the impact threw the solider backwards. It wouldn't kill him, but enough of my enhanced blood fae strength remained that he wasn't going anywhere anytime soon. Quickly, I threw the second torpedo, and another guard dropped.

It would be smarter to dispatch rather than incapacitate, but running around in the open was a bad idea. I still didn't know where Hielmal was, and the last thing I needed to do was run into the street and give her a target.

Mae came outside, moving to my left.

"Two down," I told her. "Not permanently, stay alert."

I reached for my sword hilt but changed my mind. The building fronts were too cramped. Tri-blades were deadly, but push daggers were easier to maneuver on the run, becoming almost an extension of my hand. Palming one in each fist, I waved to the left, toward the building where Mae had been held captive. She nodded, and I hustled in that direction.

Keeping my focus on the soldiers still running for cover in the street, I stepped off the porch and onto the strip of grass between buildings.

The sound was subtle. A foot scuffing the ground. A shoulder brushing a wall.

Light burst from Mae. Her shield flared. A filmy orb of translucent gold circled us. Lazy swirls moved around my sister and me, like glitter powder caught in a slow current.

I felt the impact rather than saw it. A malignant oil slick moved over my sister's shield. Death magic. My stomach hollowed while my hearts galloped against my sternum. I breathed through my mouth and focused on the source of the magic.

Hielmal stood with four guards positioned around her. Remnants of black magic oozed from her fingertips. At her feet, blades of grass curled in on themselves and turned to dust. An older version of Mae, rumor had it she'd once been stunning. Now, her sapphire eyes were crowded by red and black, and her golden complexion drowned beneath the corruption crawling over her from head to toe.

"Baby girl," Hielmal cooed. Eyes on Mae, she smiled, the reddish-black veins of corruption stretching and pulling. "You're stronger already."

Mae's breath came in heavy pants. I didn't think it was an emotional reaction. Sweat dampened her hairline on her neck and ran beneath her shirt. A wet stain spread like an ink blot along her spine.

"I asked you once, and you refused, but I understand." Hielmal moved closer. "You weren't ready, but you are now. Come with me."

A thin shield was the only thing between us and the magic. As I watched, the black pushed against the gold, but Mae's magic pushed back. It ate away at the death magic, absorbing it.

Converting it? Where the gold and black met, the gold burned brighter.

Hielmal took a step closer. She reached toward the shield. I didn't understand how magic worked, and I didn't know if she could reach through the shield to Mae.

"Do you always try to kill those you love?" I asked, trying to draw her attention.

Swords at the ready, the guards closed rank around Hielmal. One didn't hold a sword, he held magic. It sparked across his knuckles.

Not good. Even if that wasn't the same magic, it was still nasty stuff. I didn't think Mae could hold back another hit.

He'd have to die first. Push daggers tapping against my thighs, I began mapping a path to my target.

"I was aiming for you." Hielmal pointed toward the spot where her magic had struck—directly in front of me. Her finger stopped just short of touching the shield. Suddenly I was less curious about her ability to reach through my sister's shield, and more interested in what would happen to her if she did.

The splotch of death magic still warring with Mae's gold, was indeed the right height to hit me in the face. My sister had saved me.

"Lane." Mae's voice was strangled. Tension lined her face. "You've got to go."

"I—"

"Get out of here," she hissed through her teeth.

My gaze flew to the guards, and then Hielmal's smug expression. *Gods damnit!* An empty pit opened in my belly. Sacrificing herself to save me was such a Mae thing to do. Maybe she believed with her shields and her blades she could escape, but she couldn't wield them against one trained combatant, let alone four.

Motes of writhing magic sparked across the guard's knuckles.

Limbs trembling, Mae looked about to collapse. I edged closer.

She turned her face toward me. Eyes pleading, she mouthed one word —*go.*

I hesitated.

"Go!" she yelled, and then softer, "Please."

The note of desperation in her voice finally struck a chord. Belatedly, I felt the heat from Mae's shield. Perspiration ran from my hairline.

Eyes wide, I watched Mae as I dragged a hand across my forehead. She nodded.

My sister was about to go nuclear.

I spun away. The torn grass felt slippery beneath my heel. For a split second, I scrambled for purchase, and then I was sprinting toward the house we'd just left.

"Snow fairies, hide!" I shouted. "Now!"

I sent a desperate prayer to the universe that for once, Y'sindra would do what she was told.

Footsteps pounded in the street. Shouts came from behind me. More shouts from the street.

I threw myself through the still open door, landing in an awkward belly flop. My push daggers clattered across the floor. Eyes squeezed shut, I folded my hands over the back of my head.

Time pulled like taffy. Seconds, maybe minutes passed. Footsteps and shouts drew closer, growing louder outside. Had I misread the situation?

I'd left Mae all alone.

Sliding my palms beneath me, I started to rise.

A concussive beat thrummed the air, throwing me back to the ground. Heat lashed across my back. Behind my eyelids, white-gold light eclipsed the midday sun.

21

MINUS THE BONE SPLINTERS

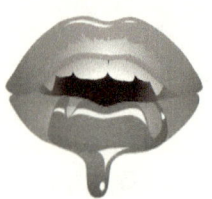

STUNNED, LUNGS WORKING OVERTIME, I STAYED PUT ON THE FLOOR. A halo of light spun on the inside of my eyelids. Thank the stars my eyes had been closed. The exposed skin on the back of my neck felt like I'd slept face down for a full day in the sun. The hilt of my sword was warm against the back of my skull.

I surged to my feet and stumbled toward the door. Was this Mae's doing? Was she okay? Was Y'sindra okay?

Blinking rapidly, I tried to clear the black shadows dancing in the center of my vision. If my eyes hadn't been shut, there was a good chance I might have been permanently blinded. Each time I blinked the black shapes turned to blazing white lights against my lids, while daggers drove into my eye sockets. The wooden porch planks creaked as I stepped outside.

"Oh, gods." My stomach dropped to my toes. No one was left standing. Hands trembling, I scanned the street. The soldiers caught in the open were all down. I pressed my hand to my sternum in relief. No small, winged forms were visible.

Dots still distorted my direct vision. In my peripherals, I could make out movement from the soldiers to differing degrees. Farther down the street, where a few had tried to find cover, they rolled and crawled in the grass. Those closest to where I'd left Mae were deathly still.

Mae!

I shuffled toward the corner of the house. Canting to the left, my shoulder hit the window. One foot in front of the other, I kept going, dragging my shoulder along the glass. The leather caught and stuttered, but I kept going. Fuck it. No point wasting energy trying to stand straight.

Single-mindedly, I put one foot in front of the other. I had to get to Mae. Why had I left her alone? So stupid. I had to assume this...this...explosion, whatever it was, had been Mae's doing. What if it hadn't?

Oh, gods. I was the protector. My sisters always stood behind me, and I'd left her.

I continued to fan my lashes as I bumped my way along the wall. Slowly, the residual dots obscuring my vision scattered. Yet, as my vision cleared, I couldn't make sense of what I saw in front of me.

As I stepped off the porch, something crunched beneath my feet. Shocked, I did a weird dance backward, looking at the ground. Grass. The grass was burnt, as if someone had wielded an industrial blow torch.

My gaze snapped up, finding Mae. She stood perfectly still, her back to me.

"Mae?" She didn't react. I hurried to her, put a hand on her shoulder and froze.

In front of my sister was one of the most gruesome things I'd ever seen, and I'd seen a lot of gruesome stuff. Much of it by my own talons and blades.

A leg stump, shorn off just below the knee was the only thing upright in the scorched grass, aside from my sister. Blackened bits split along the top of the leg. Wet crimson showed in the grooves of the blackened cracks. The leg belonged to a barbequed body I assumed was Hielmal, based on where I'd seen the sun fae standing last. It was mostly bits of flesh curled on a charred skeleton.

"I did that," Mae said, staring at the remains of her mother. She stood straight, like brittle iron, ready to snap.

Moving carefully, I wrapped an arm around her waist and pulled her against my side. "Yes. You had to. Are you okay?"

Sure, she'd told me to take out Hielmal, but it was done. Her birthmother was dead and literally dusted.

Turning her face toward me, she smiled. Fortunately, it wasn't an I-lost-my-marbles smile, but full of joy. Weird, but considering Mae was all light and goodness while the female who birthed her was truly, irredeemably evil, and her mission would have destroyed Eodrom, ultimately killing everything and everyone my sister loved, it made sense.

"I did that," she said again.

Hielmal wasn't the only one who had been near Mae. Three guards had also been turned into extra-crispy skeletons and piles of melted fae goo. One had retreated directly behind another guard. The lack of weapons confirmed my suspicions it had been the magic-wielder.

"I think this makes you an official badass." My voice broke on a laugh. Adrenaline and anxiety still vibrated my nerves.

As if stepping out of a dream, Mae looked behind me, and then to me. She gripped my arms. "Are you okay? Y'sindra?"

"I'm fine. I didn't see any fairies in the street." Reaching over my shoulder, I unsheathed my sword. "If you're up for it, why don't you look for our sister while I take care of the guards?"

I made quick work of the soldiers. Three had been caught in the direct path of...whatever Mae did and were in similar shape as Hielmal's guards. Only a few had gained their feet, and they were in no position to defend themselves. I had zero regrets. It was a kinder death than they deserved.

Doors slammed open. Mae's footsteps pounded from building to building as she searched for any trace of the fairies. Her pace was frantic, but with each place she checked and abandoned, the knot of fear loosened in my chest. If there were no fairies to be found, they got away in time.

With seven soldiers disposed of by Mae's blast or my sword, I had a pep in my step as I headed for the three soldiers who had been farthest from the blast. Doing little more than moaning and rolling in the grass, they weren't going anywhere anytime soon. I still had a hard time believing Hielmal—the most wanted sun fae alive—was gone. Just like that. And Mae, my amazing sister and her daughter, was the one to do the deed.

I stopped by the crumbled body of Enode lying where it fell. The ice had melted, leaving him looking like Y'sindra's favorite type of cheese. Minus the bone splinters pushed outward from the impact.

The holes she'd put in his sternum and belly were large enough to reach my arm through. Two ice spears that size would have burned through almost all her magic reserves. Not to mention she pushed herself to fly on a wing that wasn't one hundred percent.

Mae jogged into the road to join me. "I can't find her. I can't find any of the fairies. Even the body we saw on the roof is gone." She pointed to where we'd seen the fallen fairy. Sure enough, the roof was bare.

"I suspect they retreated as soon as we came outside." A quick look down the street confirmed the remaining soldiers were still down for the count. I sheathed my sword and nudged Enode's body with my toe. "Check out the size of those holes. Y'sindra would have left as soon she threw the second spear."

Taking an audible breath, Mae nodded. "You're right."

A fluttering sound built—like a flag picked up by a breeze and steadily whipped into a frenzy.

"Sounds like Y'sindra times one hundred," I murmured and swiveled in the direction of the approaching noise.

"Mother sun." Awe filled Mae's voice.

From the tree line in the distance, behind the row of buildings where the bar was located, fairies emerged from high in the branches. One after another, they separated from the foliage, and I realized they all wore some form of camo. No doubt Lo's influence.

A cluster of four fairies emerged, each carrying the corner of fabric draped between them like a hammock. Another group of fairies followed in the same formation. I eyed the bulges in the fabric. "That's how they carry their injured. I bet one is Y'sindra."

"Injured?" Mae's head whipped toward me and then back to the incoming fairies.

"I doubt it. She's too cantankerous to be hurt." Despite my words, I smiled as I spoke. "Tired or lazy. Take your pick."

Mae giggled. "Why not both."

Laughing, I pointed to the first group. "I think that's ahwal'Tam, so I'm betting that's our troublemaker."

All around us, snow fairies alighted on rooftops, in the streets. They watched us with wary curiosity. A few entered buildings along the street. After twenty landed, I stopped counting. There were still many more coming.

Eyes wide, Mae turned to me. "What the..."

"Fuck. I'll say it because you won't, and this"—I waved my hand at the veritable cloud of snow fairies—"this is a what the fuck sort of situation."

A poof of white hair spilled out from the litter carried by ahwal'Tam and three other snow fairies. Y'sindra peeked over the hammock-like edge. She shot us a lopsided grin and a wobbly thumbs up before she toppled back into the depths of the cloth cradle. Those ice spears she'd skewered Enode with had drained so much power, it left her in a loopy, drunken-like state.

I snorted. "She has so much explaining to do."

"So much," Mae echoed.

The fairy escort gently eased their magic-drunk cargo to the ground before landing themselves. True to character, Y'sindra threw fists at the cloth material she managed to wrap around herself.

Sighing, I picked her up from the blanket and placed her on the grassy ground, where she immediately fell to her butt again. She gave me the stink eye as if her lack of equilibrium was my fault.

"Nice aim," I said, distracting her from whatever tirade she was about to launch into and nudged Enode's corpse with my toe again.

Her gaze swung to the crumpled body of shadow shifter lying several feet away, as if she only just realized where we stood. A slow grin spread across her lips. "I can't wait to tell Lo."

"He'll be cool with you...you know?" I gave a meaningful nod toward the corpse.

"Putting an ice pick through his brother?" Y'sindra wobbled and grabbed my leg to steady herself. "Yeah, he'll be fine."

As the flash-frozen wound thawed, the body had begun to collapse around the large holes. Glistening pink innards slithered like bloody snakes from his belly. *Gross.*

"I'm not so sure. We're talking about his brother. It wasn't that long ago he'd begged us not to hurt Enode. I can take the blame for this." As I spoke, Y'sindra used a stick to scramble the shadow shifter's guts. "Disgusting."

Grinning, she waved the stick at me. I took several steps back. I'd made it this far without any blood or body fluids ruining another set of leathers. Maybe I'd actually make it home with clean clothes.

"He'll come around." Y'sindra went back to poking. Gross as it was, I realized she was trying to peel up the shifter's shirt, as if she was looking for something.

"Because Enode pumped him full of poison?" I asked.

"Nah." Y'sindra managed to separate the shirt fibers from frayed skin and pushed the material to his neck. A chain with a pendant lay on Enode's chest. She pointed at the gore-covered pendant with her equally gory stick. "Grab that."

"And get shifter guts all over myself? No thanks. Why can't you do it?"

She made a face. "Because I'll probably fall in the shifter guts, which would be way worse, doncha think?"

"I'll get it," Mae volunteered.

As she knelt to retrieve the pendant, I asked, "So if it wasn't Enode shooting him with the dart, why did Lo change his tune?"

"Because," Y'sindra said as she held her hand out to receive the pendant from Mae. "Teddy informed him Enode tried to kill me."

"What? Why?" It had happened, but telling Lo would have been cruel. I couldn't imagine Teddy ever doing that.

Y'sindra dropped the pendant into a pocket on her tunic and buttoned the flap. Lips pursed, she turned her face up to me. "Lo thought it would be a good idea to request his brother be released into our custody. He thought Enode might be influenced by our family unit."

"Ha!" A laugh burst from me.

She grinned. "My little muffin is sweet, but naïve. Teddy set him straight. He told Lo what happened, how Enode had almost taken a shot at me."

I dragged my lower lip beneath a fang. "Poor Lo."

"He found out right after everything happened. It was rough for a little while, but he's good now." Y'sindra patted the pocket with the pendant. "He'll be relieved when I show him this."

After we all made it home from Shadwe, and Lo recovered from the poison that nearly killed him, he hadn't been his usual chipper self. I'd chalked it up to what happened between he and his brother. No, it'd been because my sister's life had been threatened. "He'll share an affinity for your bloodthirsty ways in no time."

"Right?" She held up a fist. Laughing, I gave it a bump.

"Let's hope not." Mae chuckled.

Pointing to the par-baked soldiers in the street, Y'sindra gave Mae a sideways look. "So, all the fairies can talk about is the light they saw from the trees. Want to explain?"

"You want to explain the fairies?" Mae asked.

"Touché." Y'sindra gave a roll of her hand and a half-bow.

"Both of you have a lot to explain." I pointed at Y'sindra. "Give us the quick version." Her lips pressed together and her face screwed up in a mulish expression.

"I'll go first," Mae said, and we both looked at her. "The quick version is I don't know what I did. I suspect it had something to do with my magic using the death magic. That's how it felt, but I need to talk to Iola."

"Okay, fine." Y'sindra smoothed a hand over her tunic. She gripped the hem while she looked around the town and at the snow fairies who had remained outside. "You know how snow fairies cull their weak? How they sent me on a pilgrimage when I couldn't summon my winter magic during the trials?"

"I do," I answered, my hearts clenching in my chest. Snow fairies were as long lived as any fae, but had no population control other than what they themselves implemented.

"Lo asked to see where I came from. I was...embarrassed." Y'sindra bunched the hem of her tunic in her fists, stretching the material. I resisted hugging her. She'd hate that. "I told him how I'd failed my Winter Within trial. How the elders had sent me on a pilgrimage to Eodrom."

Mae knelt and put a hand on Y'sindra's shoulder.

Tugging at one of her tight, white curls, Y'sindra looked at Mae. "I told him how the elders meant to be rid of me and this orphan sun fae who had been dumped in our camp."

Mae smiled. She was the orphan.

"So, you and Lo set out to collect other snow fairies who failed their Winter Within trial," I said. It was a statement, not a question. Pride for my sister nearly overwhelmed me.

She nodded. "We found ahwal'Tam barely surviving in the base of the Drifta Mountains, and I knew I had to."

"You're amazing," I said and meant it.

A vivid pink blush blazed a path across her cheeks. She smoothed a hand over her fuzzy curls. "Dad's lessons, how he taught me to coax my winter magic to life? That's the reason these snow fairies are here and alive. It's the reason they won't stop calling me Ellri, no matter how many times I tell them to stop."

"You made a new home for them." Mae squeezed our sister's shoulder and rose. "Lane's right, you're amazing. This is amazing."

"Well, that's my news. Can we get out of here?" Y'sindra patted her pocket. "I want to get this to Lo."

"Sounds like a great plan." There was more to her story, but I didn't want to pump her for more information, not right now. I was truly proud of her and didn't want to diminish what she'd done. Fishing a portal disk from a side pocket on my jacket, I tossed it to the ground. "There's not much reason to stick around here."

"What about them?" Mae pointed in the direction I'd been heading before I'd been distracted by the shadow shifter. I followed her finger to the guards who'd graduated from rolling in the grass to crawling.

I winced. "Right, them."

"We should probably call Duskmere and have them transported to the dungeons," Mae said.

Narrowing my eyes, I noticed ahwal'Tam watching us from the house we'd been hiding inside. "What is he doing in there?"

Y'sindra turned and spotted the snow fairy who waved in our direction. "It's his house."

A squeal of surprise came from Mae.

"His house? I have an idea." Grinning, I exchanged the portal disk for one of Duskmere's portal stones and made my way over to awhal'Tam. "You got some rope in there?"

22

BLOOD, GUTS, MORE BLOOD

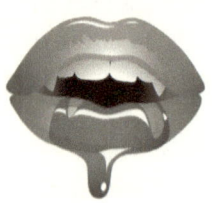

"Was the red bow really necessary?" Mae asked as we stepped through the portal, onto the penthouse balcony.

Unable to hide my self-satisfied grin, I bent to unlace my boots. "We needed to bind those moon fae before we tossed them in the dungeon. Is it my fault those fairies only had sheets?"

"No," Mae said, following me inside. I watched with envy as she slid the blades out from the hidden, outside holsters in her boots, and then unzipped the panels on the inside of her calves. "But it is your fault we spent an hour hunting down every scrap of red cloth they possessed."

"What can I say, perfection is my middle name." My communication crystal vibrated from inside a jacket pocket. Light, musical bells tickled the air.

Y'sindra blew past me and cannonballed onto the sofa. "A perfect pain in the ass, maybe. You're gonna replace every sheet, towel, and tunic you borrowed."

"I thought Lo was training them for stealth. What do they need red anything for?" I swiped my thumb across the crystal before she could do more than squeak a retort. My gaze shifted to the moon fae I hated-grew to respect-grew to like-hated again. "Before you say anything, you're welcome, Duskmere."

Duskmere rarely showed emotion, but I could virtually feel the gratitude radiating through the crystal connection. "Malaney Callaghan."

He bit off my name. Nope, that was anger. Still an emotion, but opposite end of the spectrum.

"Duskmere Blademoon," I retorted and he blinked. I'd bet a whole package of Ho Hos he hadn't thought I knew his full name.

Jaw working, he glared. "Why are there two and a half trussed corrupt in my dungeon?"

"Yeah, sorry about the half part. I thought I could get that last guy through the portal." I looked at the front of my blood splattered legs, I'd almost made it home from a job gore-free.

"That does not explain what they are doing here." Duskmere's teeth were clenched so tight he was going to crack a molar.

From the sofa, the peanut gallery—otherwise known as Y'sindra—snorted. "Look who's got some explaining to do now."

"I told you it was a bad idea," Mae called from the kitchen.

Duskmere's eye twitched. This was the most fun I'd had in weeks. I strolled to my favorite chair, scooted into its depths, and crossed my feet on an ottoman. "I thought you'd appreciate the gift. Delivered with a red bow and all."

His nostrils flared. "You sent two prisoners into a dungeon cell without any knowledge of its occupants or if it was even locked."

"Listen, if you go around leaving your cell doors unlocked, that sounds like a you problem." I made a show of tapping a talon to my chin. "No, wait. It's also a me problem since I put most of your prisoners there."

"Now, you listen to me—"

"No." I flung my legs from the ottoman and sat forward. "You listen to me."

"My man, Duskmere said the wrong thing." Y'sindra raised her voice. "Shoulda just said thank you."

I jabbed a finger at the projection of Duskmere above my palm. "I—we—just did you a huge favor. Hielmal is dead."

Eyes widening, Duskmere's head jerked and his mouth fell open.

"How's Miro?" I switched subjects fast enough to give him whiplash. "How about Enode? He's such a small, delicate thing. How's he handling being kept behind bars?"

"We...we determined he would be of better use outside the dungeon." Duskmere reeled in his momentary fluster.

"How's that working out? Is he fully reformed? Where did he go?"

"We—" Duskmere paused, visibly pulling on his cloak of superiority. "Last report had him exploring the Illigrad Plains."

"Bullshit," I snapped.

His silver brows angled low over the beaten steel of his glinting eyes. "How dare you—"

"How dare *you*!" I thundered. "Have you checked the satchels we sent along strapped to the prisoners?"

Silence answered me. The tight line of his mouth bled all the color from his dusky lips. His glare disconnected from me, and he snapped his finger at someone out of view of the crystal and then pointed at, what I assumed was the prison cell and its two new gift-wrapped residents.

"Let me ruin the surprise. Hielmal's head is in one, Enode is in the other."

Shock once again washed over his features.

I smirked. "Enode's in pretty bad shape. He's got a few holes in him, courtesy of Y'sindra. "

"Right on," she crowed.

"You know the sister whose advice you asked for and chose to ignore because, what was it you said?" I tilted my head and tapped my chin, pretending to think about it. "I remember now. You said, and I quote, *you determined he was better outside the prison*. Where was it your expert team tailed him to?"

He didn't answer, so I answered my own question.

"I can tell you where Enode wasn't. He was nowhere near Ta'Vale. He led Hielmal and her soldiers right to us in Outerlands." I sneered. "Crack team of trackers you've got over there."

Duskmere's jaw worked. His gaze flicked in the direction he'd sent whoever he'd snapped his fingers at. Grunts, moans, and the shifting of gravel indicated someone was manhandling the corrupt moon fae we'd dropped into the dungeon cell.

"This is the last time I'm going to tell you this, Duskmere." I met his steely gaze. "If you continue to behave like my sisters and I do not deserve your respect, or should be brought in on matters that might put us in harm's way, do not ask for our help again."

Clenching the crystal in my fist, I cut off the connection.

"You sure do know how to get under Duskmere's skin." Mae chuckled weakly and leaned her full body weight against the chair railing. Her scrunched forehead and pursed lips drew exhaustion on her face with grooves and lines.

I went to her and took her hands in mine. "Hey, are you okay? That was a lot, and I think what you did got lost in the mix. You...you just harnessed the sun as a weapon."

Sun magic was defensive magic. Effective and powerful but wielded for protection in battle. Moon fae magic was the opposite. It was the reason those who did not fall to the corruption during the Great Fae Divide were welcomed into Eodrom. The two races were bound together, and why my father strove so hard create a hybrid magic. I wondered what he would make of what happened today.

"No," she said, smiling. "The sun harnessed me. Or it used the death magic trapped in my shield. I'm not sure."

"You should rest."

Mae shook her head. "I need to talk to Iola and father, but I do need to clean up. For once, I smell like you."

I made a face.

"You do normally smell like Eau de Death," Y'sindra quipped as she fluttered to the top of the stairs. "You know; blood, guts, more blood."

The spray of gore across the front of my leg was testament to their words. "I was doing so well today. And this was not my fault."

"We both did tell you three full grown fae would be too much mass for the portal." Mae shook her head.

"Well, one thing I can say is I never smelled like barbecued fae," I snapped.

"I distinctly remember—"

"I can't help it he wasn't watching where he was running!" I glared up at Y'sindra. "He ran right into that bonfire."

"Ha." She bobbed in the air. "Because you were chasing him with a sword."

"If he—" My cell phone rang. I clacked my mouth shut and went to the coffee table where I'd unloaded my pockets.

SUGAR BUNS lit up the small screen. The tension knots in my back unwound. I swiped a finger on the little green telephone icon. "Hey, you," I said and glanced at the clock. "Home soon?"

"No." Teddy's sigh held weight. "Things are worse than we thought."

Hearing his words, his tone, the knots returned and then some. I met my sisters' gazes. "What happened?"

Instantly, both of my sisters returned to the room.

"Is Lo okay?" Y'sindra alternated between hopping and hovering.

"Putting you on speaker." I held the phone between the three of us. "What happened?"

"First, he's fine, Y'sindra." As bone-deep weary as Teddy's sounded, the smile in his voice was evident. "Everyone is fine."

A soft scraping sound followed by a long breath came through the phone, and I could virtually picture Teddy scrubbing his face.

Tapping my toe, I stared at the phone and waited.

"That's about to come down. Get away from there," Teddy bellowed.

I winced, my gaze flying to my sisters. Mae shrugged and I returned the gesture. *What the seven layers of bean dip is going on?*

"Everyone is fine, but everything is obviously not," I said, since Teddy seemed to have forgotten he was on the phone. "What happened?"

"Sorry, let me step outside." He let out a humorless laugh.

Strange reaction. My brows pinched. Background voices faded quickly.

"The bar is gone."

Nerves tingling, muscles pinching, I gasped. "Gone? How?"

"Did it get up and run away?" Y'sindra asked.

Mae and I glared at her.

"Right, not the time." She scrunched her nose. "Sorry."

"Don't worry about it." Teddy chuckled. "Humor is exactly what we need around here right now. The building isn't completely gone, but two walls and most of the roof are ash."

Shock sucker punched the breath right out of me. I met my sister's equally startled expressions and asked, "How? When?"

"They'd just gotten the fire under control when they called earlier."

"Shit, electrical fire?" Despite Dexter's claim, fireballs did not fall from the sky. However, due to crappy wiring, electrical fires weren't uncommon in Interlands, and every time they happened, the already outrageous cost of electricity went higher.

"No." Teddy did not elaborate.

The lack of explanation felt like a gathering storm. The dark clouds were scraping across the horizon, but the ferocity of what hid behind them was unknown.

Fae light illuminated the bar, but surely electricity was needed for other aspects. "If not electrical, do you know how it started?"

"I do."

I wanted to have empathy. I *did* have empathy, but damn, he needed to spit it out! "I have to assume there is a reason you aren't telling me what that reason is."

"Dacian," Teddy ground out the name. "My dear brother happened."

23

WE WERE SET UP

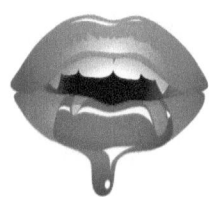

THE PORCH I DEARLY LOVED, WHERE I'D SHARED SO MANY SPECIAL moments with my sisters, with Teddy, had crumbled in on itself.

We sped past the horrible sight so fast I jumped the curb into the parking lot. My trusty Bronco shimmied through the sharp turn. Only Teddy's Jeep filled a spot at the far end of the large gravel lot. All other vehicles had been relegated to further down the street.

Along the bar's wall closest to where we'd parked had been turned to ash. Some of the back wall remained. The roof was a dome of blackened ribs, open to the elements. Only the wall furthest from the parking lot remained fully intact, reminding me of a life-sized diorama. People moved around inside the sodden remains of the bar's interior, sifting and sorting debris. Fortunately, the furniture and beautifully carved bar appeared untouched.

"Teddy wasn't kidding about being lucky there'd been a water mage here." I pocketed the keys and looked at Y'sindra. Mae had wanted to join us, but I put my foot down and insisted she visit Eodrom. She needed to speak to our father and Iola more than she needed to be on a cleanup crew.

"Someone needs to descale that wyvern." Y'sindra flung open the passenger door. "I'm going to find Lo."

I followed, hopping down from the Bronco, and was immediately assaulted by a soggy, acrid scent. A stench so thick it clung to the back of my throat. The smell of woodfire was divine, but this was not that.

An ogre spotted me. He lumbered from the rubble, a large slab of wood tucked under his arm.

Nose scrunching against the unpleasant odors, I started forward and met Rip halfway. "Hey, big guy. What's up?"

His hairless brow rippled. "Fire. Fire is up."

"So I heard." I jutted my chin toward the wooden plank pressed against his side. "You taking a souvenir?"

"Yous know I's moving to the new bar?"

"I do."

Rip held the wooden plank toward me. One of his conical, chameleon-like eyes rotated toward the burned-out bar, while the other fixed on the piece of wood. I smiled sadly at the plaque affixed to the wood.

"Teddy said I could take for the new bar." The enormous ogre drew his fingers over his name on the sooty brass plaque declaring the booth his with unexpected gentleness. He turned his face toward the bar. "I's miss this place."

"Yeah, me too." I'd run my business from this bar right up until we relocated to the penthouse. At least once a week, I still did. Business in Interlands hadn't stopped after we made the move. If anything, it had picked up. "See you on the other side. Be prepared. The place is fancy."

Showing his big blocky teeth, including a substantial chip in the front, Rip grinned. "I's can do fancy. Yous see." He tapped his neck. "I's have bowtie. Special made."

I said my goodbyes and hurried toward the bar, needing to find Teddy. I stepped from the gravel lot across the ashy remains of the wall and shimmed between two of the still-standing booths. It was a tight squeeze, and soot drew a dark line across my belly and no doubt my butt.

A thin layer of gray water swirled over the hardwood floors and splashed beneath my steps. I grimaced. Even if Teddy decided to rebuild, everything but maybe the bar would need to be replaced.

The saddle seat of my usual stool was filthy and wet. I drew my finger through the thin layer of ash as I rounded the bar and was greeted by a spectacular view. Bent over, back to me, my sugar buns transferred bottles to boxes. I took my time appreciating the view. Pursing my lips, I let out a low whistle.

Teddy turned to smile up at me. He laid the rag he'd been using to clean the bottles over the edge of the box and brushed his hands together as he rose. "Hey, you."

Without hesitation, I walked into his arms and laid my cheek against his chest.

"I'm filthy," he said.

"I don't care." I squeezed tight and then stepped back in the loose circle of his arms. "How can I help?"

He grabbed a towel from the bar, took my hand, and led me toward a table in an area that appeared to have been cleared out. Without releasing my hand, he wiped a seat clean and sat. He pulled me onto his lap, as if he needed the connection.

I happily obliged.

"I'm sorry," I said. "You can get this place rebuilt in no time. I bet we can borrow the construction crew that worked on *Blood and Wine*."

Arms draped around my waist, he used his thumbs to swirl a lazy pattern on my hip. "I know. I'm not upset about the bar."

Despite being seated on his legs, our height difference put us at eye level. I studied his expression. All I could read was sincerity. "If you aren't upset, what's wrong?"

"I'm angry." A muscle ticked at the corner of Teddy's tightly clenched jaw. "It's pure dumb luck the water mages stopped for a drink on their way to the tower."

Water mages were paid well to keep Interlands in clean water, and they normally came on the first day of the month, which today was not. Dumb luck, indeed.

"According to Dexter, they're the reason the interior went untouched, while the walls burned hot and fast." Teddy looked at a group of men who looked like bikers, because they were. But they were also water mages, and they had stuck around to help with the cleanup. "From now on, those guys drink free."

"Anyone injured?" Or killed?

"Thankfully, no. A few minor burns, one twisted ankle, but that's all. The fire came in from above, burning the roof and most of the walls before anyone knew what was happening. I suspect an accelerant was poured first and the fire followed." Teddy tapped his foot in the thin layer of water. "I was told the water mages reacted quickly. Dexter did something as well, but I'm unclear what."

As if summoned by the mention of his name, Dexter carried several empty boxes in from the street and lined them up on the bar.

"That guy is an enigma." One I would eventually figure out. I turned my head to the roof and then the walls, taking in the destruction. At last, I addressed the wyvern in the room. "What makes you think it was your brother?"

A thin red line pulsed around Teddy's irises. The black wolf was near the surface. Angry had been a gross understatement. "Someone saw a dragon in the sky. No one around here would know the difference between a dragon and a wyvern, but you and I know it was Dacian."

It explained why he'd not been with Hielmal. But that paved the way for much more troubling thoughts.

"Hey." Teddy gave me a quick squeeze. "You went stiff. What are you thinking?"

Taking his face between my palms, I kissed him. Right in front of everyone. It was slow and deep...and necessary. When I pulled away, I tipped my forehead against his. "I think we were set up."

"Go on," he said.

I stood and waved over Y'sindra and Lo. While they flew toward us, I wiped the rest of the chairs clean and took the seat adjacent to Teddy.

"Ain't this some shit?" My sister stepped from the tabletop into the seat across from me holding what looked like an unopened jar of maraschino cherries. She looked at Teddy while she unscrewed the cap. "They probably have a smoky flavor. I figured you wouldn't mind."

"I doubt smoke can make its way through glass, but no, I don't mind."

"Right on." She shoved a fistful of bright red cherries into her mouth.

Ignoring my completely inappropriate sister, I watched Lo. He was his usual smiley, if extra-dirty, self. Pulling my lower lip beneath a fang, I turned back to Y'sindra. "Have you told him?"

"She did," Lo answered for my sister and slid the pendant and chain she'd taken from Enode's corpse onto the table.

"You okay?" I asked.

"I am. Ted-D helped me understand there was no bringing my brother back." He traced a finger over the pendant. "This represents the oath my family takes to the Barbout they are bound to. Enode would have never betrayed Dacian."

"Aw, buddy. I'm so sorry." Teddy's big hand engulfed Lo's small fist over the pendant. "He was still your brother, and I know he meant something to you. I will go with you to return this to your family, if you would like."

"I would. Thank you, Ted-D." Lo's big round eyes were luminous.

Y'sindra kissed his cheek, which blew my mind.

Lo smiled at her and then to the rest of us. "I'm okay. Really."

I wasn't so sure, but he was putting on a brave face, and we'd let him.

Taking a deep breath, Teddy turned to me. "So, you think you were set up?"

"First, I think the fire was intentional." I tapped my talons on the tabletop.

"Obviously," Teddy drawled. A smile kicked up the corner of his mouth, and I was amazed even now, he could find humor.

"I mean, the timing was intentional."

The metal lid from my sister's confiscated jar of cherries clattered on the table. Catching onto my train of thought, Y'sindra stared at me, open-mouthed.

Beneath my palms, the table was hot, from the sun and lack of roof, not the fire. I made small, swirling motions with my hands flat on the tabletop as I formulated my thoughts. "It started with the food poisoning. I don't know how, but I suspect the RFG ceremony attendees were dosed with something. Dacian was sent to the bar so you wouldn't be in Outerlands."

Y'sindra stood in her chair, screwing the lid onto the confiscated jar. "I see where you're going. I agree, but how did they know the three of us would be there?"

"They probably didn't." I sat back and threaded my fingers behind my neck, thinking my thoughts through as I said them aloud. "They knew patrols were often in pairs, so they were rolling the dice on which of us showed up."

"Pretty sure they didn't know about the fairies," Y'sindra said.

"You're right." I tilted my head, considering. "I wouldn't have known if ahwal'Tam hadn't shown up. I'm pretty sure Hielmal's plan was to grab Mae if she was there or use us as leverage to bring Mae to her if she wasn't."

Reaching for the cherry jar, Teddy popped one in his mouth. "Let me make sure I understand. You are saying somehow Hielmal and my brother found a way to incapacitate the entire Royal Fae Guard, keep me from going with you to Outerlands, all so they could grab Mae or one of you so they could draw Mae to their side?"

I looked across the table to Y'sindra. We shrugged at one another. "Yeah, pretty much."

Teddy laughed. Once, twice, slowly building to great guffaws. It was infectious. I laughed. Y'sindra laughed. Lo looked confused, but he laughed.

Shaking his head, Teddy dragged a finger beneath his eyes and then stretched his arms up and behind him. "Man, I wish I could be there when Dacian realizes what happened to Hielmal and Enode."

A smirk kicked up the corner of my mouth and I told Teddy what I'd sent to Duskmere.

The soothing scent of lavender washed over me, and a shadow fell across the table. Y'sindra looked past me and began laughing all over again.

I twisted in my seat to find an extremely out of place, Fate. She faced the bar, watching Dexter.

"You here looking for a date?" I asked dryly.

She jumped and a deep red blush burned up her chest. "Oh, no. I was just...I was looking for you, but it seems I might be too late."

"Oh?" Without thinking, I hooked a foot around a neighboring table's chair and pulled it to us. Either I was tired, or I'd given up on hating the world. "Have a seat. Tell me why you're here."

Ever the gentleman, Teddy grabbed the towel and wiped off the seat. The white cotton came away with a thick streak of black. *Oops.*

"Thank you." Pastel skirts swirling, Fate dropped into the chair. Placing her palms flat on her thighs, fingers splayed, she slowly lifted and dropped her fingers—pinkie to index—in a rolling wave motion. She craned her neck, looking this way and that, taking in the damage.

I cleared my throat. "How did you find me? *Why* did you find me?"

A tentative smile teased her lips. "The how is simple. Duskmere placed a call to Maerwen. She told me where you were and told me to use your father's portal to come to her at your Las Vegas home. From there, she gave me one of your father's ingenious portable devices so I may return to Ta'Vale when I am done here. She then brought me to the front desk where they agreed to transport me to this location."

"It's a short drive." Depending on the time of day and traffic, using the portal to the Interlands house and driving from there could take longer. "You must have called Mae right after we left."

"Yes." Fate nodded, her long blue curls sliding on her shoulders. "Your sister said I just missed you."

"Okay that's the how but more importantly, why?" I shifted sideways to face her. "I didn't think there was anything left to be said. You told me not to come home, I agreed."

"I saw...." she lifted her hands and gave an expansive wave to encompass the burned-out bar. "Not this exactly, you know how a *see* works."

"I don't," I said. "I really don't."

Smiling, she shook her head. "You never did."

"She's hardheaded like that," Y'sindra said.

Before I could launch into a rebuttal, Teddy placed a hand on my knee and asked Fate, "Will you explain?"

"Yes, I can try." Turning her gaze to her lap, thick waves of hair fell forward. She tucked it behind the delicate, tapered points of her ears. A silver loop winked in the sunlight filtering in from above. She took a slow breath and looked up, meeting all of our eyes but ending with me. "It isn't a clear picture as the name implies. Often, it's just a feeling, something I know. If an image does come, it's an abstract impression I must interpret."

"You're good at detecting lies," I complained. "I remember that."

Fate grinned. "You always tested me. But yes, our ability to *see* untruths is our primary purpose."

Which was why, not so long ago, Torneh and Iola had considered bringing in the Iomas to read the residents of Eodrom to locate the traitors in their midst.

"But you saw something?" Y'sindra asked.

Fascinated, Lo scooted to the edge of his seat. "What did you *see?*"

"Mostly colors, with a few flashes of abstract images." Fate leaned forward and tapped Enode's pendant. "I saw this, but there was blood and fire."

Lo gasped.

Surprise burst through me like a shock of electricity. "The pendant links Enode and Dacian. Enode was killed. That was the blood. Dacian set fire to the bar."

Fate nodded slowly. "This makes sense."

"Okay, cool, but how did you link all of this to me?"

"I didn't," she answered.

"Why, in Freya's frozen fruitcakes are you here then?" Y'sindra's forehead puckered.

I raised my hand. "I'd love to know that too."

"Duskmere," Fate answered.

"Ugh," I groaned. "It's always that guy."

"That troll-licker is a piece of work." Y'sindra kicked the table. "Ow! What are these things made of?"

Teddy snorted a laugh. "Wood."

"You misunderstand." Fate leaned toward me but stopped short of touching my hand. "Rather, I did not explain well. I was visiting with Iola when Duskmere arrived to speak with Torneh. He reported due to an illness brought on by the tainted food he placed a request with Maerwen for YML Investigations to take over patrol on the Shadwe border."

My brows climbed in disbelief. "You know what YML Investigations meant?"

The look she gave me implied I was a stupid question to ask. "I know you and your sisters—Y'sindra, Maerwen, and Lane—and I know you have always favored Lane to Malaney. After you returned the sun stones, everyone in Eodrom is aware you have an investigative business. So yes, I knew what he meant."

"Well, when you say it like that," I mumbled.

"When Duskmere mentioned the tainted food, something felt false. Not from him, but..." She pursed her lips.

Fate was here, confirming suspicions I already held. "I don't think it was an accident, either."

"Duskmere concluded the food was tainted by something in your father's shipment mixed in with the food." Fate pinched her lip in thought, and then shook her head. "That part felt truthful, so I did not press the matter."

Sitting back, I stretched my legs out in front of me and crossed my ankles. "It's possible both things are true."

"Come again?" Y'sindra asked.

"Someone might have intentionally mixed our father's spell ingredients in with the food shipment intended for the RFG banquet."

Eyes rounding, Y'sindra scooted forward. "Someone would have to know what Dad ordered."

"Precisely," I said and hooked a thumb toward Fate. "She was right when she said something, or someone was still up to no good in Eodrom."

Fate smoothed the folds of her skirt across her lap. "Those weren't my precise words."

I shrugged. "Close enough. But how did you link any of this to me?"

"It was the mention of YML Investigations." Fate shrugged. "I thought of you, and I fell into a *see*. The feeling of something dark and dangerous being set in your path was overwhelming. I wanted to warn you."

"That's...considerate." I gave her a sideways look. "Duskmere could have called."

"He did. He called Maerwen."

"No one was concerned about the dark and dangerous bit?" I was annoyed, but not really surprised.

Lips pressing together, Fate shook her head. "Duskmere believes all of the major threats within Eodrom have been dealt with."

I snorted. "And at the border, now. You were right. We were ambushed. Hiemal and Dacian's spy have been dealt with."

"It seems you have handled everything. I should return." Fate patted her thighs and stood. "You should not. The bridge appeared within the collage of images that included that pendant."

On impulse I stood. "I appreciate you coming. For someone who until recently probably never stepped outside of Ta'Vale, I know this wasn't as easy as you made it sound."

"I've always been curious." She smiled shyly.

"We should catch up," I said, shocking everyone, including myself. "Maybe for the grand opening of Teddy's new bar?"

"I would like that." Fate withdrew one of our father's portal devices from a small bag slung diagonal across her chest and turned toward the missing wall. She stopped and looked again at the bar and Dexter. "You always were sneaky. No one knows you found the moon fae prince."

Maybe Fate wasn't such a good Iomas after all. "Old news. I sent Miro to the dungeon months ago. Please don't say you're here to tell me he escaped?"

"What? Stars, no." She pointed to Dexter. "The missing moon fae prince. You found him."

24

TWO RUNAWAY PRINCES

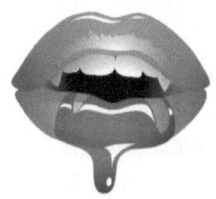

"You didn't know?" I asked Teddy.

He rubbed a hand thoughtfully over his stubbled chin and shook his head. "I knew there was something different about the guy, but I had no idea how different."

"Right, well, you see the irony, don't you?"

"Irony?" Teddy regarded me with his head tipped back.

"Two runaway princes. One bar?"

Laughing, he leaned down for a quick kiss then spun me and patted my ass. "Go save Dex from your sister. We'll head home when you're done."

Adding an extra swish to my hips for Teddy to appreciate, I made my way across the room. I was rewarded by the deep, melted chocolate chuckle I loved.

Standing atop the bar, Y'sindra stared at Dexter, giving him the crazy eyes. One brow arched, the other slanted over her scrunched eye. "You don't look very royal," she declared, and looked at me when I leaned against the counter. "Does he look royal to you?

I shrugged. If I'd learned anything in my short life, it was to believe Fate. That blue-haired bane of my existence, and apparently also my friend, just knew things. Weirdly, though, she often didn't know why she knew things. Socially oblivious, she also wasn't aware everyone around her didn't know those things.

"Moon fae prince, hmm?" I tapped my index finger on the bar top. "Why have I never heard of you?"

Dexter tossed a dirty rag on the bar and tucked his hands into the front pockets of his jeans. His pale pink shirt, damp from sweat and who knew what else, highlighted the muscled wall of his chest and sharply defined, lean torso. It was easy to see why he was a bar patron favorite.

"Because everyone assumes I was either dragged to Shadwe with my brother or died during the migration from the Lann Ridge to the Grian Valley."

My tapping talons came to a standstill. "I wasn't there, but I've heard."

By all accounts, the roads between Dealga and Eodrom—the moon fae and sun fae palaces—were littered with the corpses of moon fae who'd attempted to flee the rule of the corrupt both before and during the war.

"You must have been young." A knot formed in my chest realizing what this easy-going, fun-loving jokester had been through. To not bear the taint of corruption and have gone unnoticed by the sun fae when he arrived in Ta'Vale, he had to of been extremely young. Much younger than I had been when I left home.

Absently, he took up the rag and wiped lazy circles on the already clean counter. "I was. It was easy to get lost in the crowd. Since I never appeared with my family in Dealga, no one knew my face."

"I can't believe no one recognized you," I said. "None of the royal fae guard? None of the court?"

"Nah. They knew I existed, they asked questions, but no one outside of family and close advisors knew what I looked like, and they were all dead or exiled." He shot me a sly look. "I've heard you were a lot like me. You avoided court."

"You'd have a better chance of convincing Lane to poke a bukbah hive than stepping foot in court," Y'sindra told him.

"If no one knew who you were, why'd you leave?" I watched him closely, trying to gauge his emotions.

A groove appeared between Dexter's brows, and his eyes tightened. "Too many questions, and I got tired of lying. It was either admit who I was or get out."

I thought of the moon fae I'd met in Uru, the new home they'd made for themselves within Eodrom. "Your people could use you."

"My people?" he laughed, not unkindly. "I'm just a moon fae with paltry magic. I have no idea how your friend knew who I was."

"She's an Ioma. She knows things." And I wouldn't call his magic paltry.

Excitement lit his expression, chasing away the momentary glimpse of sadness I'd seen. "Cool, never met one of them before. Still, I promise there isn't a moon fae alive who believes I exist this side of Shadwe."

"All the more reason to surprise them." Y'sindra stood and hopped from the bar to a stool, barely keeping her balance. "You don't have to, but it might be fun, and I bet our dad would love to meet you. Magic is his jam."

My sister and I shared a look. She took pity on abandoned things for a reason, and for once, she didn't have a snide word. With a wink, she hopped to the floor and water splashed up her legs. She let loose a string of colorful curses and took wing. Cussing and dripping water as she went, she flew through the open wall to where Lo waited in the parking lot.

Dexter chuckled. "Your sister is something else."

"You have no idea." I studied him. Until this moment, I hadn't known another moon fae prince existed. "May I ask what your name is?"

He tipped his face to the side and smiled. "It's Dexter."

Whether he was born with that name or assumed that name, it was the name he wanted. I'd respect that.

Changing the subject, I gestured to the thin layer of water on the floor and asked, "You can do more than what you did, can't you?"

The devilish look he gave me would have curled my toes, if it wasn't for my super sexy sugar buns busy hauling tables out of the standing water.

"I knew it!"

He laughed. "I'm pulling your leg. I can feel the magic inside me, but the best I can do with it is a few party tricks."

"Would you like to do more?" I asked, growing serious. "Y'sindra was right. My father would sell a piece of his soul—which for him means a lot of sun stones—to talk magic with you. He's the chief royal wizard, and a damn good teacher when it comes to magic."

"Oh yeah?" Dexter leaned his palms on the bar. Genuine interest lit his face, and he hadn't outright said no.

"Do you want to learn? I don't have to tell him who you are."

He bit his lip. "I..." Dexter looked around the bar. "If I knew more about my magic, I probably could have done a lot more to help. Yeah, I think I'd like that. It doesn't matter if he knows who I am, I've not been hiding or anything. When I left Eodrom, I was scared. I'm not anymore. It all happened a long time ago, and Ta'Vale is no longer my home."

"Don't need to convince me. You're preaching to the choir on that one." I pushed away from the bar but paused. "Does Blackthorne know who you are?"

Dexter pulled an empty box toward himself. He took a deep breath, his gaze following the motion of his hand as he wiped down a bottle of some sort of clear liquor and put it in the box. "He's never said anything, but I get the feeling he does."

"That sly old druid knows everything." I wrapped my knuckles on the counter. "Good chat. Expect Mae to show up as soon as she finds out who you are."

Outside, Y'sindra had the driver's door open, and was digging around for something inside. I angled away from where Teddy was staging what appeared to be the last of the furniture from inside, and instead strode for my sister.

"What are you doing?" I asked and banged on the hood. She screeched and tumbled backwards from the SUV. Wings flapping furiously, spraying snow, she caught herself just before she hit the ground and glared up at me. "Just testing your wing strength." I grinned and gave her a thumbs up. "Doing good."

Lo giggled. He'd finally caught on to the fact we did not hate each other. These barbs and taunts were how we expressed our affection. Poor guy used to get so upset.

Rolling her shoulders, Y'sindra worked her wings. "Mom's salve smelled like dung, but it worked. I finally understand how bad the medicine you drink must taste."

"So bad," I agreed and pointed to the open Bronco door. "What were you doing?"

"Oh, that." She looked to the ground and then inside the SUV. Finally, she reached in to grab something from the footwell. A glint of amber caught the light, and I knew immediately what she had—one of our father's portal devices.

"Did that fall out?" We were missing a lot more disks than I believed we'd used. Were we losing them? I patted my pockets but found all the devices I'd brought with me to Outerlands where they were meant to be.

White curls bouncing, Y'sindra shook her head. "Nah, I brought this one, but it must have fallen out of my pocket on the ride over."

Which made my theory plausible.

"I don't think there's anything here for me to do, but let me check with Teddy." I swung the Bronco's door shut.

"Lane," Y'sindra said. The seriousness of her tone had my full attention. "Lo and I are heading back to Outerlands. We're going to check in on the snow fairies. Since my secret's out, you might as well know we moved into Lo's rooms above Teddy's old bar."

Pressure built behind my eyeballs. This was the thing I'd feared all along. The beginning of the end. I nodded. "I'll miss you, but I'm proud of you."

Y'sindra guffawed. "Do you think you're getting rid of me? I'm milking the penthouse for everything it's got until Blackthorne decides to come back and give us the boot."

The weird emotional tickle in my nose from aborted tears pissed me off. "You just said you moved into Teddy's old bar."

"It's like a second house. Or third, I guess, if you count the place here." She grinned up at me. "Look at your face. Your nose is all red. You really luff me."

She fluttered up to pat my cheeks. I half-heartedly swiped at her.

"It's allergies." I sniffled. "So, what did you name your clan?"

She stopped trying to pinch my nose and scowled. "I don't have a clan."

"Okay, Ellri." I rolled my eyes. "Maybe you need to tell your snow fairies."

Lips pursed, she turned away. "I only taught them how to survive outside of the mountains. Lane, you should have seen how they were living."

Her voice broke off. An ache built in my chest seeing my strong-as-steel sister emotional.

"There are so many living in the mountains, on the edge of death, but no one knows. They hide because they have no means to protect themselves. With no magic, they're vulnerable." She swallowed. "If traders catch them, they take their wings. Their wings!"

Gasping, my hands flew to my mouth while my gaze snapped to her newly reformed wing. For several heartbeats, we stared at one another. The fury and anguish in her eyes nearly broke me. I knelt and took her hands in mine. "I meant it, I'm so proud of you. What you are doing is amazing."

She stared at her feet as she ran her toe through the gravel, back and forth, drawing a line. "I only find them and teach them how to summon their magic. With patience, the same way Dad did, not the archaic life-or-death method the clans use."

I squeezed her hands and stood, brushing away bits of gravel stuck to my knees. "Don't be so humble. You are giving them a life."

"I'm doing all right. You saw the amount of magic they have. Most can't do more than summon a few ice pebbles." A pink so deep it was nearly neon burst across her cheeks.

"It's enough they can survive outside the Driftas."

She nodded. "I'm going to ask Dad to help."

Thinking of Dexter, I looked toward the bar and grinned. "He's going to have more magic pupils than he'll know what to do with."

"It's his happy place. He might even crack a smile." She tossed the portal device to the ground and held her hand out for Lo who took it without hesitation. "We're just making sure everyone is okay. I'll be back for dinner."

She activated the portal and left. I went in search of Teddy, feeling like I'd shed a thousand pounds of emotional baggage. Y'sindra was gone more often than she was home. I hadn't known what she'd been up to, but I'd anticipated the worst. Instead, she'd been out there being a real-life superhero.

Halfway across the lot, Teddy stepped outside. He smiled and waved before heading in my direction.

Still riding the emotional high from Y'sindra's news, my hearts performed a little tap dance. I didn't know what forsaken god had their eye on me, but I'd really hit the sisterly jackpot.

"Hi," I said, walking into Teddy's arms.

He curled a finger beneath my chin and tipped my face toward his. "Hi," he said and then came in for a kiss. It was slow and gentle. He ended the soft exploration, brushing his thumb over my lower lip. "That looked like a serious conversation. Are you okay?"

Patches of soot and debris were so thick on his shirt, the original color was indiscernible. I didn't care. I rested my cheek against his chest. "Better than okay. I'll tell you about it when we get home later."

"How about on the drive home? If you don't mind talking about it in front of Zee."

"No portal?"

He shook his head. "I drove, remember? You can leave the Bronco in the lot. I'll take it to your house later this week."

"Okay." Stepping back, I looked at the bar. The furniture had all been stacked in the parking lot. A cluster of employees carried a tarp toward the only pieces still vulnerable to the elements. "Are you done?"

"Yes. We're lucky, everything inside is fine. It's just structural damage. All the staff showed up to help as did other businesses on the street."

In his now filthy uniform of white button up top and crisp khakis, I spotted the grocery store owner returning to his shop. A guy meticulous about his appearance had jumped right in to help. The owner of the only movie theater in Interlands had tied her skirts above her knees and waded in along with several of her employees. They, along with Teddy's competition, the owner and staff of a bar down the street, were all slowly returning to their business.

This place might be full of degenerates, but they were degenerates who had each other's backs. I smiled at the thought.

"I'm sorry this happened," I told him, watching Zee step from the building and veer in our direction.

Teddy snorted. "He's my brother."

"But he's our problem." I slid my arm around his middle, hugging him to my side as I turned us to both to face Zee.

"Am I interrupting?" Zee looked between us.

"Just ruminating on the many ways to scale a wyvern," I said.

"Count me in." She grinned and then looked at Teddy. "You can just drop me at my place."

"Don't be silly, we have plenty of room," I told her. "Plus, my sisters will kill me if I come home without you."

Holding his hands up in surrender, Teddy backed away. "I only do as Lane commands."

Zee shook her head at me and laughed. "You're the best, babes. Right, I'll stick around on one condition."

"I'm sorry. I didn't realize the penthouse was such a hardship," I teased.

"It's not, but imposing is. Ever noticed the *lone* part in lone wolf?" She arched a brow. "I appreciate all you and your sisters do, but I'm a control freak."

"Let's walk and talk." Teddy led us toward his Jeep.

The gravel hissed beneath our steps. "I understand," I said at last. "What's your condition?"

"Since I'll be working at the new bar, it makes sense for me to move into the hotel too. As soon as an apartment opens, I'm out of the penthouse."

Not what I'd been expecting. Zee opened the rear passenger door, gave me a wink, and hopped into the SUV. I scrambled into the Jeep and turned in my seat to face her. The vehicle dipped slightly as Teddy slid into the driver's seat.

Kneeling on my seat, I curled my hands over the headrest. "You want to live at the Blackthorne?"

"Road's bumpy, Lane. You shouldn't sit like that." Teddy started the Jeep.

"What a mom thing to—"

We pulled out of the parking lot, the front right tire dropping into a deep rut. My knees momentarily lost contact with the seat. My head thumped the roof and my teeth clacked together. Somehow, I didn't bite my tongue.

Glaring at Teddy's profile, I planted my butt in the seat and snapped the seatbelt in place. "You did that on purpose."

The corner of his mouth curled. "I would never."

25

BIGGER AND BADDER

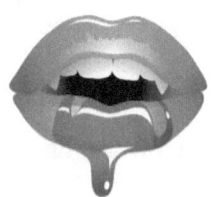

Teddy's black Jeep idled in stops and starts down Las Vegas Boulevard. Ever since the walking overpasses had been built along the strip, there were less pedestrians crossing the boulevard, but plenty still moved along the wide sidewalks and flooded the crosswalks. Vehicles clogged the streets.

We'd worked until dusk, and the Strip was coming alive with bright lights and glammed up tourists on their way to a show or dinner or both.

I popped off my shoes and drew my legs up in the passenger seat. Wedging my right foot flat on my seat, my arm draped over my right knee, I twisted to look at Zee. "So, let me see if I understand this. Your dad has no pack, but all other pack alphas answer to him?"

"In North America, yes."

"And Mexico?"

"Yeah." Zee flopped back against her seat. "Sort of. It's a whole political thing. Some answer to the South American Vargr, some my father."

"Your father, Hati Gunnulf, the son of Fenrir?" I reached between the seats and slapped her knee. "Wait until I tell Y'sindra. She will die. We're talking turn to fairy dust, die. You know she grew up in the Drifta Mountains where a lot of Norse deities settled after their world fell during Ragnarök?"

It occurred to me then every world had some sort of world-altering war, but I'd never heard of one in Shadwe. Had I figured out the purpose of the black wolf? A ripple of unease fluttered in my belly.

"Named after," Zee said, pulling me back to our conversation. "He's named after Fenrir's son."

"Brothers or sisters?" I asked.

"Two brothers. I'm the youngest." She flashed a grin full of teeth. Very wolfy. "I'm the trouble pup."

"Okay, so you're what? Third in line? A wolf princess?"

"A what? Girl, have you lost your mind?" Zee tilted her head and made a face. "Do I seem like a princess?"

"But you're in line to inherit your father's title? Sounds pretty princess-y to me."

"I'm going to agree with Lane on this one," Teddy chimed in.

"I didn't ask." Zee scowled at the back of his head but added, "Boss."

Beneath his breath, Teddy chuckled and shot me a wink. Warmth—the feeling of home—flooded me, all the way to my toes, which I wiggled inside my socks.

I shook my head at my world-ending musings. Teddy was no impending apocalypse. The only thing he threatened were my hearts if he ever chose to leave.

We pulled through a stoplight but quickly joined a long line of idling vehicles at the next.

Curiosity still unabated, I turned back to Zee. "When your brothers take over the Vargr title, will they force you to come home, wherever that is?" Something clenched in my chest. For nearly ten years, Zee had been a background character in my life, but she was my friend. With my sisters' slow slip away, this just added to the chasm of emptiness opening inside of me.

"Colorado," Zee said, pulling me from my emotional slip. "And much to Dad's dismay, they're betas. They won't—can't—become the Vargr."

"If they can't take over your father's title, and you don't want it, what will happen to him? To it?"

She flipped her sooty blonde hair from her shoulders and shrugged. "He's an immortal, so I guess he'll just keep living and being grumpy about it."

My mouth opened, but only a breathy croak came out. I shook my head and made a show of jiggling a knuckle in each ear, as if cleaning it out. "I'm sorry, did you say immortal?"

"Yup."

Brows climbing, I asked, "And that makes you?"

She snorted. "Not immortal."

Teddy looked at Zee in the rearview. "You know that for sure?"

"I mean, I haven't died and lived to tell the tale, but I think I'd feel it if I was." She scrunched her nose. "I would be able to tell, right?"

Not answering, Teddy grinned and eased his foot down on the gas as cars moved ahead.

Zee looked at me. "Right?"

Laughing, I held up my hands. "I'm the wrong fae to ask. I don't even know what I am or how long I'll live. Besides, immortal does not mean unkillable."

She tilted her head to the side. "Fair enough."

Arching my back, I stretched and then pulled both my legs into the seat. "Why not just ask your dad?"

"Asking requires speaking, which we've rarely done since I was sent away at ten to—and I quote—learn werewolf pack politics."

"Ten?" I sat straight. Much younger than when I'd left home. Younger than when Y'sindra had been cast out of her clan. Younger than—I wasn't sure how old Dexter had been when he'd left Eodrom. "And your brothers?"

Ahead on the strip, I saw the Blackthorne towering over its neighbor, the Wynn. We were almost home.

"I barely know them. They'd already been sent to different packs before I was born, and those pack alphas determined they were betas. One still lives with his pack, one returned home to Dad a few years ago." Zee pulled a scrunchie from her pocket and piled her curls into a frizzy bun atop her head. "I won the lucky alpha lotto."

"Your tone is screaming sarcasm."

She snorted. "My tone does not lie. Life in a pack as a second alpha means hostility and constant challenges. It's impossible."

"So, you left."

"It was that or take a pack I didn't want," she confirmed. "Mom was gone, and I didn't want to go back to Dad, so, I wandered. Eventually, I landed in Interlands and stayed."

I poked Teddy in the arm. "Your bar had two princes and a sort-of princess, all under one roof."

"And then there's you," Zee said.

The Blackthorne's driveway appeared between impossibly landscaped planters and a massive marque advertising the casino's sellout shows and restaurants. A splash of gold and crimson announced *Blood and Wine* -*COMING SOON*-.

Teddy steered the car into the outside lane.

"We were all drawn to Teddy, I think. I mean, I was." Zee looked at me and then turned to stare out her window.

Maybe being a lone wolf meant she was lonely. Had Teddy's black wolf felt like an alpha to her? Had something about him felt safe to Dexter too?

"It's like you have a gravitational field tuned to the outcasts," I teased, watching Teddy's profile. I'd certainly fallen into his orbit.

He glanced at me as he turned right, toward the front door of the Blackthorne. "Not outcasts. Misunderstood, maybe."

"Dangerous," Zee said. "We're all considered dangerous, and Teddy here is the only thing bigger and badder than all of us."

Teddy barked a laugh. "Have you met my mate?"

Mate. An electric thrill shot through me. Would I ever tire of that word?

We pulled in front of the Blackthorne's grand entrance. A valet came toward our vehicle. Teddy left the SUV idling while he stepped out and made his way around the front.

"I suppose if anyone can give our boy a run for his money, it's you babes." Zee hopped out, lifting her arms above her head and snaking her spine in a languid stretch.

At Zee's words, an ice bath of reality dumped over me. I remembered Dacian's laughing words. Teddy's explanation. *The black wolf chooses a mate who can end him if he can't come back to himself.*

Never, I promised myself, my gaze meeting Teddy's through the window as he came to my door and opened it.

"Hey." Teddy frowned. He reached inside to cup my chin, stroking a thumb along my jaw. "You okay?"

"Yeah." I tilted my face into his palm.

"You feel a million miles away."

I felt as if I'd gone a million miles away. Smiling, I planted a kiss on his palm and swung my legs out the door, forcing him to back up. "Just thinking about dinner."

"Of course, you were." He threaded his fingers through mine and led me toward the rotating front doors.

Despite an appetite that knew no bounds, I didn't think he bought my explanation, but I appreciated he didn't press for more. He always let me work things out for myself and come to him in my own time.

As soon as we stepped inside, the relentless air conditioning peeled away the oppressive layers of desert heat. Cool air spiked with exotic spices splashed across my senses. We moved toward a wide hallway that led through a parade of high-end shops and ended at the casino floor. There were elevators off the lobby, but only one elevator on the casino floor had access to the penthouse.

Movement pulled my attention toward the reception area. A woman waved furiously in our direction. "Ms. Black!"

"Callaghan," I muttered beneath my breath.

Teddy squeezed my hand. "I'm going to take Zee to *Blood and Wine*, then meet you upstairs."

"Okay," I answered, and tipped my face up for a kiss.

As they headed for the bar, I turned and went to the front desk. The woman who had flagged me down was hurrying from a back room, a familiar vampire in tow.

She smiled at me as Vaughn moved around from behind the counter, heading in my direction.

"Vaughn," I said.

He held a box toward me. "Mr. Black asked I provide you with footage of the two moonbit victims from—"

"Two?" Shock zapped my nervous system, my spine straightened, and shoulders went back. "Why didn't you tell me there was more than Beast?"

"Why would I?" His brows came together. "It was before you took up residence, and as I continue to remind you, you are not the owner. You are not the boss. Mr. Black was immediately made aware of the vampire we lost."

My jaw worked. I chewed on my retort. Vampire—Blackthorne told me about that one. This wasn't something new. "What happened?"

He tapped the box. "It is all on video here. Both incidents in question as well as the week leading up to the events."

"A week leading up to the events? That must be..." I trailed off. The hotel had cutting edge facial recognition. It would have captured every moment they were inside, in view of a camera.

"Thousands of hours, plus the thumb drive you were expecting." He pressed the box toward me until I was forced to take it. Laughter rumbled from his broad chest. "Enjoy."

26

GOOD AT LEARNING LESSONS

I came awake, my arms and legs tangled with Teddy's and the sheets twisted around our torsos. Confused, I blinked at the slip of light coming from the horizon. Unsure what woke me, I slid an arm back across my personal radiator and snuggled against his side.

In seconds, I drifted in that gray space, tumbling toward—

The banging came again. I sat up and threw a glare at the bedroom door. "Someone better be dead!"

"They are," Mae answered.

Leaping from the bed, I ran for the door and yanked it open. "What happened? Is Y'sindra okay?"

Mae's wide eyes dropped to my bare toes and climbed back up my body. She smirked. Vaughn stepped behind her, buttoning the cuffs of his shirt. His fingers froze when he spotted me.

Cold air brushed across my nipples. "Oh my gods!" I threw an arm across my chest and slammed the door in my sister's face. Her musical laughter followed my completely naked ass back into the room.

Hands folded behind his head, Teddy reclined against the headboard, watching me with a half smile. His bent arms highlighted the swell of his biceps. The sheets pooled at his hips just above...

I gave myself a mental slap.

"Forget something?" he drawled.

"No," I snapped and rooted through the piles of clothes next to the bed. "She said someone died."

He yawned. "She didn't say who."

"Blah, blah, I care about my sisters, okay?" I tugged on a pair of black leggings from the small pile. Deep down, I knew this couldn't be about Y'sindra. Mae would have plowed through the door. She wouldn't have knocked. "Maybe a little less after Vaughn just got a view of me naked because of that stunt."

"Lucky man." Teddy chuckled. "Maybe you'll stop making threats when you wake up."

"Probably for the best." If nothing else, I was good at learning lessons. I tugged on a white shirt that read *Bite Me* in bold black letters. *Me* was crossed out and *You* was scrawled in red. My sisters were forever buying me gag gifts, and I loved every single one.

Crawling across the mattress, I gave Teddy a quick kiss. "Not sure what this is about."

He wrapped an arm around my back and pulled me onto his wonderfully naked chest, delivering a much deeper kiss. When his tongue sought entrance, I parted my lips, allowing him in. The heat and flavor of him scattered my urgency.

After too brief a moment, he slowed and pulled back. I sank onto him, really hating the idea of getting up.

"Should I join you?" he asked.

"Nah." I kissed his lips one last time, more than a peck, less than the toe curling, bone melting pleasure he'd just delivered. "It sounds like YML stuff. I'll be down and back in no time." I rolled off the bed and adjusted my clothes. How did I get so rumpled so quickly?

"I'll text if I need to go anywhere before you're back," Teddy assured me, and I headed for the door, grabbing a light jacket as I went because casinos were cold as the Driftas.

Mae and Vaughn were no longer in the hall. They were making out by the elevator. "Ugh, why did you wake me up if this was what you planned?"

Since it wasn't the best idea to traipse through a casino barefoot, I snatched a pair of gray canvas sneakers from the pile next to the door and slipped them on.

"Nice seeing you," Vaughn drawled and pushed the elevator button. "With clothes on."

I sputtered while Mae laughed.

The elevator doors slid open. Looking quite pleased with himself, Vaughn stepped inside.

I crossed my arms and glared.

"Stop being a baby. Don't let him fool you. He liked what he saw." Mae grabbed my elbow and tugged me into the elevator. She turned a look on Vaughn. "Didn't you?"

I rolled my eyes. "I don't actually care."

"You seemed to care," Mae said.

"It's early. I can't be held responsible for my actions, but I assure you, I do not care." Which was the truth. The only opinion I cared about was Teddy's. "It was a shock, that's all."

"Perfectly understandable." Vaughn pressed the casino floor button. "Besides, most of the staff have seen a lot more of you, from several different angles."

"Positions," Mae said with an innocent smile. "He means different positions, Laney. I saw the tape. You're more adventurous than I gave you credit for."

"Oh, gods." I turned away and leaned my forehead against the back wall. Chilly glass cooled the fevered flush of embarrassment consuming my entire body. That damn camera. One romp on the roof with Teddy, and now everyone had seen my bare ass.

The elevator raced downward, its motion so smooth, if it wasn't for the view, I wouldn't believe we were moving. Beyond the glass, a waterfall tumbled down a strategically tiered rock wall. Colorful flowers and vivid green flora bobbed in the water spray. Hired water fairies flitted in and out of the stream, amusing tourists. Y'sindra occasionally joined them, she said, to help regain the muscle strength in her wing. A smile creased my lips, remembering Vaughn's tirade when she froze the waterfall, and the fairies treated it like a slip and slide.

Staring at my face superimposed over the fantastical view, I asked, "Did someone actually die?"

"They did," Vaughn confirmed. In the reflection, I saw him check his watch. "I was notified a half hour ago. The body was moved, fortunately with few witnesses, thanks to the early hour."

The elevator came to a stop and the doors slid open. I pushed away from the wall, following Vaughn and my sister as they strode across the casino floor.

"Another werewolf?" I asked.

"No." Instead of continuing through the walkway all the way to the lobby, Vaughn took a left down a narrow hall. We passed the large, decorative arches that opened to restrooms on either side. At the end of the passage, we reached a plain set of double doors marked Employees Only.

"The bodies are being held here until local authorities clear us to transport the presumed moonbit victim to Mr. Black." Vaughn pushed open the door and bladed his body, allowing Mae and I room to enter.

"What a gentleman," I murmured, and Mae elbowed me.

I thought about Vaughn's use of "presumed" to describe moonbit. Zee had initially believed that while rare, other paranormals were susceptible to moonbit. Was Vaughn repeating the same line he used with the authorities, or did he know the truth?

"Mr. Black suggested I allow you to view the body before he takes custody." Vaughn let the door swing shut behind him and stepped around us to lead the way.

Because I could, I'd explored most of the casino, both the glitzy front and efficient, if sterile, back of the house. I wasn't familiar with the entrance we'd used, but I recognized the direction we took. We were headed to the in-house kitchen and a central storage area which included large communal coolers for the resort restaurants to store new shipments and overflow.

As we continued, I glanced toward Vaughn. "If not a werewolf, who was it?"

"You spoke with Mr. Black. You know this cannot actually be a moonbit victim, correct?" he asked, which wasn't exactly an answer. Not to what I'd asked, but it did answer what I'd just been wondering.

We rounded another corner and moved to one side of the wide hall, allowing a train of employees pushing carts with multiple cloche platters to pass. Room service breakfast. My fingers itched to grab a tray, as did my stomach when it rumbled.

I looked up from the passing food to find Vaughn watching me. Right, he'd asked a question. Or made a statement and expected an answer. "Yes," I answered simply.

One thing I'd learned early in my investigative career, the less information I provided, the more the person I was questioning filled in. I didn't want to overplay my hand, mostly because I doubted Blackthorne had told me everything he knew. I didn't trust anyone beyond Teddy and my sisters—and lately not even them—to ever give me the full truth.

"It will be easier for you to see rather than walk and explain." Vaughn steered us into the large industrial kitchen. Immediately, he peeled away to speak with two members of his staff who had clearly been waiting for us.

Somewhere, food popped and sizzled on a grill. Metal spatulas rang out as they hit cooktops and scraped up food. A deliciously scented melting pot of bacon, sausage, and sugary breakfast treats lulled me toward the kitchen pass. The aroma of fresh baked bread filled the air like a warm hug.

This place was, in my opinion, the fragrant heart of the Blackthorne. It serviced the resort's room service orders twenty-four hours a day, seven days a week. I was on a first name basis with several of the kitchen managers, one of whom spotted me. She smiled and waved. Grabbing a plate, she piled it with their special Billionaire Bacon and presented it to me. At the sight of the thick sliced bacon baked, drowned in maple syrup, sprinkled with a secret recipe, peppery spice blend, and then baked again, my salivary glands kicked into overdrive.

"You know the way to a girl's hearts," I declared, accepting the plate. I was definitely putting in a good word for the chef with Gramps. She deserved a raise.

Vaughn returned and reached for my plate. I bared my fangs. His lip peeled up in an automatic response, flashing his own fangs. They may be bigger, but I was more ruthless, and he knew it.

Shaking his head, he held up his hands and backed toward a large metal door. "I don't think you want a meat snack while you are in a freezer full of corpses."

"There you go thinking." I locked eyes with Vaughn and folded an entire strip of bacon into my mouth.

"Suit yourself." He turned and opened the heavy-duty latch on the door.

"Never fear, my sister has a stomach of steel." Mae patted Vaughn on the chest and strolled past him into the freezer.

"Want some?" I held the plate out toward Vaughn.

He rolled his eyes and shaking his head, trailed behind Mae, letting the door begin to shut behind him.

I shrugged and grabbed another piece as I hip-checked the door to keep it open. Licking the sticky, sweet-and-spicy syrupy coating from my fingers, I wandered to where my sister and her vampire waited by the first sheet-draped body.

Pinching the cover between his index fingers and thumbs, Vaughn waited for me to approach. The white sheet was stained with all shades of wrong; the gray of a wet, white sheet, yellows and browns from who knew what, and red. So much red, I didn't have to lay eyes on the body to know this would be a gnarly sight.

When I reached Vaughn's side, he flipped his wrists dramatically and fanned the sheet off the body, or as much as a sheet soaked with various bodily fluids could fan. Because I knew he was doing this to prove a point, to try to get a rise out of me and my stomach, I leaned in for a closer look while slowly taking another piece of bacon and tearing off a bite. As my sisters often reminded me, I was very immature.

"You are disgusting," he said, tone wielding the same adjective he'd used to describe me.

I grinned, showing off the pig bits stuck to my fangs.

"Lane," Mae snapped. Brow pinched, she shook her head at me. "Many are dead here. Show some respect."

"Sorry," I muttered. Properly chastised, I put the bacon on the plate and the plate on a shelf. Licking my fingers clean, I tore off a paper towel from the roll mounted near the door and dried my digits.

Returning to the table, I looked from Mae to Vaughn. "Sorry," I repeated. "Who do we have here? Is this the *suspected* moonbit?" I repeated his words but threw in air quotes.

Vaughn watched me, as if waiting to see if I had anymore snide remarks. Little did he know, Mae was the sanity-glue holding us sisters together. A pang of worry rose inside me. Rapid fire thoughts of what would happen if—when—my sisters left to do their own thing bombarded my brain, but I shoved all the minutia aside to focus on the task at hand.

Two jagged lines scissored across the dead man's throat. The cuts were so deep, the center where they overlapped had snagged and twisted tissue, muscle, sinew, and every other pink-and-red thing inside a throat. I spotted the tail end of the tongue. My stomach did not approve, but I fought to keep the level of gross factor off my face. A scan of the rest of the body revealed a few puncture wounds in the chest and abdomen. A cream-colored button-up shirt covered the wounds, but the rings of blood gave them away. Judging by the relatively small amount of blood on the torso, it was clear the attack to the throat had come first.

"The victim?" I asked again, relieved by my steady voice.

"We do not know." He pulled the cover over the body and moved to a draped form separated from the rest. "Staff is sorting and bagging belongings to identify these victims."

Scowling, I followed Vaughn's very deliberate path. "You knew that wasn't who you brought me here to examine, didn't you?"

"I did." He began to gently roll the sheet back, showing much more care.

I looked at Mae as I spoke. "That was just for shock value? Because I said I could handle it?"

He grunted and I raised my brows at Mae.

Crossing her arms, she tipped her nose into the air. "You did deserve it."

"Whatever," I mumbled, and rounded the gurney to stand opposite Vaughn. I waited as he finished peeling the blanket to the woman's ankles. He didn't need to tell me who this was, I recognized her. I didn't know her well, couldn't remember her name, but I'd seen her in action on the job.

A middle-aged human who chose to spend most of her time in her office, knitting and watching security footage, was the on-staff clairvoyant.

This woman was, or had been, the reason no one—other than Y'sindra—got away with card counting, or any other method of cheating in the Blackthorne. My sister had been hauled in front of her more than once. Rather than turn her in for freezing the inner mechanisms of slot machines and scoring big wins, the two struck a deal. So maybe she wasn't the best at her job, but it was still a shame. The woman had been harmless.

Harmless. My head whipped toward the body with the torn-up throat.

"I know who this is. How could she possibly have done that?" I jabbed my finger at the mangled corpse. My breath wheezed from my chest as I took in the number of bodies. Nine in total, and all had various splotchy red blobs spaced out over the white sheets covering them.

"With knitting needles, I am told," Vaughn said and had the good grace to grimace as he, too, took in the carnage.

"How?" Mae asked, her voice reflecting the shock I felt. "How was a human of her age, with nothing to enhance her physical abilities, able to dispatch this many other humans?"

"With knitting needles," I added, because seriously, how?

Vaughn rubbed a hand over his face, stretching the skin beneath his eyes.

"I was made aware of several crime scenes. None of these attacks occurred in the same location. She probably caught people alone or in small groups, and shock held their hand long enough for her to do this"— he waved a hand at the covered carnage—"and move on."

Taking a deep breath, I approached the woman. If I didn't count the blood coating her, she looked peaceful. The tangle of scents assaulting my nostrils indicated none, or very little of the blood, was hers. A single gunshot wound punctured her chest.

Slowly, I walked along the side of the gurney, looking for...I wasn't sure what. While I appreciated Blackthorne extending me this opportunity, showing me respect, I had no idea what looking at a dead body would get me.

If everything Gramps said was true, and I had no reason to think it wasn't, this woman had somehow been dosed with a version of the potion that created the blood fae. Many had died then, and they were fae. Human paranormals were coping far worse.

Gently, I pushed up the woman's shirt to examine her torso. Aside from the gunshot, she had no other wounds. I didn't know what the potion had done to her, but she must have had a momentary burst of strength and maybe speed, as Vaughn implied, to overtake all these victims, even if one at a time. Smoothing her shirt back into place, I lifted the woman's arm. It was coated in sticky blood, but she had no wounds. Not even a bruise.

Still unsure what I was looking for, I moved around the body, finding the same thing. No wounds, no bruises. I checked her pockets, all empty. A baggie lay against the woman's side. Bloody knitting needles were tucked inside with bits of what had to be pieces of her victims.

Biting my lip, I was about to step away when my gaze snagged on the oversized knit sweater balled up in another clear bag, tucked by her feet. I held up the bag and looked at Vaughn. "She wasn't wearing this?" Casinos were kept cold, and she wore the sweater—a cardigan, she called it—everywhere, telling anyone who asked she'd knitted it herself.

His brows furrowed. "I don't know. Since it's with the body and not on it, she must have dropped it at one of the scenes."

I sliced through the red sticker sealing the bag with a talon and shook out the beige sweater threaded with colorful bursts of oranges, reds, and blues.

"You shouldn't handle evidence," Vaughn objected.

"Local authorities have my fingerprints on record. They can exclude me." My sisters and I had to supply our prints when we went legit and applied for a P.I. license here on Earth.

The thick yarn was soft and heavy. It had absorbed quite a bit of blood, but not nearly as much as the rest of her clothing. "She must have dropped this early," I murmured, moving to a clean table, and laying it flat. A woman after my own heart, it had several pockets, and I dug into each.

I pulled out a slim, silver case the size of a business card. Setting it on the table, I popped it open and discovered it did, in fact, hold business cards. A small box of mints and a slip of paper with a phone number, damp and stained with blood, were in the next pocket.

A weird mixture of scents rose from the paper. A cloying floral fragrance, like roses gone bad, a mixture of herbs from sharp to subtle, and fruit. Something soft and sweet, not citrus. Who knew how many sources of blood were on that paper? I frowned and held it out to Mae. Most of the numbers were smudged beyond recognition.

"I think it's a local area code." She squinted at the paper. "This could be a three, or maybe a five."

"Careful not to tear the paper. It's still damp," I warned and dug to the bottom of an excessively large pocket. Something bumpy and hard brushed against my fingertips. I wiggled my fingers and rolled the object into my palm. My stomach dropped, and I held the fae communication out for Mae to see. The crystal rolled in my palm, revealing a crack.

Mae pointed to the defect. "We can take it to Duskmere, see if there is a way to figure out who this belongs to."

"Let's see if we can figure it out before we include him in this." I tucked the crystal into my pocket, meeting Vaughn's gaze as I did. "You can write down an inventory of anything I take, but the locals would have no idea what to do with this."

"Agreed," he said, surprising me. "We have a healthy fae client base. That could belong to any of them."

"Fair enough. Did she socialize with fae?"

A small, sad smile pulled at his lips. "Yes, quite often."

Which probably made the crystal irrelevant. Nothing more than a cell phone with no way to trace who she'd been in contact with. I found a tube of pale pink lip gloss, an actual cell phone, and a matchbook. "I didn't think she smoked."

"She didn't," Vaughn confirmed. "But the matchbook is from a popular club in the area for paranormals. The footage dropped off for you yesterday is from there."

Pocketing the matches, I held the sweater out and shook it. A few chips of bright blue glass hit the floor. "Any broken glass at the scenes?" I asked Vaughn and crouched to pick them up. Mae got to the broken shards first, putting them in a small plastic baggie.

"I haven't seen the scenes yet, but I was told they were chaotic. A lot of damage," he said. "I imagine broken glass was involved at more than one location."

I pocketed the baggie Mae handed to me, folded the sweater, then returned it to its bag. "What could possibly be gained by turning a clairvoyant into...something else." I sighed and looked at Vaughn. "We're done here."

With more care and respect than I would have expected, Vaughn guided the sheet back over the woman.

"Nothing else has worked, maybe this person is getting desperate." Mae tapped her chin and then leaned closer to me. "Your eye is still red. Does it hurt?"

"Which one?"

"Left. Since you didn't know which, it must not bother you." She tilted her head, studying me, and then straightened. "It's not as bad as I thought. Must have been the light."

Blinking my eye several times, I didn't feel a thing.

"We are in a walk-in freezer, the lighting isn't the best," Vaughn said.

"Good point. Let's get out of here." I snagged my plate and left the freezer.

27

LIVING MY BEST LIFE

T HE ELEVATOR OPENED TO THE PENTHOUSE AND THE RICH SCENT OF BACON and warm, savory smell of toasting bread flooded inside. Mae frowned at me before striding down the hallway and into the kitchen.

"What?" I called and followed, smiling because that smell meant I'd find my sexy sugar buns at the stove.

Toeing off my sneakers in the hall, I padded barefoot into the kitchen, the hard wood cool beneath my soles. Teddy, wearing only his apron and gray sweatpants that highlighted all the muscled ridges of his perfect derriere, used tongs to move bacon from pan to plate. My toes curled as I watched the smooth lines of his back ripple with his movements. Yum. Yummier than the bacon.

Mae passed behind Teddy, breaking my line of sight and the spell that man's bare flesh never failed to put me under. She took a plate from Zee and moved down the assembly line of food laid out.

No doubt about it, I was living my best life. I went to Teddy who bent toward me so I could kiss his cheek. "You're the best."

He winked and waved the tongs at a grease-stained paper towel covered plate. "Some bacon already cooked."

"Lane's had enough already," Mae said, and took her plate to the other end of the island where she slid onto a stool.

"You wash your mouth out with soap this instant." I added an extra slice to the three I'd already taken, just because. "I can't help it if people like to feed me."

Mae rolled her eyes.

"Billion Dollar Bacon?" Teddy asked. Talulla twined around his ankles. He chuckled, broke off a piece of bacon, and dropped it to her.

"Maybe." I popped the top of the compostable to-go box. "For you, not Talulla."

"Minus the two slices Lane ate in the elevator and two more in the kitchen downstairs," Mae said.

"Oh my gods, Y'sindra, is that you?" I glared at Mae. "Suddenly, you're all vinegar and snark. If you're still angry because I ate bacon over the corpse, I apologized."

Palms flat on the cool marble counter, I stared across the island at my sister. She continued to chew and stared back. The cat mewled and Teddy discreetly tossed another piece to the floor.

With a full plate balanced in one hand, Zee pulled out the seat next to Mae. The scrape of the stool's stuttering and thumping feet seemed excessive. "Oops," she winced.

Mae puffed a breath. Her shoulders sagged and she wiped her hands on a napkin. "You're right. I'm being unfair."

"Nah." I waved a dismissive hand. "I was being an asshole."

Mae laughed, bright and light. "That's normal. And..." She stressed the word, cutting off my objection. "We love you for it. For every aspect of you."

"Aw, shucks," I joked, making light of her remark, but deep down in my belly something warmed. Hopefully, it had nothing to do with all pig product I'd consumed.

Nibbling a piece of griddle toasted bread, Mae's gaze went distant, staring into the corner of the kitchen. "I just feel...overwhelmed. Yes, we've had big cases. And yes, some of those cases have had massive consequences."

"Like me gaining a mate and you, a sun stone."

Her blue eyes snapped to me, and she grinned. "Like a mate and a sun stone." She licked her lips, growing serious. "I was kidnapped. Duskmere almost died. Y'sindra lost a wing."

The last statement landed like a gut punch. Whether I'd cut off her wing to save her or not, it was a feeling—physically and emotionally—I would never be able to run far enough from.

Teddy eased down next to me. His heat pulled me from the dark headspace I so easily fell into.

"Hey," Mae said, and I lifted my gaze. "I'm not trying to pick scabs on old wounds."

"I know. You would never do that." She was the best of all of us. She'd sooner sever her own limb than see Y'sindra or I in pain.

"I only mean we've dealt with weighty repercussions before—good and bad—yet something about this feels different." Mae wrung the napkin clutched in her fists.

As if sensing the weight of my sister's emotions, Zee placed a hand on Mae's arm. Maybe she could sense emotions? Animals were intuitive, not that Zee was an animal. Not all of the time, anyhow.

A yowl preceded a fluffy body landing atop the island. "What...no! Lulla, that's unsanitary. Get off of there," I chastised the enormous feline.

Teddy laughed. "Y'sindra walks on the counters. I doubt a bit of fur is going to make it any worse."

He wasn't wrong. Proving my point about animal's intuitiveness, Talulla padded to Mae and bumped her silky head against my sister's cheek. Mae smiled and stroked the cat, who tilted her head for chin scratches.

"Lulla. I like the name." Mae used both hands to cup the cat's jaw and scratch. "Where's she been?"

I frowned and looked from the food bowl to Teddy, only now realizing I hadn't seen her around the penthouse for a couple days.

The elevator doors slid open. Wheels rattled along the floor, and a gurney rolled into view. The clairvoyant had been moved to a black body bag. When Vaughn drew even with the kitchen entry he stepped inside and went to Mae, who turned into his arms.

Wiggling her brows, Zee looked from the pair to me.

I scrunched my nose and tossed my napkin onto the counter. "I'll go open the portal for you."

"No need," Vaughn said.

Before I could move, Talulla—Lulla—jumped off the island and bolted out of the kitchen. The scrambling clack of her claws traveled through the living room and all five of us watched her patchwork tail end gallop onto the balcony and make a sharp right toward the garden stairs.

"Where is she going?" I asked.

"Mr. Black's," Vaughn said and returned to the body.

"What?" Mae spun on her stool to face Vaughn.

"How?" I looked from him to the back door.

"I have no idea." Ensuring the wheels were locked, he maneuvered the body from the table to his shoulder. The clairvoyant hadn't been a large woman, but dead weight was never easy to manipulate. I was reluctantly impressed with the ease with which he'd made the transfer. He wrapped an arm around the legs and faced us. "All I know is Mr. Black said to follow the cat through the portal. This shouldn't take long."

Readjusting the awkward weight, Vaughn strode away from the kitchen entry and down the hall. A moment later, we all watched him pass through the living room and exit onto the balcony.

For a moment, we picked at our food and pretended like everything was normal. A minute passed, two. Unable to stand it any longer, I looked at the others. "I mean, we've gotta, right?"

"Absolutely," Mae agreed, and jumping off her stool, she ran for the sliding glass door, Zee and myself following close behind.

Realizing Teddy was not with us, I stopped and looked through the pass through to the kitchen. "You're not coming."

"Nah." He waved. "You go."

I took off toward the stairs. Despite taking the steps two and three at a time, Vaughn and Talulla were already gone. I dug my hands into my sides and bent forward slightly. "Sun scorch it, I'm out of shape."

Mae and Zee spilled onto the garden behind me.

"You blew past us on the balcony." Zee tilted her head and gave me a weird look. "I'd hardly call that out of shape."

My brows pushed together. I looked from my friend and sister standing behind me, to the stairs behind them, and shrugged. "I guess I was more motivated." Scrubbing a hand through my unbound hair, I shook out the ends and started toward the druid circle.

"You got a secret stash of cheesy poofs up here you were worried Vaughn might sink his fangs into?" Y'sindra winged past me, touching down halfway between me and the circle. She glanced back. "Your boy told me where you were, and that your cat has some sort of magic portal juju."

"Not my cat, and I have no idea what Lulla has."

"Hopefully, not fleas," Mae said as she caught up. "Do we have to worry about fleas up here?"

"What are you looking at me for?" Zee scowled at my sisters who were, indeed, looking at her.

"You're the only one of us who sprouts fur," Y'sindra said at the same time.

Zee held out her arms. "And then I lose the fur."

"There is that." Y'sindra fluttered into the air to perch atop one of the stone pillars.

Desert heat was already beginning to creep in, drying the last drops of dew. I scrunched my bare toes in the grass. Then again, the water could be from the sprinkler system Blackthorne had installed up here. I lowered myself to the damp ground, waiting for Vaughn and Talulla's return.

I tilted my head back to look at Y'sindra. "Where have you been?"

"Outerlands." Legs dangling over the side of the pillar, she bounced her heels against the stone. "I told you yesterday."

"Are the fairies okay?" Mae asked.

A genuine smile lit Y'sindra's face. "Half of them passed out from spent adrenaline, and the other half are buzzing around like live wires. They were so excited."

"We saw a fairy..." *Dead.* I couldn't say it. Lips pressed into a tight line, I turned pleading eyes on Mae.

"There was a fairy on the roof," Mae said gently.

Legs kicking out, Y'sindra rocked back with laughter. "That was Matilda. Silly fairy fainted."

I blinked at her, unsure what to say, and turned to Mae whose mouth hung open. "Fainted?" I asked.

"Yep. Girl has the constitution of a goat."

"What are you talking about, a goat?"

"You've never seen those videos? Goat gets scared, screams, faints?" Y'sindra hoisted herself up on the pillar and demonstrated, scream and all. Wings fluttering, she caught herself before she hit the ground.

"Y'sindra," Mae snapped. "Is the fairy okay?"

"That's what I said." Y'sindra brushed off her leggings. "Daft girl spotted Enode, which was good, but then screamed and fainted."

Laughter bubbled out of me, and I pressed my fingers to my mouth. Ridiculing the fairies felt inappropriate. Straight faced, I asked, "Which wasn't good?"

"No, it was not. But she's one of the youngest fairies, only recently sent on pilgrimage." Y'sindra put air quotes around the last bit. "She's learning fast."

"Just a few goat incidents," I said.

Mae giggled and Y'sindra grinned.

Legs stretched in front of me, I leaned back on my palms. "We should grab Jason and Eli, plus all these sun fae who have migrated to Vegas through the portal to Outerlands for a barbeque with the snow fairies."

Mae straightened. "I love that idea! Our friends in Ta'Vale can join us as well."

"Your friends," I muttered, and Mae frowned at me.

"Pru? Odo?" she asked.

"Well, sure them." I leaned forward and rubbed my damp palms on my thighs, the sweatpants working like a towel.

"Duskmere, and Cirron," Mae added. "Oh, maybe I could convince Brenyn!"

I rolled my eyes in the direction of Y'sindra. She shook her head. We were of the same opinion on those suggestions, but if it made Mae happy, we'd acquiesce. Even if it meant accepting Duskmere's former-maybe still partner, professionally and personally.

"What about me?" Zee finally wandered over from the row of fruit trees she'd been exploring. I'd almost forgotten she hadn't been up to the garden yet. "I don't want to miss Jason's green chili."

"You're a given," I assured her.

"Of course," Mae exclaimed.

Y'sindra fluttered around her. "Like it or not, you're one of us now."

"Thanks, babes." Zee fist bumped Y'sindra and then offered me a meaningful look. "Lone wolf no more."

A fizzy feeling settled inside of me. Happiness, I decided. This was happiness. I wasn't sure how I'd stumbled into all this goodness, but I had, and I sent a big fat *thank you* to the universe for all of it.

Unsure what impulse drove me, I added, "And Fate. We should invite her."

An approving smile lit Mae's face.

"Aw, look Mae, our girl's all growned up." Y'sindra twirled through the air.

Shaking my head, I pushed up and strode toward the portal circle. Vaughn and Lulla had to be back anytime now.

Behind me, Zee added, "Don't forget Dexter."

"Oh, yeah!" Y'sindra buzzed to Mae. "I bet you were excited about that news."

"What news?" Mae's brow pulled together in confusion.

"Oh..." Y'sindra drew out the word in a sing song voice. She looked at me. "You didn't tell her."

Mae's confusion shifted to suspicion. "Tell me what?"

Salty air washed over me. The sound of crashing waves came from inside the circle a fraction of a second before the grass shifted to sand. Vaughn and Lulla appeared beneath a dome of darkness splashed with the barest hint of white-gold light. On the other side of the country, the sun was just making an appearance.

Vaughn passed over the perimeter of the circle and into the garden. Talulla yowled and raced over the perimeter on the beach.

The dome disappeared and the sand returned to grass.

I looked from my sisters, to Vaughn, to the empty circle. White noise buzzed in my ears. My mouth opened and shut. I ran my hand over my hair, winding the waist-length ends into my fist. "Did that cat open the gods damned portal?"

28

WHAT WICKED THING

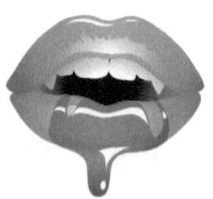

AFTER HEARING THE NEWS ABOUT DEXTER, MAE HAD IMMEDIATELY grabbed her keys and was on her way to the elevator when Teddy let her know Dexter would be downstairs, at the new bar, in a few hours. Reluctantly, my sister returned her purse to the table near the elevator.

Vaughn, who had been saved from a thousand questions by a phone call, hung up and went to Mae in the kitchen. He slid onto the stool my sister indicated, while she picked up another plate and began piling on the breakfast offerings.

He looked up as I entered. "That was the front desk. They are working on a video for the last two weeks with the clairvoyant."

"That will be a lot of footage."

Sending Mae a grateful smile as she slid a plate in front of him, he gathered a forkful of fluffy scrambled eggs. "It won't be too bad. She was an on-call employee."

I'd been shocked the first time I witnessed Vaughn eating normal food, which taught me not to put stock in movies. Vampire physiology was different from humans, and I had no idea how he processed the food, but I also wasn't going to ask.

"Are you talking about Caroline? Why are you looking at tapes of her? She get fired?" Y'sindra and Lo joined us in the kitchen. "I had nothing to do with whatever she was into."

I rolled my eyes hard enough to give myself a headache.

"Y'sindra," Mae hissed, her tone bringing our snarky sister up short. "She was killed last night."

"Dead?" Darting a look between my sister and me, Y'sindra curled her hands around the hem of her tunic. Suddenly, her eyes widened and her fingers froze. "Freya's frozen fruitcakes! Did she get herself spelled?"

"Suspected moonbit," I told her. I didn't mention Blackthorne or the potion. Being aware not all cases were moonbit infections was a far cry from knowing his boss's full history, including how the false moonbit cases were, in a way, a result of his past deeds. I could care less if he knew, but I had neither the desire nor patience for explanations.

Teddy eased an arm around my waist, drawing a lazy pattern on my hip with his fingers. I leaned into his heat and tilted my head to the side, against his chest. My breakfast lay unfinished on the counter, and for once, I didn't have the appetite to finish. Which finally answered the question, "Did my stomach know no limits?"

Everyone else settled into a more subdued meal while I, to the astonishment of all, began cleaning up.

Mae's head swiveled, her blue eyes following me as I moved empty pots, pans, and platters from stove and counter to sink. With a damp cloth, I wiped down the counter.

"I'm not sure I have a purpose if I don't have to clean up after you," she said.

"Wouldn't want you to lose your reason for living." I tossed the cloth at the sink. It didn't land inside, but close enough. "I promise not to do it again this year."

Y'sindra snorted. "For you, once a year might still be too often."

Leaning back against the counter, I studied my talons. All dry and cracked, they were a disaster.

"I will begin looking at the video we have today," Mae said. "Can you help, Y'sindra?"

"I'll help," Zee volunteered. She was such a trooper. Looking at Teddy, she added, "If the boss doesn't need me at the Interlands bar?"

"Nope, everything is done there. Just waiting for quotes from the contractor. Actually"— placing a palm on the counter, he shifted his weight forward and eyed Lo—"with the corrupt out of Outerlands, the new snow fairy residents, and the door to Ta'Vale reopened, I was considering reopening that bar. What do you think, bud?"

Overcome with excitement, Lo leapt to his feet on the stool with such force, the seat toppled with a loud crash, leaving Lo hovering in the air. "Oh, yes! Y'sindra and I spend much of our time there already."

I went around the counter to right the stool.

Teddy nodded. "We'll need a few full-sized employees."

"Why do I think this is being mentioned for my sake?" Zee chuckled. It was a smoky timbre I could only dream of possessing. I'd seen an animal on a documentary series called a hyena. That was me.

"Not my intention, but you are more than welcome to check it out, see if you'd rather work there," Teddy told her.

"I can't believe I'm saying this considering the memories I've built in Outerlands, but it's a really great place. It's lush and green." Mae looked at me. "If Lane's Grandpa can be convinced to open the gate to Earth, it leads to a gorgeous beach."

"A beach?" Zee asked, her voice distant and dreamy. Her plump lips pulled into a wide smile. "I do enjoy working on my tan."

Conversation dwindled to hums of agreement and soft clinks of utensils on plates. Teddy kissed the top of my head and excused himself to get dressed while I tackled the stack of dirty cookware I'd piled in the sink.

Finished, I wiped my hands dry on a towel and once again leaned against the counter to quietly watch everyone. I had the distinct impression I was standing at the edge of a cliff, leaning into the wind, all the possibilities stretched before me, but then there was the drop. The wind would eventually die. A fall would happen, and it felt like it was only matter of time. Too much was coming at us, all at once, and at increasing frequency. The best we could do was figure out what wicked thing stirred before it had the opportunity to show itself.

The heavy thump of Teddy's steps coming down the stairs preceded his reentry into the kitchen. Mae had been trying to splash color into all our wardrobes, and it looked like she'd succeeded. He wore a burnt orange T-shirt, loose enough to move in, but clingy enough to show off his muscles. Paired with denim and his typical work boots, which he knelt to lace.

Even Y'sindra wore the sunflower-yellow leggings Mae had slipped into her closet. Not me. With the exception of letting her dress me for the big night out the other day, it was better than anything I'd done. What was the purpose? As I told Mae, clothes should be comfortable, or they should provide protection from on-the-job injuries. Ideally, they would do both.

A smile lit Mae's features when she spotted Teddy. "I knew you were an autumn. That's your color, Teddy."

I had to agree. It did bring out the lighter notes of golden brown in his shoulder-length hair. I'd never noticed before, but his deeply tanned complexion also had a slight gold undertone.

Boots laced, he rose and gave Mae an amused smile. "Thank you for the additions. I could probably use something beyond white, gray, or flannel."

"Hey!" I objected. "I like you in those flannels. Actually, I like you in—or out—of anything." I slow winked.

He met me halfway across the kitchen, enfolding me in his arms and leaned down for a kiss. A soft, but insistent press of his lips was over too soon.

Hopping off her stool, Zee looked at Mae. "I know I said I'd help with the video, but do you girls mind if I head down with Teddy? I'd like to hear more about this Outerlands bar, plus I want to be there when Dexy boy shows up. It'd be good to get a feel for what he wants to do since Interlands won't be up and running for a while."

"Of course, Y'sindra and I've got this." Mae rose and took her and Vaughn's plates to the sink. She rinsed them and slipped them into the dishwasher. "Call when Dexter arrives?"

Mae sounded calm and casual, but I knew beneath the surface she had to be a cauldron of frenetic energy. My sister was only a fraction less obsessed with magic than our father. Her attempt to hide her excitement was cute. I tucked my chin to my shoulder, hiding a smile.

"Absolutely, babes." Zee added her plate to the dishwasher. She joined Teddy beneath the large opening from the kitchen to the hallway. Pausing, she faced us. "I'm thinking it might be a good idea to call my dad. I figure he should know the difference between moonbit and this potion thing. He can get word out to the packs."

"Good idea," I said. "We should know if this is isolated to our area, or if whoever this is has been testing the waters elsewhere."

Smoothing a hand down the oversized sweatshirt she wore, Zee sucked in a shaky breath. "This isn't going to be a fun conversation when he realizes what this means."

"What..." I winced as the implication settled. Her mom was dead because her father *made* her.

"How old was your mom when you lost her?" Mae asked.

Gaze going distant, Zee nibbled on her lip. "It's been so long. I think she was one hundred and thirty-three. Maybe thirty-four, or, Hell, I don't actually know."

Knowing Zee was not the twenty something she appeared, but rather somewhere in her forties, I didn't blame her for not remembering. I rarely remembered what day it was. "That's close to twice as long as he would have with her if he hadn't *made* her."

"You wouldn't exist, and that would suck," Y'sindra added.

Zee snorted. "Dad might not agree."

"I bet you're wrong," I said.

"He loves his kids in his own way, but nothing compares to the love he had for Mom." She slipped her hands into her hip pockets. "This will hit him hard, but the reminder of the extra time he had with her will soften the blow. Thanks, babes."

In short order, only my sisters and I remained in the kitchen. Before long, Mae and Y'sindra settled in at the dining room table to search video feed, putting the two laptops we owned to use.

Not even noon, and I had nothing to do. Deciding to catch up on lost sleep, I made my way upstairs and faceplanted onto my bed. Beneath me, something crinkled. Rolling over, I sat up and looked at the mattress. Nothing on the bed. I patted down my jacket

and felt the source of the sound in my pocket.

I held up the baggies of collected evidence, though I wasn't sure any of this meant anything. A matchbook of a location we already knew about. A sodden piece of paper with a smudged phone number that could never be recovered, and a chip of blue glass.

At least the matchbook confirmed a link to the club. Whoever was inflicting Blackthorne's bastardized potion on unsuspecting paranormals could be using that place as their hunting grounds. The victims could be dosed there, but my gut told me they left the club together and they were doing this in the privacy of the victim's home. If we linked more victims, looked through more feed, maybe we could get lucky and identify one person in contact with more than one victim.

Holding the bag to the light, I twisted it for a better look at the glass. It hardly seemed like evidence, but something about it struck me as familiar. Maybe it was the unusual shade of blue. It could be stemware from the resort, but I didn't think so. I squinted. Then again it didn't exactly look like broken glass.

I grabbed a white washcloth from a bathroom drawer and spread it atop the nightstand, preparing to dump the evidence for closer examination.

My cell phone rang. Very few people had this number, and two of them were downstairs. Already suspecting what I would find, I flipped up the edge of the cloth that had fallen over the screen and scowled at the name.

Rolling my shoulders as if about to enter battle, I answered. "What?"

"Is that anyway to speak to your grandpa?" Blackthorne asked.

"Depends on who the grandpa is." I smiled at my retort. "Why are you calling?"

"I have some information, but if you don't want to hear from me..."

My smile fell. He always won. "You know I want to hear it."

"Good, good," he said. The rush of wind and crash of surf came through the speaker. "I'll see you in five."

The line went dead.

"What the...?" I glared at the phone and then threw it at the wall.

29

BLAH, BLAH

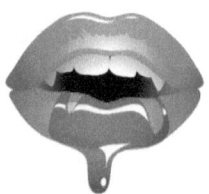

T<small>EDDY HAD BEEN RIGHT. EVEN</small> I <small>WOULD HAVE A HARD TIME BREAKING</small> the case he'd put on my phone. As I made my way up the path leading from druid circle to the hotel, I turned the phone screen down in my hand and examined the hard, rubberized backing. A little scuff mark, but nothing that wouldn't wipe off. I flipped it and once again examined the screen. No crack or scratch there either.

Remembering the dent I'd left in the wall, I grimaced. Mae would lecture me for sure, but I could just keep her out of the room for a while. Maybe hang a picture to hide the damage. Teddy, though, would be all disappointment, and that would be worse. He didn't mind my violent streak, quite the contrary, but he'd been trying to get me to think before acting. So far, not so good.

Halfway to the hotel's back deck, a constant quiet murmur I'd heard since arrival coalesced into soft strands of lively music. Some sort of current pop station. Not the choice I would expect for Blackthorne, but maybe he was catering to tourists, even if the hotel had yet to open. Word would spread. The guy was good at drumming up business.

As I mounted the stairs, the back door pushed open with a hiss and pop of suction. Blackthorne stepped outside, a patchwork of fluff on his heels.

"Traitor," I whispered.

Lulla's ears, one orange, one black, swiveled in my direction, and she gave her tail a quick twitch.

"If I remember," Blackthorne said as he made his way to the single opening on the backside of the big, square bar. He crossed the interior to the front counter. "You did not want a familiar."

Heat from the sun-warmed wooden stool seat pushed through my leggings. Yikes, that was hot! I rocked side to side, letting the wood cool. "You need some sort of padding for these seats. This thing is going to leave welts on my thighs."

"I have plans drawn up. What do you think about a cover over the bar?" He pointed behind me. "The deck will be extended, and a pool added over there."

I was both impressed and curious, but I wasn't here to talk about construction. "Hotels are your thing. You don't need my input." Lulla pranced along the bar top to where I was seated. She was so big, she had to physically tilt her furry face down to look down at me. Pausing, she ducked to bump her head against mine, a purr rumbling from her fluffy body to rival the boat engines crashing through the waves behind us. "Want to tell me how this cat got through the portal?"

A tilted smile pulled up the corner of Blackthorne's lips. "She's bonded to you. You can use the circle, therefore, so can she."

The cat in question curled up in front of me and went to work grooming herself.

"Are you kidding? It took me months to figure that thing out, and you're telling me she followed me through once and now she can travel at will?"

"Hm. Yes." Blackthorne punched a code into a small refrigerator, retrieved a beer, and held it out for me.

"Ew, no. It's like ten A.M.. What is it with you drinking this early?

"We're on island time here."

"Florida is not an island."

"Last time you passed on a mimosa. Bloody Mary, then?" he asked.

A flashback to the half-melted Bloody Mary I'd had in front of me the day everything changed with Teddy, with my life, sent a tendril of happiness twisting through me. I still hated the drink, though. Absolutely disgusting stuff. I cleared my throat. "No."

Blackthorne shrugged and popped the cap off his bottle. "Suit yourself, but you might change your mind after you hear what I have to tell you." He took a long pull.

My shoulders tightened. I sat stiff and straight and counted backwards from one hundred as I stared at Blackthorne, practicing patience. Sundering the veil between worlds aside, if I'd learned nothing else in my short acquaintance with dear old great grandpappy, it was that he would get to everything in his own time. His time rarely aligned with mine.

Eighty-seven, eighty-six, eighty-five.

After another pull of beer, Blackthorne swiped a napkin across the bar and then set down the half-empty bottle. A sense of wariness tickled my neck.

His nostrils flared and chest expanded as he drew in a deep breath. "I finished testing your blood."

I blinked. My shoulders released their tension. Not the calamitous news I'd expected. I wasn't actually sure what I'd expected, but a blood test was not it. "My DNA is a hot mess. That isn't exactly news."

"Your DNA is exquisite. The parts of many far outweigh the strength of one, but that isn't the point."

Through the cryptic messaging, I got it. The fae valued purity of a being. Magic resided in the blood, and blending blood weakened the primary magic. Apparently, in Blackthorne's view, possessing the strands of many magics outweighed the power of one. I was slowly coming around to the same conclusion, which shocked the hell out of me.

I traced my tongue over my dry lips. "I'll take a water."

Blackthorne grabbed a large plastic cup, not the cheap kind. This looked like opaque glass but wouldn't break when a customer inevitably knocked it to the ground. He turned on a tap identical to the fancy filtered stuff installed in the penthouse kitchen and filled the cup.

"Thanks." I took a long swallow. "Okay, I'll bite. What's the point?"

Grinning, Blackthorne crooked an arm onto the bar and leaned his hip against the counter. "I knew you couldn't resist."

"Blah, blah, why am I here?"

Talulla stood, and then three feet of cat stretched in front of me, chest lowered onto her front legs, tail end arched into the air. Yawning, she showed off fangs as large as mine before she performed two full circles, found her comfortable position, and laid back down.

I looked at Blackthorne and then back to the cat who regarded me with round, unblinking—and if I wasn't mistaken, judgmental—eyes. "What? It's a valid question. Ugh, I don't have to justify myself to a cat."

"Familiar," Blackthorne said mildly.

"Whatever." I accentuated my extremely mature response with an equally mature eye roll. "Why am I here? What could you not tell me over the phone? And give me a beer." Cold drops of sweat already turned the dark brown bottle Blackthorne handed to me slick. I hooked a talon beneath the bottle cap and popped it off. It plinked once and then bounced behind the bar as I took a long drink.

Blackthorne crouched to retrieve the cap and tossed it into the trash, his brows climbing when he noted the empty bottle in front of me. "Another?"

I shook my head and idly stroked the long length of Lulla's side. Her fur was like fine strands of silk.

"All right, well, as I told you, I got the results of the blood tests I ran. Not poor Caroline's of course, but the rest."

Scrunching my hand in the feline's fur, I watched thick tufts emerge between each finger. "You did."

"I ran the tests again since we met, several times in fact, the results were always the same."

Letting my head fall back dramatically, I groaned at the sky. "This seems more drawn out than it needs to be."

"While each victim was riddled with paranormal pathogens, they also contained sun fae, blood fae, and druid markers. Primarily blood fae and druid. The sun fae was nearly insignificant." He finished his beer in a single long drink. "And shifter, can't forget the shifter."

My forehead wrinkled in confusion. "This is what I came all the way here for?" I tapped out my building irritation on the bar. "I'm a hybrid. I came from your potion. This is old news."

Eyes the shade of an eggplant, vivid and startling in color, burrowed into mine. He kept staring.

"Dude. If you are trying to telepathically impart some sort of message, you do not possess that power." Not that I knew of. Afterall, I was the one who kept trying to skewer people with eyeball lasers.

He sighed, longer and deeper than, in my opinion, he had a reason to. "I spoke with Meghan."

That got my attention. My tapping finger stilled, and my hands curled into fists atop the counter. I leaned forward. "Why?"

He squinted at me. "To compare notes, of course. See if she has ever researched the composition of your DNA. She confirmed you always presented with sun and blood fae markers in your genes, while the druid began to present later."

"Something she never told me."

"Hm. I was probably a dirty little secret in your family tree. Well, the last time she ran a test, your druid and blood fae markers were about equal strength, while the sun fae was greatly diminished."

I flexed my fingers, flattening my palms on the glossy wood. A tiny warning bell tickled the back of my brain, but nothing was obvious for me. "Still don't see how me having a DNA melting pot is news."

"This isn't about your blood, Granddaughter," he said with no small amount of exasperation, and what was with the attitude? He was the one drawing this out. "This is about the results from the victims of whoever is using a version of my potion."

I puffed a breath. "Then why are you talking about my test results and calling my mom about my blood?"

Lines bracketed Blackthorne's mouth. "You did not hear me. The victims all had ..." Words trailing off, his chin dipped, and he watched me, as if waiting for something.

The stool's seat stuttered in protest as I slid off. Lulla raised her head at the noise, ears rotating in all directions. "I get it. They had sun fae blood..." My mouth opened on my next words but didn't close. "Blood fae and druid."

"The potion created blood fae."

I slid back onto the stool. "And it brought the druid out in latent DNA I already possessed."

Dizzy, I planted my elbows on the bar, pressing the heels of my hands into my eyes. Tullula's exquisitely soft fur brushed against my forearms. "It's my blood, isn't it?"

"Yes. It's a version of my potion, but using human paranormals, your blood, and Aventheo's."

I jerked upright on my seat. "Teddy's. How..." I groaned. "Mom. Not only does she keep some on hand to be used in my medicine, but he was injured and in her care after your spell almost killed him."

Blackthorne scoffed. "It would take much more than a sleep spell to kill the black wolf."

"So I keep hearing," I mumbled. "Okay, so I assume she tested the sample you sent to compare and confirmed all this."

"Yes."

Idly curling a length of hair around my finger, I smiled. "Cute. You know she is also your granddaughter?"

"She is a long distant relative, yes. But you, Granddaughter, are druid."

"Blood fae druid. Your words," I said. "This is all interesting, but I still don't understand why I'm here. You could have called about all of this."

Blackthorne approached the other side of the bar, leaning toward me. He searched my eyes—specifically, my left eye. Talulla stood and bumped her head against his cheek. "I just wanted to see you. In person."

Despite the rising heat of the sun prickling my neck, a wash of cold rolled through me. "Why?"

"I tested your blood."

My nostrils flared. "You said as much. And?"

"The good news is, your fae DNA killed off all the human pathogens after the bite, except a trace amount of vampire. To be expected, since that particular magic-born disease has its roots in blood magic. Not to worry. I am certain it's only a matter of time before that, too, is flushed from your system." His wide grin immediately made me suspicious. "In the meantime, I hear vampire blood tastes wonderful to those who imbibe, and as I told you before, it can do astonishing things. Your Aventheo might enjoy those benefits."

Instead of abating, the tension in my neck increased. No one started with good news unless they had a steaming pile of bad news to impart. "And?" I asked again.

"You, my dear, are the proud new owner of shifter DNA."

30

BIGGEST BADDEST BOGEYMAN

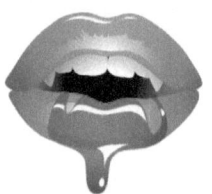

I TOOK MY TIME CROSSING THE ROOFTOP GARDEN TO ABSORB THE NEWS Blackthorne had delivered. Ultimately, he hadn't believed the miniscule amount of shifter—specifically, black wolf—DNA inside of me wouldn't amount to anything other than an extra dab of color in my eye. What he wasn't certain about was whether my body had absorbed and assimilated the shifter genes because of the shared blood magic between shifters and blood fae, or because of my mate bond with Teddy.

I steered toward a tree, its heavy limbs dipping low with large globes of varying shades of red. I didn't know when any of the fruit planted up here was meant to be in season, but these trees yielded fruit year-round.

It didn't take long to locate a pomegranate which was less round, with flattened sides. I placed my palm beneath the fruit and pressed up, transferring the weight from the branch to my palm. It was heavier than it appeared. The sides and heft indicated it was ripe.

A quick stab and pull with a talon cut the stem. I palmed the fruit and made my way across the garden, toward the stairs. Mae had tried to introduce the strange fruit over salad, which did not go over well. Then she dumped the seeds into a pitcher and made pomegranate water. I was hooked. It was what drove me to learn how to determine when the fruit was ready for harvest.

As I neared the stairs voices floated up from below. I recognized Dexter's laid-back tone. When Mae responded, her typically melodic voice was loud and jumpy, like an excited puppy. I chuckled to myself and jogged down the spiral stairs, catching the pair just as Mae steered Dexter toward the portal stone.

"Lane!" she said and left Dexter to rush over and hug me.

Weird, but okay. I patted her back and then stepped away. "Someone's in a good mood."

She beamed. "I'm taking Dexter—Dex—to see Dad. I already called him. He is beside himself!"

"I bet he is," I murmured, not failing to miss she already felt familiar enough to adopt Zee's pet name for the guy. Behind Mae, I met Dexter's eyes. "You're okay with this?"

Gasping, Mae swatted my arm. "It sounds like you think I would force him."

"Well..." I drew out the word.

Dexter slung an arm across my sister's shoulders. "It's all good. I'm—" He paused. "It's time I went back. I'm eager to see what your dad can teach me."

"I'm so glad." A warm fizzy sensation bubbled up inside my chest. I was happy—for other people. My inner circle kept growing, which was probably good considering my sisters' growth away from me. I swallowed and looked at Mae. "Find anything on the feed?"

Head shaking, she sighed. "No, but we barely scratched the surface. There are so many people in each video, a lot of tall blondes. This is going to take forever."

"Don't stress. We should hurry to stop whoever is doing this, but we should be thorough." I glanced toward the sliding glass doors. They were closed all but a crack just large enough to squeeze through. Their mirrored coating reflected the heat and my view. I grimaced at my image superimposed on the glass. Still wearing the same clothes I'd thrown on when I'd been dragged out of bed and a half-assed braid, I was a mess. "Anyone else around?"

"Sort of," Mae said. "Y'sindra and Lo took off to Outerlands. Zee is inside packing."

I straightened. "Packing?

"She... It's nothing bad, but I'll let her give you the news." She squeezed my hand and then smiled up at Dexter. "We should go."

They were gone before I reached the doors, taking their lively, bright chatter with them. Quiet stole over the balcony and followed me into the penthouse. It was stifling. "Anyone home?" I called out, kicking off my shoes and carrying them to the front door.

Zee's footsteps thundered down the upstairs hall. "Babes! I hoped I'd catch you before I left." She greeted me with her typical, overexuberant werewolf hug. There was so much hugging going on lately, which I didn't love, but I was slowly resigning myself to accept. At least I no longer punched people who came at me for an embrace.

I shuffled back and folded my arms over my chest. "Mae said you were packing. Real estate in this joint is hard to come by. Did a place open already?"

"Nah, but—"

"You aren't moving to Outerlands?"

She laughed and shook her head. "No, at least not yet. I need to visit before I decide anything."

"Good. There are still corrupt just across the border. Who knows if they grow a set and decide to come for the sun fae again. And let's not forget about Dacian." Which frankly, I had. Having Y'sindra, Lo, and a tribe of snow fairies so close worried me. Or maybe Dacian should worry. A single snow fairy with the full strength of their winter magic was a menace. An entire tribe... I grinned. Yeah, Dacian should be concerned.

Zee wrinkled her nose. "Politics."

"Hm," I said, sounding eerily like Blackthorne. Ugh, no. I cleared my throat. "So, what's up then?"

A soft smile slipped onto her face. "I called my dad." Her mouth twitched to the side and her gaze fell.

Very un-alpha-like behavior. My interest was piqued. "And?"

"He wants me to come home." She looked up at me through her lashes. "It's been years, but he asked nicely. I should go. Right?"

"You're moving to Colorado?" I shifted my weight. The lightness I'd felt seeing my sister and Dexter so happy evaporated. Sure, more and more people were barging their way into my life, but surprisingly, I also loathed letting them go.

"No way! I'm not leaving my girls." She winked and checked her watch. "Gotta hurry, you know how security is at the airport."

"I'll call down for a car to take you."

"Thanks, babes. You're the best. Okay, the quick and dirty summary of my conversation. Dad was..." Her face scrunched and she made a waffling motion with her hand. "He didn't take the news great, but he recovered quicker than I thought. I think it's why he wants me and my brothers back home."

I nodded. "Makes sense."

"Anyhow, he said he'd heard about an increase in moonbit cases, but they were all coming from this area. Specifically, within a couple hours of Las Vegas."

"So, whoever is doing this, is definitely based here."

"Right-o." She pointed a finger at me. "Okay, I'm almost done packing, then I need to head to the airport. I'll be back." Her mouth twisted to the side. "I'm not sure when. It's an open-ended trip right now, but no more than a month." Zee turned to leave but stopped. "Almost forgot, Teddy's still at *Blood and Wine*. He said to let him know when you got back."

The mention of Teddy worked its usual magic. A sense of home and belonging washed over me. I placed a call downstairs, reserving a car for Zee, and texted Teddy to let him know I was home.

Home. It was disconcerting how easily I'd assimilated to this place. Sure, the amenities were awesome, but I hadn't expected to get comfortable so quickly in the home of a male I'd thought until less than a year ago, was the fae's biggest baddest bogeyman. Now I lived in his place—no, his old place, mine now—and I had taken to day drinking with the guy.

Pomegranate in hand, I headed for the kitchen. Loud footsteps and the rolling of luggage wheels came up behind me. Zee said her goodbyes, promising to call if she heard anything else, and punched the elevator call button. The ornate wood panel doors slid open almost instantly, and she was gone.

I had the fruit split and seeds scooped into a pitcher when I heard the soft hiss of the elevator doors opening again. Moments later the sexiest male alive eased behind me. Sliding his arms around my waist, he bent and kissed my neck. With our height difference, poor guy's back would be a mess in no time. Maybe Mom could make a pain salve. She whipped up something to regrow Y'sindra's wing. Back pain should be a breeze to tackle.

Turning in his arms, I tilted my head to meet his eyes. My neck pinched. Ugh, Teddy's back wouldn't be the only thing in need of Mom's magic touch. "Hi."

"Hi." Gripping my waist, he lifted me onto the counter, careful not to bump the fancy crystal carafe.

The chill from the granite pushed through my leggings, while his delicious heat burned through to my thighs. I hooked my legs behind the small of his back and pulled him closer.

Palms braced on either side of me, he leaned in for a slow kiss. "I've missed you," he murmured, and then really turned on the heat. His lips, somehow soft and firm at the same time, moved with mine.

My breath floated in my chest, airy and light when I opened my mouth to his seeking tongue. It felt the entire universe existed in this single place, right now, right here.

He slid his hands down my back, gripping my butt and pulling me closer. The heat of him against the apex of my thighs sent sparks of awareness through me.

Withdrawing my arms from around his neck, I cupped his face. A day's growth of stubble scratched my palms, and I liked it.

The voracity of our kiss slowed. His hands rose along my sides, tickling my ribs. "My mate."

"My mate, I like that." Careful not to break skin with my fangs, I took his bottom lip between my teeth I tugged. "I'm not complaining, but what was that about? I wasn't gone that long."

"A minute apart from you is an eternity."

I jerked back and met his gaze. He kept a straight face for exactly five seconds before we both broke into a fit of laughter.

"Maybe I just like kissing you?" And he demonstrated again.

"I'll allow it." I licked the coffee and cinnamon taste of him from my lips. The guy knew how to make my toes curl.

"What, you don't like kissing me too? Ouch, my ego." All drama, Teddy clutched his chest.

"Your ego is just fine, and I didn't think it was necessary to tell you something you already knew."

"Fair enough." Teddy patted my thighs and then grabbed the pitcher. As he began filling it with filtered water at the sink, he glanced back at me. "Your sister mentioned you were pretty worked up when you left."

Sliding off the counter, I filled two glasses, and took a sip. Just as subtly sweet as I remembered. "Yeah, Blackthorne."

"I assume there is a hole to be patched in the bedroom?"

"No," I said automatically and then wrinkled my nose. "Maybe a little one."

He chuckled and drained his glass. "This would be good with vodka."

"Don't tell Y'sindra. I don't know if pomegranate would have the same effect as berries, but I don't want to find out, either."

"What's the news?" Teddy rinsed his glass and put it in the drying rack. So domesticated. So sexy.

I grabbed the front of his shirt and tugged him down for a quick kiss.

"What's that for?" he asked.

"Maybe I just like kissing you?" I winked.

A loud laugh erupted from him, but the wink drew his attention to my right eye. He leaned close. "Your eye is still a little red. Does it hurt?"

"About that, let's sit down."

"Is it serious?" Teddy asked as we settled onto the sofa.

"No. At least, I don't think so." I gave him the rundown of the conversation with Blackthorne, ending with the news that Talulla, who hadn't returned with me, could use the circle by herself.

"Well," Teddy said thoughtfully. "I can't say this is the first time you've had a bit of black wolf in you."

My mouth fell open. I sputtered.

Laughing, he fended off the barrage of throw pillows I sent toward his face. After he blocked the third pillow, he grabbed me and pulled me sideways into his lap.

"So rude," I said.

"But I'm not wrong."

Pillows lay scattered on the floor around us. I turned on Teddy's lap and bent forward to pick them up.

He gripped my hips, fingers digging in as he pulled me against him. His heat scorched my backside, and something moved beneath me. "Keep that up, and you'll have more black wolf in you than you know what to do with."

"Such a dirty boy." I reclined, my back to his chest. "I like it."

He slid his hands from my hips to my legs, drawing them slowly upward. His thumbs tracing my inner thighs.

"So, is that all the news?" he asked against my ear.

"Yes," I said breathlessly. My brain slowly slipping into incoherency. "I just can't figure out where whoever this is got our blood."

He nipped my earlobe. "Eodrom."

Shock pounded into me like a brick from that single word. "Son of a goat!"

"One goat bites you, and the entire species is maligned." He let go of my thighs and leaned back, no doubt to avoid another black eye from my flailing elbows.

"Not only did it hurt, that thing tore a hole in my pants." Pushing up from Teddy's lap, I paced across the room. The absence of heat on my legs was acute. I scrubbed my hands down my thighs. "Gods! How did I not see it?"

"Did you have to figure things out right now?" Teddy adjusted the bulge behind his zipper.

"You brought it up." I stabbed a finger at him.

"Technically, you did."

"Ugh, you're right." I made a face. "Still, you figured it out."

One brow rising as he watched me, he slid his arms out on either side on the back of the sofa and shrugged. The posture only accentuated his muscled shoulders. "I'm surprised you hadn't. The fae hospital is the only place that would have both of our blood on hand."

"Which means whoever is doing this, is fae." I squeezed my hands into fists until my talons pricked my palms. I looked at Teddy. "He knows."

"Who knows what?"

"Blackthorne. He knows who is doing this."

Teddy scooted to the edge of his seat. "How can you be certain?"

"I can't, but there's one way to find out." I strode into the hallway and stomped back into my sneakers. Teddy was standing when I returned. "You want to come?"

Strands of brown hair fell across his brow as he shook his head. "Not unless you need me. I have a meeting at three in Interlands."

"I'll be okay." I flashed a fangy grin. "Can't promise the same for good old Grandpa."

31

HANDED THEM A BOMB

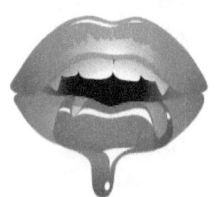

I CAME THROUGH THE DRUID CIRCLE LIKE A BANSHEE WITH HER BOG ON fire. Sand flew in every direction from my angry steps. "Blackthorne!"

The male in question appeared as a dark cutout, leaning against the railing where the wooden path ended, and three wide steps led from the beach to deck. Late afternoon sun bounced off the back glass wall of the hotel, wreathing him in orange-gold light.

"You!" I stabbed a finger in Blackthorne's direction as I stomped toward the stairs.

"Me." He smiled and straightened.

My hand itched to slap the smile from his face. Though, I wasn't stupid. Most of the time, at least. Also, not true. I did do a lot of stupid things, but I tried not to do the ones that could get me dead.

Putting the sun at my back, I squinted at Blackthorn, my sensitive eyes still adjusting to the blast of light coming off the windowed wall. The special contacts I wore allowed me to walk pain-free in the same light as any other fae—or human—but my eyes still adjusted slower.

I blinked rapidly to clear my vision, which effectively ruined the menacing glare I was going for. "You knew," I said, squinting at his blob.

"You must be specific, I know many things, Granddaughter." He eased away from the rail and headed for the back door of the hotel. "It's very hot, and you don't seem like you are in the mood for a cold beverage. Come, let's move this conversation inside."

It occurred to me as he pushed his way into the lobby, he'd been waiting for me. "Do you sit around and watch the garden all day? Is that thing set up as some sort of nanny cam?"

"No," Blackthorne said, moving to the large, separate dining area. He held up his phone so I could see it over his shoulder and gave it a little shake. "There's an app for that."

"Seriously?" I lengthened my strides to catch up.

Chuckling, he shook his head as I drew up even with him. "No. I mean yes, it is an app, but that was my attempt at humor."

I followed him into the dining area. "You failed."

"Yes, I know." He went to a booth and gestured for me to sit. "Wait here. I was on my way to retrieve the dish my new chef left when I received the security alert."

"Damn it, Blackthorne, I'm not here for a family dinner."

"Maybe not, but I'm hungry." He leveled a deadpan stare at me. "We both know you can't make me do anything. You, apparently, want some sort of answer. I want my dinner. You can join me while you ask your questions, or you can ask and watch me eat. It makes no difference."

Stung by the brutal honesty, I stood stiff until he disappeared into the kitchen and then I collapsed into the seat. I was full of fire and bravado, but if push came to shove, I knew I couldn't take down Blackthorne. My druid powers were growing, they were turning my blood fae abilities into something different and greater than they'd ever been, but I had a feeling he could level cities.

Pulling the napkin out from beneath the utensils, I wrung it like a wet towel. If I was honest with myself, I wasn't certain he was even fae. I wasn't sure what he was. Of the universe, like dragons—isn't that what Teddy once said? What did it mean? Moreover, what did that make me?

"Not important," I told myself. At least, not right now. Straightening in my seat, I smoothed the napkin and watched the kitchen door. I'd prefer he didn't see how much he'd rattled me.

I kept my hands busy, straightening the fork on my left and knife on my right. Where did the spoon go? If I remembered correctly—a big if—next to the knife. Mae took some ridiculous class on etiquette and insisted Y'sindra and I sit through her instructions, as if we were destined for fancy human parties. Fuck etiquette, I'd told her, to which she'd informed me I had bad manners. Y'sindra's "no shit" had been the last straw, and the lesson had ended.

A small smile curled my lips, and I snapped a picture.

Proud? I typed and sent the text to Mae. She was in Eodrom, but when she returned, she'd get a kick out of the text.

With a huff, I put the phone on the table screen up and slumped into my seat to wait. Eventually, Blackthorne returned with two plates of food. He slid something resembling a fried sandwich in front of me and returned to the kitchen. Generally speaking, I was all about fried food, but I still hadn't been hungry since my appetite left me this morning.

I started to push the plate away. Was that powdered sugar? Dipping my finger into the sprinkle of white stuff, I tentatively took a taste. Yep, sugar. And fried bread with meat and cheese? Maybe just a bite. I pulled the plate back.

Setting two glasses of what looked like iced tea on the table, Blackthorne slid into the booth across from me. Despite having an identical sandwich in front of him, he pointed at mine. "It's called a Monte Cristo. Thick brioche bread, baked here yesterday. Ham, gruyere cheese, and a thin layer of raspberry jam are put together. The bread gets lightly buttered and then dipped into an egg wash before a turn on the griddle. A sprinkle of powdered sugar and done." He grinned, clearly proud of himself, and then pointed at plate once again. "There is extra jam for dipping."

"You made this? Just now?" Ugh! I'd come here with the fury of fire and brimstone, and now I was swapping sandwich recipes. Blackthorne had cracked a little, and I'd seen a hint he was not a "good guy," yet he had a way of disarming me—disarming anyone who spoke with him for longer than five minutes.

He fanned his napkin out in his lap and arranged his utensils on the right side of his plate. "I did. Well, not entirely. Chef LeBlanc left everything in the fridge. The only thing I had to do was to dip the sandwich in an egg mixture and get it golden on the griddle." He pointed at my sandwich. "That was intended for my breakfast tomorrow, so eat up."

If he sacrificed his breakfast for me, it would be rude not to take a bite. It also sounded—and looked—very good. I dipped half of the diagonal cut sandwich into the little cup of jam and took a bite. Divinity exploded on my tongue. My eyes slid shut as I savored the melty, crispy, sweet-and-savory goodness. Dear gods, this was amazing. For once, grateful for my long-winded relative's food talk, I filed away the recipe. Teddy would for sure be able to recreate this.

Smiling around a mouthful of his sandwich, Blackthorne set the delicious mess on his plate and wiped his hands on one of the extra napkins he'd wisely brought. "Thank you for eating with me. Now, you had questions."

Caught off guard by how willing he was to answer, I slowly set down the sandwich. Accepting a clean napkin Blackthorne held out, I took my time wiping my hands. I avoided meeting his gaze as I gathered my thoughts. He didn't rush me but continued to eat.

Out of nowhere, Talulla jumped on the seat next to me. Grateful for the break in what had been, for me, an awkward silence, I scratched between her ears. "Where did you come from?"

"She comes and goes." Blackthorne waved his sandwich in her direction. "Been here most of the afternoon, stealing bits of ham from LeBlanc."

"From bacon to ham, you eat pretty well." I tore off a piece and placed it on the table in front of her. The cat was as tall as I was while sitting and had to bend down for the food, not reach up. I took another bite and spent some time chewing. Maybe the sugar on the sandwich would sweeten the sour words on my tongue.

Forearms extended along either side of his plate, Blackthorne leaned forward. "As much as I enjoy your visits, I believe you came here with a purpose?"

I licked my lips and then rubbed my mouth clean on a napkin. I finally got to the point. "You knew whoever this is doing this must be fae."

He dipped his chin once in acknowledgment.

An incoming text lit my phone's screen, and it buzzed. I caught the flash of words before the message faded.

Left Dex with Dad. Home looking at video.

"You need to get that?" Blackthorne asked.

"No." A question pushed to the forefront of my brain, one I hadn't anticipated asking. I met my ancient grandfather's vibrant purple eyes, watching for any reaction. "Do you know who it is?"

His gaze literally darkened. The dip to deeper purple was so brief, so subtle, I would have missed it if I hadn't been anticipating some sort of cue.

"I do not know."

"Liar," I said, a quiet accusation.

Nostrils flaring, he leaned against his seat, arms folding across his chest. A defensive posture, my years as a private investigator told me. Knowing, didn't break me of the same habit.

"I truly do not know," he repeated.

I narrowed my eyes. "But you suspect?"

He rubbed a hand on his chin. "I do."

"Will you tell me?"

"No." His voice was flat, final.

Everything in me wanted to argue, but I recognized the steel in his tone. He wouldn't bend, yet I had to try. "Why not?"

"This is my business. It is a death owed to me," he said with a force that straight up terrified me.

The scent of ozone hit my nostrils. Goosebumps rolled across my skin as power like I'd never felt crowded the room, pushed against me. I hunched beneath the weight of it. The air filled with something unexplainable.

Gods, was this the *thing* unlocking inside of me? Changing me? The day I'd first tapped into my druid power to crack open the veil between Ta'Vale and Outerlands, I'd felt the shift. I fisted my hands against my thighs.

A cool wind brushed over me. All the small hairs loose from my braid lifted and danced. Tiny electrical charges nipped my exposed flesh.

"Stop," I said, hoping my gut told the truth and Blackthorne wouldn't decide to smite me with magic or use that extra steak knife on the table to shut me up. He gave no indication he'd heard. The plates on the table rattled. My hearts gave a nervous little skip. "Stop!" I slapped my hands on the table.

Blackthorne jerked as if I'd struck him. He blinked at me and then shoved up from the booth. Pacing the dining room, he shouted in a language I'd never heard. The words evolved into a litany of curses I understood, and his breathing evened. Eventually, he returned to the table and stood over me. "I apologize. This is deeply personal."

"You don't say?" I used sarcasm to disguise the relief I felt at still being on this side of conscious. Not much scared me, but now that I'd had a peek at Blackthorne's monster, I was adding that to the list.

Excusing himself, he went to the kitchen and returned with a pitcher of tea and a bottle of liquor. He held it up as he slid into the booth. "This conversation calls for alcohol."

Without asking, he topped off my glass with more tea and then added a healthy shot of bourbon. Two shots went into his own glass. Capping the bottle, he drank deeply before settling back in his booth.

"No more games." I straightened my spine, sitting taller, and dredged up the shred of bravado I had left after Blackthorne's intimidating display of power—and I was not intimidated easily. "People are dying. Fae are dying, and you won't help?"

"So?" He tilted his head. "I don't know them. I have lived lifetimes with this single death on my mind."

"You are being selfish." Inwardly, I winced. There I went, speaking without thinking. Hopefully, my runaway mouth didn't get me dead. Beneath the table, I squeezed my thighs to stop myself from nervously shredding the napkin in my lap.

"Yes," he said simply.

I blinked slowly. Of all the responses I'd anticipated, agreement hadn't been one. "And you're fine with that?"

"I am." He took a long slow breath. "A fae lifetime is a slow burning candle. Mortals, like a match, here and gone. I have seen the cycle of both many times."

Eyes narrowing, I pushed my plate aside and leaned forward on my elbows. "You're fae."

"Am I?" There was that smile I itched to smack.

"Are you?"

Reaching across the table, he placed my barely touched sandwich on his plate and tsked. "This is too good to let go to waste."

Talulla's head popped up and she watched the plate move. She rose and followed the food to the other side of the table, curling up against Blackthorne's hip.

Talons clacking on the table, I watched him give the cat yet another piece and then he proceeded to polish off the untouched half of my sandwich. "You aren't going to answer, are you?"

He took his time wiping his fingers clean and then leaned back, hooking his elbows over the back of his seat. "I'd like it if you spent more time here. Learn what it takes to run a hotel."

The absurd turn in conversation had my head spinning. I sputtered, "I have a job."

"Hm. You are going to live a very long time. It would benefit you to have more skills."

Dull pain pulsed in my right temple, a sure sign a headache was on its way. I pinched the bridge of my nose. "For once, can we please stay on subject?"

He sighed, loudly for effect. "Just because you didn't like my answer doesn't mean the conversation wasn't over."

"If you know who this is, or think you know, and you want them dead, why haven't you done it already?" I waved a hand up and down in his direction. "It pains me to say it, but you're clearly powerful enough."

"Why, thank you, Granddaughter."

I rolled my eyes. "Wasn't meant as a compliment, more a commentary on your character. You could do something, but you haven't. That just makes you lazy."

"Immortal does not mean unkillable," he said, an eerie echo of words I'd spoken to Zee.

The declaration also confirmed he was, in fact, immortal. What did that make me? Scary stuff. Maybe I did need to diversify, but unless he planned to sign over The Blackthorne, it probably wouldn't be hotel management.

With a shake of my head, I circled back to the conversation. "I get the impression you didn't just figure this out. You could have done something by now."

"What makes you think I haven't?"

My brow puckered. "Because I'm still dealing with the fallout of what you did over a hundred years ago."

"No fae would dare try me out here—"

"Except me." I smirked.

"Except you, because you didn't know better." He winked. "Good thing I didn't take it personal."

Lips twisting from smirk to scowl, I folded my arms across my chest and slumped against my seat. As if he let me live. I mean, he did, but he didn't have to rub it in.

"Everything I have done—my connection to the corrupt—has all been to get me closer to my goal."

"But you're here and they're in Ta'Vale."

He nodded. "In Eodrom, where the keepers are their most powerful, and make no mistake, they are powerful."

"Come on," I said throwing my hands in the air then thumping the table.

"I've seen you in action, and now you say you're an immortal. Are you telling me you can't handle a couple sun fae?"

"Because sun fae magic is thought of as defense, most believe they are weaker than their moon brethren."

"Yeah," I agreed. "And your magic laid Teddy, who, according to everyone is nearly indestructible, flat."

"The black wolf is incredibly difficult to kill, but it happens."

"Thanks for the pep talk."

"If I went into Eodrom after this fae, I would not make it out alive," he said.

My Great Grandpa was as cagey as I aspired to be, yet he'd let information slip I was certain he hadn't noticed, nor intended, to reveal. The fae responsible wasn't just in Ta'Vale, but inside Eodrom. He might have calmed down from his earlier slip of power, but was obviously still rattled.

"You should kill the corrupt prince."

"Way to give me whiplash." That statement came out of nowhere. "What does Miro have to do with anything?"

"Unlike sun stones who choose their keepers, moon stones are inherently linked to one family."

I groaned and dropped my forehead to the table. "Why does everyone want to teach me a sun-scorched lesson?"

"All moon fae benefit from the stone's power, but that power is amplified in the presence of a keeper," he continued, as if I hadn't said a word. "And in the keeper themself."

Arms folded on the table, I sat up enough to glare. "What is your—Oh, fuck. Miro is a moon stone keeper."

"Glad to see you're as smart as I believed."

I traced fang to fang with my tongue as I thought through the situation. "Just one big problem. If he's in a cell warded to neutralize magic—a ward you created—he won't benefit from the extra moon stone juice."

He drained his tea and refilled the glass, this time without the bourbon. "Correct, so long as he stays in the cell."

Cold terror hit my veins. My face felt numb.

Someone was still inside Eodrom causing havoc. Someone who was probably responsible for many of the escaped prisoners. And I'd handed them a bomb named Miro.

Mumbling words I didn't remember, I pushed from the booth, crossed the hotel's main floor, and went outside. My breathing grated against my eardrums, like a wind tearing through a tunnel.

Somehow, I made it to the beach on lifeless legs. Salty air clung to my skin, bringing me back to my senses. Tiny shocks pinched my neck, down my arms. I rubbed my tingling fingertips against my thumbs.

A starless night had fallen in the short time I'd been inside. I walked toward a great black void. Only the barest hint of silver reflected from the moon playing peekaboo in the cloud revealed the presence of water. The quiet thunder of surf meeting beach still filled the air. It was peaceful. Not for the first time, I wondered if I could stomach the humidity for the view.

Face tilted to the ground, I watched the wooden planks pass beneath my steps. The muggy gulf breeze kicked up, swirling sand across the walk. A physical representation of the many thoughts circling my skull.

I grabbed the tail end of the most pressing thought. One thing was certain, I needed to get word to...to everyone. Miro needed to be dealt with, but I doubted I'd get anywhere near the dungeon. At the very least, I needed to convince them to double the guards, or have guards at all. The few times I'd been there, the only security I could recall were the wards.

Youth might be my excuse for ignorance, but many of the Royal Fae Guard would have been alive during a time when the moon fae royals ruled. They would know the threat they had locked up.

Fate warned me to stay away, but I could call. I would convince them.

"Malaney." Blackthorne's voice pulled me to a stop. I looked up to find I'd made it to the druid circle. Blinking, I turned toward him.

"You forgot this." He handed me my phone, while Talulla pranced around us and continued to the circle.

"Thanks."

With his hands in his front pockets, he looked past me as he spoke. "I could see you blamed yourself. Don't. You did well taking Miro out of play."

"You said—"

"I am aware of my words." His gaze snapped to my face. "You did what needed to be done, removing the others involved. Now the one responsible will have no choice. Releasing the prince will be a move of desperation, and believe me, they will be desperate."

Needing his words to be true, I nodded. "I'll pass along the warning, and if they won't get rid of him, I will."

"The warning is good, but you need to stay away. The keepers of the sun stones are not the only reason I have not already taken my due," he said. "She has the stolen power of the gods inside of her."

"I'll be..." My gaze widened and my breath froze on a surprised gasp. He'd done it again. He'd let something else slip. "She. You said she. You don't mean Iola, do you?"

Nostrils flaring, his expression shuttered. "Heed my warning and stay out of Eodrom." He strode away without a backward glance. The conversation was over.

32

FATE'S SENDING A MESSAGE

I wasn't sure how long I stood there. Long enough for Blackthorne to disappear into his hotel. Long enough for the deck lights to be turned off and then the lobby, bathing the beach in absolute darkness. When I finally turned away, it felt as though I'd come out of a trance. My breath stuttered on an inhale.

I'd learned so much, yet so little. Still lost in thought, I entered the perimeter of the circle, and my unconscious desire to be home took me to the garden. Travel had become that simple.

Tail high, Talulla slunk through the grass, disappearing down the stairs. I stopped just outside the circle, tipping my face up.

While the sun had already fallen in Florida, here it was just dipping its toes over the horizon. Strands of fluffy clouds strung across the sky appeared to be on fire, bright orange, haloed in gold against a deep, cobalt canvas.

This was the type of sunset that inspired poetry, but it did nothing to distract my racing thoughts. I cast a glance at the security camera as I passed, wondering if Blackthorne was watching.

I should be creeped out or angry. Instead, I felt...sad. Our conversation had a note of finality. I couldn't say what or why, but I half suspected the next time I tried to cross through the portal, I would go nowhere.

My brain catapulted back to a conversation and what Blackthorne let slip. The warm grass whispered beneath my steps as I crossed the garden, mulling over his words.

She has the stolen power of the gods inside of her.

"She," I murmured as I rounded the final spiral to the balcony. Who could possibly be that powerful? Aside from the keepers, my father was the most powerful sun fae. Maybe Mae would have an idea. She spent enough time in Eodrom.

I toed off my slip-on sneakers and padded inside. My sisters and Lo were busy in front of laptops, a bowl of popcorn between them. Talulla had already curled up in my favorite seat, watching me with "I dare you to try" eyes. The cat was eating my bacon, using my portal circle, sitting in my favorite seat. Familiar my ass, she was a free-loading roommate.

"Hey!" I said, and my sisters and Lo almost came out of their seats. "Geez, jumpy?"

"We've been at this for hours," Y'sindra whined. "It's like meditation, but we have to pay attention."

"So, nothing like meditation." I knelt on the sofa, facing the dining room where the group gathered. Leaning my elbows on the back, I rested my chin in my hands. "Haven't found anything?"

"Nothing at the hotel, but look at this." Mae jotted down the time stamp location of the video she'd been reviewing. A lonely thumb drive to her right replaced the one in her laptop. "This is the video delivered from the club."

"You won't be able to see anything from there. Pull up a chair," Y'sindra said and plopped down in her seat.

Lo remained standing, grinning and waving at me. His perpetual joy never failed to make me smile.

Deciding I was too tired to climb over the back of the sofa without faceplanting, I stood and went the long way around. "Where's my sugar buns?"

"Didn't he ask you not to call him that?" Mae asked while she scrolled through the video feed.

"He asked me not to call him that in front of others. I don't consider you others, if I'm not calling him that to his face."

"Your logic is perfection." Y'sindra gave me her nod of approval.

"I knew you'd agree," I said and spotted Teddy's boots in the hallway at the edge of the living area, as if he'd stepped out of them and kept going.

"Your sleeping wolf went to lie down." Y'sindra pointed to the upstairs hallway. "Said to wake him up when you got home."

"Ted-D must slow down." Lo shook his head. "He is busy with the bar downstairs, the clean-up in Interlands, and now Outerlands."

"You're right." I rested my hand on the back of Mae's chair. "We need to force him to get some rest."

"Blood will also help," he said.

I went still, and then experienced a full-body flush. "I thought shifters were blood magic, not that they drank the stuff." Aside from the mating bond, of course. My blush cranked up the heat at the memory.

"Oh, we do not! Not for pleasure." Lo clapped his hands to his chest. "But mate blood does help shifters."

His gaze left my face to stare adoringly at Y'sindra's profile. She made a point of pretending she didn't notice, but the blush that roared to life on her pale cheeks made a liar of her. At least I wasn't the only one turning pink around here.

Would they try the mate bond? Had they tried the mate bond? I wanted to ask so badly, but Y'sindra would leap from the balcony before she answered that sort of question. Of course, she could fly away, but the point would be in the drama.

"Makes sense. Thanks." I smiled and then leaned over Mae's shoulder. "Okay, what am I looking at?"

"Besides a sick club?" She craned her neck to see me, a wry smirk tilting her lips. "Y'sindra's words, but I definitely want to go."

Too many flashing lights and people for me. Mostly, too many people. I was pretty sure I'd filled my annual crowd-quota attending Taboo. "Didn't Vaughn say he'd go with you?"

"He did." She smiled brightly and then turned back to the laptop screen. She scrolled through a few minutes. Despite the fast-moving frames, I recognized Lincoln's strong build and lustrous complexion. His braids were tied at the nape of his neck, the long strands swinging with his animated movement. He was laughing, drinking, and dancing, always surrounded by large crowds. "Here." Mae paused the video, went back a few frames, and tapped her screen.

Squinting, I leaned close. I could barely make out Lincoln, who was in profile. But next to him... Adrenaline sputtered into my system and my hearts sped up. He was on the far side of a large open bar with his arm around a blonde woman's waist. The woman, who looked to be as tall as him, had her back to the camera.

"Is this the only angle?" I asked.

"Unfortunately." Mae paused the video and stood. She pressed her hands into her lower back and arched her spine, releasing a series of rapid-fire cracks and pops.

"Wow, how long have you been sitting here?"

Mae tilted her head. "What day is it?"

"A couple hours. Lo and I got up to stretch our wings, but this one"— Y'sindra hooked a thumb at Mae—"hasn't moved."

Had I been gone that long? I pinched the bridge of my nose. It felt like I'd packed a year into days. Fatigue pressed on my shoulders. I pulled out the chair at the head of the oval table and collapsed into the seat. Not quite ready for the whirlwind my Blackthorne conversation would stir up, I eased into an easier subject. "How did Dexter cope?"

As expected, Mae's face lit up. "Very well. Dad's spirits are soaring with the sun."

"Good enough he agreed to shack up with our folks for a few days," Y'sindra said and closed her laptop.

My brows shot upwards. "He's staying in Eodrom?"

Sucking on her bottom lip, Mae nodded. "Do you know how long he's been gone from Ta'Vale?"

"Roughly," I said. "Sometime after the Great Fae Divide ended."

"Holy Hell!" Y'sindra exclaimed. "You're telling me Dexter—Dexy-boy— is over a hundred years old?"

"He told me he stayed in Eodrom for a little while before splitting," I said. "The war ended over a hundred years ago. So yeah, he is."

Her face scrunched in thought. "He acts a lot like a surfer guy in a movie. Like he doesn't have a care in the world."

"Maybe he doesn't." I pulled my braid over my shoulder and ran my hands down its length. "Well, this is as good a segue into the Blackthorne convo as I will get."

"Oh." Mae slipped back into her seat. "This sounds serious."

I picked at the edge of the table with my talons. "Do you know who the moon stone keepers are?"

Going still, Mae watched me. "I never thought about it, but I would assume same as sun fae. The stones would choose."

"Since you're asking, that ain't it?" Y'sindra asked. She leaned into Lo's side. He reached for her hand.

A brief smile tugged at my lips watching them. If only life could always be so simple. "Nope. Apparently, the keepers are born to it. One blood line. Dexter's." I paused. "And Miro's."

"That's a good thing, right?" Forehead puckering, Mae twisted her hands together in her lap.

"With Dexter, yes. Miro? Clearly not. If he ever gets out."

"He won't." Mae tipped her chin up, speaking with confidence I didn't feel.

Y'sindra's eyes made an exaggerated tour of their sockets. "Are we talking about the same dungeon?"

Wind pounded into the sliding glass doors, rattling them in their frame. All three of us swiveled to look.

"Ooo," Y'sindra said, modulating the "o" to make it spooky. "Fate's sending a message."

It was my turn to roll my eyes. "You know that's not how it works."

She made a face. "So? I know Odin has more than one eye, but it's still my fav curse. Same diff."

"Our typical evening thunderstorm," Mae said. "Lots of thunder and wind, five minutes of rain."

After so many years living in arid Interlands, the frequency of storms we'd encountered in Vegas—albeit brief—had come as a surprise.

"Let's assume Miro gets out." I crossed to the sliding glass door and shut it before we let the rain in.

"Hmph," she grunted, and it was not the sound of agreement. Mae might be incredibly intelligent, but she was often blinded by her stubborn belief in others.

"He'd be in the company of whoever is behind all the subterfuge to oust the sun fae, and he'd not only have scary black magic, but he'd be pulling power directly from the moon stones that are planted in Eodrom." I held Mae's stare, watching the transformation of her features from irritated to understanding to horrified. "He'd do irreparable damage before anyone could bring him down."

"But he's locked up," she insisted in whisper.

"For now." I returned to my seat. "That gets to the core of what I got out of Blackthorne. He won't say definitively he knows who is behind all this, but it's obvious he does."

Wings shivering, Y'sindra dusted snow. It evaporated before it hit the ground. "Why the hell not?"

A humorless laugh left me, and I shook my head. "He said it's his business. A death owed to him."

Y'sindra's wings folded tight to her back, and she whistled low. "Sounds personal."

"Sure does." I leaned forward, resting my forearms on the table, and gave them a rundown of my conversation with Blackthorne.

The whites of Mae's wide eyes were startling against the blue. Her mouth had fallen open as I spoke, and she clacked it shut.

"You're telling me that super old, super powerful druid was too afraid to confront whoever *she* is?" Equal parts acid and awe spilled into Y'sindra's voice. She threw up her hands. "Well, I guess Mom and Dad need to pack up and hit the road. They can have the Interlands house."

"I'm not sure we're there yet. I think this fae is out of options. Blackthorne says she'll be desperate since we took away the other players involved." I looked at Mae and repeated his words. "Releasing Miro will be an act of desperation."

Head bowed, Mae rose from her seat. She carefully tucked the chair under the table. "I will tell Iola."

"Not sure that's the best idea," I said.

Her head snapped up. "Why not?"

"Because you're softer than a half-cooked marshmallow." Y'sindra fluttered to our sister and poked her in the arm. "Fun as always, but Lo and I have an early day at the Outerlands bar. Text if you need me."

We watched her fly to the top of the stairs, Lo winging behind her.

"She's right. You're a pushover. You believe the best of everyone." I took Mae's hands and squeezed. "And we love you dearly for your squishy center."

Golden hair tumbling over her shoulders, Mae shook her head. "I'm not that soft."

"You are. Maybe one day my cynicism will rub off on you."

"It will be the day my optimism gets into you." She flicked my braid over my shoulder. "There is nothing wrong with giving everyone the benefit of the doubt, which I choose to do until they prove me wrong."

I snorted. "Like Duskmere did? So many times, I've lost count."

"True, he has made mistakes. Will I still believe what he tells me?" She shrugged. "Probably, but not in this. I understand why Miro must be dealt with."

"Killed. He needs to be killed." Outside, heat lightning lit the sky while the patter of rain slowed.

My gaze flicked to the clock. It wasn't late, but I was exhausted. I could hardly think straight. "Let's talk about this in the morning."

"Sure thing, and maybe we should contact Fate? See if she still feels like you need to stay away?" Mae suggested. "You never know, she might also get a feeling on how much danger Miro poses."

"Maybe." She was probably right. Still, just because I extended an olive branch to Fate when she showed up at the Interlands bar, it didn't mean I wanted to start calling her for her Iomas fueled opinions. "We can talk about it in the morning."

"You look like you're about to fall over. Why don't you go snuggle up to your man?"

Exactly what I'd been thinking. "You staying up?"

She pulled her chair back out and opened her laptop. "For a bit. I just started on the footage of Beast. The guy liked hanging around the bars here in the casino. There's a lot to sort through."

I left her to it and headed upstairs. The bedroom was cool and dark. Soft, rumbly snores came from the bed. Quickly, I washed up and changed into thin cotton shorts and a loose tank top. The chill of the sheets shocked me, but I warmed as soon as I scooted next to my personal radiator.

His murmurs melted the tension knots this day had twisted into my neck. He tunneled an arm beneath me and pulled me against him. I curled my leg over his thigh and rested my face on his shoulder, soaking in his woodsy, vanilla scent.

"Everything okay?" he asked, voice thick with sleep.

"Fine." I slid my arm across his torso. Already, my eyelids drooped. "Nothing that can't wait until tomorrow."

"Mmm." Teddy kissed the top of my head. "I planned to go with Lo and your sister tomorrow, but it can wait."

"It's okay." And it was. There was nothing Teddy could do about what I'd learned.

"Love you." He squeezed me against him.

Sleep dragged me under.

33

OUTCAST

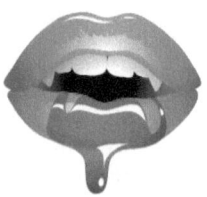

SOMETHING VIBRATED ON MY NIGHTSTAND. "MAKE IT STOP," I MUMBLED into my pillow.

The sound came again. Lying on my stomach, I pressed up on my forearms and glared at the table. The phone vibrated a third time, and I slapped it to the floor.

Unrelenting, it vibrated again, but the sound was muffled from the nest of shed clothing it had landed in. Communication crystals were so much easier to ignore. Groggily, I rolled over and sat up, blinking at the dark glass doors. Sun scorch it, it wasn't even dawn. This was happening much too frequently.

I ignored the phone and flopped backward, rolling toward Teddy. Instead of a hard, warm body, my hands found the silky texture of cold sheets. The sound of running water finally penetrated the web of sleep cocooning my brain. Rising on an elbow, I looked toward the light leaking from beneath the closed bathroom door.

Memories of my last shower with Teddy heated me from the inside out. I'd take more of that. Though maybe turn down the intensity a notch or two. It had been hot, but a little overwhelming. I had no idea what came over me.

That wasn't entirely true. Beast's attention had kicked the mate bond into overdrive.

At least I could get a good eyeful of Teddy's sugar buns before I started the day. Grinning, I flung my legs over the side of the bed. The bed was tall, and I was short, forcing me to hop to the ground.

My thoughts about the mate bond drew me toward Teddy's side of the bed. A vial hung from a hook above his nightstand. The length of my finger, the heavy-duty glass was flat on two sides so it rested neatly against the chest. I'd purchased two from summer fairies as a sort of "break in case of emergency" gag gift.

Like Y'sindra with her winter magic, summer fairies manipulated the summer sun to create glass. The vials were magicked to keep anything inside fresh, which currently meant mine and Teddy's blood. I slipped the leather tether from the hook and palmed the vial, which was several degrees warmer than the room.

Dacian had tried to turn the Interlands bar to ash. He couldn't easily access *Blood and Wine*, which left Outerlands, where Teddy planned to go today. I squeezed my fist around the vial and headed for the bathroom. After Lo's comment about mate's blood, I wasn't letting my mate step one foot out of this penthouse without this vial hanging from his neck.

The first thing I saw was denim sliding up to encase Teddy's delicious derriere. Bummer. Our gazes met in the mirror, and he turned to face me, bare chested. Not the view I'd come here for, but almost as good.

"Hey you." He walked forward and took me by the waist. Turning, he set me on the counter. He did that a lot, but I wasn't complaining. With a hand on either side of my hips, he leaned in for a kiss, but I quickly slapped a hand over my mouth and shook my head.

Twisting, I looked for the mouthwash.

Teddy straightened. The flex of his biceps momentarily distracted me as he crossed his arms over his chest.

With my eyes glued to all that glorious naked flesh, I reached for the mouthwash and missed. "Dang it!" I ripped my gaze away, grabbed the bottle, swished and spit. "Ah! Minty fresh. Where were we?"

"Moment's passed." He shrugged, and his powerful shoulders bunched in all the right ways.

Outraged, I gasped. The corner of his mouth rose in a lopsided smile.

"Get over here." I looped my arms around his neck, pulling him to me. He only resisted for a heartbeat before he chuckled, and his lips met mine. The kiss was slow and sweet but over all too soon.

Teddy raised his head but remained between my parted knees. His fingers lifted my hair from the back of my neck. "You're sweating."

"You take hot showers." I gestured to the top half of the mirror, still opaque from steam.

"What's in your hand?"

"Oh." I plucked the leather tether from my palm and held it up, letting the vial dangle between us. "Since we have these, I thought maybe you should wear it."

Those deep brown eyes I'd once mistaken for black tracked the swaying vial. "I'll wear mine if you wear yours."

"Deal." Honestly, that was much easier than I'd expected.

Though he bent forward, I had to stretch to reach behind his neck. Drawing my lip beneath a fang, I focused on ensuring the knot would hold.

He straightened, and looking at his reflection in the mirror, he turned the tube one way and then the other. "We've had these for a while. What made you think we should wear them now?"

Leaning forward, I pressed a lingering kiss to his chest, directly over his heart and just above the blood vial. "Something Lo said."

"Oh yeah?" Brows arching in question, he grabbed his shirt from the counter and slipped it on. Thanks to the cleverly designed flat sides, only a slight bump from the tube was visible beneath the shirt's grayish-blue material.

"He said shifters can benefit from mate's blood, which I knew, of course."

"Of course." He pulled on a pair of socks.

"The reminder just...I had them made, we might as well wear them."

He swung me from the counter. "You're worried about me going to Outerlands."

A statement, not a question. Was I that transparent? "No."

"I'm just going there to see if the idea of getting the bar up and running again is viable. I'll be fine."

"I know." Logically, I did know, but my hearts had a mind of their own.

"But this is a good idea." He took my hand and squeezed. "It's early, you should get some more sleep. I didn't mean to wake you."

"You didn't. Someone was texting." I scowled at the far side of the bed, as if whoever dared message me at this hour would see the expression. "It was probably Y'sindra."

"I wouldn't put it past her." He glanced at the clock. "I've got a few minutes. Want to tell me what happened with your grandpa?"

I made a face. "Why do you insist on calling him that?"

"Because, technically, he is." My big, strong male playfully tapped me on my nose. "Plus, you're adorable when you're annoyed."

Despite myself, I smiled. "You're not so bad yourself."

"Your sister will be pounding down the door soon." Taking my hand, he drew me with him toward the door. "Tell me what happened?"

"I was right. He knows who's behind everything going down in Eodrom, with your brother and the corrupt in Shadwe. He won't tell me who, though."

We stopped just shy of the exit. Teddy pulled me against him. Placing his palm flat on my back, he drew slow, soothing circles. "Did he give you a reason?"

"No good reason, no. Something about a death owed to him."

Delicious warmth seeped from his palm into my back. "Sounds personal."

"Mae said the same thing, and I agree. He also said something about her being too powerful, but he was probably just trying to scare me away." I looked at Teddy. "Blackthorne was more flustered than I've ever seen him. He let something slip."

"Oh?"

"He called this fae *she*."

Someone thumped against the door. A single loud bang. I jumped but then laughed beneath my breath, shaking my head. It seemed my sister's patience with me not answering my phone had run out. "I'm surprised she was so subdued."

"Me too. Your sister is something else." Teddy chuckled and then patted his pockets until he located his phone. "Lo says the reception in Outerlands is spotty, but I'll have my phone. Text if you need me. It's bound to get through eventually."

"I'll probably be here all day." I went up on my toes for another kiss.

Teddy opened the door. Y'sindra was already gone. He paused on the threshold. "By the way, how much do you know about Blackthorne's past?"

"About as much as any fae who's read a history book." Not that I'd read many. "Why?"

"Because it sounds like your grandpa has a case of love gone bad."

Shock rooted me in place long after Teddy had left. The conversation I'd had with Blackthorne when he'd been locked in the Eodrom dungeon came back with brutal clarity.

She is like you.

Not she was like you, she *is* like you. I rubbed my fingers against my thumb, a weird prickly sensation beneath my skin. I'd been so blinded by desperation to save my kidnapped sister and find out how to wake Teddy who'd been knocked unconscious by a mega dose of Blackthorne's sleep spell, I hadn't paid attention when he'd discussed the female he'd bound himself to all those years ago. His love for her was the reason he'd created the potion for the moon fae during the Great Fae Divide. The same potion that was twisted into something else and being used now.

It had been right in front of me all along.

She has the stolen power of the gods inside her.

A powerful, highly respected druid, when Blackthorne left Eodrom, many druids left with him. The monster I'd been taught my distant relative to be had drained his followers of all their power and left behind their dried husks in the desert.

That was how fae history had it, but when I'd accused Blackthorne of the atrocity, he'd denied it. Simply said it wasn't him.

What if it had been her? What if Teddy was right and it was a case of love gone bad—very, very bad. Gods, but it made sense. Blackthorne had already been immeasurably powerful. Why would he kill the druids who followed him, probably his friends, maybe even family? But if she devoured that kind of power...

My brain spasmed at the thought. The jumpy, prickly sensation had stopped. My body and my brain felt as if they had been rolled in cotton. I flopped face first across the bed. What good did it do me to figure this out now, or ever? I had no way of knowing this fae's identity, other than it had to be one of the old ones. But a lot of fae were old.

The fact that they were bonded to Blackthorne led me to believe no one had known. If he were the monster the fae believed, she wouldn't continue to walk the halls of Eodrom freely. Or at all. Due to her allegiance to the corrupt, I can't imagine she'd be allowed to live.

Then again, Miro still breathed.

I dragged a pillow beneath my face and screamed into it. I took a breath and screamed again, until my throat caught fire and lungs ached. Pressure pushed against my eyes. Gods, I hated feeling so...helpless.

Rolling over, I threw an arm across my eyes and focused on slowing my breath. Blackthorne had talked a lot in the dungeon. If I picked at the threads, maybe I could unravel some sort of clue Mae could run with and research.

I squeezed my eyes and focused. My memory wasn't my best attribute, and at the time, every piece of me had been focused on getting answers I'd needed.

"Outcast," I whispered. He'd call her an outcast. It was the comparison he'd made between us. My brows pinched. The recent case of the missing fae revealed the sun fae's dirty little secrets. There were a lot of lonely outcasts. I huffed a breath. It was somewhere to start, but at the rate these events were escalating, it wouldn't be enough.

Gods damn Blackthorne to the bottom of the Boiling Bay. I'd never been, but I'd read about the salty waters that could melt flesh from fae. It would be awful and exactly what he deserved. I yanked my arms from my face and pummeled the bed at my sides. The mattress shook.

Breath coming in harsh pants, I groaned my irritation. Fuck it. I'd call the guy. I still had that weird feeling he was gone, but maybe he'd answer.

Rolling over once again, I crawled to the side of the bed and reached down to grab my phone from where it had landed on a twisted T-shirt. With my elbows resting on the edge of the bed, I thumbed through my contacts— less than ten—and called Blackthorne.

It rang, and rang, and rang. I glanced toward the liminal pale gray light trapped between dark and dawn leaking up from the horizon. Despite it being three hours behind where he was at, this only solidified the vibes from our last goodbye. Sadness clung to the back of my throat, but anger overshadowed that emotion right now.

A death owed to him. What a crock of cheeseless poofs. I sent off a quick text telling him what I'd figured out and a demand we talk. Maybe making demands wasn't the best approach, but if I begged, I doubted he'd respond.

The little missed call icon reminded me of what woke me this morning. I pulled up recent history and frowned. Unknown number. My hearts beat faster with false hope that it might have been Blackthorne calling from a different phone. Afterall, not many people had this number.

I hovered my finger over the call icon but then I noticed the text bubble at the bottom of the screen and tapped that instead. The message wasn't from Blackthorne.

A long series of texts popped up along with a photo taken of Lincoln surrounded by a group of laughing people on someone's front lawn at the Split Sands pack compound. I didn't recognize the actual location where the image had been captured, but the style of home was familiar, and the arrangement of the neighborhood was the same as what I'd seen during my brief visit.

Momentarily distracted from my Blackthorne conundrum, I scrolled to the to the top and read.

hi this is roger we met at pack grounds
i told you about linc u gave me ur info
my brother works at that club

"Good gods, dude. I got it as soon as you said pack grounds." I scrolled past a few more dumb reminders lacking grammar and punctuation.

forgot I had this pic of linc with the blonde hope it helps

In other words, he was too drunk to know he took it. I dragged my lip beneath a fang and looked at the picture again. Nothing jumped out at me at first glance. I hadn't even noticed a blonde woman.

A large group of people who were obviously having a good time filled the frame. Most held some sort of beverage. A lot of beers, wide grins, and open-mouthed laughter. The crowd was mixed with people standing on their own and standing together as couples, I presumed, even if only for one night.

Placing two fingers on the screen over Lincoln, I spread them apart, zooming in. Like the others, he looked happy. The guy had been tall, and he had an arm slung around a woman of equal height.

My hearts tapped. The same woman from the video. This must have been after they returned from the club. I squinted, scrutinizing the photo. While everyone still wore their nightclub finery, Linc wore loose-fitting pajama bottoms and plain T-shirt. The clothes on the blonde woman at his side had the oversized look I'd only seen on Mae when she padded around the penthouse in Vaughn's boxers and shirts.

This must have been taken at Linc's house. Roger had said Linc left first, but it appeared the group had brought the party to him. Probably a prank for leaving early. Poor guy had likely already been poisoned with the potion.

As with the video feed, I couldn't see the woman's face. Beneath Lincoln's arm, she stood in profile, leaning against him. Her face pressed against his shoulder hid her features, but I had a clear view of her thin frame and long golden hair.

A dot of blue grabbed my attention. Throat suddenly tight, I forced myself to swallow. The longer I looked, the more blue I saw woven into tiny braids, along with onyx and amber stones.

Or beads.

"No." A wave of horror swept over me, into me, turning sharp and frigid, slicing into bone. It couldn't be.

I scrambled from the bed and stumbled toward the evidence bags haphazardly thrown on the dresser. Dumping what I'd mistaken for blue glass into my palm, I switched on a lamp and held it under the light.

Hearts thumping in my ears, I spotted the nearly invisible hole drilled through the center of the bead. Blackthorne's words pounded into my skull.

I opened the bag containing the bloody paper with the smudged phone number, stuck my nose inside and inhaled. Herbs and fruit. Caraway and honeydew.

Her moon fae mother abandoned her to her noble father at the sun fae court.

A mere shadow to her exalted half-sister.

The fae behind everything was Iola's sister. The fae who was never seen with Iola. The fae my sister idolized.

Brenyn.

34

DON'T BE MAD

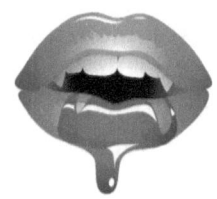

"Mae!" I shoved open her bedroom door. It flew inward on its hinges. Something cracked. The doorknob punched into the wall and stuck. I raced out, down a hallway, past a bathroom, into the main room, and came to a stumbling halt next to the bed. It was empty.

Hearts thundering in my throat, a sense of foreboding raised goosebumps along the back of my neck. I rubbed my hand over the tiny bumps and turned in a slow circle. My gaze landed on the cluster of sun stone necklaces Mae never failed to wear if she left the house. Relief swept over me, nearly bringing me to my knees.

"What was I worried about?" I turned and strode toward the door, shaking my head at my ridiculous over reaction. Who did I think I was? Fate?

Fate does have awesome hair. Maybe I should go blue? Better yet, purple, to match my oddball eye. I had a feeling Teddy would approve.

Smiling, I hit the landing and found the dining room and living area empty. I took a right and headed for the kitchen, still thinking about hair. I'd ask Mae her opinion. Hair was more Y'sindra's thing, but Mae was our fashionista. She'd have all kinds of opinions.

"Mae?" I called as I rounded the corner and stopped. The room was empty. It had that cold, no one had been here for a while feel.

Belatedly, I realized I didn't smell coffee. I looked at the empty pot. The early riser of the three of us, Mae always made coffee. That light-headed, panicky feeling reemerged. And I was supposed to be the calm one.

I looked through the kitchen pass to the living area and the pastels painting the sky outside. The sliding glass doors were wide open. Of course! Mae had her morning meditation in the garden.

Pajamas were appropriate attire for meditation. I would join. She would be all at peace and whatever when she was finished. It'd be easier to tell my sister about Brenyn, who she had a low-key worship complex for when she was in that frame of mind.

Several pairs of slippers sat by the door. I slipped into a fuzzy pink pair. The pink had started as an ironic joke, but like my attempt to annoy Pru with kindness, it had backfired. I owned a lot of pink.

Trails of steam rose from the lounge chairs. The desert heat, already reaching into the stratosphere, evaporated remnants of last night's storm from the vinyl mesh material. Slowly, I climbed the stairs, taking care not to make too much noise. I'd jogged up the steps to glares and scowls from sun fae who had joined Mae in the garden enough times to learn better.

I hadn't heard anyone this morning. Thank the holy Ho Ho, Mae must be alone. It was enough of a chore dealing with strangers on my best day, which today was not. Not to mention the news I needed to break to my sister wasn't fit to be shared in the company of others—especially sun fae.

At first glance, the garden was empty. At second glance, it was still empty.

"Shit." I was ninety-nine percent certain she wouldn't have left to deliver the message about Miro without speaking to me—that was something I would do. Yet, that one percent margin dug its beastly claws into my brain and wouldn't let go.

I curled and flexed my fingers, trying to dislodge that jittery sensation. Faster than I'd come up the stairs, I jogged down.

Every creak and groan the building made snapped against my nerves like a rubber band.

Though Brenyn had never made a move against Mae, that wouldn't last forever. She might even genuinely like my sister, but she was a ruthless monster who had been hiding in the shadows, planning, manipulating, and now she was out of moves. Thank the stars I discovered this before she made a move, and I could warn Mae to stay away. She'd hate it, but until Brenyn could be apprehended, it was the only option.

Vaughn's apartment was the likeliest place Mae would be if she wasn't here. Knowing the odds of him picking up were better if the call came from the front desk, I strode for the house phone.

Warning Mae might not be all I needed to do. She liked Iola's evil sister far too much to outright condemn her. Her blind faith in others would embolden her to talk to and hear Brenyn out.

I called downstairs and asked for Vaughn. Rather than ringing his room, they put me on hold. The vampire was already at work. Mae never stayed in his room alone. A knot formed at the base of my throat.

"Lane." Vaughn came on the line.

"Have you seen my sister?"

"Often."

Now was not the time for this guy to develop a sense of humor. My hand tightened on the receiver. The hard plastic ground against my bones. "Today. Have you seen Mae today?"

"No, but I worked the graveyard shift last night. We were supposed to meet for breakfast when I get off in…" There was a pause and rustle of movement. "I get off at eight. We have plans to meet then."

My gaze flew to the clock. "That's almost two hours from now."

"You can tell time."

"Listen," I snapped. "I don't know where Mae is. Do you have any ideas or not?"

"She…no, I don't know. I'm assuming you've checked the garden?" Vaughn was around enough to know my sister's routine almost as well as I did.

"Of course. She isn't in the penthouse." I looked through the kitchen to the hallway, where I could just see the edge of the elegant elevator panels. "Wait, do you guys have cameras in the elevators?"

There was only a moment's hesitation, as he decided whether he should give away Blackthorne's secrets, I imagined. "We do."

I wasn't offended. I'd expected as much. Elevator surveillance for safety was common practice. If I owned this joint—and I liked to pretend I did— I'd have done the same. "Will you see if Mae used it. Or…" I licked my lips. "Or if anyone came up to the penthouse between last night and now?"

"I don't have to."

"Vaughn!" I stomped my foot.

"Lane, I have been here since midnight. The front desk receives an alert every time the penthouse code is used. A precaution Mr. Black had installed after your uninvited visits last year."

I sank onto a stool. Closing my eyes, I rested my elbow on the counter and forehead in my palm. Despite knowing the answer, I asked, "It wasn't used?"

"No." His tone had gentled. "Your sister is the most capable female I have ever encountered. I'm certain she's fine, but I will check the cameras like you asked."

Though he couldn't see me, I sat up and nodded. "Thank you."

"Lane?"

"Yes?"

"Have you tried calling her?"

My eyes widened. I was a dumb ass. "Of course," I lied. It wasn't so strange I hadn't thought to call her. For years, Mae only carried a fae crystal. Recently, she finally got her own cell phone.

"All right. I'll be in touch if I find anything."

The moment the receiver hit the cradle I raced upstairs for my cell phone. As I returned downstairs, I dialed. Across the room, a gentle chime trilled. Instantly recognizing Mae's ringtone, something twisted inside my chest.

I took the final four stairs in one leap and raced to the dining room table and found my face staring up at me from my sister's phone. Punching end call, my gaze snagged on the open laptop. She would never walk away and leave the laptop open. Her scent was faint, stale, as if she'd been gone for hours.

A folded piece of paper was tucked beneath the laptop. On its own, I wouldn't think anything of it, but the placement had been intentional to grab the attention of anyone who looked. Only enough of the paper was beneath the keyboard to hold it in place. The rest stuck out and draped over the side of the table.

"Oh, Mae, what did you do?" I pulled the paper out and unfolded the note.

Don't be mad.

Love you

Hands trembling, I tapped the keyboard to bring up the screen. Somehow, I knew what I'd see. Dread clung to the back of my throat. I breathed through my mouth, chest rising and falling. *Please let me be wrong.* I curled my talons into my palm. The wait was excruciating.

Something whirred to life and the screen lit up. The sight sent shards of denial through my hearts. Sharp pain flared and then everything inside me went dead.

I'd been right.

On the screen, Mae had paused the video feed.

She'd been going over footage of Beast. This did not look like the man I'd had the misfortune of meeting. His head was bent forward, speaking intimately to the woman he embraced. His face was in profile, an easy smile lifting the corner of his mouth. The camera looked down on his broad back. Inside his embrace, Brenyn smiled, seemingly right at the camera.

35

SOMETHING WAS VERY WRONG

"Oh, gods, Mae." I heard the words come out of my mouth but couldn't feel my lips move.

Staring at the screen, a rush of heat burned through the paralytic terror holding me hostage. As if coming alive, I gasped on a breath.

Brenyn possessed an otherworldly beauty. A quality not uncommon among the sun fae or the moon fae, but she had a face that could coax the stars from the sky, just so they had the privilege of shining in her presence.

How had she gone unnoticed within Eodrom? Like the relentless push of the incoming tide, Blackthorne's words in the dungeon came back.

She was unwanted.

Her mother's abandonment and father's rejection.

It ate at her, rotted her from the inside with every taunt and blow she took.

Without my sisters, was this who I would have been?

I squeezed my eyes shut, once again feeling pressure build. Helplessness pushed down on my shoulders. It was all too much. I was too small in this great big universe. My breathing turned ragged. I wanted to sink onto the floor and curl into the fetal position. This past year was like a heavyweight boxing match, but no one called the round. It just kept going and going.

Shoving my fingers into my hair, I shook my head. "No."

I'd always believed myself a monster, but Brenyn was the real deal. My hearts might be tarnished, but the crust of cynicism had begun to flake away.

I would never do it for myself, but I would tear every world apart between me and those I loved without looking back. Zero regrets.

Eyes still squeezed shut, I inhaled deeply. The cool air soothed my emotion-ravaged throat. I released the breath. My hearts slowed. The gulf of powerlessness torn open inside me began to mend.

My eyes popped open. "The crystal."

I turned and raced for my bedroom, suddenly there and sweeping junk from the dresser with no memory of climbing the stairs. Desperation to contact Mae must have blurred everything. While I used to be quick, I was never that fast, and certainly not anymore.

Or was I?

Hands freezing mid grab, I looked into the mirror mounted behind the dresser. A fissure of red rimmed my right eye. I swallowed and shook my head. It had been that way since the bite.

Right now, Mae mattered, not my stupid eye. Staring at the cluttered surface, I opened and closed my hands. *I swear I left the communication crystal right here.* Even if it was right in front of me, I probably wouldn't see it in this mess.

Gods, I sounded like Mae. Maybe all these years, she'd been onto something?

I clenched my hands, only then realizing I still held my phone. Shockingly, I hadn't thrown it. That wasn't baby steps, it was an emotional baby leap.

A quick scroll through my contacts brought me to *Sassafras*. Y'sindra's doing. Drunk on a sassafras martini—with berries, of course—claiming it sounded like sassy fairy martini, she'd programmed the name into all our phones.

The call went straight to voice mail. I stomped my foot and hung up, almost tossing the phone. "Not her fault, Lane."

My shoulders were pinched. A quick side to side roll of my head shook loose the tight hand of frustration from my muscles.

I called again, this time leaving a message. "Mae's gone. She discovered something, and I think she did something stupid about it. I need to know if you've talked. Call me."

Though I knew I'd gone through everything, I searched again. Each second that passed without locating the crystal, frustration built. Not under the discarded shirt. Not under the empty bag of cheesy poofs. Not in the cute box Teddy bought me for the express purpose of keeping small, important stuff.

The fae did crazy things with their magic, why couldn't they put a "find me" spell on the damn things?

My gaze came around to my nightstand. I was up, over, and across the bed almost before the thought solidified. The nightstand was clear of everything except a lamp, a napkin, and a half-empty soda can from I-had-no-idea days ago.

I wrinkled my nose and slid a look to the neat surface of Teddy's table, then to his clean floor, and finally back to my side, and the pile of clothes. Dear gods, I truly was a slob.

Left with no other alternative, I dropped to a crouch and shook out every shirt, sock, and...something fell from a pair of pants. I followed the muffled thumps to the thimble-sized communication crystal where it had bounced against the baseboard.

"Gotcha." Immediately, I brushed my thumb across the crystal's warm, smooth surface and spoke. "Mae."

The soft pings came like razors scraping across my nerves, each one slicing deeper. I squeezed my fist over the crystal and tried again. Still no answer. She had to be there! My hearts double-tapped my ribs, and I tried a third time. I left the unanswered connection open much longer than necessary.

"It's okay," I told myself. The sound was so soft and vibration so subtle, calls were easy to miss—or ignore—I did it all the time.

A call on the crystal to Y'sindra had the same result. That worried me less. If she was in the air, it would be nearly impossible to notice the alert.

Dampness crept into the creases of my palms. I put the crystal on the table and rubbed my hands on my shirt while I decided who to call next. Would Mae have woken my parents? I doubted it, but there was a chance our father had been awake when she went through the portal. I wasn't entirely sure the great Finnlay Callaghan ever slept. He might even have been at his lab.

I glanced at the window. Eodrom and the Pacific coast ran at roughly the same time. An early riser, Mom would be awake. I swiped and said her name.

And waited.

No images or voices rose from the crystal. Small nips, like tiny electrical zaps, pricked across my neck. My mom, who had never missed a call, did not pick up. Cutting off the connection, I counted to ten and tried again. The fae communication device remained dormant.

What was going on? This wasn't like Earth where service got cut off for unpaid bills. These damn crystals worked from anywhere, and as far as I knew, forever. Three separate calls going unanswered was unheard of.

"Not impossible," I said, doing a real shit job of convincing myself.

Clenching the crystal in a tight fist, I paced across the room. I didn't want to call Duskmere. I really, really didn't want to.

Pru, I'd call Pru.

She, too, did not respond. Twitchy and light-headed, as if I'd chased an entire pot of coffee with a case of full throttle energy drinks, I tried Odo with the same result. At last, I tried Duskmere. I pinged his crystal five times. He did not answer.

Something was very wrong.

Crystal in one hand, phone in the other, I sank slowly onto the bed. I'd always prided myself on my small inner circle, on my lack of dependency on others. Admitting, but more importantly accepting, I needed Teddy's blood had been huge.

That stubborn independent streak left me with no one else to call, no one who could help.

Through a watery haze of despair, I blinked at my phone and found Teddy's name. Y'sindra hadn't answered, so I didn't expect Teddy would, but if I ever needed anything, right then, I needed to hear his voice. When the call went to voice mail, hot tears finally spilled over my lashes.

I ended the call without leaving a message. Head bent, I let the tight ball of helplessness and desperation unravel. A scream ripped from my lungs. The twin dragon of misery and fury scorched my throat. I screamed again and again until the tears were dry, and my voice turned to gravel.

Time continued its relentless slog forward. The morning sun climbed in the sky, and the room grew brighter. Minutes dragged like days. In the tense silence, the ticking of Teddy's clock seemed to rise to the decibel of a jackhammer.

While I didn't know what was happening or what to do, the only thing I knew with certainty was where Mae went and who she went to confront. And now no one was answering their phone. I didn't believe in coincidence.

Honoring Fate's warning to stay away from Eodrom hadn't been difficult.

I'd been happy to have the excuse. Would someone waiting for me there matter if I lost everyone to keep my own ass safe?

Absolutely not.

As concisely as I could, I summed up the situation in a text to Teddy. Did I need him? No, but he had become my partner, my strength. Hopefully, he got the message and could meet me in Eodrom—and not be too angry I'd broken my promise to stay away.

After all, at this point, Fate's warning was irrelevant. I knew who waited. Unlike the anonymous shove that sent me over the bridge, I'd see her coming.

I tossed the phone and crystal onto the bed and headed for my closet. My gaze skipped over my work leathers, landing on the dragon skin. Without thinking, I pressed my hand against the hard surface of the wyvern scale embedded in my chest.

Yeah, time for those.

The supple dragon skin slid up my legs in a smooth glide. As if coming alive, the skins heated against my flesh. Without warning, the ground shook with the rumble of a train coming through my bedroom.

Did Las Vegas have earthquakes? I sprinted from my closet, but quickly stumbled to a stop. Nothing was happening. My gaze skipped over the room. Despite the fact the building had felt like it was about to come down, nothing had fallen over, nothing had moved.

"Ayo?" I whispered.

Teddy's old-fashioned bedside clock ticked. A drip hit the shower floor.

There were tales about dragons tracking thieves who helped themselves to the prized shed skin. It had to be bullshit. And if it wasn't, I came by my dragon skin fair and square. Mine had been a gift.

The air conditioning kicked on.

I shook my head at myself. I'd let an urban legend spook me. Returning to the closet, I pulled on a tight black, light-as-air undershirt made of spider silk before fitting the matching dragon skin jacket over top.

Pixies were master tailors, and the one I'd entrusted with making this armor was incomparable. I ran my hand down the fathomless onyx scales which flared to turquoise, peach, yellow, violet, and red at their tips. They fit together so seamlessly, Ayo, the dragon who gifted me the rolls of shed skin had seemed to carry a nebula on his massive body when we met. In the dimly lit closet, I saw the same slice of universe on me.

I took my time weaving a tight plait from the crown of my head all the way to where it ended at my waist. My hair would not become an impediment during a fight. Undoing the jacket clasps, I tucked the braid beneath my collar. When the weight fell against my spine, I refastened the hooks and snaps.

Last, I went to the wall of weapons and got to work strapping on an arsenal—sword, push daggers, tri-blade daggers, torpedo daggers. Beneath the weight of steel and determination, I grabbed my phone and crystal and headed into the hallway. Remembering my promise to Teddy, I returned to the bedroom and grabbed the twin to the vial of blood I'd forced him to wear, only this contained his blood, not mine

I went downstairs.

Locating pockets in the new armor took time. Beneath the layers of weapons strapped over my chest I managed to work the jacket open. I let the vial fall beneath my shirt while I secured the phone and crystal into an inner jacket pocket.

"On second thought..." Biting my lip, I wiggled my fingers into the tight space until I snagged the crystal with a talon and worked it back out.

I'd kick myself if I didn't check with everyone at least one last time, which I did. Same results.

The crystal went into the pocket, and I gave the phone the same final check. There were no messages. It took longer than I would have liked to snap and adjust everything, but I was finally done.

Stars help me, but if I needed to pee... Well, damn. I thought about it, and now I had to.

A quick trip to the bathroom later, and I was finally digging into the basket containing our stash of portal devices. I collected a disk to Eodrom, Outerlands, the penthouse, and just in case, Interlands.

I started to push the basket away but pulled it to me and looked inside. Was I crazy, or were there even fewer disks? Either one of my sisters— probably Y'sindra—was fibbing and using more than she was willing to admit, or one of these strange sun fae traipsing through here on their way to meditation was a thief.

Something I'd deal with later.

Hopefully, there would be a reason to deal with it later.

With the other devices tucked into pockets, I slapped the Eodrom portal disk against my palm as jogged toward the open door to the balcony. From the corner of my eye, I saw Talulla raise her head and watch me from the sofa. Hopefully, she still had food. If not, she could go scavenge for fish on the beach.

The disk fit perfectly into a slot carved into the portal stone on the balcony. I traced a rune above the device. A moment later an oval opened above the platform—a doorway to my parent's yard.

I stepped through, into chaos.

36

FULL OF DEATH

MAGIC CHARGED THE AIR. SO MUCH, IT HAD A PHYSICAL PRESENCE, A scent. Hairs too fine for my braid lifted. The scent of musky moonlight and sundrenched stones coated my senses. And death. I could smell rotting things.

My foot continued the momentum of my steps and skidded forward a few inches. I caught myself, looking down as I did.

"Oh gods!" My breath left me. Everywhere I looked, slick gore painted the grass red. Bodies and various body parts were scattered across the yard. There were fae who were not my family upright and moving. I finally looked. Really looked.

"Mom?" I whispered.

On the far side of several broad backs mostly blocking my way, my extremely petite and extremely vicious Mom ripped the throat from a fae twice her height. With her hands. Spitting blood and globs of I didn't want to know what, she jumped out of their reach and bared her long fangs at the group. They glistened with blood.

How did this happen? Where was my father? I smelled his magic. Was there an insurrection? Was everyone dead? Where was Mae?

Oh gods, oh gods, oh gods.

"No!" Hands clenched, I controlled the air flow in and out of my lungs. *One thing at a time. Focus.*

Pushing down my panic, I took in the situation. Slipping two push daggers from the bandolier, I glided forward silently on the balls of my feet. No armor protected the back of the threat in front of me. They were fae, but not Royal Fae Guard and not the corrupt. They wouldn't be trained.

The fae I moved behind was shorter and stouter than his golden-haired companions with the oak-brown hair of a wood fae. Dagger grips resting horizontal against my palm, blades extended between my fingers, I punched both fists into his kidneys.

Grunting a half-shout, he tried to turn. His leg gave out. He came down on one knee, almost facing me.

I stepped directly in front of the sun fae and met his startled gaze. We stared at one another for a heartbeat. Recognition flared in his eyes. He was a stranger to me.

A quick lash of my arm, and I whipped my blade across his throat. He clutched his torn flesh. Blood geysered through his fingers.

An angry shout I recognized hit my ears. My gaze shot up, locating my mom. A sun fae with a weak sun magic shield grabbed her. He had some sort of rope looped around her. She slapped her taloned hand against the side of his head. The impact jostled him but left no blood.

Breathing slow through my mouth, I stalked past the dying fae. A thump sounded behind me. He was dead.

One fae held my mom, while the rest stalked toward them. Seven in all. There had been so many bodies on the ground. How many had come for my parents? Why had they come for them?

A high-pitched shout of pain scattered the questions crowding my brain.

"Try that again," my mom shouted. Long trails of blood and something gloopy dripped from her talons. My gaze flew to a sun fae female clutching the side of her face, and I laughed. I couldn't help it. Dumb bitch got too close and paid.

At my laughter, faces whipped in my direction.

"Hi." I smiled and waved, the push daggers still seated against my palms catching the sunlight and glinting.

I loved my mom. She was vicious. I was her daughter.

As one, the group took a step away from me. Unfortunately, that put them in range of my mom.

One went down. A loud crack snapped across the yard.

"Don't get close to her," the man holding my mom said and grunted. He was out of breath. I laughed again. Trying to hold her would be like trying to bring down a wild aloughta.

The rope. It had to be spelled, weakening her.

"But the daughter—" someone tried to argue.

"I don't care!" The fae bellowed and then wheezed. "Sun scorch it, someone stab this female."

My laughter died. Stepping toward the group, I sheathed the push daggers and pulled my tri-blades.

Focused on my legs, I put on a burst of speed, launching into motion.

The fae fell over themselves to get out of my way. One ran at my mom, short sword in hand.

I bolted to my right and then arced left, ramming my shoulder into his ribs. With his sword arm outstretched, he went down on his side. The blade swiped inches from Mom's face.

Her captor took a step back, forcing Mom to move with him.

"I know your mother, Jarhod," she said as she tried to dig in her heels, but the rope seemed to have drained all her strength. "I will send you back to her in pieces."

A dark grin curved my lips. It was no mystery where I got my violent side.

With a quick twist, I looked behind me, startling a fae who had been reaching for the fallen guy's sword. Startled me too. She tripped over her own feet and wasted no time scrambling away on her hands and knees.

I snorted and looked back to the man who had retreated further with my mom. The laughter dried in my throat. My stare went flat, face expressionless. "Let her go."

His tongue flicked out to lick his lips. "No. You...you should leave. Miro will be here any minute." Quickly, he glanced behind him and then back.

Hoarfrost coated my insides. Icy claws scraped at my guts, but I kept my face blank. My eyes darted from the male's nervous face to my mom and back.

"That corrupt filth is no match for Finnlay Callaghan." Mom laughed, and then looked at me. The intensity of her stare willing me to...I didn't know what?

Shit, Miro? Fighting Dad? I looked past the pair in front of me. There was no one there, but I smelled the magic. Sun, moon, death.

The fae laughed. "Miro has more than just moon magic."

Eyes still locked on me, Mom smiled. "And my husband has his brother. You aren't old enough to know the power of sun and moon magic combined."

Oh, stars. Dexter hadn't even been here a full day. His party tricks wouldn't do a thing to stop Miro.

Discreetly, I holstered the tri-blades and then angled my chin over my shoulder, checking behind me one last time. The remaining fae who'd snuck behind me paced my forward movement, but wisely kept their distance.

If Mom's talons hadn't punctured the shield of the fae holding her, my blades wouldn't. I clenched my hands. He was too jumpy to be trained. He was just lucky enough to be born with enough magic to manifest into something useful. All I needed to do was force him to lose his focus.

"This is going to be fun," I said and sprang forward. His eyes widened, and I was on him. Like a felled tree, he tilted backward. I held on, pummeling his face, his torso, any exposed body part as we went down.

His grip loosened on my writhing mom. The shield would dampen the blows, but his brain told him to protect himself. Screaming, he struggled to block my hits. The gold sheen molded to his skin flickered.

Untrained. I grinned and went at him harder, faster. The back of the fae's head slammed against the ground beneath a nose-breaking blow.

I drew my elbow back. His shield flickered. Another quick jab. Bone crunched and blood sprayed across his face beneath my fist.

He howled in pain and covered his nose.

Mom rolled from his hold and shook off the rope. She loomed over him, her baby blue nightgown fluttering around her knees. Before I could pull a dagger, she had her talons in his throat. She yanked back, pulling his trachea free and spraying me with yet more blood.

I blinked and swiped my forearm across my face, which probably only made it worse. "That's one way to do it."

Footsteps pounded the ground behind me. In a single motion, I pulled a tri-blade and rose.

The fae weren't coming for us. They were running away. I met my mom's gaze. We stared at one another and then laughed.

She pulled me into a fierce hug. Her hair, full of damp, sticky things I didn't want to think about, pressed against my cheek. "Laney."

"What happened?"

A thunderclap shook the ground. It didn't come from the sky, but somewhere ahead of us. My head snapped toward the house. Light flared, brighter than the sun and then dimmed.

The brief burst was enough to paint dark spots across my vision.

"Dad." I was up and racing for the garden.

Mom caught up and grabbed my elbow. Her talons glanced off the dragon skin. "Lane, wait!"

I ignored her.

"Do not!" she shouted with such urgency, I rocked onto my toes with my sudden stop.

"What are you talking about?" I asked incredulously, my nerves doing a jittery dance. "We have to—"

"Do nothing," she finished. "We will do nothing."

Spots in my vision fading, I looked toward the house. The garden was destroyed. Mom's herbs looked like spilled salad. Flower petals carpeted the ground. Deep craters churned soil. Chunks of stone had been blown out of the house. In the center of the destruction, my father and Dexter stood, hands clenched.

Déjà vu hit me hard and fast. I looked at their joined hands and knew what my father had planned. He was going to try to draw Dexter's moon magic out. He'd channel it, combine it with his sun fae magic. I knew because when I was very young, he'd tried to pull the kernel of dormant sun fae power inside of me to the surface the same way. It had failed.

My hands shook as I looked at the semi-translucent golden orb surrounding them. An opaque black film oozed across the shield's surface. Miro, the source of that magic, stood facing them, near the stone portal pad —one of the few things that remained upright in the garden.

Death magic crawled over the pale gold orb, slowly dissipating. A jittery feeling weakened my knees. Thank the stars Dad's shield held. But unlike Mae, his didn't flare with light. He couldn't turn Miro's magic against him. He couldn't control Dexter's magic. What was he thinking?

Mom put a hand on my arm. "I meant what I said. The strength of sun and moon magic combined is more powerful than anything Miro might possess. It's why your father has dedicated his life to recreating hybrid magic."

Her grip was steady, but she couldn't control the tremble in her arm, as if she didn't quite believe her words.

"But Miro can channel moon magic directly from the stones here in Eodrom. He's a keeper."

She smiled. "So is his brother."

Suddenly, the familiar scent of gingerbread reached me. My head whipped up, and I took a step back to really look at her. "Mom?" So much blood, and I realized a lot of it was hers.

"I'll be okay." She swallowed and shook her head. "You need to find your sister."

"Mae," I whispered. My lungs were suddenly too tight for words.

"Enough, old man!" Miro shouted.

Out of instinct, I ducked. Muscles spasmed between my shoulders. I twisted toward the garden. This was all too much, too fast. My hearts pinched. A splash of cold washed over me. How much damage had Miro done inside Eodrom before he came here? Was Mae there?

"And you, little brother." Laughing softly, he paced forward. "You came back in time to die."

Time seemed to slow. My hearts kicked against my ribcage, trying to escape.

Miro's raised his arms and thrust his hands forward.

Dad would die! I had to stop this.

I shook free of the loose hold Mom had on my arm and sprang into action, making a beeline for Miro.

A thick stream of silvery light erupted from his palms.

The glare of light drove pain into my eye sockets. Throwing an arm across my face, I fell, momentum carrying me forward. My knees hit the ground. The impact rattled my teeth.

Jaw clenched, eyes throbbing and watering, I forced myself to lower my arm. Through a wash of tears, I could make out the blurry figures of my father and Dexter. Together, they shoved their clenched hands forward. A thinner, but somehow brighter beam of white-gold light shot from their hands and arrowed toward Miro.

Holy shit, it worked!

The light from their combined magic pierced Miro's, shattering his light. Tiny filaments floated away. Dad and Dexter's white-gold magic continued forward, cleaving everything Miro had until it reached him. It didn't stop. It punched into his chest. It didn't come out the other side but poured into him, every last drop.

He let loose a scream, loud and shrill and full of death—his death. His back bowed, and he curled forward, over the light continuing to pour into his body. Fissures of silver and gold streaked beneath his flesh. His wail continued until a crack of light erupted from a tear in his throat.

"Look away, Lane!" Mom shouted.

But I couldn't. The intense light was agony. Tears soaked my cheeks. Still, I watched. Horrified. Fascinated. It was terrible and beautiful. More skin ripped open. Small lines at first, but then great gaping slashes.

His screams had stopped, but the tearing of flesh and cracking of bone hadn't. They were so much worse.

My breath stuttered. The brutal similarity to Etta'wy, the banshee whose death started this entire thing, was uncanny. Darkness, death magic, had consumed her from the outside. This light shredded Miro from the inside.

Fine lines raced across Miro, covering him like a spiderweb. They pulsed.

"Look away, now!" Mom shouted again.

My burning eyes widened. A seam split wide down Miro's front, and the brilliant white-gold light spilled out. "Shit!"

Still seated on my legs from my fall, I tucked my face to my knees, and threw my hands over the back of my head. Even with all that, the light continued to build, turning the back of my lids a flaming orange. Intense cold and heat licked over me. What had my father and Dexter done?

All at once, it stopped. The sound. The light.

My rough and ragged breathing sawed inside my ears. I squinted one eye open. Nothing seared my retinas. Opening the other eye, I rolled my head to the side and saw nothing but bright green grass under regular sunlight. Slowly, I sat up.

"Finn!" My mother raced past me to where my father and Dexter lie motionless in the garden.

Gods, no! I ran after her, coming to a sliding stop. Mom bent over Dad's chest. Powerful wrenching sobs shook her back. I looked past her, at the multitude of sun stones hanging around his neck, now shattered within their settings.

"Meghan." Dad's voice was a croak. He moved his hand to cover hers on his chest.

Dexter groaned.

My dad smiled. He fucking smiled. "You did good, my boy."

"Are we dead?" Dexter asked.

Laughter rattled from my dad's ravaged throat. He coughed and clutched his ribs. "Do not make me laugh."

Mom laid her hand to Dad's forehead and then Dexter's. "You're both too hot. We need to get you inside. I have herbs. You need poultices."

I moved to help, but she rose and shook her head. "No. Miro came here to use your father's portal pad. He meant to get to you."

Her lips folded together. She looked at Dexter and my dad struggling to sit up and wagged her finger at them. "Do not move." She took me by the elbow and drew me a few feet away.

"It's Brenyn," I told her.

Her forehead pinched and mouth trembled. "I know. Miro said he planned to bring you home, to her. To where your history together began on the sun bridge." Her nostrils flared and she stared into my eyes. "Where she pushed you."

37

MY MONEY, LANE CALLAGHAN, IS ON YOU

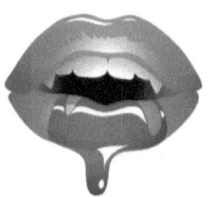

THE SUN BRIDGE WAS A MAGICAL AND ARCHITECTURAL WONDER. RIGHT now, it was too fucking long.

It stretched to the four corners of Grian Valley. Some of the massive pillars supporting the long, sloping ramps contained stairs, but I didn't know which. That forced me to run miles to the closest ramp. From there to the walkway ringing Eodrom, it would be about a two-mile climb.

Brenyn held Mae there. I tried to keep my mind clear as I ran, but questions continued to interrupt my focus. Where were Iola and Torneh? Where was the entire Royal Fae Guard? Brenyn might be powerful, but surely against the entirety of those adversaries, she wouldn't stand a chance.

Yet she did. Because she had my sister. She'd been confident enough to send Miro away from her side, to bring me to her.

Beams of sunlight kicked off from the multitude of sun shards embedded in the entrance to the ramp in front of me. The slick, dark scales covering my dragon skin leathers acted as a mirror, sending each ray of light reflected onto me in a different direction. Anyone who saw me from a distance would think they were under attack by a disco ball.

I sprinted up the ramp, distantly amazed by my speed and endurance. The constant thrum of panic was probably numbing me to aches and exhaustion I would feel later.

Because there would be a later.

Like the scattered outer edges of an exploding star, the number of sun shards slowly dwindled. I forced my mind blank, to focus on each step. My gaze remained on the distant reaches of the ramp. That point became my entire world. I ran and ran, moving faster than I'd ever run before.

The verdant tips of trees passed in a green blur until the ramp rose above them. The bulky stone tops of support pillars came and went in a flash. I was moving so fast the widely spaced sun shards created a vertical amber line in my peripheral.

Wind ripped against my eyes, forcing me to squint.

Eventually, as he always did, Teddy crept into my brain. Would he get my message? I didn't need him, but holy Ho Hos did I want him with me right now.

A queasy feeling rolled my stomach. My steps slowed. Mae and Y'sindra had a special bond. Y'sindra would…I wasn't sure what she'd do when she found out Mae was missing.

Gods, how had Mae escaped Hielmal only to fall into a web woven by Brenyn, who was so much worse? How had she fooled everyone, including her sister, a sun stone keeper. One of two de facto rulers of all the sun scorched fae!

Shaking my head, I scattered my thoughts. These questions and worries would not help me. They would not help Mae.

I gulped air, letting it fill my lungs until they burned. I released it in a single, elongated breath. Imagining sweeping an eraser across a chalkboard, I cleared my thoughts. My battle calm returned to fill the empty void left behind.

While it hadn't been long, it felt like ages since I'd existed in this place. I embraced it now. Folding the clarity that came with a blank mind around me like a familiar cloak.

The steady thump of my footsteps and even push and pull of my breathing became all I was.

Thump, thump, thump, thump, whoosh. Thump, thump, thump, thump, whoosh.

With a gentle curve, the ramp widened to my left. I angled toward the center of the walkway that eventually opened onto the circle. Almost there.

Shouting filtered into my empty space. I slowed and blinked my surroundings into focus. A fae ran down the ramp toward me. Another followed. Another, and soon a crowd of fae bore down on me.

I tensed. Eyes narrowing, I zeroed in on one face in the crowd.

Duskmere wasn't the tallest, but he was the most stabbable. My palms itched for a blade. I curled my fingers into my palms. Plunging a dagger into his chest would be satisfying, but it would be a delay I did not need.

Silver eyes wide, he sprinted toward me. His usually well-kept hair poked out at different angles. Skin pulled thin across the sharp angles of his tight expression, turning his luminous charcoal complexion a waxy gray.

Of course, he'd be the first to spot me. Could this get any worse? *Don't ask questions like that, you idiot*. Whether I believed it could happen or not, I knew better than to think something into existence.

"Brenyn! It is Brenyn," he shouted before he drew close, loud enough for anyone to hear. Very unDuskmere-like. That guy was a secret, wrapped in a secret, hidden from a secret.

"No shit." I stopped walking, forcing him to come to me. Anger toward this male was a churning ball of acid in my belly. I couldn't help but wonder if he'd been up front and open all along if I would have figured out it was Brenyn before we reached this point.

I looked past Duskmere, at the huge crowd surrounding us. A tall, copper-headed sun fae stood out. My lip curled. Cirron. Fuck that guy. We locked eyes. His gaze tightened and he turned away. The dislike was mutual. Shaking my head, I directed my attention to the massive gathering of fae. Tall, slim, golden sun fae were interspersed with their moon fae kin, creating a living picture of day and night. Wood fae, stone fae, every kind of fae, even nymphs with their bright, multi-hued hair.

"Seems unwise to have so many targets in the open," I said and then nearly groaned when I spotted two imposing figures near the front of the crowd. They stood taller than any other fae. If their height and postures didn't scream keepers, the buffer of space between them and everyone else did. "You might as well have painted bullseyes on Iola and Torneh."

"At the moment, Brenyn is keeping her distance," Duskmere replied. "But we are unsure how to proceed."

Unsure. A word that had probably never crossed his lips.

Most of the fae nearest to the keepers wore the RFG insignia, but not all. I recognized a number of sun fae wizards who trained beneath my dad. Snooty members of the court milled about in their finery, however the bulk of the masses appeared to be average fae.

"You could start by not throwing juicy bait out there for Iola's unhinged sister to take a pot shot at."

Duskmere looked from me to the keepers. It dawned on me then, he'd been brave during the Great Fae Divide and helped save many sun fae who had been captured by the corrupt, including my parents, but he had been a child. For more than one hundred years, a true threat had not existed—not one they'd been aware of.

I had neither the sympathy, nor patience, to coddle him. He'd dwelled in that false sense of superiority for far too long and ignored the red flags. Concerns I had repeatedly sounded the alarm on, but he had brushed aside. Now my sister's life was on the line.

The crowd jostled. Someone pushed through. Shorter than most of the surrounding fae, but with a much more powerful build, the wood fae shouldered his way toward me.

Seeing the familiar face, one I didn't want to stab, a tiny measure of relief washed over me. I left Duskmere and strode toward the RFG general.

"Odo," I said, and we clasped forearms like equals. I flicked a glance over the crowd keeping their distance. "Why is everyone here?"

"Brenyn has your sister. For the moment, they remain at the section of the circle I am told you fell from. We should be able to see her from here, but the lookout appears empty."

"Pushed. I was pushed, and she's the one who did it."

He dipped his head. "Apologies. I learned only moments ago."

My gaze skated to the left, to the picturesque lookout that extended like a balcony off the walkway. I hadn't returned since it happened. As Odo said, it appeared empty. My stomach wobbled. "Why is everyone here, not there? Why does she still have my sister?"

Deep grooves carved between his pinched brows. He waved his hand at the seemingly open space at the top of the ramp. "There is some sort of barrier."

I allowed my senses to wander, to focus on the surroundings. Almost immediately, the smell of hot metal and the sharp, clean scent of chlorine hit me. Well, shit.

Frowning, I looked in the direction I imagined the barrier to be. "Stretchy, like the shield protecting dungeon cells?"

"Yes, precisely. How...?"

All that druid power inside of her. I squeezed my eyes shut. My pulse throbbed in my suddenly too tight throat. I forced myself to swallow. Despite everything, it felt necessary to absolve my great(ish) grandfather. In the end, Blackthorne might have withheld the full truth, but I knew down to my bones his guidance was the only reason I might still save my sister. The only chance I had to survive this day.

Lifting my chin, I squared my shoulders and met Odo's questioning look. "Brenyn is Angus Blackthorne's bonded."

He hissed a breath. I'd dropped a massive bomb, but I wasn't done.

"She asked him to create the potion that ultimately resulted in the blood fae, in me. She is the reason he left Ta'Vale. She is the one who killed the druids who followed him." I paused to let that sink in.

As I watched, he paled until the white scar running from his hairline to his jaw nearly blended with the pasty shade of his usually ruddy complexion. He shoved a rough hand through his hair. "Fuck. Their power was stolen..." His words trailed off on a weighty exhale.

"Drained," I said. "They were drained of their power, lifeforce, everything. Brenyn did that."

"I was there. When they were found, I mean. The...the emptiness of it was somehow worse than the aftermath of a battlefield." Brows dipping low over unfocused eyes, Odo seemed to stare into the past. After a beat, he blinked away the ghosts.

"Do you have a plan?" I asked him, aware Duskmere had eased into hearing distance.

"We can't do a thing." His lips pressed into a tight line. That expression and the amount of direct eye contact he was making had me bracing for his next words. "I'm sorry, but you're the only one who can get through the barrier."

And there it was. How things got worse. Prepared or not, shock strummed my nerves. I swung a look from Odo to the invisible barrier and then groaned. "Druid. I can get through because of the druid bits twisted up in my DNA."

Odo said nothing. There was nothing to say. Duskmere, too, wisely held his tongue.

"All right, I'm going in. I don't know what is going to happen, but you should clear these fae out of here."

"That would take too long," Duskmere said.

I slid him a dark look, loathe to admit he was probably right. "Then move them back. Far enough not to be hit by any wayward spells, if Brenyn starts throwing them." Which I had no doubt, she would.

"Agreed." Odo snapped his fingers, and several guards ran to join us. He passed on orders to set a perimeter and then turned to Duskmere. "They won't like it, but you need to escort the keepers to their chambers."

It was a miracle Brenyn hadn't taken a shot at her sister already.

"Brenyn holds a deep grudge toward Iola. If I can't stop her, she will come after her sister."

"Understood." Odo nodded. His gaze slowly assessed me, and a satisfied smile pulled up one side of his mouth. "You appear prepared. My money, Lane Callaghan, is on you."

"Thanks." I grinned. "I have no idea why of all fae she wants me, but I guess it's time to find out if you get to keep your money."

The crowd parted as I made my way up the ramp, toward the barrier. Seeing Duskmere steer a confused and irate Iola and Torneh toward the left side of the bridge, I veered right. For once my height was an advantage, allowing me to disappear into the crowd. I had a feeling if Iola saw me, she'd make a beeline in my direction. Duskmere wouldn't be able to stop her. I didn't have the time or patience to rehash the situation. I also didn't want to be the asshole who explained why her sister was a monster.

Why me? I wondered as I cut through the group like a knife in hot cheese. Cheese, not butter. These damn fae got out of my way, but then they hung behind me at a distance like hot, stringy cheese.

Ahead, a cluster of RFG were dispersing a large group. A face I recognized came into view. Pru. She left her colleagues and headed toward me. Anxiety to reach my sister crawled over me. It pinched and scraped.

Mae was leverage. Brenyn wouldn't hurt her, not until she got what she wanted. Me, apparently. For that reason, I was a tiny bit relieved for the delay. At last, the crowd broke apart as the guards ushered fae away from the barrier, leaving only Pru, me, and a handful of stragglers.

Her pitch-black eyes dropped to my toes and rose as she approached. "Dragon skin. I'm truly jealous."

"The red leathers still make my ass look great."

A laugh burst out of her. She gave a rueful shake of her head and gestured toward the sword pommel rising above my shoulders. "My compliments on your choice of weapons."

I grinned, a light feeling pushing against the big ball of dread that had taken root in my sternum.

As with Odo, she clasped my forearm just below my elbow, and then moved past me.

Still smiling as she left, I looked up, meeting Fate's eyes. Her blue curls fell in a wild tangle over the smooth dark skin of her bared shoulders.

"Sun scorch it, what do you want?" Ugh, where had she come from? I resisted the urge to stomp a foot. Or to grab a dagger. Instead, I planted my hands on my hips. "Don't tell me you're here to deliver another warning."

"I wasn't." Her tongue darted out to wet her lips. "But then I saw you."

"Great."

She put her hands on my shoulders and stepped close. "Be careful. Today, someone will die because of you, but someone will also live."

Heat prickled against my neck. My hands tightened on my hips. "Don't suppose you can be more specific?"

"You know I can't."

"For a seer, you suck."

Fate laughed. "If I was a seer in that sense, I might take offense."

"One day, you can explain exactly what you do." I narrowed my eyes. "If there is a *one day*. Don't suppose you can *see* that?"

"It's no guarantee, but I don't get the impression today is your final day." The scrunch of her brows made her smile a little sad. "Try to ensure it isn't. After all, you just promised to spend time with me, a promise I intend for you to keep."

"Can't wait," I said to her back as she walked away.

Alone at last, I slowly approached the area where I assumed the barrier rose. I could see the place where I'd been pushed, where Brenyn was supposed to be holding my sister. As Odo said, no one was visible. She was here, though. I would find her.

I tilted my face toward the sky. Was this a dome-type situation, or was the perimeter of the barrier only walls? If they were walls, how far would they rise?

Rubbing my fingers over my thumbs, I inched forward. Blackthorne couldn't pass through the shield he'd erected inside the dungeon. I didn't understand why I, then, could pass through this.

Different magic. My gut told me that was the answer. Brenyn was using a perverted version of druid magic. She stole the power, but didn't have a lick of druid DNA inside her. I could barely use druid magic, but I was, in fact, part druid.

I'd also seen druid barriers turn into a vicious vine ball with the power to lay Teddy flat. My gaze skipped over the wide space where the ramp met the circle walkway. I didn't think this was that sort of shield, but what did I know?

Glad to see you are as smart as I believed. Blackthorne's words. From the moment he realized who I was, he'd believed in me. It was a little creepy and a whole lot weird, but maybe he'd been onto something. His lessons more or less instructed me to allow my instincts to guide me, to let them shape how I used my magic. So far, it had all worked out.

Blackthorne hadn't been willing to name Brenyn, but he'd told me things from the very beginning. It was as if he'd handed me jumbled pieces of a puzzle, leaving it up to me to fit them together.

Tipping my chin up, I rolled my shoulders back. Time to put my gut to the test with something other than an ultimate burrito. I took a tentative step forward. Even though my gut, which I was suddenly so keen to trust, said the barrier wasn't about to sprout thorns and turn me into a fae kabob, my head wasn't so sure.

I held my breath until I stood in the center of the circular walkway, well past where the barrier had to be.

The sheer drop-off directly ahead carved a hollow space inside of me. I licked my suddenly dry lips, unable to look away. The only thing to stop me from falling was a flimsy guard rail that barely reached my hips.

My hearts fell out of sync, quadrupling their beats as I approached the edge and pressed my knees to the barrier. I focused on my breath while I stared at the treetops so very far below. Slowly, the pinch and twitch of my nerves eased. I wouldn't be pushed again.

Fate hadn't felt today was my day. As much as I hated to admit it, she was pretty good at sensing that type of stuff. If Brenyn wasn't meant to be my end, I sure as stardust was meant to be hers.

Someone will die because of you. I smiled. There was no scenario where Brenyn left this bridge alive.

I turned my head toward the outlook and froze. Brenyn waited there. Alone.

The same railing I'd approached enclosed the balcony edge of the lookout. I strained, trying to see below the railing, but couldn't. Mae could be there. If she was unconscious, she would be on the ground.

Glancing behind me, I could clearly see the last of the fae retreating down the ramp. Like the barrier Blackthorne had laid over the rooftop garden in Las Vegas, this one blocked the view from anyone on the other side.

Brenyn waited just on the edge of my vision. I could see her there—I assumed it was her, because who else would it be—but couldn't make out any details beyond tall and blonde.

With each step, I shed all thoughts of Duskmere, Odo, Pru, Fate, and every other fae I'd passed. I let concern for Y'sindra, and even Teddy, fade to the background. Two thoughts remained—save Mae, kill Brenyn. I went through my battle preparations as I walked, checking my weapons were present and secure.

It seemed simultaneously both hours and minutes before I could see Brenyn had her back to me. I wasn't trying to be quiet. She had to hear my steps. Yet, she didn't turn to face me as I drew closer. Fangs tingling, I glared, itching to bury a blade in her spine. My fingertips brushed the hilts of my tri-blades.

Showing me her back wasn't the biggest insult. Leaving herself vulnerable while looking out from the precise location where she'd once pushed me, was.

I rounded the corner and finally had a clear view of the platform. My sister was nowhere in sight. Was this a trick?

Some sort of rope lay across the bridge, extending over the bump out, a balcony of sorts, where Brenyn waited. It creaked, moving slightly against the edge of the platform.

As if it held something swaying beneath.

My lungs shriveled. I went so cold, the tips of my ears burned. This time, the tingle in my fangs came from an entirely different emotion—unfiltered terror. Mae was not on the bridge, because she was underneath.

"She's alive," came a disturbingly melodic voice. "But one wrong move and unlike you, I am certain she will not survive the fall."

38

BE A FLEA

My gaze snapped up. I gasped when I saw Brenyn and took an unconscious step back. Her face, with its otherworldly beauty and smooth golden complexion, had been replaced by a roadmap of dark veins throbbing with multi-hued corruption. Her hand was covered with the same snarled lines of corruption.

Steadying my breath, I crossed my arms over my chest and smirked, letting a hint of fang show. "I'd say nice finally meeting you face to face, but I try not to lie. Have you seen yourself in a mirror?" I shuddered.

She smiled, completely unfazed. "The corruption is power. There is nothing more beautiful than power."

"We're gonna have to agree to disagree. How did you hide"— I made a circular motion in front of my face—"all that?"

I wasn't calling her ugly, more like undiluted evil.

One slim shoulder lifted in an elegant shrug, so contrary to her monstrous appearance. "Who do you think cast the illusion spell on the handmaid who took Hielmal's place in the dungeon?"

"Hielmal," I said, joining Brenyn at the edge of the platform. "Obviously."

Laughter that reminded me of a bubbling brook rang out, shocking me at the pleasant sound so contrary to everything else about her. "That's rich. It took years for her to master enough death magic to make an attempt on Iola's life."

"Right, your sister, the keeper." I rested my arms over the railing next to her and smiled into her corruption filled eyes. "I wasn't the best student, but remind me, was it my dad who saved the keepers?"

An especially large vein throbbed below her right eye.

If Mae could hear me, she'd say I was trying to catch a tiger by the tail, but it was more like I was trying to be a flea, biting and annoying. Brenyn wasn't going to kill me.

No, that wasn't true. She definitely planned to do just that, but not yet. It was clear she wanted me alive for some sort of purpose I hadn't yet figured out. Since leaving Ta'Vale, it wasn't like I'd been in hiding, living a sheltered life. She could have come at me anytime between then and now.

"I wasn't certain you would come, but I should never have doubted. Miro is very convincing." She leaned her hip against the railing to face me. Her gaze was steady. The whites of her eyes were almost entirely gone. At first, the irises appeared to be an unpleasant muddy color, but they were so much worse. Thin veins of rusty red, chalky green, charcoal gray and others coiled around each other like snakes.

"Miro is dead," I said flatly.

Her jaw ticked. If I hadn't been staring so hard into her eyes, trying to keep my stomach from rebelling, I wouldn't have seen it. Point to me.

"Oh, no!" I pressed my fingers to my mouth. "I'm sorry. Did you like him? Did you think he'd make it back to you alive?"

She tapped the knife on the rope. Everything inside of me seized. "I admit," she said smoothly. "You aren't what I expected. Had we met under different circumstances, I think we would like one another."

"Us? Friends?" I laughed in her face. "We're living in two different realities, and mine isn't the one that's made up."

The corruption writhed beneath her skin. Her jaw flexed, but relaxed. "I understand why you feel that way. I did push you, after all. Right here. I admit, I anticipated a much different reaction to us meeting at this location."

It wasn't only my sister's life holding that particular nightmare at bay. Something about seeing her, the faceless hands that pushed me, the source of so many nightmares, obliterated the fear.

"Why did you do it?" I asked and used her proclamation as an excuse to look down. Mae wasn't there.

"Jealousy."

I whipped toward her. "Say what now?"

Her lips bent into a wistful expression. "I'd heard the rumors of a blood fae hybrid. I knew what you were."

"An abomination?"

"His masterpiece."

My mouth dropped open. No words came out. I had no idea what to say to that. I'd already called her a crazy bitch. Maybe not in those words, but the sentiment was implied. Did I need to use those words for her to get the message?

Demurely, she angled her face toward the ground and shrugged. "I was so enraged when I realized he got what he wanted—"

"Blackthorne?"

"Of course," she answered in a tone implying it was obvious. "Who else?"

"Miro, Dacian, the guy Mae told me about who stepped on the baskets you left outside the garden and didn't apologize. Literally anyone."

Her pale brows drew together. They stood out grotesquely against her corruption-darkened face. "Yes, I was speaking of Angus Blackthorne."

"Thanks for the clarification."

Brenyn tipped her chin in a regal nod, my sarcasm flying right over her head. "I have a confession."

"Can't wait."

"I thought he died with his followers in the desert." She pressed her hand to her chest, and I'd be damned if those weren't actual tears gathered on the heavy fringe of her lashes. "It broke my heart to do it, but he had abandoned me."

I paced away, across the platform, as if I was just here for a girl's chat. As if my sister's life didn't hang in the balance. "So, you admit you killed the druids?"

That bubbling-brook laughter followed me. "Come now, you already knew."

Alarm rattled my bluster. This was the part of the movie where someone died. The bad guy was revealing all. I'd need to navigate this carefully or she might decide to kill me before I figured out why she needed me.

Which would suck.

Because I'd be dead.

"True," I said. "Let me see if I've got this. When I was still a knobby-kneed teen, I reminded you of something Blackthorne wanted. You got mad, and you tried to kill me?"

"Not exactly how I would have put it, but yes. I suppose that is the sum of the events."

She could have at least denied the knobby-knee part.

Gripping the opposite railing, I leaned out and looked down. No Mae there either. Gods damn it, this was ridiculous. I twisted on my heel to face Brenyn. "Are we going to do this dance where you try to bait me, I say something to irritate you, and on and on. Or are you going to tell me where my sister is and what you want from me?"

We stared at one another. Her jaw flexed.

"Your sister is unconscious, suspended directly beneath this walkway."

I couldn't hide the stutter in my breath. Who needed careful when I could bulldoze my way through a situation? "What do you expect in exchange for her life?"

"One of my creations bit you. I couldn't believe my luck when sweet Maerwen told me the news." She waved the knife at me. A statement, not a question, so I chose not to answer. This topsy-turvy conversation felt a bit like dealing with Y'sindra. That gentle, serene smile once again tilted her lips. "The answer to your question, is your life."

Ice turned to sludge in my veins. "Normally, I don't take threats seriously, but I think you mean it."

"Oh, I do. You were already everything Angus wanted, but then you were bit. Your fae DNA would have burned off the paranormal pathogens. But the black wolf..." Her smile turned predatory, and my vision grayed at the edges. "That, sweet girl, is blood magic. If you were not mated with the black wolf, I'm not sure what would have happened. Like the rest, you might have been too weak to survive. But you are mated. You took his blood. And now, thanks to the bite, the black wolf's DNA is a part of you."

The insinuation I was weak cut a little too close to the bone. I bristled and forced air past the vise clamping down on my chest. A reflexive action to her words, my hand covered the vial of Teddy's blood hidden beneath my jacket. The magic keeping the essence of him fresh and warm cut through the cresting panic.

"You have a lot of power that wasn't yours to take." I tilted my head. "And now you want whatever is in me."

"Correct. Your essence, in exchange for your sister's life." She tapped the knife on the rope again.

"You must think I'm really stupid."

"On the contrary, I think you love your sister. Admirable, but ultimately, love is a weakness." Her smile fell and her expression turned to stone.

Behind her on the circular walkway, a figure approached from the opposite direction I'd come. Tall, loose clothing, a walking stick. No, not a stick, a staff. Blackthorne met my gaze. Son of an ogre humper, how did he get here? The better question was why?

He lifted the staff—my staff—and gave a little wave. It was his staff first, but he gave it to me, and it had been in my closet since we moved into the penthouse. He'd been in my fucking closet. Again, his closet first, but it was mine now, and it was full of my stuff. He and I were going to have a serious talk about boundaries when this was over.

The monotonous tick from the staff striking the bridge grabbed Brenyn's attention. Her head whipped around. Despite not having seen him for over a hundred years, instant recognition flashed across her face. Her eyes sprang wide when she saw who leisurely strolled toward us. In a matter of seconds, the number of expressions that contorted her face were more than I could count, until the spinning wheel of emotions landed on unbanked fury.

Contrary to her emotions, she threw back her head and laughed. "Tired of our game? Finally come to die, my love?"

Instead of answering, Blackthorne smiled at me. "Duck."

He lifted his staff, twisting it perpendicular in front of him. Green light exploded beneath his clenched fists.

"Shit." I dove forward. My knees cracked against the stone bridge, followed by my chest. The air left me in a pained wheeze. Lying face first on the walkway, I craned my neck just in time to see a wave of light punch into Brenyn, who hadn't reacted to the warning he'd given me.

The light landed a physical blow to her midsection. She folded around the light. The knife flew from her hand and clattered on the stone walkway as the blow threw her at least ten feet past me. She hit the guardrail with a thump. The whiplash of impact flung her to the ground. With an unpleasant, meaty thump, her face bounced against the rough stone.

I didn't wait around to see if she got up. Scrambling to my feet, I sprinted toward Blackthorne who, staff still held aloft, advanced on Brenyn.

"Get your sister and go home." He didn't look at me, didn't take his eyes off the female he'd survived all these years to destroy. "If I don't leave here, see that Talulla has a home."

"Talulla..." The cat had been on the sofa. She'd watched me leave. "Are you here because of that cat?"

"I told you she is special. Take care of her," he said, and then he passed me.

A fissure of worry cracked inside me, but I didn't pay it any attention. I had tunnel vision for the rope Brenyn had threatened to cut.

Reaching for the knife, I fumbled with the handle. I didn't need another knife, but if Brenyn made it back this way, she didn't need it either. It dropped and clattered from my fingers three times before I caught hold.

I skidded to a stop against the railing. Going up on my toes, I leaned over the rail. Too close to the lip of the platform for me to have seen on my first glance, what looked like a green net dangled at the end of the rope at least twenty feet below the bridge. It swayed, the net rotating. I saw Mae's distinctive honey-and-ice blonde hair falling through the webbing and cried out.

The relief ballooning inside my chest came on so hard and fast, it hurt. Hands trembling, I took hold of the rope. She was close, so close. All I had to do was get her onto the bridge and she'd be okay. Abs flexing, biceps straining, I pulled.

"Come on." Hand over hand, I kept pulling. Between the considerable length of rope and Mae, the weight was tremendous. A year ago, I might have had an easy time, but now I was barely more than a regular fae.

Behind me, Brenyn's shrill scream ripped through the air. My neck pinched, and I ducked. The rope slipped in my sweaty grip. Gritting my teeth, I dug my talons into the fibers, stopping its fall.

I looked over my shoulder, my vision bouncing with my ragged breathing. Blackthorne had Brenyn pinned to the ground. Evergreen light flared around the knotted head of his wooden staff he had pressed against her chest.

She'd been no match for Blackthorne. My grandfather, who had come here, now, for me. I laughed a little, flexing my hands on the rope. Because of the cat. Lulla was getting a whole tuna for dinner.

Flexing my arms, I prepared to pull.

Before I could register what was happening, Brenyn's head turned in my direction. She flung out a hand. Blackthorne yanked back his staff and swung. A multi-hued cone of writing magic shot from her hand a moment before his staff connected with her head.

The magic flew toward me. I shouted. My fingers tightened. Talons dug deeper into the fibers. Fight or flight locked my muscles. I couldn't do either while I leaned over the railing, Mae's life in my talons.

Magic slammed into me, jolting me forward. The world spun around me, or maybe I was spinning? Twisting? Falling. I tried to reconcile what was happening. Couldn't. Darkness didn't fold me in its gentle embrace, it smashed into me like a brick.

39

I DIDN'T RUN FROM ANYTHING

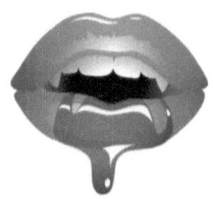

I broke the surface of consciousness. My pulse hammered at the base of my skull and against my eardrums, amplifying each ragged breath inside my head. Why was I spinning? Not quite spinning. A jerky twist one way followed by something pressed against my hands, pulling taut. A hard thrum heralded a twist in the opposite direction.

The moment I moved, a wave of pain threatened to knock me back unconscious. It felt as if my shoulder had been pulled—no, ripped—straight from the socket. Maybe both shoulders. I tried to contract my hands and screamed.

White hot pain tore me apart. My stomach heaved while my vision flashed gray and thready at the edges. I hung there, vaguely aware my cheeks were damp, and my breathing was loud. I'd felt this one time before, when a year ago, upon my first meeting with Blackthorne, I'd leapt from the penthouse balcony and half-fallen, half-scaled my way to the parking lot below.

The wooden slats in front of me made no sense. Whatever was happening in my brain turned my thoughts swampy, slow to understand my situation. Ready for the pain this time, I wiggled my feet. There was nothing below me, but my toes bumped something. It moved.

Steeling myself, I looked down. A long rope dangled in front of me. Far below, the net containing an unconscious Mae rolled violently back and forth.

I whipped my gaze up to look above me. As if detached from the situation, I couldn't quite make sense of anything. Like molasses, my thoughts coalesced. My ribs collapsed around my hearts, my lungs.

I was dangling by my literal fingertips on the wrong side of the bridge.

"No, no, no." I repeated the word over and over. A prayer. A denial.

Footsteps thundered on the bridge.

Forcing my dry throat to work, I looked down again. The wild tilt of the net slowed with each twist. I turned back to my talons caught in the rope. Blood seeped from the beds. Thin trails ran over the backs of my knuckles.

I'd almost gotten used to the burn of my talons pulling against their roots. I looked at my dangling legs and then back to my hands. Somehow, I had to grip the rope. That meant either hoisting myself up by my talons, which were barely clinging to their nailbed free or pulling one hand loose and grabbing hold. I would be supported, even if only for a second, by the talons of only one hand.

Both options sucked.

"Hold on," I called to my sister who was too far away to hear me, not to mention unconscious. But talking to her made me feel better.

Teeth gritted, I stared at the rope. This was going to hurt.

Blackthorne's head popped out from above the balcony. One hand curled over the railing, the other still gripped his staff. Crimson stained the knobby top.

His violet gaze, much lighter and brighter than usual, swept to my fingers, to my face, to my sister dangling below. "Good girl," he said. "Let's get you up."

He leaned his staff against the railing and then bent over the barrier, stretching his arm toward me. A good two feet separated his hand from mine.

"Can you climb up to my hand?"

"I don't know. I…" I squeezed my eyes shut and refocused on his face. "Yes. I'll try."

"Wait." Blackthorne retrieved his staff. Gripping the knobby end he'd used to bludgeon Brenyn with, he lowered the straight end toward me. "Grab hold of this."

A massive shadow fell from the sky behind him. Wings flared. Sunlight glinted off pink, orange, and cobalt blue scales. He came in so fast.

"Watch out!" I screamed.

My wide eyes locked on my grandfather's. Dacian was suddenly there. His powerful hind legs lifted. His clawed feet grabbed Blackthorne.

The staff fell toward me. I twisted, taking the hit on the shoulder and then the ancient relic tumbled away.

Time turned to molasses. I saw every detail in Blackthorne's expression as Dacian lifted him into the air.

This couldn't be happening.

Dacian brought his feet forward and let go. Blackthorne sailed over the railing.

"No!" Tearing my talons free of the rope, I reached for my grandfather with my free hand. As if someone hit play, time caught up. Wind rushed between our hands, and then he was gone.

Frantically, I gripped the rope and searched the area beneath me. There was nothing but varying shades of green. It was so far. He was immortal, though. How could he die?

Immortal did not mean unkillable.

Oh gods, he was dead. Dead, dead, dead. Something vital inside of me had been severed. I was bleeding out, emotionally. I thought I'd hated him, but I hadn't.

The air I gulped didn't make it into my lungs. The screaming. I was still screaming. They were ragged, inarticulate sounds. Shredded and broken. My throat burned.

Laughter came from above me, and I whipped my face around. Dacian, no longer in his wyvern form, looked at me over the railing. "Hi." he said and waved.

I snarled and ripped the talons of my other hand from the rope, reached up, and pulled. Pain nearly knocked me loose. I slid several feet, the rough material tearing my palms before my fingers convulsed, and I caught myself.

Chest heaving, I looked down at my still unconscious sister. In all of this, she hadn't moved, but she was alive. I would know if she wasn't. Somehow, I would know. Mae was there, under a sleep spell, and I had to get ahold of myself. Grief, or whatever this was, could come later.

In the distance, a roar sounded, raising the hairs on my neck. My entire body tensed. If I'd been on the ground, I would have run away. And I didn't run from anything. I looked around, searching the sky, the trees.

"Will it hold?" Dacian asked.

What was he talking about? The rope? I was the one dangling here. I sure hoped it held.

"The shield will hold," a light female voice answered. Brenyn appeared above me next to Dacian.

My nostrils flared with a renewed sense of anger. Anger was better than whatever I felt for…I blanked my mind. "You're alive."

"Of course," she said. "That was an inconvenient interruption, but perhaps a convenient outcome. I thought I was rid of him years ago."

Beneath my palms, warm blood from my fall turned the fibers slippery. "If you have something to say, you better make it quick."

I dropped a few inches before I was able to tighten my hold and catch myself. Things were not looking good.

Another roar accompanied a loud thumping.

Brenyn's lips pursed and she looked at the trail of red I'd left on the rope. "In exchange for your sister's life, you will allow me to have your power."

Despite the situation, I laughed. "Okay, sure. Bring us both up and we have a deal." Not. The minute I was on that bridge I would rip out her throat, Meghan Callaghan style. Maybe Iola would like her windpipe for a trophy.

"I'm afraid that is not how this will work. We will bring you up, and Dacian will retrieve your sister. Once the transfer of power begins, Dacian will fly your sister to safety."

Exactly what sort of dumb did she think I was?

"That requires a lot of trust on my part." The rope was winning this battle. I kept trying to tighten my grip, but I couldn't do this much longer. "What sort of assurance do I have he won't just, I don't know, have her for a snack?"

"I'm vegan." Dacian draped an elbow over the railing, looking far too relaxed.

I shot him the darkest look I could muster.

He held up his hands and laughed.

"No assurance," Brenyn said, and I transferred my glare back to her. "But what other choice do you have?"

The banging I'd heard grew in intensity. Another roar, and Dacian looked at something over his shoulder.

My jaw worked. Fury bubbled inside me. She had me. She'd won. Either I let her take my power and hope she kept her word to let Mae live, or I sentenced us both death.

"I am truly sorry I was forced to use Maerwen in this. I care for her." Brenyn's declaration was soft and lilting. "You have my word, if you don't fight me, she will live."

I rested my forehead against the rope. "Do it."

40

I BROKE THE DAMN BRIDGE

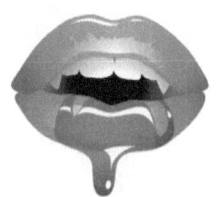

THE ROAR CAME AGAIN. THE SOUND OF AN ENRAGED PREDATOR. Something so primal and terrifying, I once again fought against the urge to run. Of course, my feet had to be on the ground to run.

Dacian's grip on my arms tightened, and he flinched. It was there and gone, and he hauled me over the rail. My vision flashed white hot and then black before slowly coming back into focus.

I was on the ground, my back against the barrier. Dacian crouched until his face was in front of mine. It was sort of sideways—or I was sideways. I realized I was halfway between sitting up and lying on my side.

"The black wolf, your mate, has the ability to see through the barrier. He will watch you die. Do you know you will accomplish what I never could?" Dacian chuckled. It was a horrible sound. "You will break my brother."

My hearts fell into an offbeat rhythm. The roaring. It couldn't be. I searched Dacian's eyes, seeing the truth reflected back. Teddy had done what he'd sworn to never do. He'd shifted. For me. The black wolf was here.

I bit back a sob. He would hate me for sacrificing myself. There had been no choice. Would he figure that out? Would he understand?

"Dacian," Brenyn snapped.

He rose and climbed onto the rail. Looking down at me, he winked, and stepped off. Light flared from behind me. It broke through the slats in the railing to momentarily turn the gray stone brilliant white. In less than a heartbeat, the light was gone and the velvety whoosh of wings beat against the air.

"He did not need to be so cruel. I am sorry." Brenyn stood in front of me, hands folded together at her waist.

The moment was surreal. "You're about to turn me into a husk, and you're apologizing because Dacian didn't play nice? You realize how fucked up that is, right?"

"If we could do this without it resulting in your death, I would."

"Wow, okay. You tell yourself what you need to sleep at night."

Her expression contorted into something angry and ugly, but she recovered quickly. "The black wolf will not see this. Not where we are, hidden behind the railing."

I laughed. "I sincerely hope you live long enough to feel it when he tears you apart, into tiny pieces."

From beneath the bridge, Dacian rose into the air. A long section of rope dangled from his jaws, the net swayed beneath, not far above the walkway. He hovered there, waiting for something.

The sweet, earthy scent of honeydew undercut by the sharp, vibrant aroma of caraway hit me. I rolled my eyes toward Brenyn, who had knelt in front of me, so close, her knees touched mine. I shifted my gaze to the side of her head and grinned. "Blackthorne got you good."

Either because of the angle or the sun behind her in the sky, I hadn't seen the injury when she stood. Now, crouched in front of me, her head and face were a bloody mess. It matted her golden hair. From the crown of her head to her right ear, and smeared across her swelling face, the blood was so thick, it looked black. Fresh rivulets tracked onto her neck.

"Don't fight or Maerwen dies, and that would make me very unhappy," Brenyn snapped. All the friendly, love and peace bullshit had left her voice.

It took precious minutes I couldn't spare, but I finally got it together enough to push myself into a vertical sitting position. "You said Dacian would take Mae to safety."

"He will." She trailed her hand lightly down my arm. "As soon as we begin."

In the distance, the black wolf roared. My hearts shriveled. They strained to beat. When they did, it felt like twin explosions against my ribcage. I wondered if Brenyn could hear the *thump-thump*.

I squeezed my eyes shut and whispered, "I'm sorry."

Something cold hit my cheek.

"There is nothing to forgive." Brenyn was back to benevolent.

Stupid bitch thought I was talking to her.

Cold-wet hit my face again, and then again. I frowned and scrubbed my cheek. As I pulled my hand away, a snowflake landed on my fingers.

Tension flowed from me at the speed of a raging river, leaving me weak and shaky. Smiling, I tilted my face toward my lap and covered my hand. Y'sindra was here. She would make sure Mae was safe. Dacian needed to go so that Y'sindra would follow. I didn't want her to see what happened to me.

"Do it, then." I glared into Brenyn's multi-hued eyes.

She struck like a cobra. Her fingers circled my wrist, flesh to flesh, just beneath the jacket cuff. Nothing felt different. Maybe this wouldn't work on—

A great wrenching sensation twisted my insides. It happened at the very core of me, that place I felt the druid magic move. I groaned.

Something rose inside me, sluggish, resistant.

Her brow puckered. The tendons stood out along her neck from strain.

Power brushed against the underside of my flesh. It kept pulling back. I wasn't fighting her, but it was. Her will drew everything toward the contact she made with my flesh, but for every inch the power eased forward, it skittered back half as far, a push and pull of hot and cold inside of me.

Growing lightheaded, I groaned and slumped forward.

It happened then. A tiny wisp shot from me into her.

When I'd tapped into my druid power, I was slowly becoming something else, but I'd been powerful before that. She could take what I'd only recently discovered, and I still had a chance. I couldn't pass out. I had to hold on—at least until Dacian took Mae away.

With effort, I straightened and looked at Brenyn. Her eyes were glassy, mouth slightly ajar.

I felt it. The dam blocking my power from leaving me had cracked. Slowly, bit by bit, she was absorbing threads of...me. And she looked drunk on it. My insides were so cold, too cold to survive, but my flesh was on fire. My leathers scalding.

"Mae," I said. Barely a croak. "You promised."

Blinking, her eyes came into focus. She turned to look up at Dacian. His wings beat and he rose higher.

The momentary distraction cut off the transfer of power, and suddenly, I could breathe. The awful pulling sensation was gone. This was my chance. As soon as Dacian was far enough away.

She gave me that false smile I wanted to claw from her face. If only my arms weren't so heavy. She tucked a strand of hair behind my ear. "See? I keep my word."

A massive black cloud dropped from the sky. Weird, clouds didn't fall. Was this what happened in death? Was I imagining things?

Where Brenyn held me, my wrist felt frozen, but beneath my leathers I was roasting alive as I watched the cloud draw closer.

Was that... No. It couldn't be.

Wings with scales that looked like they held the universe scattered across them unfurled. Wings like the scales on my armor.

It was!

Hope became a living thing, taking up too much room in my chest. My breath stuttered around the swell of emotion.

Ayo rose behind Dacian, the dragon eclipsing the much smaller wyvern. Despite his size, his wings were silent.

"Lady of the universe," a voice boomed.

Who of the what?

The dragon's thunderous voice shook me all the way to my bones. I was pretty sure he meant me, but how was this happening?

My gaze shot from Dacian to Brenyn. Neither reacted to Ayo's voice. Nostrils flared, I focused on the push and pull of air, on keeping my expression blank.

The dragon was in my head. We'd had an entire conversation in the caves. I'd been speaking out loud. His voice was so booming, so all-consuming, it never occurred to me he hadn't also.

"Ayo?" I thought, focusing mentally, staying blank physically. "How are you here?

You wear my gift. It links us. I felt your need."

His voice filled all the nooks and crannies in my head, until I was sure my brains were about to leak out of my tear ducts. Everything he'd said was all kinds of weird, but now wasn't really the time to dwell on that.

"That structure will not support me." The deep rumble returned, and I fought not to wince. "The fae is too close to you for me to burn."

Picturing Brenyn turned into a pyre, I smiled into her eyes while I sent my thoughts to Ayo, praying to the universe he heard me.

"The wyvern has my sister. Get him. I'll take care of the fae."

In the sky, Dacian hovered then began to bank right. His wings flexed, preparing to beat.

Dacian was oblivious to Ayo, who hung far enough back not to be noticed yet. He would soon, and I wanted to laugh.

Long neck whipping around, Dacian's wings thrummed wildly against the air, pushing away from Ayo, whom he'd almost careened directly into. He shrieked so loud I couldn't tell when he stopped. The horrible sound continued to ring in my ears. The rope dropped from his jaw.

Mae crashed onto the bridge. The net didn't open, and she didn't move. The thick rope followed. Its weight, far greater than my sister's, sent a tremor through the walkway.

Brenyn spun and squeezed next to me. She didn't let go of my wrist, and I didn't have the energy to shake her loose.

I tried to move away, but only managed to fall over.

"Y'sindra." Pure desperation gave me the energy to speak, hoping she heard. "Get Mae out of here!"

Nothing happened. No buzz of wings or snarky answer. She had to hear me! Pressure pushed against the backs of my eyes. I blinked.

Someone would live. Mae had to live!

In the sky, the two beasts snapped and twisted. Ayo shot a huge plume of black fire toward Dacian. The much smaller wyvern was fast. He spiraled away but came around and stabbed with his spear-tipped tail. He landed several blows before darting away. Undeterred, enraged, Ayo pursued. The terrifying battle drew them farther and farther away.

"Please, Y'sindra, please." Maybe I imagined the snow.

Breathing hard and oblivious to my pleas, Brenyn huddled close, the melon and spice scent of her overpowering. She adjusted her grip on my wrist. The slow pull continued to draw everything inside me toward that point of contact. The power felt too big for my veins. It was like trying to suck an ice cube through a straw, and oh gods it hurt. I squeezed my eyes shut against the pain.

A flurry of fluffy snow drifted over us. I blinked my eyes open. Two, four, ten—more and more snow fairies flew toward Mae. Relieved, I shook with tears that didn't fall.

The fairies each grabbed a section of rope. Instead of joining the others preparing to fly Mae from the bridge, Y'sindra winged toward me. I shook my head. She stopped but hovered nearby. Too close.

Go, I mouthed.

The others flew straight up. I had my answer. The shield was a wall, not a dome. Mae and that rope were heavy. We were already so high, and they were going higher. I hoped to all the forsaken gods they would come down over the ramp as soon as they could.

Still, Y'sindra remained far too close. She wrung her hands on her tunic.

Go, I mouthed again, desperate, afraid to speak and draw Brenyn's attention to her.

Lo appeared and whispered in Y'sindra's ear. Her head snapped toward the barrier and the black wolf. Wings humming, chest heaving, she sent me a determined look and then flew in the opposite direction the fairies had taken Mae.

I didn't know where she was going, but that was okay. Mae was safe. Y'sindra was safe. She just needed to stay—

A deafening boom came from the left. Brenyn and I turned toward the sound. A succession of pounding followed. Another boom and a massive web of frost grew across the barrier.

What was Y'sindra doing? That took so much magic. She'd be vulnerable. *She has to stop!*

Another boom. Somehow, I dredged up enough strength to sit a little straighter, enough to see over the railing blocking my view of the barrier. This time, I could just make out a dark shadow slamming itself over and over into the far side in time with the pounding I'd heard. *Is that Teddy?*

Brenyn's grip on my wrist fell away. Power that had been resisting the pull rushed into hiding places inside me. My head seemed to float away from my body momentarily. Chest heaving, I swam in a wavy, gray space for what felt like hours but had to be seconds because when my vision cleared, Brenyn was barely two steps away. She stared, transfixed at whatever was happening at the barrier. As if she didn't believe what she saw.

"Run!" I tried to scream, to get Y'sindra out of here, but my voice came out a scratchy whisper.

Brenyn didn't react. Maybe it hadn't even been a whisper.

I clenched my fists, furious at the feeling of helplessness holding me down. My talons pricked my palms. The sharp bite of pain, a pain I was accustomed to, pain I knew how to channel, beat back the feeling of defeat that had come over me.

One slow step at a time, Brenyn moved toward the center of the walkway. She'd taken some of my power, maybe a lot of my power. It felt like someone had taken an ice cream scoop to my insides. I pressed my hand to the hollow in my chest.

Beneath my jacket, I felt the hard ridge of the vial. Teddy's blood. I shot a look toward Brenyn, as if she might sense it. She might know. She might take it from me.

Her entire focus was centered on the barrier and whatever was trying to come through.

Quickly, before she could stop me, I reached for the strip of leather tied around my neck. Shaky and weak, it took three tries before I managed to drag the vial out from beneath my collar.

Gritting my teeth, I wrapped my hand over the glass tube and gave the strap a hard yank. The burst of pain was so intense, I heard it in my ears. But it came and went, and I held hope.

The deep shudder of ice cracking split the air. Something, whatever was coming, roared. It had broken through the barrier. Even with the ice turning it brittle, the power it would take to break through that barrier was unimaginable.

My fingers were too numb and stiff to remove the wax seal holding the cork in place. I made the decision and acted before I could tell myself what a stupid idea it was. I bit down on the top of the vial. Glass sliced into my lips. I spit the shards, but tiny slivers burrowed into my tongue. It didn't hurt yet. It would.

Footsteps pounded the walkway. Black magic swelled in Brenyn's hand. It dripped from her fingers, pinging against the bridge. The magic hissed when it hit the walkway. Small pockmarks burrowed into the stone where it fell.

I put the vial to my lips and tipped my head back. Teddy's life force poured down my throat, healing, even as slivers of glass slid down with it.

As if the world shifted from black and white to living color, strength flowed into my limbs. It was enough to keep me conscious and on my feet. I could tell pieces of magic were missing, but enough remained. Pressing my back against the barrier, I rose, wobbling a little. My core tightened, and I planted my feet, righting myself.

The roar came again, much closer.

My gaze shot toward the sound. Something surrounded the enormous creature—smoke or fog—and it was a blur. A huge intangible thing. It couldn't be Teddy. It would be too cruel to be so close, for one of us to watch the other die. I didn't want to believe it. I wouldn't believe it. Dacian had played this trick on me before. He'd said things to hurt me, to get in my head.

The shadow figure didn't rush, but stalked up the ramp, where Brenyn waited.

I flicked my gaze to her.

She was steady, but her hands shook.

Vicious satisfaction swelled inside me. I smiled. This thing frightened her. Good. I hoped it ate her face.

Watching Brenyn, wondering why she wasn't throwing her magic, I edged my way behind her. If this thing didn't kill her, I planned to.

Magic dripped from her hands. A swirl of violet and green in one hand, black in the other. Insurance in case one missed.

Peeling my gaze from the magic, I looked toward the creature. A writhing cloud of smoke or fog did, in fact, surround it. I couldn't be entirely sure where the beast was in the haze.

I reached the edge of where the lookout met the main walkway, and shimmied farther to my right, away from Brenyn. The smart thing to do would be to run, but I wasn't always smart. I was very determined, and in this case, I was determined to see her dead.

The closer the creature drew, the eerie swirl of gray fog parted long enough for a brief glimpse of the thing inside.

I forgot how to breathe.

A wolf. A black wolf. He was enormous, both in height and in breadth of body. Muscles upon muscles. Like Beast, he walked upright, but bristly fur covered him from face to feet. The glimpse came and went too fast to see much else. Fog consumed his form—there and gone before Brenyn could aim and react.

My vision narrowed to the creature. To my mate. Somewhere in there, it really was Teddy. Oh, gods, the black wolf was hard to kill, but that was death magic. If she hit him...

Unable to blink, unable to look away, I licked my lips, and the sharp bite of my fang scraped my tongue. The sting immediately dissipated. "Teddy," I whispered.

Brenyn moved, breaking my trance. She widened her feet, one foot in front of the other, bracing herself. The sound of hot grease popping in a pan accompanied each drip of death magic oozing from her fingers.

I looked between her and Teddy—the black wolf. I pulled a torpedo throwing dagger and threw it, but my fingers still weren't quite right, and the throw went wide.

Dropping the second torpedo, I pushed away from the railing. Heavy and clumsy, I stumbled toward her. Each step was steadier, stronger, faster. "Brenyn!" My throat burned.

Her head came around to face me. A horrible smile twisted her lips. She angled in my direction, and the purple and green magic I'd thought was meant for Teddy flew toward me. My eyes widened.

Before I could decide what to do, the magic punched me in the gut.

I flew backward, half skidded, and rolled into the railing. My head bounced off a wood beam. As my brain continued to circle my skull, I managed to roll onto my butt and look at my midsection. Nothing. The scales were pristine. I laughed, a little hysterically. The magic had broken apart harmlessly against the dragon skin.

Maybe not harmlessly, but I was still alive.

A roar promising death tugged at my primal need to run. I whipped a look toward Teddy.

Beyond reason, he—no, the black wolf—roared again. He launched himself toward Brenyn. Beneath me, the bridge vibrated from the heavy thud of his steps. The curtain of fog that had surrounded him fell, leaving him in the open.

He was terrifying. He was beautiful. He was vulnerable.

"Teddy, no!"

Even from this distance, the burning red was visible in his eyes. Teddy was gone. This was all black wolf.

Panicked, I shot a look at the black magic clenched inside Brenyn's other hand. Dread's icy fist clamped around my throat.

Her arm came back.

I pushed from the ground, shouting with the effort.

Magic left her hand.

The black wolf and death magic crashed together. A fist-sized section of fur turned to dust. It was just...gone. The flesh blistered and the damaged section imploded. A wet ragged hole dug into his flesh. So much red and bone. *I could see bone!*

Images of Etta'wy turning to ash exploded in my mind. Of Y'sindra's wing turning to dust. The magic racing to claim her body, her life. The black wolf was strong. He could fight this!

But this magic wasn't from his world.

Time moved in that awful swampy way, forcing me to witness every horror, unable to stop it from happening. I couldn't move fast enough. I was so gods damned useless. Even with Teddy's blood, my body was leaden. My limbs would not do what they were told.

The black wolf roared and kept coming.

Brenyn stepped back.

Run, bitch.

Laughing, I again pushed the cement blocks masquerading as my feet into motion. Each step lighter, steadier, I stalked toward her.

A gurgling snarl ripped my attention from Brenyn. I turned toward Teddy.

The crater in his chest widened. His massive shoulders rolled, and he bent forward, into his next step. Another step. He shuddered, lifted another foot, and then crashed down on one knee. His hands shot out and fingers curled, claws digging great divots in the stone.

My legs locked, my insides turning to ice. I screamed. My throat turned raw and hot.

His roar cut off abruptly. Neck bent forward, his head swiveled toward me. Our gazes locked. Muzzle hanging slightly ajar, his ruptured chest rose and fell with harsh wet pants loud enough to reach my ears.

Please, Teddy, please. Get up, get up, get up!

"Please," I whispered.

He toppled. Didn't get up.

No!

My feet lifted, and legs pumped. I became fury. I became death. Feral and snarling, I collided with Brenyn's back. Her face hit the stone with a wet crack. Her head bounced.

My gaze sought my mate. Teddy, no longer the black wolf, lie crumpled and unmoving. My hearts tangled into knots. He'd told me the only way to break the black wolf's hold might be to kill him.

He couldn't be dead. I'd know. I'd feel it. He was my mate!

Someone will die because of you.

Fuck Fate!

A pitiful cry wrenched from my throat. It turned into a scream. It went on and on as something built inside of me, too big to contain.

I unraveled at the edges. Shades of red drenched my world. My ability to reason fell away. My focus narrowed to one thing. Brenyn, painted with a crimson hue, was crystal clear. My screams weren't fae, they were something else. I drew my arm up and slammed my fist into her back—through her back. Into the stone beneath.

The essence she'd stolen returned like a tornado. Like an earthquake. Like a hurricane. Darkness teased my vision. Snarling, feeling my power settle into place, I held on.

Thin cracks in the stone raced away from her body. Blood fanned out from beneath her. It filled the widening cracks that continued to multiply around us.

I ripped my hand out of her back, spraying blood across myself, and in all directions. I hit her again, and again. She didn't react to the dull meaty thumps, or the snapping bones.

Something else cracked. A deeper sound, bigger than bones breaking. Vibrations in the ground finally pierced my mindless rage. The red haze receded from my vision. My torn breaths filled my ears.

Standing, I slipped and stared at what I'd been crouched over. If I hadn't been there, I wouldn't have known who it was—what it was. Something had taken over and all I'd wanted was Brenyn's death. Blood and gore covered her body, flung away by my swinging fists. Her torso was an unidentifiable riot of bone and meat.

I shook and stared.

Jagged lines in the stone fanned out from her body like skeletal butterfly wings. The crevices continued to grow wider. The trembling wasn't coming from me. I broke the damn bridge.

My gaze flew to Teddy. He still hadn't moved. *No, no, no.*

I had to get us out of here before this thing came down. I stepped toward him, but my foot flew out in front of me. I cried out as I landed hard on my knee.

The tremors grew more violent. With my hands planted on the bridge, my arms vibrated. Pools of blood—the lake of blood—rippled.

Rather than waste time trying to walk on the slick surface, I crawled until I reached dry stone. Never stopping, I pushed up and ran for Teddy.

Glass crunched beneath my feet as I reached him. I wondered where the glass had come from, but then my eyes tracked to the ragged hole in his chest, and I saw nothing else. The black magic hadn't missed him. But it hadn't consumed him.

Gently, I brushed my hands over his face. My eyes burned. The pressure inside my head threatened to overwhelm me.

Was he breathing? Gods, I didn't think so. The bridge continued to shudder, and I couldn't tell. I looked *into* the hole in his chest.

Someone will die because of you.

I stared so hard at the wound my eyes burned. Something was missing. Something more than flesh and bone.

The vial.

My gaze flew to the broken glass and then returned.

The magic hit the vial. My blood entered his chest with foul magic. That had to be what prevented it from consuming him.

Someone will also live.

The bridge shook, and I lost my balance again. It snapped me out of the sorrow. Teddy wasn't dust. The magic hadn't taken him. Mate's blood had stopped the spread, but it hadn't healed the damage. The blood inside me was made up of even more now. Vampire blood. Blackthorne said vampire blood could do amazing things. It could save him. It had to!

Fangs punching down hard and fast, I sank them into my wrist, tearing it open. Instantly, blood flowed. I tilted my arm over Teddy's chest, letting my blood run directly into the hole, and then into his mouth.

"Come on," I pleaded. Another snapping rumble rent the air, popping over and over like a hundred gunshots.

I couldn't wait any longer. Crouching behind his head, I slid my arms beneath his shoulders and hefted his torso. He was so much heavier than I expected. Whatever brief jolt of power I'd gained from cracking open that vial was gone.

But we moved. I pushed with my legs, dragging Teddy backwards, down the ramp.

Five steps, ten, twenty.

The bridge gave a shudder of defeat and came apart. Really broke. Giant pieces fell away, taking Brenyn with them. Slow at first, and then an avalanche as piece after piece fell away. The gap widened.

I hurried past two of the massive support pillars and kept going. "Please, please, please."

A great, yawning void raced for me. I glanced over my shoulder. The ramp I'd climbed to reach the walkway was too far away. I'd never make it.

Accepting this was it, I collapsed and pulled Teddy into my lap. Bent over, lips pressed to his ear, I whispered, "I love you."

Chunks of stone large enough to park my Bronco on disappeared. There one second, gone the next. The bridge shuddered. Hundreds of fissures radiated out from the initial damage I'd done.

My teeth chattered with the building rumble from the devastation happening right in front of me. Teddy's head flopped against my shoulder.

A fast-moving break arrowed towards us. Massive sections of stone fell away in its wake. I squeezed my eyes shut and clutched Teddy to me.

The sound reached a deafening crescendo and then nothing. The rumbling ceased. Through the ringing in my ears, I heard a few small pops.

I squinted one eye open. A cloud of dust billowed where moments ago there had been an entire section of walkway. I opened both eyes. The fracture I'd been sure was about to drag us down had stopped when it reached the supports.

Muffled thunder rose from far below as the fallen pieces of sun bridge hit the ground.

With my arms still locked around Teddy, I rocked forward and back. A laugh bubbled out of me. It built into fast, high-pitched laughter.

I felt the erratic beat of my hearts against Teddy's back.

No, that wasn't me. I held my breath. This time, beneath my palm, I felt a thrum from his chest.

Laying Teddy gently on the ground I scrambled around to his side and pressed my fingers to his throat.

His pulse was sluggish, but it was there.

A different kind of pounding came from behind me. I didn't need to look to know it was the Royal Fae Guard, late to the rescue. They would have seen the shield shatter and made it up the ramp to the walkway.

Teddy's chest rose and fell. Shallow breaths, but he was breathing. The wound was disguised by his torn shirt, but from what little I could see, it was healing.

In the meantime, your Aventheo might enjoy the benefits. Thinking about Blackthorne, emotions I wasn't ready to deal with pushed against the box I'd stuffed them inside. He would have been so smug to find out how right he'd been.

Tears broke away from my lashes and ran over my cheeks. I dragged my forearms across my face and laughed, shaking my head. "Fucking vampire blood."

41

THE BLACKTHORNE TREE

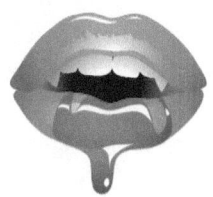

I FELT NAKED WITHOUT AT LEAST ONE BLADE STRAPPED TO MY BODY. Uncomfortable with so much bare skin on display, I folded an arm across my chest and scratched my exposed elbow. A tendril of hair fell across my face. There were no braids. I'd worn it loose today, the heavy mass falling stick-straight to my waist with nothing but a thin, ankle-length dress beneath.

For the first time in I didn't know how long, I hadn't dressed in my leathers. There was no need. There was no one left to fight. Hiemal, Miro, and Brenyn were dead. So was Dacian. His remains had been discovered at the edge of Eodrom. I no longer had to look over my shoulder. It left a strange, fluttery feeling inside me.

My hands had a mind of their own. They kept moving and fidgeting as I walked the palace halls. For the fiftieth time in the last five minutes, I smoothed the skirts of the white sheath dress.

Pru had brought all of us a change of clothes. She'd brought me more leathers. Shocking everyone—even myself—I'd asked if she had anything else. She'd returned with the dress and a pair of sandals I'd have sworn she stole from Mae. Flimsy, ridiculous things that laced to the knee. They were frivolous and impractical.

Right now, they were exactly what I needed.

Twisting a knot into my hair, I entered the hallway to the sun garden and abruptly stopped. I'd been told the wall had vanished, but I hadn't believed.

The massive stone wall only someone chosen by the sun stones could pass through had magically turned into stone columns, still covered in vines and filled with small, dangerously cute creatures. The garden was now open to any fae who wished to visit. In the span of one night, hundreds already had.

It wasn't only about the sudden access. There was something new in the sun garden, something aside from the fallen sections of sun bridge. While everyone had been distracted by what was happening on the bridge above, a new tree had sprouted inside the circle of sun stones.

On a whim, I untied the sandals. Reaching for the laces, I let them dangle from my fingertips as I crossed the transition from the palace's stone floor into the garden. Scratchy grass tickled the soles of my feet. I laughed a little, burrowing my toes into the cool soil.

Mom had descended with her stinky salves for Teddy, herbs for Mae, and medicine for me laced with something that earned me a few fitful hours of sleep. This morning, Mae finally woke, and at last, Teddy fell asleep. A deep, healing sleep. I knew then everything would be okay, and I'd snuck off to the sun garden before anyone could stop me.

I needed to visit. I needed to see for myself...

Just in case.

In case Blackthorne defied the law of gravity and survived the fall. He had, after all, defied expectations and sacrificed the death owed to him that kept him going all these years, to save me. His creation. His granddaughter.

Taking my time to really breathe, I drew air deep, to the bottom of my lungs. The heady smell green growing things and musky wooded stuff coated my senses. A strong hit of earth, from all the churned soil twined with all the other scents.

I looked out across the garden to where the bridge fell. In the same location, one tree towered above the rest. It was a long way away. I started in that direction.

Strange birds that ran on legs too long for their tiny bodies and didn't seem to fly darted across paths, chirping and chittering. Small animals scampered around and hid behind trees. There wasn't a fae in sight. Iola had cleared the garden for my visit this morning.

The walk took the better part of an hour. As I approached, an emotional knot lodged in my chest unspooled. The backs of my eyes stung and my ears burned. I breathed through it. The churn of emotions broke apart and melded together—joy and sorrow, anger and acceptance.

A fragrant pile of flowers circled the tree trunk that had to stretch at least twenty feet wide. The sight left me a little breathless.

Hundreds of fae had come to honor the blackthorne tree. A tree long thought extinct until last year when one rose alongside the Eodrom palace. I never did get around to telling the RFG that might have been (definitely was) my fault.

Remembering my grandfather's clever trickery, I smirked. He was such an asshole, and I kind of really liked him.

Long portions of the ground had split open, exposing knobby roots. Some were short and twisty, others thin and long. I stepped onto one twice as wide as me, the knotted wood pressing into my arches.

I approached the trunk and crouched, sweeping aside the stack of blossoms gathered against the ebony bark. As I stood, I tipped my head back and my gaze followed the gradient of color. It shifted to mahogany, paling more and more as it rose to the canopy. Even with my vision it was too far to see the details, but I knew the branches were pale and sported enormous black thorns.

While I'd still been laid up in the infirmary, Y'sindra had flown around the tree and told us she'd nearly skewered herself.

"We misunderstood Angus Blackthorne," someone said, voice gentle with a melodious tone.

Smiling, I turned to face Iola. "Only a little. None of this had to happen. He knew all along about your sister, yet he played a game because he thought it was his right to end her."

"I have heard." She looked past me, to the tree. "He could have done all that, but I do not know that I blame him. No one knew they were bonded, yet I understand she tried to end the male meant to be the other half of her soul."

"Yes." I didn't think she was looking for more of an answer than that, but I wasn't here to talk about Brenyn. I wasn't here to talk at all, but I couldn't very well tell the sun stone keeper to go away.

Iola sucked in a sharp breath, as if the words she wanted to push out burned her tongue. "She took many lovers, so she must have believed him dead."

Considering the reaction I'd had to Beast, the revulsion for him and need for Teddy, I supposed that was true. "Eventually, she knew he wasn't. She had Etta'wy locate and hire a druid to open the way to Outerlands."

"Many fell by her hand, but not all. Druids are nomads of the universe. They come and go, and many have." She tilted her face to the tree's canopy.

"Do you know the building where I live on Earth, Blackthorne's building, is called the Blackthorne? That is where I first tracked Etta'wy when Palough hired us to find his runaway wife." The job that started this all. It felt like decades ago, but it had only been a year.

Iola jerked, surprised. "Angus had been a god among druids, it could have been given that name in homage, but surely Brenyn had to have suspected."

I chuckled. "She did more than suspect, but not right away. Like I said, Blackthorne loved his games. I'm certain he pulled strings to bring Etta'wy to him. Dropping rumors about the druid who owned the casino would have been enough. After she recruited him for Brenyn's plan, he changed the resort name to the Blackthorne. Sort of like firing a warning shot before he made his final move."

"That sounds like Angus." The smile returned to Iola's lips and grew to a grin. "We were friends once."

It was my turn to be surprised. I blinked. "I had no idea."

"Angus was...well, I do not know his age, but he was here before me." She laughed, light and airy. "As a keeper, my father kept me apart from *his people*. I was above them, in his eyes. A member of the court, he was greedy and wished for what I had been granted."

Once again following instinct and hoping I didn't survive Brenyn to be smited now, I placed a hand on Iola's arm. She turned to me and smiled. No smiting, thank the stars.

She placed her hand over mine. "He ignored my sister, and I always thought she was fortunate for that."

"Grass is always greener," I said, and Iola gave me a quizzical look. "Earth thing. It means what we don't have always looks better than what we do. According to Blackthorne she was abandoned by her mother, ignored by your father, and shunned by the fae for her situation. It's why she grew into... what she did."

"As you were mistreated for who you were," Iola said. "But it is not who you became."

"Family is a powerful thing." I didn't point out it was my sisters, who to this day, made me better. Who knew if Iola would ever regret the relationship she didn't have with her sister? But pointing out the one I did have felt like putting salt in the wound.

Iola gave several jerky nods. "Perhaps it is time Torneh and I step into the royal roles we have so long abhorred in order to bring about much needed change. The moon fae prince you found will help return balance to our world."

Smiling, I tucked my hair behind my ears. "I think that will be good."

It would be a long time before Dexter would want to do anything... princely. Kingly? He was the last of his line, so yeah, kingly. But I'd seen him with my dad. He'd been bitten by the magic bug. He would visit Eodrom often.

Satiny petals tickled my feet as I stepped close enough to the tree to press my palm to the bark. "You haven't found any bodies, have you?"

"No," she answered and moved closer, into my peripheral. "Blackthorne was an ancient. I am considered an ancient, so then was Brenyn."

My hand slid from the bark, and I turned to face her.

"I have seen the passing of many ancients. We return to stardust, wholly. I expect that was my sister's fate. Angus, though." She tilted another smile at the tree. "I am not surprised he managed to impart himself to the land."

"Hm," I said, doing my best Blackthorne impression, neither agreeing, nor disagreeing.

"I shall leave you to remember him in peace." Shocking me to the tips of my toes, Iola drew me into a hug. "I hope to see you soon. We shall install benches here."

The whisper of Iola's footsteps faded. "Did you hear that? Imparted yourself to the land." I snorted. "You aren't that generous."

This was Blackthorne's middle finger to the realm that had turned on him—never mind he'd done worse first.

The tree wasn't his only parting shot. When the tree sprouted, the wards he'd helped create to block portals in and out of the realm fell.

Tossing one of my father's devices I'd brought with me to the ground, I crouched and drew a rune over it. An oval opened onto the penthouse balcony.

There was a cat I needed to feed.

42

YOU ARE PERFECTION

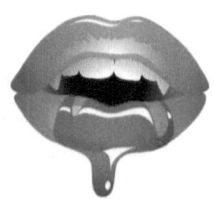

My phone buzzed. I squinted and saw sunshine. Teddy and I had been sleeping in since the events in Eodrom.

I rolled over, drawn toward the center of the bed by Teddy's body heat. The phone buzzed again. Apparently having the same feelings about being woken up, Lulla abandoned the foot of the bed and padded from the room.

"Lane." Teddy's voice was thick with sleep.

"Whoever it is, they'll leave a message."

The phone stopped vibrating on my nightstand. I resettled beneath the sheets. The buzzing started again. I sat up and glowered at the name on the screen: Sassafras.

I grabbed the phone, hit accept, and snapped, "What?"

"You need to get over here. Right now!" Y'sindra shouted.

"Shh! Do you know how early it is? Don't shout," I shouted back.

The rumble of Teddy's amusement shook the mattress. He hadn't completely healed, but he was in no danger of dying. It had been a week, and while he was back to getting the bar downstairs ready to open, Mom declared him unfit for the fun stuff. The chest wound was still open and raw, but with her stinky salves, it was better by the day.

"Lane, you have to see this. It's important."

I pinched the bridge of my nose. "You know what else is important? Sleep. And I need like a month of it."

"Bring Ted-D," Lo said from somewhere in the background.

The bedding shifted and tugged against my waist. I looked behind me to Teddy who sat up against the headboard. A rumpled T-shirt covered the bandages wrapped around his torso. Beneath the sheets, I knew he wore sweatpants, because, he said, it would be weird to only sleep in a shirt.

He yawned and shrugged, indicating he'd heard Lo.

"Fine." I pulled my legs back onto the mattress, fully intending to go back to sleep. "We'll be there in an hour."

"Lane, you need to come now," Y'sindra said. Something in her tone had me out of bed and on my feet.

I looked at Teddy who did the same. "We'll be right there."

WE STEPPED THROUGH THE DRUID CIRCLE...

"Why are we in Outerlands?" I spun, looking in every direction, sure I was seeing things. "*How* are we in Outerlands?"

"You aren't." Y'sindra followed by Lo, ahwal'Tam, and a bunch of snow fairies whose names I did not know, came flying toward me. "Outerlands is over here. You're still on Earth."

"How?" I repeated. Shouted, more like. My feet burrowed into the sand as I turned in another circle, slower this time. For the most part everything was the same, but directly in front of me was green and lush. The grass gave way to sand and then, improbably, an ocean inside Outerlands.

Up the beach, on the side of the hotel where Blackthorne had torn open a door and then swore he'd closed, was where downtown Outerlands began.

I looked at Teddy, who only shook his head. I turned to Y'sindra. "Explain."

She thrust her arms out at her sides. "I'm not a druid or a...what are they? A physicist? Astrophysicist? Astronomer? Whatever it is, I am not it, and I don't freaking know what happened."

Lo fluttered around as excitedly as I'd ever seen. "We heard a loud tearing sound. The ground shook, and when we came outside this was here."

"The door tore open," I whispered and then my brows crashed together. "Blackthorne did this. I don't know how, but he set this up."

"Lane," Teddy said gently.

"I don't mean he was here and did something. He's gone, I get it, but somehow, he did this."

Excited conversation from the snow fairies who'd hung back and the murmuring of an ocean on a calm day were the soundtrack to Teddy and Y'sindra's silence.

At last, my sister shrugged. "Anything is possible with that guy. But what do we do with your hotel?"

"It's not—" I started to object, but then snapped my mouth shut and stared dumbfounded at the beach hotel, I did, indeed, own. I laughed, because how dumb was it to give me—*me!*—a hotel? Not just this hotel, but the Blackthorne, with access to the financials to support them.

Or to go on a really great shopping spree. The lockbox Vaughn had delivered with the deeds and information was on a shelf in my closet, next to my secret stash of emergency Ho Hos.

Still looking at the hotel, I thought about the note I'd found in the bottom of the lockbox and started to laugh. *Remember you are not a mistake. You are perfection. Don't destroy my hotels.*

43

GRAND OPENING DAY

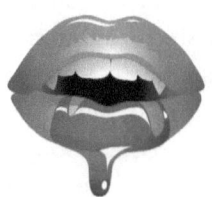

IT WAS GRAND OPENING DAY. NOT FOR *BLOOD AND WINE*, THAT HAPPENED five months ago. There were the usual hiccups—not enough of this or that, double-booked reservations, frazzled staff—but overall, it had been a huge success and was still going strong. Though both Dexter and Zee were there, they'd spent the last few months training new staff.

While they had been doing that, and Teddy had been at his other properties, I took business classes. To my utter astonishment, Vaughn had been helpful. My first decision as new owner of the Blackthorne had been to promote him to general manager.

A fae and a human walked directly toward me on the packed grassy street, oblivious to where they were going. I swiveled to avoid having to push them out of my way.

Main Street, as we'd so cleverly come to call the main thoroughfare in Outerlands, was packed with foot traffic. As business had moved in, the grassy roads had been clipped and flower planters hung off nearly every railing. The roar and hiss of surf played background to the lively chatter in town.

Today was much busier than it had been since the veil between Earth and Outerlands fell, but as new businesses continued to open, a steady stream of visitors arrived daily. Sun fae, moon fae, wood fae, you-name-it-fae, even a couple dryads had shown up. Shifters came from Shadwe, while humans, from Earth.

Several buildings had been converted back to businesses. The snow fairies had happily agreed to share living quarters while work was underway to build them new homes off the main strip, away from the tourists. I'd offered the hotel I had not yet opened, but they weren't keen to live on Earth. Despite the building being in plain sight of downtown Outerlands, it was, technically, a whole world away.

Zee would eventually take over as general manager of the hotel. When she did, I strongly suspected she'd tempt some snow fairies onto the staff. These days, she shadowed Vaughn to learn the hotel management ropes. I knew she wouldn't stay there forever, but for now was good enough.

A large corkboard had been erected along the street with plexiglass doors that opened and closed to protect the contents. Between the fliers and business cards, almost no cork showed.

My gaze moved over the colorful posts as I approached the board. The center featured a square black frame with the contact information in bold, blocky script for Barbout Building Management. Since the Barbouts were originally responsible for...everything in Outerlands, Lo suggested—begged —Teddy to take up the reins. He'd agreed, but he laid all the power in Lo and Y'sindra's hands. Terrifying thought.

The wind shifted. A smoky, spicy, slightly earthy scent reached me over the brine of the nearby ocean. My salivary glands went into overdrive. The doors to a restaurant Elisette owned were thrown open. A long line stretched from the building into the street. Customers exited with paper bowls filled to the brim with Jason's secret recipe green chili. I restrained myself from stealing a bowl from a group of humans who wandered dangerously close.

I let them pass, despite the timely rumble that erupted from my midsection as they neared. I'd come prepared with an empty stomach and a huge appetite.

"I heard that!" Y'sindra yelled, despite appearing only a foot away. Grinning, she hovered in front of me. "Jason and Eli made a pot special for you. Lo stashed it at the bar."

My gaze slid down the street, to the sign above a building declaring *LO & DEXTER'S DRINKERY* in stylish calligraphy cut from shiny silver metal. I didn't think drinkery was a real word, but Lo had been so pleased with his suggestion, none of us were willing to say differently.

Y'sindra looked me up and down. "You sure are showing a lot of skin."

I peered down at myself, shaking the loose T-shirt I'd thrown over a swimsuit. "This is what people wear to the beach."

"And not a dagger in sight," she teased.

"You guys keep telling me to stop stabbing people." I winked and stepped around her.

She fell into step at my side and proceeded to give a play by play of how the day was going, starting with the moment they opened the doors. I smiled and nodded, probably in the right places, but my mind was on this dead town that had come to life.

To everyone's surprise, I'd taken this business thing seriously. Every time I thought about blowing off a class or a day of shadowing Vaughn, I remembered—*don't destroy my hotels*. Ha, ha, funny guy. I gave a mental eye roll. All the effort that went into not ruining things kept me busy. It had been over a month since my last visit to Outerlands, and the amount of new business was staggering.

I craned my neck to see into each building we passed. Several clothing stores filled previously empty spaces, as well as a café, a bookstore, and oh my gods, a place on the corner offered "rides." There was a picture of each creature available painted on a large sign out front. A horse, snake, wolf, big cat, and... I squinted. Was that one of those weasel-bear things I'd fought a few months ago?

"Do I want to know what kind of rides that place is offering?" I asked Y'sindra.

She stopped in the street and hovered to look at the place in question. Her brows dove together as she swung around to face me. "Aren't you a gutter brain? It's for tours of Outerlands and Shadwe, ya perv. For your information, the shifters have the most popular business on the street."

"With humans?" I asked.

"Ya'd think it was just them, but fae around here are dying to get a safe look inside Shadwe." Turning, she buzzed ahead.

I followed until a bright red-and-white rendition of a peppermint candy with googly eyes caught my attention. I slowed and waited for the slow-moving group of tourists to get out of the way.

My eyes expanded into dinner plates when the full scene came into view. Candy of every type had been painted on the plate glass window. Gumdrops played jump rope with pulled taffy. Blocks of fudge sat laughing and melting on a bench. The scene was fun and hilarious. It gave me a sugar high just looking at it.

"Nope." Y'sindra grabbed my hand the moment I angled toward the store and towed me in the opposite direction.

Sighing, I let her, but then I smelled it. Roasted coffee. I stopped in the middle of the street, looking for the source.

"Your boy toy is waiting." Y'sindra grabbed my hand again, this time not letting go as she dragged me toward the bar.

A crowd spilled onto the expanded deck where outdoor seating had been added. There wasn't an empty table in sight.

"How are Lo and Dex handling the crowd?" I asked, following my sister inside. The yeasty scent of beer and distinct, mouth-watering smell of fried food washed over me.

"Great. Most of the Interlands staff moved over here, and of course Zee is helping out. Girl can throw down behind a bar." Y'sindra hovered into the air. "We have that booth over there."

Following the direction she indicated, I found two large tables pushed together. Mae sat between Vaughn and Pru. Odo chatted with a cute moon fae female. Duskmere and, *ugh*, Cirron, were seated next to one another. A few fae I vaguely recognized both from the hotel and from the RFG sat with them as well.

"You can head over. I'm gonna check on my muffin first. See if he needs help," Y'sindra said and then flew toward the bar.

A smile pulled at my lips as watched her go, barely avoiding a collision with a snow fairy flying drinks to a table. She'd done that. Given those snow fairies a home, a purpose, a new life.

Emotion rose inside me. A swift, hard knot balled up in my chest. *Don't you dare cry!* I blinked rapidly, pulling air in and out of my mouth. What was wrong with me?

"Hey." Teddy's caramel-coated tone melted over me.

Without thinking, I walked into his arms, careful to rest my head against his biceps, not his chest. "Hey."

Taking my hand, he drew me back toward the door. Laughing, I let him. Maybe I could score some of that candy. And chili. I was so hungry.

Outside, he pulled me into the space between his bar and the building next door. We weren't exactly out of sight, not even close, but the moment

Teddy backed me against the wall, I didn't care. Instead of bending down, Teddy lifted me, and pressed his lips to mine.

I'd been working on that whole shy thing. Considering how eagerly I locked my ankles around his back, baring my barely covered ass to anyone who looked, I was doing a great job.

Careful not to break skin, because I'd not reached that level of public PDA, I nipped Teddy's lower lip. With a satisfied hum, he smiled against my mouth.

He traced the seam of my lips with his tongue, and I opened to him. I tasted the spicy cinnamon flavor of his favorite gum as he explored my mouth. My legs tightened. I tunneled my hands into his hair, lightly scraping my talons over his scalp.

His hips pressed into me. I laughed against his mouth, realizing the wall at my back wasn't the only thing hard. Teddy was well on his way to making an impressive spectacle of himself.

In his defense, it had been a while. His chest still wasn't completely healed. He insisted I was being ridiculous, but I reminded him of the days when I didn't drink his blood and he'd denied me sexy time. Besides, we had a lifetime of days and nights to be together.

"I have this idea." Teddy lowered me to my feet and adjusted himself. Pity. He took my hand and steered me back into the street, in the direction I'd just come from.

Frowning, I looked behind me to the bar where a pot of chili waited. Maybe he was taking me to the restaurant. "Does it involve chili? I'm hungry. We're VIP enough to jump the line."

"Nope." Teddy was walking awfully fast.

As we drew even with Elisette's, I caught a glimpse of her inside and waved. She made a wild motion with her hands, beckoning us to come in.

"They're waving for us to come in." I slowed and tugged on Teddy's hand.

"I'm hungry for something else."

"Just a quick stop." I pulled toward the restaurant. "I've been looking forward to that chili for weeks."

Teddy paused. He looked inside to Elisette and Jason, who had joined his now wife, and waved. Satisfied I was getting my chili, I smiled, already imagining the sharp bite of tomatillo's dancing on my tongue.

Turning away from the building, Teddy barely paused as he swept me into his arms and continued down the street. "I've been looking forward to something else."

At that rumbling tone, a shiver rolled over me. As if they had a mind of their own, my traitorous arms wound around my sugar bun's neck. I pressed my suddenly full and aching breasts against his chest.

Horrified I could have caused him pain, I pulled back. "We had a deal. Not until you're healed."

Teddy chuckled. "You had a deal. I never agreed."

The grassy street gave way to patchy tufts of green poking from sand, and eventually, to a wide cement sidewalk that circled the hotel. He walked to the deck, which never did get a pool, and to the back door where he set me down, to fish a key from his pocket.

I wrapped my arms around my middle and stepped away. On one hand, gods yes, I wanted this—him—but on the other hand, he'd had a giant hole in his chest.

Someone will die because of you, but someone will also live.

Because of me, Teddy had done both of those things. That terrified me. I could admit it was irrational, but I couldn't move past it. My arms fell to my sides, and I bunched the loose coverup in my fists against my thighs.

Teddy inserted a key beneath a keypad and then entered the code. The locks on the glass door next to the pad *thunk*-ed. Coming to me, he pulled my arms from my sides, and grazed a kiss across the knuckles of each of my hands. "Come inside with me." That damn crooked smile appeared. "All these people, and we have a whole hotel to ourselves."

"When you put it like that." Laughing, I let him lead me inside.

Teddy hit the lock button on the indoor keypad as soon as we entered, and then I was in his arms, my legs around his waist. He smiled, and the expression in his eyes undid me. Love. I saw love.

I lifted my hands to frame his face. "My mate."

"Yes," he said and carried me to the sitting area. "Your mate."

"Hey, isn't that the part where you say you're my mate, or you love me, or can't live without me?"

Pressed against him, I felt the rumble of his laughter in my bones.

"All of the above." He kissed my nose and maneuvered to sit on a sofa with its back to the floor to ceiling windows. Pulling me to straddle his lap, he worked his hands up my bare back, beneath my shirt.

Biting my lip, I looked past him to the empty deck. "Anyone could walk up."

"They could." His warm lips moved against my throat until he reached my earlobe. "They won't."

I tilted my head to the side. He swirled his tongue along the length of newly exposed neck. My lashes fluttered. "How do you know?"

When he reached the area above my pulse, he sealed his lips against my skin and sucked, ending in a light nibble.

I gasped. My knees squeezed his hips.

"The closed sign we mounted on the deck will do it."

"The what?" I blinked, moving restlessly against Teddy.

He grinned. "You asked how—"

"Oh, yeah." I licked my lips. "Right, the closed sign."

His hands slid down my back. He kept going, fingers sliding beneath me to cup my butt, fingers teasing the hem of my bathing suit.

My hearts pounded. He had to feel them. I couldn't control my breathing. "Teddy," I groaned his name, bending my forehead to his shoulder, careful to keep my chest from crushing against his.

"Lane." His voice had turned rough, full of gravel.

The puff of air from my name teased the fine hairs at my nape. It caused my insides to clench. This was the point where I climbed off and took him into my mouth. That weightless quivering sensation took up residence low in my belly at the thought. I loved the salty taste of him on my tongue. The satin and steel feel of him in my palm.

Digging my fingers beneath his waistband, I began to slide off his lap. His hands tightened on my ass, a hand beneath each cheek. His pinkies so close to my entrance. He teased, and I knew he could feel me getting wet.

"I'm fine, Lane." Teddy pulled his hands from beneath me and yanked his shirt over his head, baring his strong, broad, scarred chest.

My hearts beat for a different reason as I stared at the reminder of how close I came to losing him. He drew my hand from his waistband to his chest. It trembled as he pressed it to the angry, pink ridges of skin. That's all it was. Not even a scab remained. I'd seen it. I knew, but I was so damn scared of seeing him that way again.

Helpless. Dying.

"I am fine, Lane," Teddy repeated, his dark gaze refusing to release mine, forcing me to see. To believe.

He lifted his hands from mine to rub his thumbs along my cheek. They came away damp. Oh, for stars sake, was I crying again? Bending forward, I tucked my head into the crook of his neck. He wrapped his arms around me, and this time, I didn't pull back when he pressed me against his chest, squeezing my hand between us.

"You okay?" he asked, and I nodded. His hands moved lower. "So..." He let the word hang.

Filling my lungs with a deep, satisfied breath, I smiled and sat up.

My gaze shot to the deck. My brain malfunctioned. Large red eyes. Scales. Wings. Big teeth.

I shrieked and fell backwards off Teddy's lap.

He leapt to his feet and spun toward the window. On the other side of the glass, a large, sapphire-blue wyvern watched us.

"Fuck! I knew I should have brought my sword." I scrambled to my feet and made for the dining room. "There are knives in here."

Laughing, Teddy stopped me.

I looked from his face, to his hand on my arm, to the big ass wyvern. "What are you doing?"

"That, sweet fangs, is my sister."

"Your...sister?" My lips felt numb. My entire face felt numb. Maybe I'd hit my head when I fell off his lap.

"My sister," he said again and pulled me against him. "Welcome to the family."

***

Thank you for reading! Did you enjoy? Please add your review because nothing helps an author more and encourages readers to take a chance on a book than a review.

And don't miss new books from Choi coming soon. Until then read more great urban fantasy romance like CATCHING HELL, by City Owl Author, D.B. Sieders. Turn the page for a sneak peek!

Also be sure to sign up for the City Owl Press newsletter to receive notice of all book releases!

SNEAK PEEK OF CATCHING HELL

BY D.B. SIEDERS

Life goal number 666: Be the kind of woman that when your feet hit the floor each morning, the devil says, "Oh, crap. She's up!" — T-shirt worn by Jinx McGee, demon hunter.

I saw my first demon when I was five. I was looking in a mirror.

I'd been brushing my teeth when I glanced at my reflection and noticed I wasn't the only one there. A presence lurked behind my eyes. It wasn't nice. It was angry, and it wanted out. I don't know if the demon living inside me had always been there, but that was the first time I saw her. My scream almost burst my own eardrums—and my older sister's since she'd been standing beside me. She didn't see the demon. Neither did my mom. They both thought I was imagining things.

They were wrong.

Still, when life gave you lemons, you were supposed to make lemonade. Life gave me a demon, so I became a demon hunter. I never learned how to make demonade, let alone market it.

Since becoming a demon hunter, I'd seen six hundred and sixty-four demons...not that I was counting. Demon number six hundred and sixty-five targeted the man I was currently surveilling on my latest stakeout. The man and his demon stalker were my latest demon-hunting assignment in downtown Nashville, and shit was about to go down.

Like the fact that said demon stalker was currently speeding through the air on a collision course with a wagon full of drunk tourists who, being strictly human, couldn't see it.

"Look out," I yelled. Damn it, where was my partner? She'd texted to tell me she was stuck in traffic, but I could've really used some backup. While unseen, the freaking demon could do real, visible damage.

Crap, I couldn't wait for Lacey. I'd have to break protocol and go after the demon and its mark on my own.

The demon, who was a streak of black only I could see, whizzed past the man it was targeting and through one of those pedal taverns clogging up Broadway and Second Avenue. The damned demon knocked the penis headband right off one of the intoxicated bachelorettes. Bummer. I enjoyed phallic party favors almost as much as I enjoyed drunken revelry. It would've been fun to pick it up and crash the party. I could shove one of those drunk gals off her stool and take her spot, pretending to be a sixth cousin twice removed who no one really knew, but she endeared herself to the group anyway.

Jane McGee the jolly bridesmaid had a nice ring to it. It was what a gal my age should be doing.

Too bad I was working.

I was Jane "Jinx" McGee, demon hunter, and would be until I figured out how to get rid of the demon currently possessing me. Long-term relationships, marriage, white picket fences, and a whole lot of normal weren't possible for me at the moment. I'd have to settle for keeping drunken bridesmaids and the rest of humanity safe from unauthorized demon shenanigans.

"Oh! Sadie lost her wiener."

The shout came from another one of the rolling bar's occupants, who nearly fell out of her seat laughing, blissfully unaware she'd been dive-bombed by a demon. Damn it, tempters moved fast. I hoped this one was corporeal. They weren't necessarily easy pickings, but easier to catch than the immaterial variety. Corporeals were still fast as all get-out, even with a body, but at least they couldn't transform into ether and vanish into vents or gutters.

I needed to slow the demon down, but first I had to follow it to the more private location it had chosen to claim the human it was after.

One of the gals on the pedal tavern handed me a shot glass as they passed, and I downed the contents in a single gulp while they hooted and hollered, giving me high fives and shouting, "You go, girl." The bachelorettes had good taste in tequila, at least. Ah, to be an ordinary human, blessedly unaware of creatures that go bump in the night. With a nod of thanks, I returned the glass and set off at a light jog to catch up with the demon's target.

The oblivious human hadn't noticed the demon tracking him, of course. Poor sap. He just had the inexplicable compulsion to go wherever the demon had chosen. Demons had all kinds of nasty mind tricks they used to manipulate their prey. If they went around openly on the attack, people would soon become too afraid to leave their houses and hunting would be harder.

Demons were ambush predators.

I'd been watching the demon's target, a middle-aged father of two, for over a week. He'd been demon marked, and when one of our patrollers spotted the demon's mark—invisible to humans but a clear signal to other demons the bearer was already taken—she'd called us in. I'd been waiting for the demon, intent on siphoning his soul—or stealing his life-force for those who didn't believe in souls and such—to lure him to a secluded location so it could claim its next meal.

The poor guy looked more like Santa Claus than demon chow with his jolly round face, salt-and-pepper beard, and generous belly. The red Hawaiian shirt really tied the look together, but thankfully he wore khaki pants instead of red crushed velvet.

That would have been completely over the top.

I wondered what this guy had done to get a bull's-eye on his back. The case file was scant on details but flagged as urgent.

No matter. I'd find out soon enough based on the flavor of tempter demon he'd attracted. He ducked into a dark alley—how original—as his demonic stalker finally stopped zipping around and stepped out of the shadows. With my enhanced senses, I observed the demon stalker assume a form that halted the man dead in his tracks and turned him into a quivering mass of lust and longing.

Ah, a succubus had tagged him. My demon stirred within me, excited by the prospect of hunting.

She's hungry. So am I.

I shuddered as my demon's thoughts echoed in my mind along with her ravenous excitement. Fortunately for me and the rest of the planet, my demon was under my control and on a tight leash. She'd only taken over fully once when I was young, but once had been enough.

Nothing would ever be as bad as that, and the memory sent a shiver down my spine.

I couldn't afford that little trip down memory lane. I had work to do.

And I needed my personal demon, who I called Hannah, to do it. When I summoned Hannah, she gave me the strength and demon magic to subdue and capture rogue demons. The fact that she was much more powerful than the tempter demons we hunted—and currently an unknown entity in the demon hierarchy—made us a winning team if a tad unstable. The obsidian mirror Hannah was bound to was supposed to prevent her from taking over and going off on any unauthorized side quests or killing sprees.

That made the two of us unsuited for normal careers like banking or public relations. Since it took a demon to find one, however, being demon possessed made me eminently qualified for my current job.

I reached the alley and took a closer look at its occupants. The corporeal shape-shifting succubus's appearance surprised me. Instead of going all hot, sexy, and ho-bag, she went for plain and unassuming. Her baggy skirt, oversize sweater, and mousy brown ponytail screamed librarian. Maybe her mark had a book fetish?

Nah.

I unsheathed my enchanted knife, crept down the alley, and prepared to kick some demon ass.

Don't stop now. Keep reading with your copy of CATCHING HELL, by City Owl Author, D.B. Sieders.

And sign up to S.L. Choi's newsletter for news, giveaways, and a FREE novella set in the *Blood Fae Druid* world!

Be sure to follow along with real time writing updates, excerpts, and ARC opportunities, in S.L. Choi's Facebook reader group.

And discover CATCHING HELL, by City Owl Author, D.B. Sieders.

Jinx McGee saw her first demon when she was five... and looking in a mirror.

Never one to let life get her down, Jinx turns her unfortunate state of demonic possession into a lucrative career as a demon hunter. It takes a demon to find a demon, and Jinx's demon is superior at finding the others... when inclined to cooperate.

The hours suck, management's deadly, and her co-workers are almost as weird as her. Still, it beats retail. And once she's worked enough cases, she'll figure out how to separate from her demon and live happily—and normally—ever after.

But a rebellion is brewing in hell that threatens earth. The leader thinks Jinx and her personal demon hold the key to his victory. Jinx's boss believes it makes her a liability and puts her on a strict deadline to sort it out—or else.

And now the smoking hot demon who once broke her heart conveniently shows up to serve as a consultant on the case. But Jinx suspects he knows more about the rebellion than he's saying.

Trust her sexy demon ex with a second chance and her rag-tag band of fellow demon hunters, including a wolf-cursed Russian giant, a genius with a Wikipedia demon, and the twin demons of technology? Not likely. But it may be her only chance to save the world from Armageddon.

Please sign up for the City Owl Press newsletter for chances to win special subscriber-only contests and giveaways as well as receiving information on upcoming releases and special excerpts.

All reviews are **welcome** and **appreciated**. Please consider leaving one on your favorite social media and book buying sites.

Escape Your World. Get Lost in Ours! City Owl Press at www.cityowlpress.com.

ACKNOWLEDGMENTS

To Bryan. You're #1. I win. KSH

To the City Owl Press team. Thank you for putting Lane's story out to the world.

To one of my earliest readers, Lanet, whose praise and support helped me believe I could do this.

Gabi, thanks for being there through this entire journey. I couldn't have done it without you.

Charissa, thank you for being such an all-around amazing human. I'm grateful we met.

Dawn, for your continued support and kindness.

Lauri and Kelly, I don't tell either of you enough how much your support and friendship means.

The Bad Girls Club. Each and every one of you rock!

Kim Harrison and Faith Hunter, for proving the old adage *"Never meet your hero"* wrong. (Have I said this before? Yes. Is it still true? Also, yes.)

ABOUT THE AUTHOR

S.L. CHOI is an urban fantasy author with a deep love for humor, fast-paced action, and hit-you-in-the-heart feels . She grew up imagining goblins living in the rocks outside her bedroom window, while fairies flew through the flowers. When not writing, she is either photographing the beautiful New England area, tending to her small furry overlords, or gaming with her equally nerdy husband. To be the first to see news, ARC opportunities, and excerpts from the BLOOD FAE DRUID SERIES, join S.L.' s newsletter or join her on Facebook. Follow S.L. Choi's reader group for the latest news and updates www.facebook.com/groups/slchoisreadersgroup

www.slchoi.com

 instagram.com/SLChoi_author

x.com/@SL_Choi

tiktok.com/@slchoi_author

BB bookbub.com/authors/s-l-choi

ABOUT THE PUBLISHER

City Owl Press is a cutting edge indie publishing company, bringing the world of romance and speculative fiction to discerning readers.

Escape Your World. Get Lost in Ours!

www.cityowlpress.com

facebook.com/CityOwlPress

x.com/cityowlpress

instagram.com/cityowlbooks

pinterest.com/cityowlpress

tiktok.com/@cityowlpress